THE SWORD OF DARROW

ALEX AND HAL MALCHOW

To Sophie
Villeneuve

Thanks!

BenBella Books, Inc.
Dallas, Texas

Hal Malchow

BenBella Books, Inc.
10300 N. Central Expressway, Suite 400
Dallas, TX 75231
benbellabooks.com
Send feedback to feedback@benbellabooks.com

Printed in the United States of America
10 9 8 7 6 5 4 3 2 1

Library of Congress Cataloging-in-Publication Data is available for this title.
ISBN 978-1-935618-47-8

Editing by Erin Kelley
Copyediting by Debra Kirkby
Proofreading by Michael Fedison
Cover design by Melody Cadungog
Text design and composition by Pauline Neuwirth, Neuwirth & Associates, Inc,
Cover art & illustrations by J.P. Targete, targeteart.com
Printed by BANG Printing

Distributed by Perseus Distribution
perseusdistribution.com

To place orders through Perseus Distribution:
Tel: 800-343-4499
Fax: 800-351-5073
E-mail: orderentry@perseusbooks.com

Significant discounts for bulk sales are available.
Please contact Glenn Yeffeth at glenn@benbellabooks.com or (214) 750-3628.

The Sword of Darrow is part of the BenBella Cause line, which publishes great books associated with great causes. BenBella will donate a portion of its profits, and the authors will donate all royalties on this title to charities serving those with learning differences.

BenBella Books has also published a separate hardcover edition of *The Sword of Darrow* that has been formatted for easier reading for persons with learning differences. Both editions use phrase-based formatting, a scientifically developed approach to layout and spacing developed by ReadSmart. Phrase-based formatting benefits all readers.

To Astrid Weigert:
wife, mother, and editor.

THE SWORD OF
DARROW

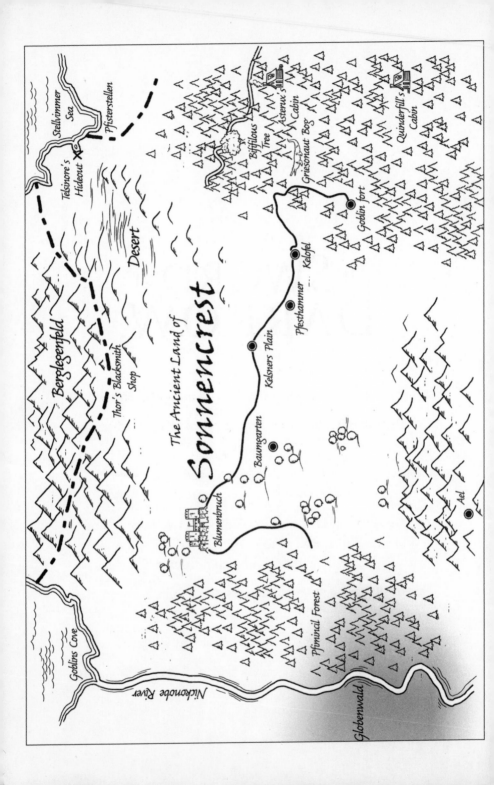

List of Characters

Aisling: A girl of sixteen who joins Darrow's band in the forest and who, in battle, hurls stones from her sling.

Asterux: Wizard who lives in Hexanwald Forest and taught Babette her magic and helps Darrow free the prisoners from the goblin prison. Darrow's uncle.

Babette: Eccentric little princess who struggles to read. She escapes from the palace the night that the goblins invade and learns magic from Asterux in the forest. See: Sesha.

Bekkendoth: Advisor to the king of the goblin nation.

Belameen: Groopus' goat.

Beltar: Great goblin general who leads the army of Globenwald.

Cebular: Mythical figure who was expelled from paradise and founded the goblin race.

Cedrick: Dwarf who joins Darrow's band in the forest and writes the songs sung by Darrow's men.

Darrow: Boy from the tiny village of Ael who is small and lame but speaks with beautiful words. Darrow seeks to form an army to free his kingdom from goblin rule.

Decidus: General who commands the goblin army in the battle of Kelsner's Plain.

Groompus: Darrow's old teacher in the tiny village of Ael.

Haidus: Mayor of Kelofel, the first village that Darrow's army visits upon leaving the forest.

Hugga Hugga: Minotaur warrior who is loved throughout Sonnencrest. Hugga Hugga was freed by Darrow and Asterux from the goblin prison and became one of Darrow's first recruits. Also known as Hugarious.

Kaylin: A soldier of fortune who joins Darrow's band in the forest.

Kilgo: Locksmith and amateur magician who joins Darrow's army in the forest.

King Henry: King of Sonnencrest and the father of Princess Babette.

Malmut: Goblin king of Globenwald.

Mempo: Darrow's younger brother.

Moakie: Thor's dragon.

Naark: Cave troll who joins Darrow's band shortly after Darrow helps Hugga Hugga and Timwee escape.

Prince Fenn: Princess Babette's younger brother.

Prince Keanu: Princess Babette's older brother and crown prince.

Principeelia: Babette's little bird.

Qunderfill: The old hermit who lived in the forest. His cabin was the hideout for Darrow and his early band.

Rildon: Tax collector of Globenwald and best friend of the goblin king, Malmut.

Scodo: Scorpion man who befriends Sesha (Princess Babette) in the forest. Scodo hideous appearance is a result of Zindown's curse. He is the greatest warrior Sonnencrest has ever seen.

Sesha: Upon arriving in the forest, Asterux the wizard changes the identity of Princess Babette to Sesha, the ugly gypsy girl. See: Babette.

Sir Fenn: Knight who helped found the kingdom of Sonnencrest and brought peace between the minotaurs and humans.

Telsinore: Evil pirate whose trickery launches the war between Globenwald and Sonnencrest.

Thor: Old dwarf and blacksmith who provides a home for Babette after she escapes from the palace.

Three Fingers Frick: Telsinore's rival pirate.

Timwee: Dwarf warrior who Darrow and Asterux rescue from the dungeon. He and Hugga Hugga are the first members of Darrow's band.

Zauberjungi: The mule who pulls Babette's/Sesha's wagon.

Zindown: The evil goblin wizard.

· 1 ·

Evil

Evil. Within this simple word lies a vast collection of deeds.

Many evils are the work of people driven to madness by love or strong beliefs. And for these, there can be pity.

But what of evil inspired by greed alone? What of those who would steal, use violence, or even kill for nothing more than earthly treasure?

If such a person holds a low place in your heart, then consider a man—if you could call him that—who would launch a war, sending thousands to their graves with many more dire consequences to follow, all for a few small boxes of precious stone.

And if the very thought of such a person makes you recoil in revulsion, unable even to consider what good deeds might yet follow, then close this book and return it to its shelf.

For it is with just such an evil that our story begins.

In the village of Fildencroft, in the great goblin kingdom of Globenwald, a thin, bony man stood pressed against a cold stone wall. His black hair was greasy and lay flat against his pale skin. On his chin sprouted a pointed beard that was crooked and thin, with white gaps revealing the skin beneath. His gleaming black eyes signaled a dastardly mind.

His name was Telsinore and he was the captain of a band of brigands that were known as the Tarantula Pirates. The Tarantula Pirates sailed the *Trap Door*, a small vessel with large sails that transported the band of thieves and murderers with terrifying speed.

He rubbed a bony finger beneath his nose and peered through the window of a house. What he saw made him tremble with delight. Inside, asleep, lay a very large goblin, who was Telsinore's target. A dangerous target to be sure, for goblins were by their nature a violent and vengeful breed who sent ordinary humans scrambling for cover, and pirates fleeing for the safety of the waves.

Twice, Telsinore had tried to kill his victim and twice he had failed. Tonight, success lay mere footsteps away. Tonight, he would kill the great goblin Rildon, the tax collector and best friend of the goblin king, Malmut II. Telsinore would cleverly lay the blame on Sonnencrest, a tiny kingdom across the river from the goblin kingdom. The death of Rildon would surely be avenged. The massive goblin army would immediately march against their weaker and peaceful foe.

And when the goblin soldiers invaded Sonnencrest, a great treasure would lay unguarded. The emerald mine.

The richest in the world. And the emeralds he would steal would buy Telsinore a great prize. They would buy the death of his rival, the great pirate Three Fingers Frick.

᠀ᎾᏒᎯᎾ

Telsinore hatched his plan, he had expected to make quick work of the tax collector, and for good reason. Rildon was fat—so fat that walking was entirely out of the question. Instead, he waddled, slowly and ponderously, at a pace that would embarrass a snail. Why was he fat? Because he ate many times a day, consuming staggering quantities of food. All day, the royal cooks would slave over their pots, concocting all kinds of stews and puddings and casseroles. Hour after hour, Rildon would eat. And hour after hour, Rildon would cry out for more.

Next to eating, Rildon had one other pastime: sleeping. Morning naps. Afternoon naps. Long evening slumbers. When he slept, it was well known to all, for he announced his sleeping with a thunderous snore that rattled nearby buildings and drove birds from the trees.

Telsinore's original plan was simple. Under the cover of darkness, he scaled the wall and sneaked into Rildon's bedroom. Lifting the bedcovers, he placed two things on the sheets. One was a note, placing the blame for Rildon's death on the small, peace-loving kingdom of Sonnencrest.

The other was Trixie, Telsinore's poisonous spider.

But when Rildon arrived in his bedroom, it was not the tax collector who perished. For as Rildon collapsed into bed, his great weight crashing into the mattress, Trixie was crushed, and her insides splattered across the note, making it impossible to read. All that remained was a great black spot that Rildon didn't notice.

But there was no time for Telsinore to mourn his beloved pet. He had a job to do. To accomplish his mission, he next chose a simpler method: a bow and arrow.

For Telsinore, the bow was an odd choice. He was a pirate, a man of the sword. Archers were sissies. His skills might be unpracticed, but how could he miss? Rildon was huge! So, in a tree overlooking the compound wall, Telsinore waited. When he saw his target, he pulled far back on the string and sighted the arrow at Rildon's heart. Unfortunately, the arrow sailed well above Rildon, through a window, and into the heart of Sindbad, the king's beloved moondust bird.

Rildon suspected nothing. But the royal archery instructor was never seen again.

Was Telsinore discouraged? Not one bit.

Two days later, a hooded messenger appeared at the compound door. He delivered an invitation from the goblin town of Fildencroft. A great pig roast would be held in honor of Rildon, the royal tax collector and King Malmut's closest friend. Rildon made immediate plans to attend.

On the day of the banquet, the goblins mounted their horses for the journey. Rildon, too large for the carriage, was lifted into an open wagon for the trip.

But when they arrived in Fildencroft, there was no dinner to be had. The confused goblins knew nothing of the invitation. They became anxious, fearing to offend Rildon, who would surely demand new taxes from their village.

So they slaughtered four large pigs. While the pigs roasted, the villagers plied their visitors with wine. By the time the meal was ready, the guests were so drunk they could hardly hold their forks. By the time the meal was finished, travel was out of the question. They bedded down for the night, which was the key to Telsinore's plan.

Finding Rildon was no problem. In the town square, covered by a hooded cloak, Telsinore sat and listened. When he heard Rildon's great snore echoing through the streets, he followed the sound to the inn where Rildon had passed out.

Now here he was, pressed against the wall, ready for his third attempt on Rildon's life. The window was open. Telsinore crept inside.

Rildon's massive body trembled and shook with each thunderous snore. Reaching into his bag, Telsinore pulled out a poisoned arrow. The arrow was marked with a yellow sun, the symbol of the kingdom of Sonnencrest.

Taking no chances, he shoved the poisoned arrow directly into Rildon's heart. After a few muddled snorts, silence filled the room.

Telesinore's plan was complete. The emeralds would be his and his rival would lie at the bottom of the sea. He smiled at the brilliance of his plan.

"That was so easy," he chuckled, "it was almost a crime."

⌘

The next morning, the royal guests found Rildon, his unmoving eyes fixed on the ceiling, the arrow deep in his chest. Attached to the arrow was a note. It read:

Trespassing on the land of Sonnencrest will not be forgiven. Let this be a warning.

BOOK ONE

· 2 ·

Vengeance

$\mathcal{T}$he fog wound through a thick carpet of fir and spruce that colored the landscape in shadows of black and green. From this landscape rose a mountain. It harbored no soil, no trees, and barely a blade of grass. From its foot to its peak was one long expanse of black rock, broken only by a door and a few small windows. Behind the door lay a castle, built directly into the stone of the mountain.

No walls, watchtowers, or large wooden gates guarded this fortress. A great door was simple and stood at the base of the mountain, but inside was a labyrinth of hallways and rooms, hundreds of them, carved deep into the mountain. At night, when lamps burned inside, the few tiny windows glowed eerily.

A road passed the castle, barely a stone's throw away. In the day, when no light shone outward, the castle seemed like no more than a stone, a silent work of nature unshaped by earthly hands. A traveler might walk past unaware that the heart of a great nation lay nearby. But on this day, from this great black rock, a voice boomed outward.

It was the voice of King Malmut II, ruler of the goblin nation of Globenwald.

"Smoke! I want to see the smoke from my window. I want Sonnencrest reduced to a landscape of ash!"

Arms flailing, King Malmut stormed back and forth, his eyes black with rage. Even among goblins, Malmut was especially ugly. His head was large and bulbous, with two tiny eyes set close together and a hooked nose that jutted out far from his face. He was oddly proportioned, with a torso barely as big as his head, and most of his height concentrated in his spindly legs, which gave him the appearance of a very large insect.

There was no hiding the stresses of the king, for when his nerves began to rattle, he began to sweat. These were no small droplets here and there that might go unnoticed. No, when King Malmut was anxious, great rivers of liquid poured forth. Today, the king was utterly soaked.

The king's advisor, Bekkendoth, spoke up in his calm voice.

"Perhaps, Your Majesty, this whole affair might be a trick. Why would such a small, peaceful kingdom provoke war with the goblins? Really, it makes no sense."

"Then who killed Rildon?" the king shot back. "Fairies? Bloodthirsty fairies?"

A smooth voice cut in, "Your Highness, perhaps we should discuss the plan."

Vinton Beltar, supreme commander of the forces of Globenwald, stood before a great map spread out on the king's table. Tall, with a broad, muscular frame, the commander looked at the king with patient eyes. To Beltar, the king's tirades were nothing new.

Beltar was a commoner, an orphan, who began his career as a foot soldier of the lowest rank. But his uncommon courage soon caught the eye of Globenwald's senior officers. Once in command, he proved a brilliant tactician and a ruthless one as well. He was a legend for his triumph at Cinidorm. Commanding the goblin force facing the army of Tolenbettle, an assemblage more than twice the size of his own, Beltar made a sudden retreat from the battlefield. His soldiers fled madly away into the woods. Hours later, under a flag of surrender, a goblin officer brought Beltar's sword to the enemy commander.

"Take it," the underling told him. "Beltar lies dead in his grave. The army is gone. The victory is yours."

The soldiers of Tolenbettle began a great celebration. Music played, wine flowed, and men danced merrily around their blazing fires. Deep in the evening, the merriment faded. The men sank into sleep, drunk and exhausted.

An hour before sunrise, a great rustling noise surrounded the camp, followed by a hideous battle cry. Out of the blackness stepped the entirety of the great goblin army of Globenwald, swords drawn and torches blazing. Before the soldiers of Tolenbettle could stagger to their feet, the goblin soldiers were upon them. Not a single soldier of Tolenbettle survived.

Now Beltar faced a new campaign against the kingdom of Sonnencrest. Perhaps Rildon's death was indeed a trick, but the general did not care. He would have a new campaign. Sonnencrest was a nation of weaklings. He cleared his throat and began to speak.

"Tomorrow, we march on Sonnencrest. We will need a day and a half to reach . . ."

The door was flung open and in walked an aging goblin, tall, wrinkled, his long, black robe swishing around him.

"At last! At last! At last!" he bellowed.

This was Zindown. His robe was woven with silk that reflected the sunlight from the window. On one sleeve, stitched in green, was a spider with twelve legs and two tiny wings. On his face, the green skin sagged with the deep creases of immeasurable age.

No one can say just how long a wizard lives. It is a secret they keep to themselves. But it is easily counted in decades, some say even a century or more, beyond the lives of ordinary mortals. Zindown had lived a very long life. But beneath his withered face rose a voice, clear and vibrant, that on this morning lifted like a song.

The king gave Zindown an icy stare.

"Your happiness exceeds the occasion."

Zindown paused for a moment. "Why, Your Highness, I do indeed mourn the death of poor Rildon. He was a fine servant of our land. It is only the possibility of *vengeance* that brings excitement to my heart."

This was not quite the truth.

For years, Zindown had conducted experiments far beyond ordinary magic. He had toyed with life itself. His goal was a whole new collection of creatures—terrible creatures that could be used in battle against enemies of the goblin land. These efforts were difficult and drew from him his last gasp of energy. Fortunately, most of the experiments failed.

Once, he had created a giant stilt crab with long legs that could walk across the land. Its shell would be impervious to attack. It could be ridden by archers, who could rain arrows onto enemy soldiers below them. And, of course, its giant claws could cut an opponent in two with a single snap.

But the stilt crab bore a temperament unsuitable for military life. Six trainers were snapped in half. Despite Zindown's pleading, the stilt crabs were put to the axe.

Another disappointment was the venomous ferret. In Zindown's mind, a small and speedy mammal like the ferret might be the perfect attack weapon. Armed with fangs and deadly poison, these creatures could be unleashed on an enemy late at night or hurled over the walls of a castle under siege!

Zindown's ferrets worked exactly as planned, but there was a flaw he never considered. When mating season arrived, the ferrets attacked one another viciously. Not a single male animal survived and the breed was soon lost.

Zindown was nothing, however, if not persistent. After many years, he had achieved two successes. They took years to reach adulthood, years to breed, and years to train. It was the work of a lifetime, and now that work would be rewarded. When the goblins marched on Sonnencrest, his creatures would be ready.

His creations. His magic. His triumph. Now, Zindown could watch his creations dismantle the army of Sonnencrest.

Beltar continued his report. "Our army will march down the Dalamath Highway. Before crossing the river into Sonnencrest, we will split into three parts to confuse the enemy."

"And what of the scorpion man?" asked Bekkendoth. "I hear he fights with the force of twenty men."

"Perhaps," sneered Beltar, "but the others are worth barely half a goblin."

Zindown broke into loud laughter. His creatures. Beltar's genius. This was going to be a beautiful war.

· 3 ·

The Festival of Sir Fenn

While the goblins soldiers readied to march, the people of Sonnencrest had no idea what was in store for them. In fact, at that very moment, a great celebration was underway. Thousands had come to the capital city of Blumenbruch to line the streets and cheer the parade that was in honor of the Festival of Sir Fenn.

A costumed dwarf soared through the air and crossed in front of the dazzling sun, briefly blinding the crowd who watched his tricks. When he landed, both feet squarely on the head of a troll, the children cheered and laughed.

Leading the way were three gigantic trolls who served as platforms for a team of six acrobatic dwarfs. Tumbling through the air from one troll to another, the dwarves landed on heads, shoulders, and open palms. They were dressed in blue and golden silks, and spun through the air like juggling balls.

Behind the dwarves came a disordered assembly of boys, small and large, pulling kites shaped like monstrous birds with teeth and soaring wings. Each kite depicted one of the celebrated creatures of the Miskerdrones, the mole people whose wizard king rose from the earth to transform ordinary songbirds into monsters, and visit his vengeance upon the surface-dwellers.

Next came the scorpion man and a hideous creature he was. He was tall with thick shoulders and arms. Atop those shoulders was a round head covered with a dark shell that was backdrop to two unmoving red eyes. His body was covered with black scales; from his back emerged a tail ending in two sharp points. It wasn't actually the scorpion man, for the great soldier himself was far too shy to walk in a parade. Still, the costumed figure reminded the crowd of the real scorpion man, who was out there somewhere and who would protect them if war ever came.

At the end of the avenue stood a great platform, adorned in blue and yellow banners of silk. There the royal family sat. Today was a special day because their six-year-old son, Prince Fenn, would read the tribute to Sir Fenn, his namesake and founder of the kingdom.

The queen rose on her tiptoes, eyes searching the parade route. Far in the distance was Prince Fenn, dressed as a knight, with a silver breastplate and leg guards. He might have been dashing, but the armor was obviously too heavy for the young prince. Under its weight, poor Prince Fenn stumbled slowly.

And why was Prince Fenn called to perform before the crowd at such an early age? Well, the answer was a scandalous fact, closely guarded and hidden from all out-side the palace walls.

Princess Babette, eight years old and the third of the royal children, could not read.

And that was only the beginning!

A tiny girl with bright, curly hair of a color somewhere between red and yellow, Babette cared nothing for the cere-monies of palace life. Her antics were legendary. Bed slippers in the throne room! A pet rat in the cathedral! A frog beneath her brother's crown!

At each such episode, the king would howl her name and demand her presence. But the queen would squeezes his arm and whisper, "Be patient, my dear. Even her younger brother comes before her. She will *never* wear the crown!" No one was happier about this fact than the little princess herself.

Prince Fenn lumbered up the steps to the stage, stopping now and then to lift one of his heavily armored legs with both hands. When he finally stood center stage, a servant handed him his papers. He raised his eyes to the crowd.

Now, Babette was ready with her surprise. She would show the kingdom that she could read. She knew the letters and she knew words, but when she looked at the page, the letters moved and came together until they didn't make sense. But for today's parade she had secretly lettered a sign—a sign to salute her brother, Prince Fenn. Standing in her chair, she called out to her brother and held a large sign, almost bigger than herself, lettered in her own hand.

Prince Fenn!
May his words make us sore!

She smiled, waiting for the crowd to cheer, but instead a murmur arose and then muffled laughter. Prince Fenn, who could both read and spell, looked back at his older sister with sad eyes. The king turned to Babette, face red, but the queen tugged at his cloak and he knew not to speak.

Babette looked about, first surprised, then confused, and finally slumped quietly into her chair.

From the reviewing stand, King Henry X rose to introduce his son. His voice boomed across the avenue.

"Today, we celebrate Sir Fenn and his lessons which have served our kingdom for more than two hundred years.

"We celebrate that love and kindness are nobler than violence of any form. And while we respect the bravery of soldiers who defend this kingdom, we know that there is no greater act of courage than the willingness to forgive the wrongdoings of others."

As King Henry spoke, the sounds of hoof beats echoed through the street. In the distance, a rider approached. The rider leaned low in his saddle. He wore a strange garment with stripes of red and green muted by dirt from the road. His face was drawn with deep lines and narrow eyes.

The rider hardly slowed before the crowd and spectators scrambled to avoid the horse's hooves. When he could no longer penetrate the crowd, he leaped from his mount and fought his way through the crowd.

"I carry a message! A message for King Henry!"

The king gave the messenger a stern glance and began to resume his address.

But the rider would not be denied. All eyes followed his course. At the entrance to the reviewing stand, a soldier tried to block his way, but the rider pushed him aside, rushed up the steps, and before he could be stopped, he dropped to his knee before the king. Bowing deeply, he raised his hands, which held a scroll.

"Later," blurted the king. The messenger lifted his face and looked bravely and directly into the king's eyes, which was a serious breach of protocol.

But upon seeing the face of the messenger, the king trembled. Slowly, he reached for the scroll and tore open the seal. His eyes darted across the writing before him. His face fell.

There would be no further celebration. Tightly gripping the message, the king turned, hurried from the reviewing stand, and entered the royal carriage. As the crowd watched in silence, the king disappeared behind the palace walls.

That night, while the palace buzzed with whispers of war, the king and his generals met to plan their defense. But alone in her bedroom, Babette knew nothing of the tragedies to come. All she could think was that she was glad that she was not queen. "If I had been queen," she thought, "I could not have read the message at all."

· 4 ·

Into the Forest

$\int$ ar from the castle, a few miles from Sonnencrest, the landscape was painted with the colors of spring. On the ground lay a carpet of flowers in yellow, pink, and blue, still moist with the morning dew.

But nature seldom sings to the deeds of men. Into this bright landscape arose a dark sound, the sound of a thousand footsteps striking the ground in unison, warning of dark deeds to come.

Beltar's army had arrived.

The army halted on the bank of the Nikanobi River. Across the water lay the edge of the kingdom of Sonnencrest. Crowding the far shore were the towering trees of the Pfimincil Forest, and at the other side of the forest lay an open highway leading directly to Blumenbruch and the palace gates.

Beltar paced along the bank, eyeing the landscape for the telltale signs of ambush or deceit. To protect his army, Beltar divided his men into three divisions. Each made separate crossings. Inside the forest, the soldiers of Sonnencrest would be waiting. To the Sonnencrest army, the forest was a perfect place to lay a trap. But Beltar had crafted a trap of his own.

One of his divisions would not march through the forest at all. Instead, they would set a trap. These soldiers would board rafts and float down the river to where the forest ended. There they would disembark and march to the road connecting the forest with the capital city of Blumenbruch. Then they would block Sonnencrest's escape, mopping up the remains of the inferior Sonnencrest army.

Beltar's advisors argued that it was a mistake to devote a third of his men to this ambush. These soldiers would be needed in the forest to break the Sonnencrest lines. But Beltar had no regard for his opponent. Sonnencrest might lie in ambush, but they would have to fight. And no army of peaceful farmers could match up to the warriors of Globenwald.

⁓

As the last of the goblins stepped into the forest, the pirate Telsinore stepped out from behind a tree. Dressed in black from head to toe, he looked warily to his left and right. Seeing no soldiers, he hurried to the water's edge. From his shirt, he withdrew a telescope and peered down river and then up. Satisfied that no goblins remained, he waved his hand. From the forest emerged his band of men, oddly attired with long hair, earrings, and strange hats. Behind them, they pulled three rowboats. With hardly a whisper of sound, they were in the water, rowing feverishly upstream.

Telsinore looked back into the forest. His scheme was working. The goblins had gone to war, avenging the murder of Rildon. With the goblins at war, the emerald mines would be left unguarded. And the emerald mines of Globenwald were the richest in the known world.

He imagined the gems, filling his boats. He imagined Three Fingers Frick, felled by an assassin's hand. His ocean would be free of rivals. He, Telsinore, would be the king of the seas. He dug his paddle deep into the water and let forth a great laugh that sent birds fleeing into the forest.

⁊

Beneath a canopy of kamilko trees stood Beltar, telescope in hand, surveying the landscape ahead. What he saw made him curse.

Off in the distance, his soldiers were chasing one of Zindown's creatures.

The skriabeasts were fast, ferocious, giant wolf-like monsters with long muscular legs, and they could be ridden like horses. They not only attacked enemy soldiers but ate them as well, a fact that gave Zindown special pride.

But although the skriabeasts were able to move with astonishing speed, they were proving nearly impossible to control. In the forest, their keen noses found temptation everywhere. Sensing prey, predators, or some mysterious scent, these skriabeasts would bolt from the path, their exasperated riders screaming orders that the hideous animals completely ignored.

Worse than that was the noise the beasts made. In designing the animal, Zindown had managed to contort its vocal cords so that they neither howled like wolves nor barked like dogs. Instead, when they opened their jaws, they let forth screams, sharp and high-pitched. At first, it sounded something like *skreeeeeee*, which gave the creatures their name. But a second or two into the scream, their vocal cords began to waver and the tone changed to an ear-splitting, hideous screech.

Beltar had hoped his army might travel ten miles a day. But his progress had been tormented by delays. Three days into the march, the army had barely traveled six miles.

Slowness was not Beltar's only setback. The forest provided perfect cover for an ambush. To avoid alerting the enemy, he had ordered his troops to remain silent. But the terrible cry of the skriabeasts signaled their presence for miles ahead and the low moans of the caged Cyclops unnerved his troops.

Beltar had wondered whether to bring the Cyclops at all. It was a violent and temperamental giant. Taken in battle from a far-away island kingdom, the Cyclops had been used to hammer tunnels in mountains and expand the caves where goblins preferred to live. Ten feet tall and stoutly built, it possessed uncommon strength. With its hundred-pound hammer, it could demolish solid rock—or a strong stone wall, like the palace wall at Blumenbruch.

So Beltar loaded the Cyclops and his hammer into a cage. To calm the Cyclops, Beltar ordered three cave trolls to march at its side. Their presence seemed to ease his torments and his moaning became less frequent, but when he did moan, the cave trolls joined in, delighted to be part of the song. Together, they signaled Beltar's advance far into the forest. Beltar cursed the Cyclops. He cursed Zindown. As he scanned the forest floor, he cursed the cowardly enemy that had yet to appear. He called to an aide.

"Unleash the ravens," he ordered and the soldier ran to the cages where the ravens were kept. The ravens were scavengers. They would find the Sonnencrest army and settle in the trees above. Their awful caws would betray the enemy long before the goblin soldiers were actually in sight.

⁕

While the Cyclops moaned in the forest, the Nikanobi River rang with a happier noise. It was a song of the sea. And from three meandering rowboats rose a raucous, drunken chorus of joy.

The life of a simple sailor
Has no appeal to me
That's why I'm a pirate
As evil as can be

My life is well rewarded
By a swig from me keg of rum
And the treasure I've a stolen
Is a mighty, mighty sum

Oh, spare me all your pity
For the hardships of the sea
The life of a heartless pirate
Needs no sympathy

The riches I have squandered
I could not count them all
Many places I have wandered
Some places I have crawled

No matter where I travel
I'm ready to do blows
And when I meet my maker
I'll punch 'im in the nose!

Oh, spare me all your pity
For the hardships of the sea
Life for a heartless pirate
Needs no sympathy

Cradled in the river's current, the three boats rocked back and forth as the occupants swayed with the song. Inside the boats were boxes of jewels and their weight pushed the boats deep into the water. In the first boat, balancing himself on the bow, stood Telsinore, dancing a careful jig to the song of his crew.

Not far downstream, goblin soldiers were loading rafts, preparing for their journey around the forest. When the pirate song reached their ears, they stopped their work and peered upstream. The singing grew louder and when three row-boats wobbled around a bend and into plain view, there were snickers and outright laughter until one goblin officer barked orders and two hundred soldiers mounted the rafts.

Perhaps those pirates might have mounted a charge had they noticed the goblins at all. Clapping in time to Telsinore's jig, shouting bawdy insults, they drifted forward, oblivious to the enemy ahead. And when one pirate sighted the goblins through a blurry eye, he stuttered, "G-g-g-goberlings!" which sent a new roar of laughter across the water.

But Telsinore, in an attempt to see the goblins himself, lifted one leg from his dance and swung round to face the river ahead. This maneuver was too bold for his condition, and he found himself wavering on one foot, his arms spread to each side, clawing for balance. He saw the goblins and his eyes grew large. But before words could leave his lips, he was swallowed by the current below.

Now the pirates saw their foe. Directly ahead stood a blockade of rafts, manned with goblins, weapons drawn.

Were the pirates frightened? Not one bit.

In one boat, the pirates rose at once, raising sabers high in the air with a blood-curdling cry. But no sooner had the charge been sounded than the rowboat tipped over on its side, dumping the crew, its treasure, and an empty rum keg into the river.

In the second boat, one of the pirates stood at the bow, preparing to strike at the goblins. But instead of reaching the goblins, the boat stuck a sandbar, launching their leader face first into the mud. Alarmed, the crew staggered into the water, tripping, falling, and stumbling into one another.

And the third boat? Oars pounded the water, but in random directions. The craft began to spin. Some pirates did not bother paddling, instead stuffing their shirts with emeralds. Faster and faster, the boat spun until it collided with goblin rafts. One pirate leaped into the water, but his stolen treasure carried him to the bottom. The rest were lifted by the goblins, one by one, drunk and dizzy, into their rafts.

Meanwhile, Telsinore was in terrible distress. Though he was a man of the sea, Telsinore was not a very strong swimmer. Driven to the bottom by the current, he bounced randomly across the riverbed, his arms and legs flailing against the water.

His head struck a rock. His body stilled and gradually floated upward. His head broke the surface of the water. Cool air crossed his forehead and traveled down to his mouth. At the first taste of air, his lungs exploded, disgorging water.

Frantically, his hands clawed, searching for something to keep him afloat, until they struck a round wooden object too large to grasp. His fingers found an edge, but the object slipped away. He reached up again and realized it was a keg. He clutched the barrel at both ends and lifted his head above the water. Another cough, this one long and helpless, followed. The cough gave way to wheezing breaths. And when the wheezing ended, he peered out from behind the keg to see where he might be.

The goblins were pulling his crew from the water and tying them with ropes. He scanned the landscape. Not a single pirate escaped. His entire crew was lost.

But Telsinore was hardly discouraged.

"A dime a dozen," he muttered and began thinking of where he might hire his next band of scoundrels. But a more alarming thought crossed his brain.

"Frick! Three Fingers Frick! Why, that lowly scoundrel has escaped his due!"

As Telsinore watched the goblins fish the boxes from the river, his heart boiled with anger. His war? For nothing! Frick still ruled the sea.

These goblins would pay. Not today. Not tomorrow. But an account had to be settled on a day and at a time when fate offered him the chance. His hands trembled as he lifted himself from the water. Steam rose from his water-logged clothes. With a grim expression and a memory etched in stone, Telsinore turned and began his long walk back to the sea.

· 5 ·

Ambush

It was the fifth day in the forest. Beltar was up at sunrise and moved to the head of his column. There on the ground lay a raven, pierced by a yellow arrow of Sonnencrest. The enemy had finally struck.

Great precautions were taken. A scouting party moved through the dense underbrush, far to the left of the path. Another advanced to the right. Scouts ran back and forth, bringing reports from the trail ahead.

Up and down his column, Beltar shouted orders, cursed Zindown's creatures, and urged his soldiers forward. Today, his curses grew louder, for there was a new delay—the mantis men.

Another creation of Zindown's, a mantis man, had the body of a man but no hands. Instead, his arms terminated in giant crablike claws. Covered in a hard red shell, these claws could snap a soldier in half so quickly the movement was impossible to see. The heads of these creatures were tiny, round, and, like the claws, covered in a bright red shell. Worst of all was the face. The yellow eyes never moved. Incapable of even the slightest expression, the mantis men were so hideous that Zindown himself was frightened in their presence.

But while the mantis men were well designed for warfare, they moved with a strange, jerky gait. They lifted each leg one at a time high into the air and then slowly folded the knee until it pointed straight upwards into the sky. At this point, the mantis men froze, not looking left or right but simply pausing. When they resumed, the foot eased forward in a reaching motion that languished in the air until the toes softly touched the ground.

These trancelike motions disturbed the goblins. They shouted at the mantis men, but the creatures were deaf. Some tried prodding them with sticks, but the mantis men turned to strike. One soldier lost an arm and the prodding ceased. The deeper they ventured into the forest, the slower the mantis men moved.

⚬⚬⚬

Beltar peered through his telescope. The forest floor had changed. Large thorn bushes, brown and without any sign of spring, rose waist-high from the ground and painted the landscape in dark, forbidding colors. Beltar smiled. No human could penetrate these thorns. There would be no ambush from the side.

He listened for the caw of the ravens. Only the moaning of the Cyclops reached his ears.

"Six days," cursed Beltar, "and we are barely halfway through the forest."

He looked down at his feet. Two more ravens lay dead in this path. Yellow arrows had done the deed.

His enemy was mocking him.

At that moment, a messenger appeared with news: "The trail is blocked."

Beltar hurried to the barrier. Across the trail lay five large trees—huge trees, obviously felled by a mighty axe. No wagon could pass this blockade. Removing it might take days. But passage was no longer a problem. For these trees spoke as clearly as a painted warning: the attack was imminent.

Beltar summoned the scouts.

"Move ahead past the obstacle and see what you can find."

While the scouts scrambled ahead, Beltar organized a defense. He ordered soldiers to man the barricade. To either side he placed archers.

But when the scouts returned they had nothing to report.

Beltar thought aloud. "If they are not ahead on the trail, then where can they be?" His eyes grew large.

"Tunnels!"

Soon, goblin soldiers moved up and down the path stabbing sharp sticks into the ground. But all they wounded were mole rats and tarantulas.

That night, Beltar did not sleep. The Cyclops and skria-beasts were blissfully silent, but the forest sang with coos and mating cries of animals he did not know. So loud were these sounds that the entire army of Sonnencrest might have marched, covered by darkness, directly into their midst.

Twice Beltar awoke his troops; twice the attack did not come. In his mind, the enemy's presence was everywhere.

Morning arrived. Around the barricade and at either side, goblin soldiers gripped their swords and tightened the strings of their bows. Once again, Beltar dispatched his scouts. Once again, they returned with no news.

The low moan of the Cyclops echoed through the forest. The skriabeasts cried in reply. The forest became a menacing force, almost laughing at a great army unable to see or hear the enemy before them.

Then, above the din, came a sound Beltar knew all too well. It was the death cry of a goblin.

A soldier was struck by a yellow arrow, not in his leg or arm or even through his heart. No, the arrow was planted squarely in his forehead, its feathered end pointing skyward to the trees above. The wound was so deadly that the soldier's scream stopped even before he hit the ground.

Beltar pulled his sword, eyes still seeking the enemy. A new sound filled the air. And this sound sent a chill right through his toes.

It was no battle cry. No footstep or clashing swords, no war trumpet or martial drums. The sound was air, rushing air, descending from the heavens above. Beltar lifted his eyes. A thousand arrows burst from the trees, a merciless rain of death that headed straight for his warriors below.

He had found the enemy—or rather, they had found him. From high in the canopy of the kamilko trees, an army of archers had located their prey, and a terrible slaughter was under way.

The goblins countered, but their response was pitiful and without effect. Arrows launched upward but fell short of the enemy every time. Soldiers hurled rocks and lances. So short was their flight that surely the enemy laughed from above.

Here and there, the mantis men, unnerved by the chaos, curled in on themselves and huddled motionless on the ground. Their still bodies made easy targets, and they were the first to die.

Without any possible defense, the goblins had but one choice. They ran. But the thorn bushes that crowded the road clawed at their garments and tore their skin. Even after they had traveled beyond the arrows' reach, their desperate flight continued without order or reason. Beltar shouted orders, but his words were but a whisper against the screaming of the wounded and the chaos of retreat.

How far they might have run, no one will ever know, for it was not exhaustion or relief that slowed the goblin flight. Their retreat stopped for one reason alone.

Sonnencrest struck again.

Waiting far down the path was yet another company of tree-dwelling archers. And this second volley of arrows was even more deadly than the first. Once again, the frightened goblins turned and ran, this time back in the direction from which they had come. But there was no escape from this attack, for the path was clogged with goblins fleeing from the first. Soldiers collided, falling to the ground. The fallen were trampled. Dozens were shoved into the terrible thorns. Jammed together on the trail, they made a perfect target for the archers above.

But Beltar did not panic.

"Fire," he ordered. "Set the forest on fire!"

Soon, up and down the path, the goblins set torches to the dry thicket of thorns. Great flames surged high in the air, moving outward from the road. Plumes of smoke lifted from the ground, forming dark clouds in the canopy above. The archers struggled to breathe and were soon unable to see the ground. Fewer arrows fell, and almost none of those found targets.

"Skreeeeeeeeeeeeee!" Frightened by the fire, the skriabeasts broke their ropes. They ran down the road and deep into the forest, their terrible screams piercing even the sounds of battle and fire.

But another cry arose, even louder and more chilling than the skriabeasts. Up the road, marching directly toward Beltar, came the Cyclops, staggering with three arrows protruding from his large eye. Without sight, he swung his hammer wildly through the air, sending terrified goblins scattering from his path. Then his hammer struck a tree and an archer plummeted to the ground, landing with a sickening crack.

Seeing the dead archer, Beltar knew what to do. Rushing to the Cyclops, Beltar shouted, "Listen to me, listen to me. The archer who has taken your sight cannot escape. There he is—to your right."

And with a thunderous stroke, the Cyclops swung his hammer against a tree, sending another archer falling from the sky.

"To your left! There is the archer who has taken your sight!" Again, the Cyclops struck. Slowly, Beltar guided the Cyclops down the path.

"The cave trolls," Beltar shouted. "Bring me the cave trolls."

When the cave trolls arrived, they followed the Cyclops, hitting the trees with heavy logs. More archers fell to the ground. On and on, the Cyclops raged. Again and again, bodies dropped from the black clouds above.

Beltar screamed at the Cyclops once more. "He has escaped! The one who took your sight has fled. Come, we will destroy him." A group of goblins took the Cyclops by the hands to lead him back to where the battle had begun.

A great black cloud filled the branches of the trees. Looking up, the goblins wondered how these archers could breathe. Some had already fallen. Others cowered above.

Again, the Cyclops' hammer struck. Furiously, the monster's club exploded into the trees. "On, Cyclops," Beltar screamed. "A Cyclops is more powerful than some coward in a tree. Slam him. Kill him. Destroy him!"

And with the cave trolls close on his heels, it was not arrows that rained, but the archers themselves. A few archers used their ropes to descend, but they were easy targets for the goblins below.

When the smoke cleared from the forest, many goblins lay dead. But for Sonnencrest the day was no better. Their soldiers retreated from the forest, hoping to make a stand behind the palace walls. But Beltar's trap was ready.

At the mouth of the forest, Sonnencrest's army met a wall of metal shields locked together in a great semicircle, blocking any path of escape. The scorpion man led the charge, but the goblins were ready, covering him with nets. Beltar followed from behind. The scorpion man cut himself free and disappeared into the forest. He was the only one to escape. No message reached the palace, and King Henry knew nothing of the defeat.

The army of Globenwald was wounded but victorious. They moved toward Blumenbruch, and a long line of prisoners followed them. They would be paraded through the streets of Blumenbruch in a show of goblin might. And when the goblin victory was complete, they would be locked beneath the palace until the last soldier breathed his last breath, a reminder to every citizen of Sonnencrest that the final remnants of their army remained in goblin hands.

· 6 ·

The Flight of the Princess

If you believe in history, grand events are the work of heroes. But in this respect, history tells little truth. Who are these heroes? They are the product of legend, of tales told over and over, until they tower in size far larger than any real memories of the time.

The truth, could it be known, is that the largest events are often shaped by the smallest hands. Tiny circumstances, unnoticed by any at the time, grow in consequence until they unleash vast powers, topple empires, crumble armies, and leave the mightiest of monarchs resting in their graves.

In the kingdom of Sonnencrest at the palace of King Henry, one such event, arising from a simple act of childish mischievousness, empowered the many great deeds that followed.

ᏩᎻᏍ

The moon was full and high in the sky as midnight approached. Though the soldiers stepped softly, the muffled drumbeat of their footsteps filled the streets of Blumenbruch. Beltar lifted his hand to signal for quiet. Among the soldiers not a word was uttered. But in the houses that surrounded them, barely a mile from the palace, citizens peered through their windows fearful and certain of the terrible events that would surely come to pass.

Inside the castle, no warnings had sounded. Few lights shone from windows. A handful of sentries manned the towers. Unaware of the impending attack, most soldiers and citizens lay fast asleep. However, *most* did not include the eight-year-old princess, Babette.

Outside the castle, beneath a pear tree, the little princess sat, waiting for an unusual visitor, a rare and precious serenading bird from the faraway island of Annisa.

The bird was a gift from a visiting prince and Babette had named her Principeelia after an angel in an ancient fable. So precious was this bird and so beautiful was her song that Babette could not bear to keep her captive. With tears in her eyes, she had released Principeelia through a window. But finding no others of her kind in the forests of Sonnencrest, the little bird returned, and every Wednesday night the princess sneaked through a window, departed the palace, and waited for her bird to return.

Principeelia landed on the branch. Barely bigger than a chicken's egg, her feathers were a dazzling yellow, accented by blue eyes and a bright red beak. Babette lifted her hands to offer Principeelia the raisins she always brought. When the little bird finished her meal, she hopped back to her perch, opened her bright beak, and let forth her song. Lost in the melody, Babette's mind wandered to faraway places.

She imagined herself a sword fighter, a sailor, or even a spy, disguised as a man, whose designs bring an evil kingdom to its knees . . . anything but a princess. Eyes closed, she galloped across a great desert pursuing evil bandits, determined to deliver the punishment they deserved.

A great thundering clap interrupted Babette's dream. Sand and small bits of rock exploded through the air, stinging her skin. A small cut appeared on her arm. The dust made her cough and when it settled, she saw a large round stone lying broken on the ground.

Another stone struck, hitting the palace wall a little farther away. Loud claps began to sound, near and far with a random but more frequent pattern. Trembling, Babette curled into a ball, wondering why such stones might fall from the sky. She reached for a branch and pulled herself into the tree.

For a moment the stones stopped. Babette crouched in the tree, ready to jump. A great bang sounded and began to repeat with an even rhythm. Next to her tree, the wall shook. After each bang, the sound of creaking wood cried out in response. "The gate," she realized. "Something is banging at the gate."

A great crash reached her ears and the banging stopped. A shrill cry, joyous and evil, filled the yard. A sea of torches floated inside, spreading like milk across a black table. Her tiny hands shook. She climbed higher in her tree. For moments, she simply trembled, eyes closed, too afraid to look.

When she opened her eyes, she saw wagons and boxes and trees alive with flame. In the stone buildings, great yellow plumes roared from the windows. Strange shadows pulsed chaotically, in a vile and wicked dance. A figure approached. Its face was dark, the light at its back. Then she knew. The goblins had arrived.

Across the yard, gleams of silver showed the rise and fall of a hundred swords. Bodies dropped to the ground. Amongst the cries, she heard voices she knew—not just soldiers but servants, craftsmen, and even their children. In and out of the palace compound, the goblins flowed, some wearing shirts stuffed with candlesticks and gold.

Torches approached, five in all. Babette gripped the trunk, trying to make herself small behind the leaves. The torches passed. She climbed higher and stepped out onto the wall. There, a watchtower cast a shadow that concealed her tiny frame.

A great cry arose. Across the yard, movement slowed. Her eyes darted frantically about, searching for the reason. The torches moved toward the palace. Her eyes rose to the balcony and she gasped.

There stood her mother, father, and three siblings, bound with ropes, motionless as statues commemorating some unspeakable tragedy. Babette clutched her heart, fearful to look but unable to look away.

A goblin wearing a black mask climbed to the rail of the balcony and lifted his hands. A high-pitched cheer arose from the yard. Babette staggered backwards. The goblin unsheathed his sword and lifted it high in the air, prancing back and forth across the balcony rail. More cheers, louder. Trembling, Babette stepped back again, but this time her foot stepped beyond the wall.

When she awoke, she lay on her back, looking up from the ground. She rose. Screams and cheers filled her ears. She was outside the wall, so she turned and ran.

She had no idea where to run as she took off across the open grounds and into the streets of Blumenbruch. As she fled deeper into the city, the noise from the palace faded. Soon, only the sound of her footsteps echoed in her ears.

She stopped, pressing her back against the wall of a small building. She had seldom left the palace, and the streets of her own city were strange and unfamiliar. They were empty and cold. She looked left and right, wondering where to go.

Footsteps. Footsteps pounding rapidly and moving her way. Again, she ran. A goblin voice shouted. She looked back to see a soldier in pursuit. Ducking into an alley, Babette covered herself with trash and listened as the soldier passed barely an arm's reach away. She feared that her heart might beat too loudly. But the soldier only muttered a curse and walked away.

Shunning the streets, Babette ran deeper into the alley, searching for an open door or lighted home. The alley branched in different directions. She did not choose. She just ran. She ran and ran until the alley came to an end.

A dog barked nearby. She froze. Then her courage was lost. She collapsed onto the cobblestones, sobbing loudly, helplessly, and without restraint.

It no longer mattered that her sobbing might be heard. She was beyond caution, reason, or any ordered state of mind. She placed her small head in her tiny hands and wept. Minutes passed. A door opened.

An older man with a cane peered out and whispered harshly, "Who are you? Quiet yourself! Do you want to bring the goblins upon us all?"

Babette looked up and tried to speak. At first, she only stuttered. But with great effort, she finally mustered these words.

"I am Princess Babette."

The man's eyes grew large. "Princess! Your Majesty." Then the man paused. "You cannot stay here. If they find you . . ." He paused again and hung his head. "If they find you here, they will kill us all."

These words jolted Babette from her sobbing. Terrible thoughts tumbled into her brain. Leg irons. A dark dungeon. A guillotine. Perhaps the good fortune of a swift sword. She lifted her head, quite unable to speak, and stared at the old man with desperate eyes.

She was covered with mud, her face bruised, and her eyes desperate and pleading. There she sat, eight years old, helpless against all the forces that conspired against her. For a moment, the old man glanced downward. Then he lifted his eyes to face Babette and spoke in a voice strong and stern.

"Leave. Run away. You must run far, far away! There is no time to be lost!"

The door slammed shut. Babette sat motionless, considering the old man's words. She climbed to her feet, but her feet did not move.

A minute later, the door opened again. Babette turned to look at the man with hopeful eyes. But the old man did not invite her inside. Instead, he handed her a small cloth bag containing a piece of bread, some dried meat, and a flask of water.

"Go," he said, almost shouting. She nodded slightly but remained still.

"For heaven's sake, run. Run until you can run no more and then keep running anyway. Do you understand? Run

until there is no city. Then hide in the woods. Travel only at
night. But run, run, run, as far from Blumenbruch as you can."

Babette looked at the man, blinking. The door shut. She ran.

〇〜〜〇

She awoke the next morning in a cornfield. The sun was high
in the sky. The stalks towered above her. Carefully, she crawled
to the end of the row to look out and see where she was.

The field stopped at the edge of a road. The road was empty
and the landscape was wooded, without a building in sight.
She wondered how far from Blumenbruch she had run.

From the cornfield, she watched the road, trembling as
groups of goblin soldiers passed. She knew the cornfield was
not safe. But she had no idea where to go.

Carefully, she peered from behind the stalks. She saw a
wagon, driven by a small man. His face was wrinkled and
what was left of his hair stood in short gray tufts pointing
straight out from his head. He had broad shoulders and big
hands. As the wagon approached, Babette could sense a kindness about him.

"That man would never hurt me," she thought. "He might
even help." But try as she might, she could not find the courage to move.

The wagon was pulled by two horses. In the back, a dirty
white cloth covered a large load. "A hay wagon," Babette
thought. As the wagon passed, Babette looked up at the man.
She tried to cry out, but the words did not come. The wagon
passed her hiding place, and she knew it was almost too
late.

Where her courage came from she did not know, but she dashed to the road and ran. Against the dusty road, her little feet made no noise. She reached the rear of the wagon and lifted the cloth. As softly as she could, she jumped up and climbed underneath.

But under the cloth, there was no hay at all! There was a warm, breathing body, enormous in size and covered with scales. It snorted and jostled against her presence. "What is it, Moakie?" the driver asked, but the animal returned to sleep.

Terrified, Babette prepared to exit, but the sound of new hoofbeats told her to stay. The animal breathed loudly; its skin was covered with hard scales that pushed against her side, scratching her skin, and almost shoving her out the back. Her fingernails gripped the old wooden planks. The great animal turned and there was more room. She lay there shaking, sure that she had made a terrible mistake. But the creature's breathing had a strangely soothing effect. Her eyes closed, and she was soon asleep.

· 7 ·

A Desperate Plea

The wagon pulled to a stop. The driver climbed down and pulled back the canvas, shocked to see the young girl lying in his wagon.

"Who are you?"

Babette blinked against the sunlight. The man was a dwarf. He stared at her, impatient for an answer.

"Me?" Babette paused, searching her mind desperately for an answer. "Just a poor orphan girl."

"You don't look like any orphan I ever met," the dwarf exclaimed. "Why, where'd you get that fine nightgown and those golden rings?"

Babette began to answer, but at that moment the great cloth lifted and the head of a dragon appeared. Babette jumped back.

"Don't be afraid," said the dwarf. "That's just Moakie. She's made some mischief a time or two, but she's a gentle soul." The dwarf led the dragon to a wooden shed.

For the first time, Babette took in her new surroundings. To her left stood a small cabin built with wooden planks that did not quite fit together, leaving gaps in the walls. At the shed, where the dwarf had disappeared with the dragon, was an open space on one side. Beneath an extended roof, the wall was hung with hammers, metal tongs, and an accordion-like blower with two handles. Here and there, pots lay scattered on the ground, shiny and new.

From where Babette stood, between the cabin and the shed, she could see rolling hills and great valleys far below. Far into the distance, she thought she saw Blumenbruch. But here on the mountain, there were no houses in sight, only trees casting their shadows across the dwarf's piece of open land. Only a faint trace of road connected the cabin to the world below.

The dwarf returned. "Come, you must be terribly hungry."

With those words of invitation, Babette scurried behind the dwarf into the cabin.

Babette's mouth fell. Dirty clothes, broken furniture, and unwashed dishes littered the cabin. A washboard lay in the corner, connected by cobwebs to the floor. An unpleasant odor filled Babette's nose.

"I'm dreadful sorry for the mess. I wasn't expectin' visitors," said the dwarf. He grabbed a piece of bread and handed it to her.

"Oh no," stammered Babette. "It is really very nice."

The dwarf threw her a cautious look. "Do you have a name?"

Babette stammered, "They call me Clarissa."

"Well, Clarissa, I'm Thor. Smithing's my trade. My specialty is pots, though you must have known that already. Thor's pots, the finest in all of Sonnencrest. Have you heard of them?"

"Indeed, I have," she replied, this time truthfully. "We use them at home."

"At the orphanage? Hmmm. I don't recall selling to any orphanages."

"They are very beautiful," replied Babette, eager to change the subject.

"I thank you," said Thor with a nod of his head, "but I can't take the credit to myself. What makes me pots so good is me dragon."

"Moakie?" Babette replied, remembering the dragon's name.

"That's right. If you want a great pot, you need strong metal. You want strong metal, you'll be needin' a hot fire. That's where Moakie comes in. She's the hottest fire in Sonnencrest. But don't tell nobody. I don't want them other blacksmiths catchin' dragons and makin' better pots. Anyway, that's why me pots are the best!"

Thor beamed.

"But wait," Thor continued, remembering his first thought. "No orphanage can afford my pots . . ." He paused to add, ". . . Although I have given them away on occasion."

"So tell me, which orphanage were you staying at? And I know a thing or two about metal. So just where did you get those beautiful gold rings all fitted to your wee little hands?"

Babette thought hard. "My father was rich," she said. "When my parents died, they left the orphanage lots of money. It was far away on the border." She paused for a moment and then blurted out the rest. "The goblins burned the orphanage. They carried away the other children. I escaped by biting off the hand of one of the soldiers."

Babette blushed bright red. She knew she had taken her story too far. Thor looked back, dumbfounded.

A thousand desperate thoughts raced through her head, but they all seemed wrong. So not knowing what to say, once again, Babette collapsed in tears.

Thor quickly apologized for doubting her story. "Those goblins are terrible," he said. "I would have bitten one, too."

Babette collected herself and, eager to change the subject, blurted out, "And where do you usually sell your pots?"

"All across Sonnencrest!" Thor pronounced. "I travel to the market at the foot of the mountains and they come far and wide just to buy."

"They even use my pots in the palace," he added in a solemn tone.

With those words, Babette's lips began to quiver, but Thor, sensing her sadness, reached over and put his hand on her arm.

"I'm a sad one, too, at least about what happened to the king. I heard what them goblins done. I would've fought 'em meself but there's no news up here in the mountains. I hardly knew there was a war 'til the whole thing was over."

Thor paused. "He was a great one, that Henry. The greatest I knew."

"I know," said Babette with a shaky voice. "But why were you and Moakie near Blumenbruch?"

"Ah, that's a long story, my dear. I'll tell that one later. Now back to that orphanage. Which one did you say you lived at?"

Babette searched for an answer and was overcome with shame. The goblins might find her. They might kill this nice old man and his dragon. But she did not know where to hide. Every answer, every action seemed it might lead to doom. There was nowhere else to turn.

"I was never in an orphanage," she whispered.

Thor looked down with a disapproving frown.

"But before I tell you who I am, you must know that my secret could bring death to us all." She paused once more. "Even Moakie."

She looked up at Thor, her little eyes hopeful and moist. "Will you promise to help? You are my last hope."

Thor just blinked. Then, he reached out and put his hand on Babette's shoulder to calm her shaking body. "How can you speak so, my child? What is it you're afraid of?"

Babette lifted her face and spoke.

"I am not Clarissa. I am Princess Babette," she answered slowly. "I escaped the palace. The goblins are looking for me. They could arrive any minute!"

Thor's eyes opened wide. He paused to compose his words, but he knew what he had to do. For once, he spoke clearly and firmly.

"For years, I have been a loyal servant to the king and the royal family. It will be my life's greatest honor to help the daughter of Henry X. I stand at your service, my princess. I stand at your service no matter what danger may come."

Babette looked back at Thor with grateful eyes that almost melted him in his chair. Before he could speak another word, she had leaped into his lap with both arms hugging tightly at his neck.

· 8 ·

Thor and Moakie

Weeks later, Babette had become comfortable in her new home. Lying next to the dragon in her makeshift bed, Babette no longer trembled at Moakie's great snores. But tonight she hardly slept. Thinking she might find rest in the cabin, she rose and tiptoed through the darkness to where Thor slept.

The door creaked as she peered inside. To her delight, Thor sat in his chair, bent over, peering through his glasses at the handle of a pot. He looked up.

"What can I do for you, my dear?"

"I can't sleep."

"Well, do you need another blanket or more straw in your sack?"

"How did you find Moakie?" Babette asked.

"Well, that is quite a story, young miss. I doubt you have time to hear it all."

But before he could say more, Babette was in his lap, arms folded and waiting. And so, Thor told his strange story.

"Well, almost twenty years ago, a dragon lived just across the border in a mountain not far from this very cabin. The dragon was a fearsome beast. Her trips into the countryside terrorized the villages.

"The king sent soldiers . . ."

"Grandfather?" Babette asked.

"No, no, just across the border in Berglegenfeld. Anyway, these soldiers never came back. And you can imagine, the king was desperate for help."

"So what did he do?"

"He did what any king would do. He offered the royal treasure and the hand of his daughter to any knight who could slay the dreaded beast.

"Far from here and there and yonder, these knights poured in, all wantin' that reward. One after another, they trotted by with their shining armor and glittering swords. And ever' one called on that dragon to step out and fight."

"Did they kill it?"

"Well, no. Not a one of 'em. That dragon would simply go to the mouth of the cave and blow. That was it. Just . . . blow. One puff and all that remained was a pile of stinking ashes and some blackened armor."

Babette's eyes grew wide. "Is the dragon still alive?"

"You are gettin' ahead of me story. Anywho, at first, the dragon loved these battles, if you could call them that. But those knights just would not stop.

"No matter how many she killed, more kept coming, each one certain that he was braver and stronger than the rest.

"Well, after a while the dragon got tired of these knights. They were no challenge at all. She hated the awful smell of burning knights that drifted into her cave. So, as new knights appeared, she ignored them. Soon, the knights were leaving discouraged but alive. The dragon simply refused to fight."

"Did she still eat the people?" Babette asked.

"You bet. But that knight business had just gotten old. Then, one day a new knight arrived.

"His name was Welbourne and he made quite an impression. His armor and lance were forged with shining silver. His sword was laced with gold. And he was so handsome that the princess ran straight to the church to pray that he would succeed!

"When he first approached the cave, he did something different. He took off his armor and dressed like a common peasant.

"Instead of going to the mouth of the cave, he hid in the bushes and watched. He watched when the dragon entered and watched when she left. He did this for months.

"Back in the town, even the princess had forgotten this knight. But every day, he dipped his quill in his bottle of ink and wrote down when that reptile came and went. When he figured he finally understood the dragon, he made his move."

Babette's eyes grew big.

"One day, the dragon returned from an especially long trip. When she disappeared into the cave, the knight gathered brush and broken limbs from the mountainside and piled them high outside the entrance to the cave. He added fallen logs, and when the pile was large enough, he stepped back to take a look. He threw a handful of sand into the air. The sand blew in his face, so he waited.

"He stood there for most of the night. An hour before sunrise, he felt a breeze blowing in the direction of the cave. Welbourne stepped out of hiding and stood ready, just like all the knights before him. Then he screamed, 'Come out, you cowardly cave lizard!'"

Babette burst out laughing.

"Not a sound came from the cave.

"'Don't hide from me, you pathetic imitation of a slow-witted crocodile!'

"Again, nothing but silence.

"For almost an hour, that Welbourne screamed one insult after another and, of course, the dragon heard him clearly. But she kept thinking of that awful smell of burning knights. She tried to go back to sleep, hoping that stupid knight would go away. Finally, that dragon got up and waddled toward the mouth of the cave.

"'I know the truth of your cowardly soul,' yelled Welbourne. 'You are no dragon at all. Those knights were killed by bears and lions while you trembled at the bottom of a puddle in your cave. Come out or I will send in a hungry poodle to rip out your cowardly heart!'

"Well, the dragon knew a thing or two of chivalry from fighting so many knights. That insult was really too much. Waddling toward the opening, she took in a deep breath of the night air. And when she blew, the fire exploded through the mouth of the cave.

"The flames struck the brush and a giant bonfire erupted. A strong wind blew the smoke and hot air into her face. Coughing, she turned, waddling to the back of her cave. The wind blew harder. Deeper and deeper, smoke poured into the cave.

The poor dragon could hardly breathe. She fell to the ground and there she found more air. But the wind kept blowing and the smoke kept coming.

"Finally, the dragon lay dead, done in by her own fire."

"I think that knight cheated," proclaimed Babette with a frown.

"That may be," Thor responded. "But it did not stop him. When the fire was all burned out, Welbourne swept away every single ash and buried it in the nearby sand. At the entrance, he scrubbed the stone to remove all evidence of fire. Then he walked to the creek to bathe and shave, for after so many months in the bush, he hardly looked like a knight at all.

"When he had his armor back on, he walked into the cave and cut off the dragon's head. Then he climbed on his horse and went back to town, dragging the dead dragon's head on a rope behind him.

"Inside the town, Welbourne had been long ago given up for dead. As he entered its streets, the townspeople came out of their houses, cheering his name. Welbourne lifted his bloody sword high and the sun sparkled on his armor."

"Did he marry the princess?"

"You bet he did," said Thor as Babette frowned.

"And after many nights of celebrating, he left with his bride and lavish treasure, never to be seen again."

"But what does this have to do with Moakie?" Babette asked, remembering her question.

"Days later, I was searching the mountain for ore. A blacksmith always needs ore. And as I was passing that same cave, I heard crying.

"It seems that the dragon had two young ones, and Moakie was the runt. When the smoke entered the cave, the bigger of the young dragons could not lie close enough to the ground to avoid the smoke. But little Moakie curled up in a hole and survived.

"So I cleaned Moakie off and took her home. I cared for her and raised her. She is my partner, my companion, and . . ." Thor paused to smile . . . "the reason I make the best pots in Sonnencrest."

"But why do you take Moakie to town, hidden in the wagon?" asked Babette.

"It's her teeth," Thor responded. "Breathin' fire is tough on the teeth. After a while, they start to turn black, and if I don't scrub them clean, they'd soon be full of holes. I cleaned them best I could in years past, but these old hands just can't do the job anymore. A friend in town does it, and I was headin' to see him when I heard that the goblins took the palace."

With her head full of knights and dragons, Babette wished Thor a good night, and made her way carefully back to her bed. She snuggled close to Moakie and fell right to sleep.

⌒〰〰⌒

The next day, Babette helped Thor and Moakie by carrying wood to the workshop. When evening came, she returned to the woodshed to sleep next to Moakie. As was his custom, Thor rose with the sun and was surprised to see that Babette was not up. He went to the woodshed and found that Babette was still fast asleep. Beside her lay a brush with blackened bristles.

Moakie lifted her head and smiled. Every tooth in her mouth was a gleaming white.

· 9 ·

Babette's Trip to the Forest

Thor's hammer struck hard and orange sparks exploded into the air. Across the mountainside, a dull clang echoed with a slow, steady beat. The old blacksmith paused, looking down at the iron handle taking shape, and wiped his forehead with the sleeve of his shirt.

Then he heard what he had been dreading for days.

Hoofbeats.

He wiped his hands on his apron and glanced quickly around the yard. Babette had gone. She and Moakie had left to explore one of the mountain trails.

Thor had warned against these trips. Babette would hop on Moakie's back and off they would go. There was no telling when or where the goblins might appear. Staying close to the cabin was safer. At least that is what he had thought.

The old blacksmith stood quietly running his hand over the stubble that topped his head. The sound grew closer. Atop an old horse sat a youthful goblin. He dismounted, barely nodded at Thor, and walked straight into the cabin.

Thor heard his table crash against the floor as the goblin overturned it and a metal plate rolled out the door. The goblin was back in the yard in seconds. He walked to the workshop and, after a quick inspection, he turned to the blacksmith.

"Have you seen a girl? A small girl with red hair about seven years old."

"Wha-wha-what girl?" Thor sputtered. He paused, looking for words, and muttered nervously. "There's nobody but me up here."

The goblin eyed Thor sternly but did not answer. He turned, mounted his horse, and rode away.

For ten long minutes, Thor watched the trail. Then he hurried down the mountainside to deliver a message in the village below.

⌒✺⌒

A few days later, Babette was carrying wood to the shed when she heard a horseman approach. As Thor had instructed, she dropped her load and ran to the forest, burying herself in a thicket of bushes. From her hiding place, she could see the cabin and the trail.

Into the clearing came a single horse. The rider was a young man, a boy really. He wore no shoes and rode bareback. Thor hobbled from the workshop to greet the rider. The rider nodded and smiled, but Thor was speaking quickly, his hands moving as he spoke. The boy's eyes grew large. He shook his head firmly, refusing whatever request Thor had made. But Thor reached into his pocket, pulled out coins, and placed them in the boy's hand. Still, the boy shook his head and tried to pull his hand away. But with the boy still on the horse, Thor grasped his wrists and shook him.

As Thor spoke words that Babette could not hear, the boy froze. He looked down at the coins, as if they were a terrible curse. Then, with a grim expression, he stuffed them into his pocket and galloped back down the path.

༄

Thor could not bear to tell Babette that she would have to leave. And he could not bring himself to stop her trips with Moakie. Every afternoon, after work, Babette would climb on Moakie's back for a ride across the mountain trails.

One afternoon, on one such ride, Babette and Moakie arrived at an open meadow. There, Babette and Moakie launched into a game of hide-and-seek.

Moakie, of course, had no talent for hiding. There was simply too much dragon to conceal. To help Moakie, Babette always counted slowly, loudly, and to at least twenty-five. But this time, when she reached the final number and opened her eyes, instead of Moakie's bulk, she saw something much, much more terrifying.

There, before her, stood two goblin soldiers on horseback.

"What do you think?" asked the younger goblin with a smile.

"Probably not," answered the other. "But you never know."

Babette, eyes wide, began slowly stepping backwards toward the trees at the edge of the meadow. As she did, the two riders dismounted and moved carefully toward her.

"Don't be afraid, little girl. Just a quick trip to town and you'll be back in no time," said the older goblin, reaching out his hand to Babette. Babette kept moving, closer and closer to the trees.

"Easy, girl. No one wants to hurt you." The goblins stepped faster. Babette kept pace, peering over her shoulder, eyeing her escape.

Babette was at the edge of the meadow, ready to run, but as she turned, her foot caught a root. She fell backwards into the brush.

The goblins leaped forward. But before they reached the princess, they met a surprise. Moakie's large green head appeared from behind the bushes. A great ball of fire exploded from her mouth. Seconds later, all that remained of the goblins were two piles of ashes on the burning grass.

Babette staggered to her feet and for a few seconds only blinked at the spot where the goblins had stood. Then she turned and gave Moakie a great hug around the neck. "Moakie, you are my true savior! I was dead for sure," cried Babette. Then she quickly mounted the dragon, and Moakie galloped down the trail to the blacksmith's cabin.

In the cabin, Babette explained what had happened and Thor shook his head in dismay.

"We'll need to find you a new home," he told her in a low voice.

Babette wanted none of this news. She loved her life in the mountains far from the cold palace walls. She pleaded with Thor to let her stay.

"I will never leave the cabin," she promised.

"I will wear disguises."

"I will clean Moakie's teeth every day!"

Thor just shook his head sadly and continued with his work.

⟡

A week later, Babette sat with Thor, sharing breakfast in his cabin. No more goblins had appeared. Thor's words about leaving were almost forgotten.

She looked up at the old dwarf.

"Were you ever married?" Babette asked.

Thor looked away and did not answer.

"What happened to her?" she asked.

"That's a long story, child. Now, off to work for both of us."

"Please tell me."

Again, Thor was silent, but he could not refuse the little girl. He started slowly.

"We lived in a village down the mountain, and in those days, I made swords. One day, I returned from the market with a lot of money. A robber followed me home. When I left to get firewood, he entered the house."

"And what happened?"

"He robbed me. When my wife tried to resist him, he killed her with a sword made by my very own hands.

"That's when I moved here to the mountains. I swore that I would never make a weapon again."

Babette gave Thor a long hug.

"You are right," she said. "There is nothing good that can come from a sword."

⟡

That afternoon, Babette returned to the cabin. Thor was polishing a new pot. Babette hopped up on a box and looked at the old dwarf.

Thor thought Babette might be sad from the story about his wife, so he offered her a story that he was sure would make her laugh.

"Did I ever tell you how Moakie set fire to my peacock?"

Babette did not hear. Her eyes were glazed over and she was staring through the window.

Thor rose and scanned the clearing. There was no sign of goblins. But his old ears heard music. It was a delicate, beautiful song.

A tiny yellow bird fluttered in the doorway.

Though the bird was small in size, her singing was loud and joyous. Now Babette trembled, her face without expression as if lost in a dream. She lifted her hand and held out one finger.

Principeelia eased herself on to her perch.

As the little bird sang, Babette began to sob in happiness at seeing her beloved bird. Thor's eyes moved from Babette to the bird and back again, unable to find meaning in these events. Then he noticed something strange.

"Babette, the paper on her leg. What does it say?"

Quietly, Babette placed Principeelia on the table and unwrapped the wire. A small piece of paper fell.

Thor took the paper, unfolded it, and tried to read the tiny handwriting. Making a face, he pushed the note back to Babette.

"I can't read," Babette said, her voice quiet and flat.

So Thor rummaged through a box until he found glasses, smudged and with one broken lens. He held the note high to catch the light of the cabin window and read aloud:

"The journey is dark. The journey is long.

But there is magic in the yellow bird's song.

Principeelia will be your guide,

Follow now, remain at her side.

Long live the kingdom of Sonnencrest."

"What does this mean?" asked Babette, suddenly thinking of her family.

Thor knew the meaning of the note. Struggling, he spoke, almost gruffly, to the princess.

"It means that you are not safe here. It means you are to follow this bird into the forest on a long journey to meet a wizard. The wizard has magic that will protect you."

Babette looked back, eyes wide.

"Who is this wizard? What will he do to me?"

"I have never met this wizard, but he is known throughout Sonnencrest. His name is Asterux. His magic is as beautiful as it is strong. He is the one person who can make you safe."

"You will go with me?"

"I cannot. This is a journey that you must make on your own."

"I won't go!"

It was more than the danger that Babette feared. She didn't want to be a princess. All she wanted was to be Thor's daughter, to help him make pots and play on this magical mountain with her beloved Moakie. But Thor spoke sternly and with an authority that Babette had never heard.

"Sometimes our lives are guided by a larger hand. Sometimes the paths we travel are not ours to choose. Hear me, child. Go!"

"I won't," Babette whispered, stunned by Thor's strange words. But Thor did not hear her reply, for as she spoke, Principeelia began to sing.

This time, the tiny bird changed her song. Her low whistle took on a slow rhythm, haunting and strange.

Suddenly, Babette was silent. Without the slightest expression, she rose to her feet.

All questions, all fears, and all concerns disappeared from Babette's mind. All that remained was the song, a song that called her forward. Principeelia was outside the doorway, inviting Babette outside.

Babette turned without speaking. She gathered some bread and an apple and folded them into a blanket. Thor took his old coat and wrapped it over her shoulders.

For a moment she paused. She leaned down and, almost mechanically, gave Thor a short hug. She stepped outside and did the same to Moakie, who could sense that she was leaving and tried to follow. But Babette turned her head and did not look back. Confused, Moakie remained still.

The bird, still singing, fluttered slowly down the trail, pulling Babette in her wake.

For two days and two nights, Babette walked across the mountain trails, unaware of the world around her. No danger of any kind crossed her mind. She felt no hunger or weariness. On the third day, Babette entered the treeless plain, still guided by Principeelia's song. She didn't speak a word and slept very little, only a few hours before each sunrise. Along the way, she found fruit and nibbled at the bread she carried in her blanket. All thoughts of family and Thor and Moakie and her new life had fled from her mind.

On the fifth day, she walked into the dreaded Hexenwald Forest. With calm and steady steps, she continued, her mind lost in the little bird's song and the magic of a wizard who waited at her journey's end.

Not far into the forest, she found a basket with bread and cheese, and she finally stopped to eat and rest. When Babette rose to her feet, Principeelia led her through a forest so dense that the sun was blocked by the trees. One day into the forest, she came to a stream, where she stopped and drank deeply. She followed the stream until she came to a huge tree, a bififilous tree that towered above the rest of the forest. From there, she left the stream and veered from the trail onto a smaller path that climbed high into the hills. Thorns tore at Babette's clothes. Her feet were bruised and covered in cuts and scratches, but she felt no pain. She did not tire. She uttered not a sound.

At the end of the sixth day, she suddenly felt cold. She looked down and saw she was standing in a stream. She collapsed into the shallow current and drank deeply for a long time. When she lifted her head, she saw a cabin. In front of the cabin stood a small round man with a bald head and bushy eyebrows. Something about this man told Babette that she was safe, for glowing in his face there appeared to be the hope and peace of the entire world.

"My princess," he said softly. "You are a brave little girl who is surely tired from this journey. Come inside and rest."

All at once, Babette was overcome with fatique and her body crumbled toward the ground. But the wizard reached out his hand and when she touched it, Babette felt love and kindness that gave her strength. She pulled herself to her feet and stumbled into the cabin.

Inside, Babette fell into a chair. Principeelia landed on the table and collapsed on her side, no longer able to stand. The wizard looked at Principeelia and spoke.

"You are a gallant heroine, my little bird, but do not sleep so soon."

At that moment, the sound of another Annisan serenader filled the cabin as a handsome male bird lit on the window-sill and launched into song. Principeelia looked upward, unable to find her feet. But her prince was a patient suitor. He dropped to the table and stepped sprightly in circles around Principeelia, repeating his song.

For a long time, Principeelia could only look. But her prince did not waver. She found her feet, clumsily at first, but with growing strength. Struggling, her wings fluttered and she entered the air as her suitor circled with dips and spins that Principeelia could not return. Then she found her voice. As she fluttered clumsily, she returned his song and the two joined together in a stirring chorus of joy. The male bird flew through the window. Principeelia hesitated, looking back at Babette and then at Asterux.

Babette blinked and her bird was gone.

· 10 ·

A Room Full of Light

When Babette awoke, she found herself on a bed in a room filled with strange and magical objects, each more wondrous than the next.

From the ceiling hung models of stars, planets, clouds, birds, butterflies, and creatures that Babette had never imagined, much less seen. One of these was a round creature, covered with spiny hair, with circular wings and eight short legs that swayed in the breeze. Unfortunately, it hung directly above Babette's bed. When Babette awoke, the bright red eyes of this creature were the first things she saw. She screamed and pulled the blanket above her head.

Asterux was there in an instant with reassuring words. "Don't be fearful. It's only a stuffed koowik! She can't hurt a thing."

Babette pulled down the blanket only slightly, inspecting the kindly wizard. His eyes, tiny and almost lost in his large face, twinkled brightly. What made him smile so, Babette could not possibly imagine. She lowered the covers and pulled herself up.

"Where am I? And who are you?" she asked, now glancing back at the koowik with a sly smile.

"I am Asterux, Your Highness. I stand here in your service and that of your kingdom." Asterux gave a great bow. "You are at my cabin, deep in the Hexenwald Forest. I am a wizard and you have been sent here for protection."

Babette looked concerned. "Are the goblins still after me? Can they find me here?"

"The goblins will never find you, my princess," he replied, his eyes sparkling again.

"How can you know?"

"Because when they find you—if they find you—it won't be you they find."

Babette blinked. Asterux made no sense, but Babette was so distracted by her surroundings that she barely noticed.

"What will I do here?" she asked, eyeing the ceiling with interest.

"My dear, you have powers that you do not know. One day, you will walk out of this cabin and into the forest and undo the goblin rule."

Babette's heart sank. Battles and kingdoms again!

"And how will I do all that?" she asked, annoyed to be reminded once more of that awful crown.

"My dear, you are about to learn the wizard's trade."

Babette's eyes grew wide and for the first time a little smile emerged. Magic. That could be fun.

"For a time, you will be my student. I have no magic to give you, for these powers can neither be given or taken from you.

But I can help you find what is within your own reach. Those skills can shape the world around you, as the world around you has shaped you. It will be the hardest work you have ever imagined. It will require patience and perseverance you may not imagine you possess. But we only have a short time, so we must start quickly. "

"How long do we have?" asked Babette.

"Merely ten years," replied the kindly wizard.

"Ten years!" exclaimed Babette. "That's hardly a short time at all! That's a lifetime!"

"And like a lifetime, it shall pass in what will seem like the blink of an eye," replied the wizard. "Now come with me."

She turned and looked straight into Asterux's eyes.

"No magic is going to make me a queen."

"Did you consider, my dear, that you may already be the queen, whether you like it or not?" Asterux asked with a smile. He stared hard at Babette's face. "Before we go, I'm afraid we need to make some changes."

Before Babette could fully consider those words, the room went dark. From the darkness exploded a display of tiny lights as dazzling as the stars in the heavens. Babette covered her eyes against the brightness. Slowly at first, but with increasing speed, the room began to spin. Babette sank to the floor, burying her face against her knees, and wrapped her arms tightly around her legs.

As the room reached a terrifying speed, the princess wondered if the cabin might be launched high into the sky, never to grace the earth again. A great hum echoed in her ears; above the hum, she could hear a voice—Asterux's voice—chanting, almost singing, strange words she could not understand.

Those words were followed by a thunderous noise that shook the cabin and bounced Babette into the air. Before she landed, the room exploded in a final flash of lights. Darkness followed by. The room was quiet.

When the princess opened her eyes, the first thing she saw were toes. They were fat, thick, and short. She was about to laugh at whoever had such ugly toes, until she realized that they were connected to *her* feet. She raised her hand to touch her hair and found that it was coarse and inky black. Her fingers, also stubby and short, touched her face and found a new nose, long and pointed, a bit crooked and surely quite ugly.

"A witch," thought Babette. "He has made me a witch! He is not kind at all!"

Asterux interrupted her thoughts.

"The goblins will search every inch of the forest for Princess Babette. But they will never look for Sesha, the young gypsy girl."

The wisdom of Asterux's plot began to dawn on her.

"Sesha. A gypsy girl." Babette grew delighted at the thought. A sly smile crossed her face. Before she could say a thing, Asterux was walking through the door to the next room.

"Come, Sesha, we have work to do."

Babette paused for a moment, then she hopped to her feet and paused again.

"Asterux."

"Yes, my dear?"

"There is something you must know. Perhaps I can never learn magic at all. I cannot read." She searched Asterux's face, wondering if he would change his mind about teaching her.

Asterux smiled at the princess. He already knew.

"My dear, you don't have to worry at all. You will not find this magic with your eyes. You will find it in your heart."

The princess followed him to the next room, leaving the name Babette behind.

· 11 ·

Sesha's Magic

On Sesha's windowsill lay a moonflower seed—the same moonflower seed that had been there for four years. Sesha sat in a chair, staring at the seed, just as she had done every day for four years, as she tried—and failed—to find the power to open the seed.

The power, as Asterux explained, came not from strange potions or mysterious powders. It had little to do with words, although more difficult magic would require a language she did not yet know. This magic was different. It was a power Sesha would have to discover inside the deepest recesses of her soul.

To begin her search, Asterux offered a simple instruction.

"Remember all those who treated you with kindness and love. Remember their deeds, each of them. Consider them. Cherish them. And from those deeds, you will find a power within."

Indeed, this task was easy, for in the life of a princess there are many such deeds to remember. Through Sesha's mind passed a grand parade of people who lived in the palace and who, eager to please, had helped her, praised her, and encouraged her. For many weeks, she thought of these deeds and they made her feel good. She thought of Thor, who had saved her life, cared for her, and sent her to live with Asterux in the forest. She thought of her mother, who always understood that she was not like the others and protected her from the king. She thought of Hugga Hugga, the great but kindly Minotaur who gave her rides as a child. She thought of Asterux himself. And when she thought of these things, she felt a glow inside and that glow made her strong.

The next step was harder.

"Sesha," Asterux told her, "now you must think of all those who have hurt you, who have given you small offenses, and who have caused you annoyance, and worse, pain. You must consider them all. You must understand them. You must understand the weaknesses and hardships that gave rise to their deeds. Then you must care for them. You must love them. And when you are able to love them, you must forgive them."

Sesha had lived the life of a princess. Who at the palace would risk bringing harm or insult to a young royal? So the annoying deeds were few, and Sesha wracked her brain to remember them. There was an episode with her brother, Prince Keanu. She had stolen his crown and hidden it behind a dung heap in the stables. When he found out, he painted her name on the wall of the cathedral. The king knew exactly who did this or so he thought. He raged at Babette and punished her severely.

But forgiving Keanu was easy. The whole matter was her fault from the start. So she thought of the goblins who tried to catch her in the meadow and she forgave them, but that was easy because they did not know her and were merely doing their jobs. Catching her would make them heroes, and Sesha could easily imagine herself in their place.

After much searching, she could find no more, so she went to Asterux.

"No one insults a princess. I have endured few hardships or wrongs. I can forgive the small deeds, but the forgiveness is too easy. There is no power from that."

Asterux thought for a long time.

"I had not considered this problem. But you are right. Not having these small offenses will make your next challenge even harder. You will have to find strength for the final step. Think of your greatest pain in your life, think of its source, think of the one individual above all others whose wrongs have hurt you in a deep and lasting way. Consider him, understand him, and forgive him."

So Sesha went back to her room and she immediately thought of the goblin, the executioner, who had held the sword on the balcony as her family awaited their fate. When she thought of this goblin, she felt hatred.

How could anyone, even a goblin, raise a sword above her family before a cheering and heartless army? How could she possibly love or forgive this creature? No matter how she tried, she failed.

After months of trying, with no success at all, she went to Asterux and told him that her magic would never come. But Asterux was nothing if not patient and spoke these words:

"What brings someone to commit acts of violence? Understand the life that stands behind their terrible deeds. Understand the burdens those deeds become. And if he bears no shame, pity him all the more because he has lost the goodness that is the true magic of life itself. Search your heart. Look deeper. It is there. And when you find it, you will find compassion and understanding, even for the executioner."

For months, Sesha thought of the goblin with the sword. She thought what it must be like to lift a sword to take the life of another—perhaps each and every day. She wondered what lived inside of him and what must have surely died. She felt his emptiness and it felt painful. And then it made her sad. She realized that somehow, in some way, this creature had been robbed of kindness, affection, and love, and that grief was the first step on the path to forgiveness. In her imaginings, she saw cruelties and humiliations and wondered, though she could not know, which of these had befallen the executioner and stolen from his soul. The more she imagined, the sadder she became. She grieved for all that he must have endured. She ached for what he had lost. From her sadness, she began to understand that he was indeed as much a victim as her own family. From this understanding, she found love. And then, after months of struggle, she forgave him.

Her forgiveness stirred a new power inside her. A deep goodness stirred in her body. It was strong. It was hopeful. With this new power, she turned to open the seed. She felt a surge inside of her. Her body shook with energy. With all her might, she focused on the seed that had stood motionless on the windowsill for four long years.

The seed still did not open.

She slumped in her chair, her body still trembling and covered with sweat. She rose, ran to Asterux, and fell to the floor before him.

"I am not good enough," she cried. "I will never find the power. Why can't I just say chants or use magic potions?"

"There are many magics, my dear," Asterux responded. "There are magics that rise from old texts and languages no longer spoken in this world. There are potions, chants, and spells that trade power for possession of the soul. But these are the magics of evil. The magic of the good is different." Asterux paused. "And far more powerful as well."

"But I have forgiven and no magic has come."

Asterux spoke slowly and gently.

"Perhaps, my dear, you have not forgiven all."

ᕮᗰᗩᕓ

Days later, Sesha stared at the seed and searched through the memories of her life. When she could not find that person— the one who caused her the greatest pain—she laid her head on the table and wept once more.

In this sadness, her memories wandered. She saw her father. Red-faced and raging, angry at Babette's endless antics, he exploded in a tirade against his young daughter, whose pet snake had almost been swallowed by the visiting king.

"You are unworthy of this kingdom! The fate of every man, woman, and child of this kingdom rests with this family to which you belong. Do you know what that means? What if our kingdom is forced to turn to you in search of a queen? What will they find? A lowly girl unworthy of the crown!"

Though this moment was years ago, the king's ferocious eyes burned in Sesha's mind. She arose and left the room.

"Father was right," thought Sesha. "I am not worthy even to live here in Asterux's home."

⌾

The next day, Sesha sat in her room and thought of her father again. Her remembrance of his harsh words, so often delivered, drove her deeper and deeper into despair.

Memories rolled by. He was standing before his subjects, thousands of them, at the gates of the palace and he spoke with beautiful words of kindness and love. But he found no such words for her, for she was not worthy.

Another memory emerged. She had entered a room and found him alone. He was seated, slumped forward, his head in his hands. When he heard her, he looked up. She jumped back, fearing his rage. But what she saw in his face was not anger but a deep sadness.

"Babette," he said, "if I have failed you, if I have failed our kingdom, please forgive me. A king, your father, is only a man."

An advisor entered the room and whispered something to the king. The king stepped out onto the balcony. There, standing before him, was the army of Sonnencrest, ready to depart for the forest to defend their land. His words betrayed none of his doubts.

His voice boomed out over the army, "The fate of our kingdom rests in your hands. Some say that a terrible destiny lies ahead. But goodness is always the greater force. Our own courage, fortified by virtue, is a mighty power. Darkness can never withstand the power of the sun. As you leave this city to do battle in the forest, know that the force of evil can never vanquish the good. We will drive these goblins from our land."

With those words, a great cheer erupted and the soldiers, confident and inspired, marched away to meet their foe. Stepping back into the palace, the king's sad face returned and he went to his study to be alone.

It had been a long time since Babette had thought of that moment. It had confused her at the time. Now, four years older, she saw her father in a new way. She saw in his life a loneliness she had never realized before. She saw the weight of the kingdom pressing down upon him. She understood for the first time that every citizen, in some way, depended upon him for their well-being, their livelihood, and their freedom itself.

As she thought of these things, his harsh words took on a different meaning. His words were meant to prepare her. She was never meant to wear the crown, but the crown might find her nevertheless. That her father never understood her could not matter. His job was to make her ready to rule.

Suddenly, a new idea raced through her mind.

"Perhaps his words were painful to him as well. Perhaps he understood her better than she knew. Perhaps he was never free to love me as I am."

From these thoughts came a new understanding of the man who had towered over her life. From this understanding, she found a new love for her father. As she did, she felt a powerful force grow inside her.

Her arms began to tremble and she climbed to her feet. More and more, the power grew until it surged with a force that she never imagined possible. With this power, her life passed before her and once again she forgave Keanu and the goblins in the meadow and even the executioner who danced across the balcony with his sword. At the end, she saw her father and the love she felt for him welled up from deep inside her soul. For a long time she trembled and shook until finally she fell to her bed.

An hour later she rose. She looked to the windowsill.

The moonflower seed had sprouted.

· 12 ·

The Enchanted Song

"Sesha, I never doubted you," Asterux proclaimed, but Sesha hardly heard his words.

On her tiptoes, she spun in little circles across the room. Though she was fat and awkward, today she floated through the air. When she stopped, she looked back at Asterux, with steady eyes and a confident smile.

"What next, my teacher? What next?"

Asterux, who had seen Sesha gripped by the torment of failure each day for four long years, laughed so loud and long that Sesha was at first offended. But soon they laughed together. When their laughter was finally exhausted, Asterux replied.

"The next step, my dear Sesha, is to make the koowik disappear."

ALEX and HAL MALCHOW

"I can do that now," Sesha teased, grabbing the stuffed animal and hiding it behind her back.

"Yes, but to make the koowik truly disappear, you will need words."

"What words?"

"I don't know," Asterux replied.

"How can you not know?" Babette asked. "You know *everything*."

Asterux just laughed. "My dear, you flatter me. The entirety of what I know could be stored in a mustard seed, with room to spare. I know the words that *I* would use to make the koowik disappear. But the words that will allow *you* to vanish the poor creature? I'm afraid you will have to find them yourself."

"Where should I look?" asked the princess.

Asterux just smiled back. "The location, my dear, is inside you."

༺༻

"From the depths of the griesonaut's soul, I command you to disappear!" Sesha practically shouted at the stuffed koowik that sat on the table in her room.

The koowik was not impressed. Even Thor's old expression did not work. In fact, for four long weeks, the koowik had endured chants of every imaginable nature.

"Koo da koo da koo da koo da doodle koo!"

"Ahhhhmmmm. Ahhhhhmmmm. Ahhhhmmmmm."

"Oh, creature of the forest, feel the power, hear the spirit, disappear before me."

Yet the wretched koowik remained.

Lately, Sesha had resorted to cursing the koowik. That brought Asterux into the room to deliver a sharp lecture about mixing bad language with the magic of the good.

Once again, Sesha despaired.

Once again, Asterux counseled patience.

"These words are inside of you, my dear. All good things come in their own time."

"But I have tried everything. Everything! I don't even know any other words."

"You might be surprised at what you know. When you find the words, you will know they are the right ones, even before you speak them yourself."

But day after day, the koowik remained.

Sesha searched her memories. What were the kindest words that were spoken to her? She remembered her mother consoling her after one of her father's rages: "You are like the Meciduous butterfly, purple and brown," she said, "unlike the rest but more beautiful than them all."

So she summoned her power and spoke: "Meciduous."

The koowik did not flinch.

Each time, before she tested her words, she first summoned her powers. She reviewed her life, loved her enemies, and forgave all wrongs. Her body would shake and tremble and the power would surge. And when she had delivered her words, always with failure as a result, she would collapse on her bed drained in both body and mind.

So, today, after another failed attempt, Sesha lay trembling on her bed. In this state, she entered a dream in which she was walking in the forest when her bird, Principeelia, appeared. The bird began to sing and its song had a rhythm that was haunting and slow. And though Sesha was afraid of the forest, the song pulled her along the trail, away from Asterux's cabin.

Suddenly, she stepped out of the forest and onto the plains. In the open landscape, she could see many villages and towns and even the city of Blumenbruch all at once, as though the kingdom had shrunk to miniature size. What she saw frightened her terribly.

Every village, every town, every city was in flames. She tried to run away, but she could not. The song of the bird was too strong.

She awoke suddenly, stunned by what she had seen. Her eyes rose and she thought she saw Principeelia standing on the windowsill, but she blinked and the windowsill was empty. Then she knew.

She rose to her feet and extended her arms. She summoned her memories of goodness and wrong. She called forth the goblin swordsman and, deep within, she showered him with forgiveness and love. And then she considered her father and the love she felt launched her power again.

Inside her, a great force was raging. Barely able to stand upright, her body shook so hard that the chair rattled on the floor and across the ceiling the creatures and planets danced in the air. She looked toward the koowik and from her lips came a whistle, a low whistle with a slow melody that was rapturous and haunting.

It was the song that had carried her into the forest.

The koowik vanished from sight.

The magic words were not words at all. They were music— the song of her precious little bird.

· 13 ·

The Legend of Scodo

The forest floor was wet and the recent rain had cleansed the air. The scents of flowers and new leaves were everywhere.

Sesha was now a young woman. After almost ten years with Asterux, she had come to know the forest and enjoy its splendor. She had no fear of goblins or griesonauts or bat spiders. When danger approached, she simply made herself disappear.

Today, enjoying the spring, she had wandered far from Asterux's cabin. The road she walked was the road that the wagons traveled to and from the goblin fort. On both sides, patches of purple flowers carpeted the hillside between the trees. The sound of a songbird caught her ear. She turned and marched upward through the brush to listen.

She gasped. Before her, in the high grass, was a body. Its shoulders were wide and its limbs thick and heavy. Its body, far bigger than that of a man, was covered with black scales. From its back emerged a tail, longer than its legs, and encased in the dark shell of an insect. At the end of the tail were two sharp points.

"Are you alright?" Sesha asked, stepping back from the body.

The body lay silent and still on the ground.

She leaned over for a closer look. It was wearing a cloak, coarse and splotched with circles of blood. She lifted the cloak away from the body to reveal deep wounds that cut through the scales and into the back. She placed her ear to the body. There was breathing, but it was faint.

She stood up to tear a cloth from her dress. Then she knew.

"Scodo," she cried. It was the scorpion man lying before her.

Sesha knew little of healing but thought that perhaps her magic might mend his wounds. So she placed her hands on the creature's back and summoned memories of goodness and found forgiveness and felt the power grow inside her. As her power grew, she felt the body stir beneath her hand. Suddenly, it lifted and rolled onto its back, staring up at Sesha.

The scales merged together into a smooth flat sheet that covered its face, which was black except for two red eyes that glowed back at her with no movement or expression. Sesha had never spoken to the scorpion man. He was far too shy to address a princess. But now she did not hesitate at all.

"You are Scodo, the great warrior of the Sonnencrest army. I thought you were dead or in the dungeon! What are you doing here in the forest? How did you escape?"

"I just walked away," replied Scodo in a calm voice. "What goblin wanted to take me prisoner? Think of the nightmares I might give the guards!"

"Do you not remember me?" Sesha asked.

"Should I?" responded the scorpion man.

"I am," she started, and then caught herself. "I am sure you wouldn't. People forget me," she stuttered. "Probably because I am so ugly."

"Don't feel so sorry for yourself," Scodo snapped back. "I'm no beauty either."

For the first time, the monster smiled. He sat up, grimacing from the pain.

"What happened?" Sesha asked, gesturing at Scodo's wounds.

"I have been stealing from the goblins for years. I leave their food for the poor villagers nearby. This time, they set an ambush. They probably think they are rid of me." He stared at Sesha for a moment. "But what about you? What young girl walks alone in this forest? Aren't you afraid?"

"Not one bit." Sesha extended her hand. "My name is Sesha."

For hours, Scodo and Sesha talked about the forest and Sesha asked many questions about life in Sonnencrest on the plains. Scodo shared tales of the hardship and hunger and his attacks against goblin wagons and patrols.

"You are a hero indeed," said Sesha as the sun started to set. "You must come with me and get the rest you need to heal."

But Scodo refused.

"Then, can we talk again?" Sesha asked.

"Come to the road where the wagons travel and whistle. Don't worry, I can protect you from the goblins."

"You think I need your protection?" Sesha scoffed.

But before the last word left her mouth, Scodo was gone.

That night, back at the cabin, Sesha told Asterux about her meeting in the forest. "Do you know of this scorpion man?" she asked.

"Indeed I do," replied Asterux.

"Do you know his story? My father only mentioned him in hushed tones, and I do not know much about him."

Asterux nodded slowly, and he told Sesha the monster's sad tale. Twenty-seven years earlier, a traveling peddler named Girodan entered a small goblin village. Girodan sold cloth and spices and tools, along with goods made by merchants in other towns. Girodan unloaded his wagon and began to organize a cooking demonstration. A young goblin maiden named Sahali was asked to assist.

The maiden was enchanted by the fast-talking human with his strange utensils, exotic spices, and elegant showmanship. A goblin maiden, even the most beautiful, holds few attractions for the human eye. But Girodan, for all his showmanship, was a lonely man and weary of his life on the road. He looked upon his new helper and he saw beauty in the girl.

The next day, Sahali appeared early, eager to volunteer once more. And when it was time for Girodan to leave the village, she begged him to stay and sell for another day or two. He did. They fell in love.

Knowing that marriage between a goblin and a human was strictly forbidden, they left quietly together under the cover of darkness. To evade the scorn their love would surely bring, they fled deep into the forest. There they lived alone, shunning contact with goblins and humans alike.

Meanwhile, shamed and heartbroken, Sahali's parents went to the elder of their village, to plead for his help. They begged him to find and return their daughter. But the elder had other designs.

Enraged at the thought of this strange and disgusting union, he sent a messenger to the wizard Zindown. The villagers had no idea where the couple was, but finding them in the forest was no challenge for a wizard.

Zindown appeared at their forest home and his timing was tragic. He arrived one week before their first child was to be born. Seeing that Sahali was with child, Zindown issued a hideous curse.

"You will pay for your deeds and you will pay well. You will not have a goblin child. You will not have a human child," he roared. "No goblin blood will run in his veins."

Sahali and Girodan looked on in horror.

"He will be a monster with the armor of an insect on the body of a man. All who see him will step back in horror. And in the eyes of all who witness his horrid appearance, he will feel the sting of this curse, every day of his life."

Sadly, upon his birth, the wizard's terrible curse came true. Worried for their son, Girodan and Sahali moved even deeper into the woods. They named their son Serkano, which in the goblin language means "precious gift."

Whatever his appearance, Girodan and Sahali raised their son with great love and affection. When the boy asked his mother why he looked so different and if, in fact, he was ugly, his mother replied that he was the most handsome child of all. It was his parents, she explained, who had been made ugly by a spell. Not knowing anyone else, the young boy accepted this story.

The boy's appearance was cursed, but in other ways Serkano was blessed.

When he was only twelve, he was attacked by a bear. He fought back, breaking the bear's legs. But Serkano refused to kill the creature. Instead, he set its broken joints and brought food to help it heal. When the bear died, he was stricken with grief.

Once, he helped his father build a new wall for their cabin. With only two or three strokes of an axe, he could fell a good-sized tree. But he soon grew bored with his axe and began pulling trees directly from the ground. Later, the family built a large house of stones because young Serkano could lift rocks from the hillsides and carry them to the site of their new home.

As Serkano approached adulthood, he yearned to leave his forest home and see the world. Unaware of how others would view his appearance, he ignored his parents' pleas and followed the long forest path to the nearest village.

As he stepped into the street, he stopped short and gazed all about him. He had never seen so many houses. "There must be a hundred people living in this city! Maybe more," he thought. He trembled in anticipation.

He would speak with these goblins, make friends, share adventures. He turned to one of the goblins walking the streets. He waved and called out.

"Hello, my friend."

A terrible scream filled the air.

"Come back," he pleaded. But the street emptied before him.

A minute later, a stone struck his head and then another. But he did not run, just stood there shielding his face with his arms.

"They will see that I mean no harm," he thought.

But a crowd formed facing him, shouting. In their hands, they held clubs and stones. Dogs barked and growled, circling the mob, eager to make noise but not to attack.

Serkano turned and ran. The mob followed, always at a safe distance. Fearing to bring the mob to his parents' home, he ran deep into the forest where no one could follow. When he was sure he had lost his pursuers, he returned to his home.

The paths of the forest were covered with the footprints that only Serkano could make. Following those footprints, the mob had found his home. The house he had helped build was a pile of broken stones and ashes. His parents were dead. His strange but happy life was over.

For the first time, a new emotion entered his heart. Hatred stirred inside him.

He left the forest. Wearing a long cloak to hide his tail and a hood with holes for his eyes, he wandered the countryside. In this outfit, his frame towering above ordinary men, he drew notice and suspicion. But at least no one ran. At least no crowd formed to chase him from their town.

In his disguise, he crossed the river into Sonnencrest. There, in a small village, a man asked him if he could fight. Serkano thought for a moment and said he could. The man directed him to Blumenbruch, where the Sonnencrest army was seeking recruits. But at the palace gate, he was asked to lift his hood. He was never even allowed inside.

Deeply discouraged, Serkano left Blumenbruch, walking down the road that led to the forest. Late that night, he came upon a terrible crime. A band of thieves had attacked a wagon carrying a woman and six children. When Serkano arrived, they were beating her with clubs.

Wielding a small log, the scorpion man made short work of these thieves, but one of them escaped carrying a three-year-old boy. Serkano hushed the woman and her other children. His hearing was keen and he alone could hear the faint sound of footsteps far away. Even at night, Serkano was a skilled tracker. Following the sounds, stepping silently and efficiently through the forest trails, Serkano overtook the criminal, who dropped the boy and ran.

Serkano lifted the child into his arms and retraced his journey. As he and the boy passed through a clearing, the light of the moon shone across Serkano's face. The boy screamed. Serkano spoke in a voice that was calm and reassuring.

"My son," he said, "fear not the face of a man, for it is his heart you must know. My name is Serkano and I have been afraid, just like you."

The softness of his voice and the kindness of his words calmed the boy, who soon hugged Serkano tightly around the neck.

When Serkano returned to the wagon, he saw the boy's father, who had ridden ahead before the attack. Seeing this monster carrying his son, he lifted his sword, but the boy cried out and the father held back. Serkano placed the boy on the ground and disappeared into the woods.

"Who was that creature?" the father asked in amazement.

"Scodo," the small boy replied.

Word of this "Scodo," half monster, half hero, spread rapidly throughout Sonnencrest. Hearing this story, Hugga Hugga recalled the visit of the scorpion monster. He went to his commander and asked permission to find the creature and bring him back.

Soon, Scodo, as he was now known, was a soldier of Sonnencrest and his deeds became legend. When a gang of twenty bandits entered the kingdom, Scodo slew half of them with his sword. The survivors climbed into a wagon to escape. But when Scodo grabbed the wheels from behind, the three horses could not move the wagon forward. He tipped the wagon to its side, dumping the thieves and their loot across the ground.

When the goblins marched on Sonnencrest, they knew they would have to be prepared for the scorpion man. As Sonnencrest retreated from the forest, a special unit was assigned to cover him with nets. By the time he cut himself free, the battle was lost. No goblin dared take him hostage. So he simply walked away and he began a new life in the Hexenwald Forest.

"What does he do in the forest?" asked Sesha, amazed at this sad story.

Asterux replied, "He steals money and food and delivers them to the villages at night. He is too shy to allow himself to be seen. I am surprised he spoke to you at all."

"Well, he didn't have much choice," said Sesha with a smile. "And I am sure that this shyness of his is not beyond my cure."

· 14 ·

Out of the Forest

As her tenth year with Asterux came to an end, Sesha's magic had grown. In the time since she had found the low whistle of her bird, she had learned magic tricks of all kinds, often to Asterux's dismay.

She changed the color of Asterux's cat!

She created a wind funnel that lifted Asterux's only flower bush right out of the ground!

And on one enchanted evening, with the full moon hanging over the clearing, she summoned the griesonauts to dance and snort outside Asterux's window!

These antics tested even Asterux's patience. But while Sesha found merriment, she proved a hardworking student as well. She mastered difficult magic. She brought dried toads and insects to life. She set bushes aflame.

Asterux grew proud of her accomplishments, but Sesha was never satisfied.

"I want to know the greatest feats a wizard can master," she told him. "I want to do them all!"

Asterux laughed.

"The greatest skills of the greatest wizards take a lifetime to master. Some are only available for evil. The magic of the good works in different ways."

"Tell me one I don't know. Tell me an evil one!"

Asterux thought for a moment.

"Have I told you of the encirclement?"

"No!" Sesha replied, almost shouting in her excitement.

"Well in the encirclement, the wizard loses his form."

"Her form," Sesha corrected.

"In the encirclement, the wizard loses *her* form and becomes a mist, a little more than fog but a little less than rain. This mist encircles the victim."

A bright sparkle danced in Sesha's eyes.

"In the encirclement, the wizard can know everything her victim is thinking. Even more, the wizard can know everything her victim knows. She can listen to thoughts. She can search memories and even find things that the victim himself may not recall. It is a robbery—a robbery of any information the mind may contain."

"And the victim will never know?"

"The victim will never know."

"And why can't I do the encirclement?"

"The evil magic is not available to you."

"And why not?" Sesha shot back.

"Because your own magic arises from the goodness of your heart. What is the magic of evil? It is dark spells, grim creatures, and powers that grow the torments of human-kind. To know these skills would plunder the goodness of your heart. All you have mastered would vanish in the blink of an eye."

"Well, okay," replied Sesha, a little disappointed. "But back to this encirclement. How many evil wizards can do it?"

"The encirclement requires so many years to master that I am not sure there is a wizard alive today who can still do it."

"And Zindown, the great goblin wizard you once described. Can he do the encirclement?"

"Zindown is indeed a great wizard. But I think the encirclement is even beyond his skills."

"Not even Zindown!" thought Sesha. Then she was back at work.

⁕

One morning Asterux entered the main room of the cabin and was surprised to see Sesha on the floor, a book in her lap.

"So, you are giving reading a try?" he asked.

"I can read!" Sesha replied. "I just can't see what I read."

"What do you mean?"

"I know the letters and the sounds. I know the words. But when I look on the page, the letters and the words don't stay still on the page."

Asterux thought for a moment. Then he spoke.

"Let me try something. Stand back from the book."

Sesha did as she was told.

Asterux closed his eyes and mumbled something she could not understand. The book popped off the floor. When it landed, it was bigger and thicker.

"Try this," Asterux said.

Sesha opened the book. Gone were the curls and flourishes that adorned the letters. Now they were simpler and larger than before. Between the lines, there was more spacing. She read slowly and carefully—

THE WONDER OF THE WONDERLICKS MADE

WONKY WONKS IN THE WESTERN WORLD.

Sesha looked up with eyes wide.

"Well?" asked the wizard.

"They still move but they don't bump together." Sesha lowered her head and returned to the book. "I guess that can get me started."

"Keep at it," said Asterux excitedly. "Sometimes, all success needs is a small assist."

⟊⟋⟊

A few days later, Sesha awoke. Outside, the birds welcomed the day with a cacophony of competing songs. The sunlight burst through the window and from the ceiling the koowik seemed to smile.

Sesha bounced from her bed and entered the main room of the cabin. On the floor were three wooden boxes. Asterux sat at the table, his breakfast before him. Through the window she saw an old mule.

"Going somewhere?" she asked in a cheerful voice.

Asterux turned to Sesha. On his face was the same hopeful smile that greeted her when she first arrived at the cabin.

"My dear, our time together is over. You have mastered many things."

"I've even learned to read!" Sesha announced proudly.

"Indeed," Asterux replied. "But now events larger than ourselves summon us both."

Sesha blinked. "We are leaving?"

"*You* are leaving."

"Where will I go?"

"I have packed things you will need. Outside is a mule. His name is Zauberyungi."

"Magic Boy!" Sesha cried, recalling the name's meaning from an old tale.

"You can ride him out of the forest to a town where you can buy a wagon and supplies. You will sell supplies from your wagon. But that will not be your main work."

"And what will be my work?"

"I think you already know." Asterux straightened up in his chair, looking directly at Sesha.

For a long time, Sesha sat in her chair. Asterux's words felt too large. Her magic felt suddenly small. But her ten years with Asterux had given her strength.

"Well, Asterux, how do I start?"

Asterux leaned across the table, a sly smile filled his face.

"Sesha, my dear, for starters, you are going to transport a hero through this forest."

BOOK TWO

· 15 ·

Darrow of Ael

 en years of goblin rule had transformed the once happy kingdom of Sonnencrest. Homes were looted. Farmlands were burned. People disappeared, never to be seen again.

There were no laws, no courts. Justice was limited to what one goblin might decide. Mere suspicion could bring terrible punishment. Fear ruled the kingdom.

But fear was not the only hardship. Looting robbed farmers of money to buy seed. Fields lay bare. Shops closed their doors. Across the kingdom, dinner tables were empty.

After ten years, the people of Sonnencrest barely bothered to complain, for the goblins had robbed them of more than earthly possessions. The goblins had taken their hope.

But in deepest darkness, even a tiny light glows like a mighty star. And in the most unlikely of places, a small light emerged.

At a far corner of the kingdom, a three-day walk below the forest where the goblins faced the archers in the trees, stood two mountains. They stood face-to-face, two sheer cliffs rising to the sky, staring at one another—almost touching but always apart. At the bottom of this slender gap ran a small stream. Beside the stream stood eight miserable cabins.

The homes were constructed of stone and held together with mud and clay. In the winter, the wind seeped between the cracks, stealing heat from the fire. In the summer, when the rains came, water trickled through their roofs. No grass or bushes or flowering trees surrounded these homes because nothing could grow in the shade of the mountains. Inside these shadows lived twenty-seven inhabitants, half of them trolls, whose homes were the grim reward for their service to the goblin crown.

This village was called Ael, although few in Sonnencrest knew its name. In this village lived a boy called Darrow. He was short, frail, and weighed so little he had to steady himself against a strong breeze. His plain brown hair was straight but tangled and never met a comb. Looking upon him, he was remarkable in only one way. When he walked, his head bobbed up and down in an odd rhythm because his left leg was two inches shorter than his right.

The boy attended a school, if you could call it that. The teacher, Empherny Groompus, was the oldest man in the village. At eighty-three years of age, he could hardly read and write himself. But old Groompus owned the only three books in Ael and for that reason alone he was given the job. Few students took interest in these books, but young Darrow had learned them by heart. So, each day in class, rather than speaking himself, Groompus would turn to the boy and say, "Darrow, can you tell us a story?"

From that moment, Darrow unleashed his beautiful voice and recited great stories of gallant knights, foolish kings, vanity, greed, and valor. His stories were embellished far beyond the content of the books themselves and his voice danced with passion, drama, and wonder.

While Groompus remained awake, Darrow was the star pupil. But soon Groompus would waver. His eyelids would droop. His head would sag. Finally, his chin would hit the desk and the first snore would rattle the walls and strands of drool would drip from his lips.

That was when Darrow's true ordeal would begin.

For with Groompus lost to slumber, the troll children rose from their chairs and began their cruel games. They would seize Darrow, tie his feet together, and hang him from the elderberry tree outside the schoolroom. Then they subjected Darrow to all kinds of schoolyard torture. They howled as they tickled Darrow with the tail of a live raccoon. They tried to stretch his shorter leg to see if they could make it equal to the other. Once, they even formed a triangle, tying poor Darrow in a ball and throwing him back and forth in an evil game. During all of these ordeals, Darrow made it a matter of pride never to cry out or show his pain.

Darrow's father urged him to leave school to work in the mines. His younger brother had already quit. But Darrow announced that he did not give in to bullies. "Better to fight and lose," Darrow replied, "than to live in fear."

But when Darrow reached his sixteenth birthday, school was over and his work in the mines began.

Deep in the mineshafts, his short leg struggled to gain traction on the slippery floor. His small frame staggered under the weight of a basket of ore. His clumsiness earned him beatings, and the beatings made him even weaker. Finally, Darrow was dismissed.

One day, as Darrow sat at home reading old Groompus' books yet again, his father shouted from outside.

"Hoofbeats!"

Darrow scrambled to his feet and ran from the house. At the edge of the village, he ducked behind a boulder and watched the road, for riders rarely meant anything good.

A horse appeared, then four more. Atop these horses were green-skinned soldiers. One by one, they dismounted and entered homes. There was no gold or silver in Ael, of course. Any valuables that survived the first raid had long ago been sold off to buy food or clothing. One goblin emerged with a hammer, cursing his meager prize.

But from another house a goblin pulled a goat, and clutching that goat was the old man, Groompus.

"Please, this is Belameen, she is all I have," old Groompus pleaded. And it was true that unlike the other goats, which were kept tethered in hidden places far from the village, Belameen lived inside the old teacher's home.

As Darrow watched from behind the rocks, the goblin secured a rope around Belameen's neck, Groompus still clutching her with both arms. The soldier lifted a whip and struck the old man again and again. Groompus cried out in pain but would not let go.

A second goblin lifted a stick and struck Groompus squarely on the head. The old man collapsed on the goat, one arm still holding on. The goblin struck a second time and a third.

Darrow could bear no more.

Emerging from behind the rocks, Darrow grabbed Groompus' walking stick and swung with all his power, knocking the goblin to the ground. But the other drew a sword and slashed—Darrow barely sidestepped the blow. Two more goblins arrived. Darrow was clubbed unconscious. When the goblins were sure Darrow was dead, a soldier stuffed the hammer in his shirt and away they rode, leading Belameen by a rope.

From their own hiding places, Darrow's father and brother hurried to the scene. Surprised to find him still breathing, they carried him into the house. An old woman set his broken bones.

As Darrow lay unconscious, he developed a fever that, to all around him, foretold a tragic end. But on the morning of the fourth day, his fever broke and his recovery began. As he lay healing in his bed, he seethed and considered the future with a new and different view.

Soon he could climb to his feet. With crutches, he could move about the house. Then he needed only a walking stick. And when he could walk at least as well as he walked before, he went to his father to share his plans.

Darrow stood, arms folded waiting to speak. Looking up, his father said, with some satisfaction, "I hope you have learned a lesson."

"I have," Darrow announced. "The lesson is that I would rather stand, fight, and die than live under goblin rule."

"You are lucky not to be dead already," his father answered.

"I will fight them again." Darrow spoke in a matter-of-fact tone.

"Darrow, what have you been reading?" his father asked, sure that his son was carried away with some new and glorious tale.

"Nothing, Father. I have just been thinking. All across Sonnencrest, the goblins are terrorizing our people. Someone has to act. And if no one else will do it, then that someone will be me."

The father was certain his son had lost his mind.

"Look at yourself. You know nothing of fighting. You are small and lame. The goblins will snuff you like a candle whenever they choose."

"They have crushed me already," Darrow replied, "but I still stand. I can find others. I can't be the only one willing to fight. But someone has to take the first step."

Now his father was on his feet. He shouted that Darrow had lost his mind. He warned him to say nothing to his brother, Mempo, who was hiding outside, listening to every word. But even in the face of his father's tirade, Darrow stood calm and firm. In the end, exhausted by the ordeal, deeply pained by the fate that awaited his son, the father decided to share his deepest secret in hopes that Darrow would grant him one request.

"My son, as you know, your mother died when your brother was born. She was not from Ael. I have never told you this story.

"She and her younger brother were the children of a noble family in a kingdom not far away, but what had been a happy childhood disappeared when they were kidnapped for a horrible task."

"What did she have to do?" Darrow asked.

"There is a rare spider that lives in narrow crevices in some caves. Evil wizards prize the venom of the spider, for it is an essential ingredient in many of their potions. Children were kidnapped for their small hands and forced to reach into the crevices of the caves where these spiders lived. Your mother and uncle were among the children taken to the caves. When their hands became too large for this task, their captors disposed of them. One day, deep within the cave, your mother and her brother met a hermit who had rescued them. The hermit had led a terrible life, performing many cruel deeds. In his downfall, he found repentance and learned a strange magic that she said arose from forgiving others.

"Your mother used her new powers to tell her father that they were alive and guide him to their hiding place. Her father sailed to Globenwald. He brought soldiers and engaged in a great battle with the wizard. In this battle, your mother used her powers to help her father, but at a crucial moment, her hatred of the wizard returned and her powers failed. Her father was killed. Your mother, now almost seventeen, fled with her brother, the goblin soldiers close on their trail.

"Once the goblins saw them, the goblins fired arrows that struck your mother in several places. Wounded, she knew that she could no longer elude the goblins, so she pretended to be dead so her brother might escape. Before he left, she gave him a gift. I asked about this gift, but she never told me what it was.

"I found her, a stranger, still alive at the side of the trail not far from Ael. I carried her to my home and after a long time she recovered. I never expected her to stay in Ael. After

Mempo was born, as she lay on her deathbed, she made one request. She told me that one day you would leave Ael. When you did, I must send you to see her brother.

"So before you go charging the goblins with swords and spears, do me one last favor. Find this uncle of yours. He is a wise man. Seek his advice. Ask for his help."

Darrow marveled at this story. He had no idea how to begin his quest. Maybe this uncle could indeed be helpful. So he turned to his father and spoke.

"Of course I will go see him. But where does he live?"

"He lives in a forest somewhere on the other side of the plains."

"And what is this forest?"

"Hexenwald."

"And what is my uncle called?"

"His name is Asterux."

· 16 ·

A Magical Journey

High in the mountains, the last gasp of winter struggled against the awakening spring. Small patches of snow lay far apart on the ground and the frozen dew painted the landscape with swaths of sparkling white.

His great journey under way, Darrow hardly knew enough to be afraid. In his whole life, Darrow had ventured barely ten miles from Ael. He did not know the way to the forest or how to find this uncle of his once he was inside. He carried no sword and possessed no knowledge of the tactics of war. He was armed only with belief—a belief in the victory to come.

Each step, awkward though it might have been, was infused with purpose. In every fiber of his body, he felt strength he had never known.

On the second day of his journey, the path rose and he found himself standing before a cliff. Beneath him lay a great forest. To the right of the forest stretched a great plain. At first, this plain was speckled with woodlands, but toward the east the trees gradually thinned, giving way to what seemed an endless expanse of grass. The grass was still brown from the winter, and far, far away, it painted a perfectly straight line between land and sky.

"It's completely flat," thought Darrow who had never seen land like this. "Perhaps this forest is Hexenwald."

To him, the tiny kingdom of Sonnencrest seemed vast and endless. He stepped back into the road, bounding ahead, eager to explore what lay below.

The sun began to set and Darrow turned from the trail to find a place to sleep. At the side of the road, behind a tree, he found a pile of leaves. With his foot, he began leveling the pile. A voice cried out.

"Can't a man sleep in peace?"

Darrow jumped back.

From the leaves rose a head. The head was hairless and covered with splotches of dirt. One ear was gone and his small eyes squinted so tightly Darrow wondered how he could see. He stood up, his hands on his hips. He was a dwarf, heavyset, and even shorter than Darrow.

"I am sorry, good sir," Darrow responded. "I was only making a bed myself. You were completely covered by the leaves!"

"You'd cover yourself, too, if the goblins were after you!"

Darrow's interest perked up. Perhaps this dwarf might join his band.

"What are you wanted for?"

"Tasting."

"Pardon? Is tasting a crime?" asked Darrow, wiping his mouth.

"It's a job, clunkhead. I tasted food for the goblin who ruled our village. He likes using dwarfs. Poisons work quicker in wee bodies."

"Were you poisoned?"

"Not one bit. But that sorry spunkernick got sick, he did. And the blame was on me. I was lucky to escape with just the loss of one ear. That fish was delicious and healthy to boot, if you want my professional opinion."

"Another citizen wronged," thought Darrow, seizing his chance.

"Then perhaps you will join me. I am recruiting an army to fight the goblins."

For some time, the dwarf looked at Darrow, a boy, small, and with no weapon. He could summon no reply.

"Well, if you won't join me, then perhaps you will help me. I need to find the Hexenwald Forest. Is it far?"

"What makes you interested in Hexenwald?" the dwarf asked, stepping back, his eyes narrowing.

"I'm looking for a wise man."

"If he was so wise, he wouldn't be in that forest. That forest is full of bat spiders. Have you ever seen a bat spider?" the dwarf asked.

Darrow admitted he had not.

"They have twelve legs and two tiny wings. They perch in the branches where they wait until their victim falls asleep. Then they leap. Those wings help them hover in the air so when they land, it's so softly that the victim never wakes.

Then they suck its blood. They roam in packs, and they can suck you dry in a firefly's flash."

"Well, I will have to stay awake," Darrow replied.

"You can't go there anyway. It is a six-day journey across the plains. And you can't travel without the goblins' permission."

"Do you have permission?" Darrow asked.

"I do not. And I do not live on the plains." With that, the dwarf grabbed his belongings and scurried away into the forest.

⌒₥₥୭

Two days later, not heeding the dwarf's warning, Darrow was walking through the plains of Sonnencrest. The fears of the taster had not come to pass. No goblin had stopped him and for good reason. Who would fear a boy, small and lame, who walked alone with little more than the clothes on his back? But he had expected to meet his uncle by now. He had no more food and his stomach ached with hunger.

He spied an old woman, moving slowly, with a heavy load on her back.

"May I help you with your sack?" Darrow asked, hoping his assistance might lead to an offer of food.

"I'll take any help I can get," the woman replied practically throwing her bag to the ground. Darrow leaned over to grab the sack. It was heavy, but with one heave, he was able to swing it across his shoulder. But almost as soon as the bag was on his back, Darrow jumped to the side, dropping his load.

"It's moving," he exclaimed.

"Of course it's moving. It's snakes, you idiot!"

"Snakes!" Darrow was confused. "Why?"

"Haven't you heard?" the woman replied, with a tone of disgust. "The goblins love them. Snake soup. My boys catch them, and I sell them. It's not much, but it's a living." She stared at him curiously. "Where have you been these last ten years?"

Darrow once again positioned the wiggling sack on his back. "I live in the mountains."

"I guess there ain't many snakes there. So where are you headed?"

"Hexenwald."

"Well, snakes will be the least of your worries there. Have you ever heard of a griesonaut?"

"Griesonaut?"

"What mountains do you come from?"

"The ones to the south."

"Well, you might want to learn some things they're not teaching over there. These griesonauts look like lizards, 'cept they're long as a man. They have fur and webbed feet. They hide in the bogs. But they travel to the edge of the forest to grab dogs, children, or even grown women. Then they carry them back to eat. People won't live near that forest anymore. There's no controlling those creatures."

She paused and looked Darrow up and down.

"A runt like you would barely make them a good meal."

Darrow considered the griesonaut attack and the tactics he might use. Thinking of none, he spoke again.

"Have you heard of a wise man named Asterux?"

"He's no wise man."

"How do you know?"

"'Cause he's a wizard."

"A wizard?"

"He has powers. Good powers, so I heard. He must be dead."

"Why is that?"

"If there was any magic for the good, do you think we'd all be catching snakes for them goblins?"

Darrow stopped, absorbing this news. His uncle was a wizard, but he might be dead, and the forest was a very dangerous place. Well, no one said it was going to be easy.

"Can you tell me how I can find him?"

"No."

"Not even which part of the forest?"

"No one knows."

Her tone was so sharp. For a long time, they walked without words, but Darrow was hungry for conversation.

"What did you do before the goblins came? Did you always catch snakes?"

"I don't catch 'em. I just sell 'em. In the old days, I told fortunes."

"Will you tell mine?"

"I don't tell them anymore. They are all bad. Yours? You are traveling alone into the Hexenwald Forest with no weapon, looking for a wizard you will never find. You don't need me to know your fortune."

Darrow smiled at this warning.

"If things were so predictable, we wouldn't need fortunetellers, would we?"

For the first time, the woman smiled.

"Give me your hand."

Darrow set the snakes on the ground, gripping the bag with one hand. The woman did not look at his palm but wrapped his hand between both of her own and closed her eyes. For a long time she stood silent, then she opened her eyes. She was shaking.

"What did you see?" asked Darrow earnestly.

"Beware of the words of a loved one, for they mark the path of death."

Darrow gulped. "And what will be the outcome?"

She grabbed the bag from Darrow's hand and turned to walk away.

"But what is my fortune?" Darrow called after her.

"I told you. I do not tell fortunes anymore."

⚬⚬⚬

It was the morning of his fifth day on the plains. He was half a day from Hexenwald. Darrow thought often of bat spiders and griesonauts, but a short life did not frighten him. A hero's death was far better than life in Ael.

What troubled Darrow was the work before him. He was heading to the forest to find this uncle of his and he did not know the way. Worse, his uncle might even be dead. With or without his uncle, he would need to recruit an army, yet he knew not a single person outside of Ael. He would need weapons, yet he had never held a sword in his hand.

The road was almost empty. Occasionally, a villager walked by and a wagon or two passed, traveling to or from a farm.

The faint sound of hoofbeats told Darrow a horseman was approaching. Darrow continued to walk, not bothering to look.

The hoofbeats grew louder and soon a rider appeared, a goblin, dressed in a black coat with shining green trim, the uniform of the goblin cavalry. He rode past Darrow, hardly looking at the lame boy, but not long after he passed, the horse reeled and the rider looked back. At a slow canter, he approached Darrow.

"Where is your permission, young man?" he inquired in a voice that was a bit too polite for a goblin.

Darrow answered without hesitation. "I have none."

"Then why are you traveling?"

"I am going to see my uncle. Why should I need permission to visit my uncle?"

The soldier was amused.

"Give me a reason why I should not arrest you or strike you down on the spot."

"There are many good reasons."

"Give me one."

"What is your reward for ruling this poor kingdom?"

"Ha! There is no reward. In this wretched kingdom, there is nothing more to steal!"

"You are right. It must be a misery to rule a people so sad and pathetic. But what if things changed? What if these people suddenly awoke, worked hard, and became more prosperous? Surely you must be weary of a kingdom in such total despair?"

"Indeed," said the goblin, enjoying Darrow's words.

"Well, then you should know that my uncle is a wise man who wants to advise me on how our people might lift themselves up and rebuild our country. He believes your reign might be changed for the better. Perhaps you should escort me to my uncle's home."

"Well," replied the soldier, laughing out loud. "That is quite a task indeed. And where does this uncle of yours live?"

"In the forest."

The soldier's just shook his head. "Well, I suppose you'll be no threat to anyone for long."

With those words, the officer turned his horse and galloped away.

〇〜〇

A few hours later, Darrow once again heard hoofbeats, these slower than the last. A band of goblins approached. It was not much of an outfit—two horsemen, a wagon, and several soldiers on foot. But when they reached Darrow, an officer stepped down from the wagon and again asked to see Darrow's permission to travel.

"I have none," Darrow responded.

This time the goblin asked no questions about Darrow's plans.

"Throw him in the cage."

Two goblins grabbed Darrow while another removed a small cage from the wagon. The cage, barely big enough to hold even Darrow, was made of sticks bound together with twine. At its base were two small wooden wheels. A goblin tied Darrow's hands. Another opened the door of the cage while a third dumped Darrow inside. They tied the door shut and attached the cage to the back of the wagon.

The soldiers gathered around to look at the prisoner.

"Where are you taking me?" Darrow demanded.

"To a place you'll never leave," answered one goblin to the laughter of his comrades.

Inside the cage, Darrow struggled to free his hands, but the rope held tight. His body pressed against the sharp edges of the sticks that stabbed him as the cage jolted over each bump in the road. For the first time, Darrow felt afraid. Where were they headed? Would he be kept as a prisoner? Would they make him a slave? Worse, they might simply dump him in the bogs. If he died, who would ever know?

As the cage bounced along the road, Darrow peered out and saw a dark row of trees that rose from the plain like a black wall. Not a shrub or even tall grasses broke up the thick barrier of trees. It was as if God had drawn a line across the earth and decreed grassland on one side and forest on the other.

As the wagon entered the forest, the sun disappeared. The tree trunks were thick and closely spaced. Above them, branches spread out and overlapped in every direction. The road was no longer a road, only a trail, barely wide enough for the wagon. But what struck Darrow about the forest was the silence.

On that afternoon, almost at sunset, the forest made no sound. The goblins themselves ceased speaking as if their words might awaken some demon or stir evil forces against them.

Darrow pushed his back against the bars to test their strength, but they would not move. He tugged at the rope that tied his hands again, which caused the knots to pull tighter against his skin. In his mind, he searched for a strategy, but the best he could do was to resolve to run when they let him out of the cage.

As the wagon moved deeper into the forest, the goblins lit torches. They moved with soft and careful steps, eyes and ears attuned to anything that might pounce from the shadows around them. Suddenly, Darrow heard a noise, a low whistle, pulsating and sinister.

The goblins drew their swords. Like statues they waited, unwilling to offer a sound that might draw this unknown creature into their midst. The whistle grew louder, its rhythm haunting, and in the flickering torchlights, eyes met eyes looking for reassurance but finding none at all. For the first time, Darrow was thankful for his cage.

"A spirit," thought the captain, but he did not share his thought for fear that his men would turn and run. Then, as suddenly as it began, the sound was no more. There was no point venturing further. The captain gave orders to camp for the night.

Whatever the noises or the creatures who made them, Darrow knew the forest was his only chance. It mattered little that his hands were bound. All he needed was an open door. Then he could flee with every bit of strength inside of him.

An hour passed before a goblin walked back to Darrow's cage. He held out a piece of stale biscuit and shoved it into Darrow's mouth. Darrow pleaded to be let out. The goblin walked away, pretending not to hear.

Night arrived and the forest grew blacker still. The silence of the afternoon gave way to a great cacophony of sounds, alien and strange. Unseen creatures competed with one another with their shrill and peculiar cries. The goblins huddled close together. Conversations were few. Before sleeping, they constructed a circle of small fires, each almost touching the next. When the circle burned brightly, they gathered inside.

"Bat spiders," thought Darrow. "The fires will keep the bat spiders away." Nervously, he eyed the openings at the top of his cage.

Sleep came to the goblins and their high-pitched snores blended with the cries of the forest to create a boisterous chorus of the evil.

For Darrow, sleep was not possible. In any position he tried, he was pierced by the sticks that supported him. Tired but awake, nothing but black before his eyes, each moment lingered in a great expanse of time.

"Mareeeokkkie, mareeokkkie, mariokeee!" The hideous shriek jolted Darrow. He heard claws scraping a tree within reach of his cage. Low and far away, a mournful call sounded: "Mockabee, mockabee, mockabee."

A deep desperation gripped Darrow's being. He was so terrified that one sound went unnoticed. It was the beating of tiny wings, a faint hum that hung outside his cage. When he noticed it, he feared a giant insect might be preparing to attack. Straining his eyes in the faint light of the goblin fires, he could barely make out its outline. But there was no insect at the door of his cage.

It was a tiny bird.

Darrow waved his hands to scare it. But the bird paid him no mind. It hopped onto a stick on the door of the cage. For a moment it paused, looking left and right. Then, in an explosion of energy, the bird was hard at work, pecking, pulling, twisting, as if some special delicacy lay hidden below.

Perplexed, Darrow strained to watch. What he saw was barely a shadow. But the shadow moved in rapid jerks, straining with all its small weight against some object on the cage. Darrow's eyes focused hard.

The bird was pulling at the rope.

The rope was strong and thick and the bird was tiny. Fascinated, Darrow watched with increasing wonderment. Peck, pull, twist, pull, peck—bird continued for what seemed to be an hour.

One of the goblins rose from his slumber and trudged to a nearby tree. Before returning to his blanket, he took a stick and stirred one of the fires. A few flames burst forth. In this flash of light, Darrow looked closely at the bird. It was yellow and barely the size of a chicken egg. The rope against which it struggled was almost gone.

Darrow could not believe his eyes. He listened closely as the goblin stepped back to his bedding. When he was sure that no one was awake, he turned and leaned against the door. The rope snapped quietly. The little yellow bird rose into the air, where it fluttered for a moment and then darted away.

Slowly, not wanting to make a sound, Darrow pushed open the door of the cage with his feet. A small creaking noise made Darrow freeze. He eased his feet to the ground, leaned forward, and emerged from his cell. For a moment he paused, looking for a path. Seeing nothing, he ran straight into the blackness of the forest.

Not ten feet from the cage, he collided squarely with a tree. The encounter made a loud noise, and Darrow fell backwards, landing on his still-tied hands. But in an instant he was back on his feet, hurtling blindly ahead. Thorn bushes tore at his legs and feet. A branch struck his forehead, sending blood running down his face. His foot hit a rock and he hurtled forward, landing on the forest floor. But each time he fell, he lifted himself and raced forward again.

When he had traveled what seemed a full hour, he stopped to listen. Nothing. He resumed his escape, this time more slowly, moving sideways so that his shoulder, and not his head, would strike against the trees. When he had traveled more distance still, he stopped and groped with his hands until he found a sharp rock. He rubbed the rock against the rope that bound his hands. His hands were free.

With his fingers reaching in front of him, he could feel his way through the forest and he made better time. Now and then, he tripped or struck a tree or branch, but his steps gained purpose and he moved steadily ahead. He fell again. He lay still for a moment to catch his breath, and before he could stumble back to his feet, he was sound asleep.

When he awoke, birds announced the morning and a dull gray light filtered through the treetops. There was no trail. He had not the slightest idea of where he was or where he should go. What he wanted most was water. He scanned the expanse of the forest and started again with no particular strategy or design. Stepping through brush and around trees and rocks, he made slow progress. After a while, he heard a trickling noise and followed the sound to a small brook. He drank frantically and ate the only food he could find—bitter onions that he pulled from the ground.

Guessing that the brook might lead to a path, he began walking against the water's flow. Eventually, he came to a primitive bridge that crossed the brook, linking two sides of a path. Darrow chose a direction at random and trudged forward down the road. He was tired and hungry and after a while, he stepped to the side of the path and slept again.

When he awoke, two goblins stood above him, swords drawn. Once again, his hands were tied, this time in front.

The soldiers marched him before them, jabbing him from behind, laughing at their pathetic captive.

"Slave boy, thank us for saving your life!"

"Anyone asleep in this forest is too stupid to be a slave."

"We'll send him to gather mushrooms in the bogs. That takes no brain."

"The job of a lifetime! A week at best!"

"Two days! This one is too lame to escape."

As the insults flowed, Darrow held his head high. He would not show fear before these soldiers. He would not lose hope.

But suddenly one of the soldiers cried out.

"He's gone!"

Darrow turned to look at his captors.

Stunned, their eyes searched the path and the forest around them. But something was wrong. He was standing directly before them.

One of the goblins ran by him down the trail.

The other cried out, "I'll check the forest," and left the path, poking amongst the bushes with his sword.

Darrow watched in wonderment until he looked down at his feet.

They were gone.

His feet. His legs. He could see nothing of his entire body.

"I must be dead," he thought. But dead or alive, he wanted to be as far from these goblins as possible. So down the path he ran. And after running for what seemed a long time, he stopped and sat on the trail, simply too exhausted to continue. He reached down to touch his leg. It was there. Frantically, his hands patted his body all around finding everything in its proper place, though he could see none of it at all.

He decided that perhaps he was not dead at all. He looked down and saw his body shimmer back into visibility.

In the distance, he heard a bell and the braying of a mule. He scrambled into the forest and ducked behind a bush. A wagon came into sight, painted with yellow birds and driven by a fat young woman with black hair and a large crooked nose. She turned to look in his direction. For the briefest moment, he thought she smiled.

Then the wagon was gone.

Darrow walked back onto the road, confused and frightened. He wondered if what he saw was true at all. Perhaps he had lost his mind. He walked ahead, not even bothering to untie the rope that still bound his hands. He had no idea where to go, but he knew he could not walk the road. So he turned into the forest and began stepping aimlessly through the thicket.

Within minutes, he stepped into a small clearing and looked at the rope on his hands. Before he could untie himself, he heard a cry. At first, the cry was faint, but it grew in volume. He froze where he stood.

Skreeeeeeeeeuhlskreeeuhlskreeuhlskreeuhlskreeuhlskreeuhlskreeuhl! Across the clearing, three animals appeared, wolflike creatures with long legs and terrifying red eyes. Darrow knew something of wolves from the mountains. His only chance was to show no fear.

The beasts charged toward him, snarling and screaming. Darrow turned and faced the beasts, his eyes soft and his face calm. He stood without defense, his hands bound, a strand of rope hanging to the ground. Though he trembled within,

the wolves saw only a smile as if he were greeting loved ones returning home.

Rapidly, the skriabeasts approached until they were within a few feet of their prey. But instead of leaping, they did something strange. They thrust their paws into the grass and slid to a stop. Darrow lifted his hands in an offering of friendship. While the other two looked on, the leader stepped forward and sniffed Darrow's hand. Then he opened his mouth and licked Darrow's fingers.

Darrow exhaled. The creature took the rope in his mouth and tugged. Darrow pulled back. The creature looked at Darrow intently. He tugged again. This time, Darrow followed him down a narrow path that wound up a hill and continued deep into the forest. For five hours they walked. Darrow stepped into a clearing and saw a light.

He looked around. He looked back at the light. It came from a cabin built with logs and mud. In the doorway, he could see the outlines of a short, round-faced man.

The man's face wore a great smile. He looked out at Darrow, who stood silent before him. In a soft and gentle voice, he spoke.

"Welcome, nephew. I see you have found your way."

Darrow looked down at his hands. The rope was gone. His eyes searched for the skriabeasts. They were nowhere to be found.

· 17 ·

Asterux's Advice

Dazed by the events of the last day, Darrow stumbled into Asterux's cabin. The wizard prepared a cup of broth and a dinner of greens and bread. Meanwhile, Darrow's eyes explored Asterux's cabin.

Above his head was a green sphere that sprouted black leaves. Strange insects swirled around it. Across the room hung lightning bolts and a thirteen-legged lizard, its last leg bearing two curved claws that protruded from the front of its body. There were planets, some connected with mobiles, creating solar systems of rotating orbs. Across the room, in the corner, hung a collection of odd birds. One had a beak that forked at the end. Another had long legs, five times the length of its body, and a razor-sharp beak. He saw a black bird with three red eyes that could scan the horizon in any direction.

Darrow turned to his uncle.

"Are you a wizard?"

Asterux laughed. "Where did you get such an idea?"

"A woman, a fortune-teller, told me on the road."

"A fortune-teller will say anything. I know no magic you could not discover on your own."

"Good," replied Darrow, eyeing his uncle cautiously. In his mind, he replayed his journey—the strange yellow bird, the wolflike creatures, and becoming invisible on the trail. But these thoughts did not linger. Within minutes, he was asleep in his chair.

When Darrow awoke, Asterux was in his rocking chair, an open book in his lap. He looked over at Darrow with a patient smile.

"What time is it?" Darrow asked.

"It is afternoon."

Darrow's face dropped. He had wasted the day!

"I will leave tomorrow," said Darrow.

The wizard just smiled. "There is no hurry, my nephew. There is time enough for all plans."

"My plans are different," Darrow replied sharply.

"That I cannot understand," replied Asterux. "Unless you would like to share them with me."

Eager to share his ideas with someone, Darrow began speaking so excitedly that his sentences tumbled out, one after another, in an almost senseless jumble.

"It is time to fight back. Our battle will tell others that it is possible to resist. Someone has to begin. I will start small. I will find men. Our story will spread. We will hide in the forest and strike in small groups. The goblins won't find us. We need swords. Men will find courage and join our struggle. One day, we will become strong enough to succeed."

Asterux smiled, greatly amused by his nephew's ideas. Playfully, he asked, "And what do you know of fighting?"

"Nothing," Darrow answered honestly. "But I will learn."

"And where will you find weapons? How will you feed your men? And where will you find men who know the ways of war?"

Darrow paused. "I am not sure."

Asterux said nothing, allowing Darrow to consider his words. Darrow collected his thoughts and spoke again.

"Uncle, can I tell you about a dream I had?"

"Of course."

"It happened three weeks ago. I could see everything clearly and the events felt almost as real as if I were wide awake.

"The dream began with a scene I have witnessed many times before. The goblins were looting Ael and they set the roofs of two houses on fire. Soon all of the houses were burning. With flames raging around us, there was no room to stand between the stream and the cliffs, so we fled up the mountain and into the forest. But the fires from our village spread to the trees and followed us close behind.

"Though we ran as fast as we could, we could barely stay ahead. We came to a clearing at the edge of a great cliff. With the fire in front of us and the cliff behind us, we had nowhere to go."

"And then what happened?" asked Asterux, his face filled with interest and concern.

"A goblin ghost riding a horse appeared before us. His laughter rang loudly and he taunted us, his voice rising even above the noise of the fire.

"'Before you lies the fate of cowards,' he howled, laughing even more loudly than before. I turned and looked at Groompus, the elder of our village. There were tears in his eyes.

"'The goblin is right,' he said. 'He is right.'"

"And did the people of the village perish?" asked Asterux quietly.

"At the moment that the fire reached our feet, I awoke. But I know the answer."

"And what is the answer?" asked Asterux.

Darrow, calmer now, composed his reply.

"The answer is that we create our own fate. Today, our first enemy is not goblins at all. Our enemy is ourselves."

"And how will you defeat that enemy?"

For the first time, Darrow smiled. "By coming to the forest to meet my uncle and making a plan."

Asterux nodded, smiling as well. Before he could speak, his nephew continued.

"Fear can be broken. It can be broken because courage, when demonstrated, will inspire other brave deeds. As that courage spreads, it becomes a powerful force that can defeat even the most powerful foe."

Asterux paused for a moment, impressed by the strong words and passion of his nephew. Then he asked, "Darrow, nephew of mine. You are not yet eighteen years old. One of your legs is shorter than the other. You have never lifted a sword in battle. You know nothing of war. Tell me, how can you succeed against the might of the great goblin army?"

"I know what I am lacking. But, Uncle, I saw the fire at my feet and the cliff at my back. Show me another, older and wiser, ready to lead, and I will gladly follow. But I know no other so I ask you, 'Why not me?'"

Again, Asterux paused. He had no answer for Darrow. So he leaned forward and spoke to his young nephew with firmness and conviction.

"You have come here for my advice," Asterux stated. "And I will give you frank and honest words. You have no experience in war. You have no knowledge of fighting. You have no men behind you."

"Mempo is coming to join me."

"Mempo knows less than you. Forget Mempo. You need warriors."

"Where can I find them, Uncle? Tell me."

"They are chained to the dungeon walls in the palace at Blumenbruch."

"Then we must set them free."

"And how will you do that?"

"Lend me your sword and I will walk to Blumenbruch and fight for their freedom."

With those remarks, Asterux pressed his lips together and shifted impatiently in his chair. "First, I do not have a sword."

Upon hearing these words, Darrow grimaced, his eyes lifting to the ceiling above.

"My nephew," the old man continued. "You will never succeed by running blindly into the fire. If you want to rescue these men, you need a plan."

"Then help me," Darrow pleaded, looking directly into his uncle's eyes. "Help me. Teach me. Join me."

"I will help you, but listen and listen well. In the palace dungeon in Blumenbruch are two great warriors, Hugarious and Timwee."

"Hugarious?" Darrow asked.

"He is a Minotaur, also known as Hugga Hugga. In his day, he possessed great strength and wielded a giant axe. He can help you. I will go with you, and we will try to break them out."

"Then we will leave tomorrow," stated Darrow.

"No," Asterux responded. "We will leave in three weeks."

⟡

Each day, the routine was the same. Darrow would arise from his bed with the sun and wait for Asterux. When Asterux had risen, Darrow would beg him to reconsider and leave that day.

Asterux marveled at his nephew's persistence. But each time, Asterux refused his request. And each day, when he was sure that his uncle would not budge, Darrow headed directly to the bookcase and began to read.

He marveled that his uncle knew so much and could read these strange tongues. But there were also books he could read, great stories of magic, heroism, gallantry, and revenge.

One day, while he was reading a tale of two wizards locked in a great contest, he looked at the ceiling and thought of the strange books. He thought again of his journey in the forest, which had been filled with magic and awe. Then he asked Asterux the question.

"Did you use magic to bring me through the forest?" he asked.

"Not at all. Not at all," Asterux replied, as a look of exaggerated innocence spread across his face. "If magic brought you through Hexenwald, it was a magic other than my own."

· 18 ·

Cebular's Ghost

The journey to Blumenbruch lasted eight days. As Asterux and Darrow walked the dusty road, they faced what seemed a wholly impossible task.

The Kirstinnex dungeon was a formidable target. Many of the great warriors of Sonnencrest were locked inside. While they remained, reasoned the goblins, there could be no challenge to goblin rule. With each passing year, these warriors grew weaker and more withered with age. With each passing year, the goblin rule grew more secure.

Beltar, the great goblin general, took no chances. The jail was guarded by twenty or more guards, all well armed. No detail was overlooked. No one but goblins and corpses ever left its walls.

On the seventh day, as the two travelers finally approached Blumenbruch, Darrow asked Asterux the question that was tormenting his soul.

"Uncle, we are getting close and you must tell me. We have no swords. No knife. No weapons of any kind. So how exactly are you and I going to break these prisoners out of jail?"

But Asterux remained silent. Then, on their last day on the road, Asterux turned to Darrow and shared his plan.

"There will not be twenty guards tonight. There may be only a few. For tonight, high in the heavens, a great spiritual event will take place. It is an event celebrated by all goblins everywhere. Tonight is the night of Cebular's Crossing."

"And what is that?" Darrow asked.

"In the night sky, at exactly this time of year, seven stars are arranged in a circle. That circle is known as Cebular's Ghost. His story is sacred to the goblins.

"According to goblin legend, there was once a time when all people lived together as humans in a paradise created by the gods. But one of those people left paradise to find adventure."

"Cebular?"

"Exactly. Outside of this paradise, Cebular met many spirits that had been banished from paradise and longed for revenge. So when they met Cebular, they whispered false words to turn him against the gods.

"One spirit told him that in the dark land, everyone lived forever. Only in paradise did people die. Another said that in the dark lands, people drank delicious wines and ate succulent foods that were plentiful beyond any possible consumption. And to prove his words, the spirit offered Cebular a magical brew that made his head dance and his body glow with delight.

"'These pleasures are forbidden in your land,' the spirit explained, 'because the gods are selfish and keep these wonders for themselves.'

"Another spirit offered Cebular gold. 'Great riches lie in the dark lands,' he explained. 'These riches are hidden by the gods to enjoy only for themselves.'

"With these words, Cebular's suspicions grew. He began to believe that where he lived was no paradise at all. Then one day, on one of his journeys into the dark lands, a strange ghostlike figure appeared before him. Cebular was frightened, but the figure lifted his hand to reassure Cebular. As Cebular trembled, the figure spoke. 'Cebular, you are the chosen one and you must know. The gods have no power at all. They are only humans. They disguise themselves to steal the best joys of life from others. Return to your so-called paradise, Cebular. Return and tell the people the truth.'

"Cebular brooded over the oracle's message and wondered if it indeed might be true. When he encountered the gods, he silently measured them, asking himself if they were indeed mightier than he. Gradually, he became convinced he was their equal. Driven by this belief, he decided their rule was only a trick.

"So one day, he decided to act.

"In the spring of every year was a great festival. And on this particular occasion, Cebular was asked to sing the first song. He rose on the hillside and from his lips came a shocking verse:

Oh, mortals present on these sands
Great imposters rule our lands
Their lies have cheated all I see
These gods, they live deceitfully.

If your powers be so great
Strike me down and do not wait
I stand here absent sword or shield
Before false gods, I will not yield.

"Well, you can imagine how the gods reacted. The ruler of the gods, Torin, rose to slay Cebular. But before he could reach for his sword, his hot-tempered brother, Tymobeer, cast a spell that turned Cebular's skin green, gave him a bulbous head, and distorted his body to appear like those of goblins today.

"But Tymobeer's powers were ordinary and his spells often contained mistakes. His spell did more than change Cebular's appearance. His spell also endowed Cebular with great courage, a fighting spirit, high intelligence, and other admirable qualities of goblins today.

"So, in this form, Cebular escaped from paradise. He walked through the dark lands and made his home in a cave. There, he found others who had suffered at the hands of the gods. He fathered many children and founded a great tribe that conquered many lands. Throughout the dark lands, the goblins grew into a feared and powerful force.

"When the gods learned of Cebular's success, they grew angry. Their ruler called Tymobeer before him and issued a command.

"'You have created this mighty Cebular. Go now. Slay him. End his reign.'

"Tymobeer thought long and hard about how he would put an end to the great goblin leader. He could have easily struck him with a plague or poison. But Tymobeer wanted the other gods to see that his magic was indeed great, so he planned to extinguish Cebular with a great display.

"Mustering his most powerful magic, he summoned a great fireball from the sky. All of the gods looked up and smiled because they knew that surely this fireball would put an end to their foe. And indeed, as Cebular looked up and saw the great fiery globe descending upon him, he knew that death was at hand."

"But Cebular escaped, right?"

"Oh, no. He perished, as surely as you or I would, if the gods hurled a fireball in our direction. But although the fireball did kill Cebular, it created an enormous explosion. The fireball broke into seven pieces that ascended into the sky, forming a circle of seven new stars. That circle became known to the goblins as Cebular's Ghost. They believe that Cebular ascended to the heavens and watches over them each and every night. And fortified with these beliefs, the goblins became stronger still."

"Okay," said Darrow. "But what does all this have to do with breaking warriors out of prison?"

"Well, on the fourth day after the first full moon of September, when Cebular's Ghost is highest in the sky, the entire goblin nation joins in a rapturous celebration called Cebular's Crossing, which is unlike any holiday known to man. They drink a strange brew that places the goblins in a mysterious trance. Once in this trance, the goblins begin a great silent dance, where their bodies move, almost in unison, but without any music at all. After the silent dance, which can last for hours at a time, great feasting begins. After the feast, the goblins drink from an enormous kettle containing a mysterious mushroom brew that launches the goblins into raucous choruses of song.

"So tonight, amidst this celebration, only a few goblins will be guarding the dungeon. And the rest will hardly notice us at all."

"But won't we still need weapons?" Darrow asked.

"Everything we need," replied Asterux, "is located right between your ears."

And with those words, Asterux began to explain the plan.

· 19 ·

Gong Farmer to the Rescue

$\mathcal{T}$hat night, at the gate of the palace, a yellow wagon appeared. It was pulled by a single mule. No guards attended the gates, which stood open, allowing any goblin to enter and join the celebration. Amidst this chaos, Sesha's wagon entered unnoticed.

Across the palace yard, the goblin rituals unfolded before Sesha's eyes. Here and there, a goblin moved in jerky motions, eyes closed, staggering about without purpose or direction. Others lay peering into the heavens, slapping their hands on the ground in a strange and unpredictable rhythm.

Sesha gripped the reins, carefully steering to avoid contact with goblins who staggered randomly into the wagon's path. She reached the stable, a structure of wood and straw that extended from the castle's stone walls. Next to the stable stood a large iron door, the entrance to the Kirstinnex prison.

"Whoa, Zauberyungi," Sesha called to her mule. The wagon pulled to a stop.

Sesha went to the back of the wagon and removed some balls. She walked out to an open space in front of the prison door. There she tossed the balls into the air, first two, then three, and finally four balls. A handful of goblins planted themselves on the ground, still twitching but spellbound by her juggling skills.

Sesha added a fifth ball and as the balls followed one another across her hands, Sesha stepped back and put her hands on her hips while the balls continued their circle as the growing crowd of goblins looked on, aghast at this amazing display.

More goblins staggered to the wagon, one of them wearing an iron helmet. While the balls continued to circle in the air, Sesha removed the goblin's helmet and walked back to the wagon. She reached into a bag and scooped three handfuls of a lumpy gray powder into the helmet. Then she walked over to the balls, held out her hand, and the five balls fell to her hand balanced perfectly one on top of the other.

The goblins cheered.

Sesha took the helmet and shook it back and forth.

A goblin lay on the ground. Sesha walked over, removed his shoe, and dropped it into the helmet. The goblin staggered to his feet and lurched toward Sesha to retrieve his shoe. Sesha sidestepped him and he fell to the ground. Helmet in hand, Sesha walked to the bewildered goblin, inviting him to reach inside. As he did, a great mass of lizards and frogs leaped from the helmet, frightening the poor goblin but sending his comrades into fits of uncontrollable laughter.

Sesha looked back at the prison door. The peephole was open. She walked over to the door and knocked. The goblins, thinking she might take her show into the dungeon, launched another roar of laughter. The door opened—but only a crack.

"Would you like to join us for the show?" Sesha asked.

"Not possible," replied the voice from inside. "Guard duty tonight."

"Well, perhaps I might serve you some apple cider," suggested Sesha in a creaky voice.

"Not allowed."

"But look at your friends, all staggering around full of brew. It is not really fair. My apple cider won't make you dance, but it is tasty enough to reward your terrible duty on this special night."

"Wait."

The door closed and for a few moments, Sesha waited. It cracked open.

"We are deserving, that's for sure. Bring us a taste, but you must leave right away." Sesha returned and pushed a pot of cider through the door. Then she rode her wagon back out through the gates.

⁊ⰊⰊⰊ⥁

An hour later, Darrow and Asterux walked into the palace grounds. Midnight approached. The mushroom brew had been consumed and the air was filled with the raucous screeching of goblin songs. Some screeched alone, others in pairs or in groups of three or four, not always singing the same song but singing loudly and with barely a melody at all.

The two humans moved swiftly through the chaos to the prison door. Asterux delivered three loud knocks. No reply. Another longer series of knocks. Still no reply. Finally, a voice.

"Go away."

It was not the firm voice that had replied to Sesha but a slow voice, wavering in its tone.

"But I cannot go away," Asterux responded. "I am delivering a gift."

There was silence for a moment. Then a slurred voice: "Th-th-the general lives in the tower. This is the dungeon. No gifts come here."

"Ah, but you are wrong," Asterux replied cheerfully. "This gift is for you, the dungeon guards. And if I leave this gift at your doorstep, it will surely run away."

Asterux thought he heard laughter inside.

"Well, it is up to you. But someone is going to be very disappointed."

With that statement, the door opened. A goblin, older but with broad shoulders and strong arms, looked at Asterux suspiciously.

"Who?"

"Sadfar, the captain who commands the fort in Hexenwald. It is his gift to you."

"Well, I do know Sadfar. So where is this gift?"

"Right here," Asterux replied, pointing at Darrow, whose hands were bound. "What is it that every warden needs?"

"A locksmith."

"No."

"A blacksmith."

"No."

The goblin giggled. The game was fun.

"A housemaid!" Inside, the two other goblins laughed uproariously.

"No, my good fellows. I bring you something better still."

The goblins stared at Asterux with rapt attention.

"I am happy to present to you a gong farmer!"

"A gong farmer!" The warden leaped from his chair. "Well, why didn't you say so?"

There was good reason for the warden's delight. In the castle, there was no harder job to fill than the gong farmer.

"He is a little addle-brained, but I think he will do," Asterux added. "Won't you, fellow?"

At that, Darrow mumbled a few grunts and snorts, proving he had no language and few coherent thoughts.

"Well, yes, indeed," said the warden. "I can see he is fit for the task."

A gong farmer, of course, grows no crops at all. In most of the palaces of the world, the nobles who lived in the highest towers would empty their chamber pots through a hole in the wall. The contents fell to a cesspool below. The gong farmer's job was to empty the cesspool and remove the contents from the castle grounds.

But for the gong farmer of the warden, the job was still worse. The dungeon was located deep in the ground. And to accept the wretched waste of the prisoners, a deep pit had been dug that reached far below. To remove this waste, the gong farmer had to lower and raise a bucket. When his wheelbarrow was full, he carried his harvest across the open ground to an opening in the castle wall where it was dumped into the moat.

Not only was the job unpleasant, it was unhealthy as well. Few gong farmers lived longer than a few months on the job.

Asterux and Darrow were ushered inside and offered a seat. The two other guards sat slumped and wild-eyed in their chairs.

"Perhaps you would like some cider. There is a bit left," one of the guards giggled.

"I think not," replied Asterux. "I really must be on my way. But I must say the odor is terrible. I am sure Darrow here would be happy to begin work right away."

"Here, here," shouted the other guard.

"Well, lead the boy to his post!"

The guard grumbled and gave the warden an angry look, but knew he had cast his own lot. So he untied Darrow's hands and led him out the door.

"And how is Captain Sadfar?" the warden asked thinking kindly of the old goblin at the fort.

"Why, he is the same as ever, grumbling about his poor post. But you know, I think he likes it actually. No marching. No drilling. No generals to order him around."

"Ah yes, that is Sadfar indeed."

Asterux rose.

"Although I would enjoy more conversation, I must be on my way. I still have hours of travel ahead. A funeral in the morning. A nephew dead of the shakes."

The warden eyed Asterux suspiciously. The shakes were caused by evil spirits and passed to relatives and others.

"Well, yes, you *should* be on your way," exclaimed the warden, now ushering Asterux to the door.

Asterux opened the door and looked out to the wall facing the dungeon. On the wall, he could make out the short, fat outline of a girl. The girl bowed. Asterux nodded. Then she was gone.

With that, Asterux turned to the warden and announced, "My good sir, your stable is on fire!"

And indeed, as he spoke these words, smoke was rising from the stable and the cries of horses began to fill the air. The warden ran down the steps, followed by the remaining guard.

Asterux ran to the well and drew a bucket, which he handed to the warden. The warden hurled the water at the fire. Asterux handed him another bucket, and the fire grew hotter. The warden wiped the sweat from his brow and removed his coat. Asterux handed him a third bucket. As the warden turned once again to douse the fire, Asterux lifted the warden's coat and withdrew the keys. When the warden turned for another bucket, Asterux was gone.

⟨∞⟩

Inside the prison, Asterux turned the stolen key and pushed the door open. The hallways were dark. Feeling with his hands, he followed a wall until he came to two doors. He pushed at the first door. It moved and he walked into the room.

He was startled by a frantic scuffling noise. Rats. He called out, "Hugga Hugga," but there was no reply. He withdrew and found the other door.

He fumbled with the keys, trying one of them in the keyhole. No luck. Another. Now there was shouting inside.

On the fourth attempt, the key turned and the door opened. The midnight visit brought panic to the floor. Prisoners pushed back to the walls, afraid that beatings might ensue.

In the firm clear voice of a human, Asterux called out, "I am here to find Hugarious and Timwee, warriors of Sonnencrest. Where are they?"

A moment of silence followed. No human had ever walked freely into this prison. A voice called out, "I am Timwee. Over here."

Asterux worked his way across the room, stepping on and tripping over prisoners along the way. When he reached the voice, he fumbled with his keys to unlock Timwee's irons. But before he could open the lock, another prisoner shouted, "Over here, I am Timwee."

Asterux found the key and unlocked the first prisoner, who began stepping across the room toward the door, not bothering to look back. Now, a chorus of voices shouted, all claiming to be Timwee. Asterux began unlocking one prisoner after another, but apparently none of them were Timwee. One and all, they fled.

Asterux stopped. In a loud voice that could be barely heard above the pleading prisoners, he shouted, "Where is Timwee? Only Timwee has the key that can free us all."

Again, a chorus of voices offered the information. He turned to the nearest and yelled, "Where? Tell me where!"

"The door. The door at the back of the room. It opens to a hall. At the end of the hall is another room. That's where they keep Timwee."

Asterux unlocked the prisoner and stepped across the room. The prisoners grabbed at his legs and pleaded to be freed. But there was no time. He reached the back door and found the room.

This time, he said nothing of rescues. Using his best goblin voice, he shouted, "I have come for Timwee. Where are you?"

From the corner of the room, a whisper of a voice responded, "I am here. Bring this life to an end."

Asterux moved across the room, stepping more skillfully in the dark. He reached the sound and without a word unlocked the dwarf's irons.

Timwee looked up at the wizard, blinking in disbelief. What was a human doing in the dungeon?

"Where is Hugarious?" Asterux asked.

"You mean Hugga Hugga? I'll show you." The dwarf eased his body upward, balanced himself on feeble legs, and led Asterux to another room.

Soon both prisoners stood before Asterux, blinking in awe.

"Make not a sound. The kingdom has come to your rescue. Follow me."

With that, he hurled the keys to a prisoner who unlocked himself and passed them to another. One by one, the prisoners rose and headed up the stairs.

Asterux led his warriors away from the stairs. They entered the latrine. The two prisoners blinked, confused. Asterux turned and pointed to a hole, the width of a medium tree.

"Go through the hole." The prisoners looked back; Timwee gulped.

"There is a bucket on the other side. Grab it. It will lift you to the palace yard."

Without a second's delay, the dwarf had leaped into the hole and slid down the stinking passageway, and then a splash sounded below. Hugga Hugga tried to follow, but his horns stretched wider than the hole.

Hugga Hugga turned to Asterux with a frightened stare. Meanwhile, they heard screams as prisoners streamed into the yard.

A cry rang out from the top of the dungeon stairs. The goblins had arrived.

The old wizard's eyes scanned the chamber. The walls were stone and the mortar was crumbling in between. He drew a knife and thrust it in a crack. He tugged on the stone and it began to move.

Hugga Hugga grabbed at the stone and pulled it free. He motioned with his hands, for a Minotaur cannot speak, pointing at the stone and his horns.

"On your back," shouted Asterux, understanding instantly.

The dull thud of batons striking bodies rang in the air—thuds followed by cries of pain.

Asterux raised the stone high and brought it crashing down on the Minotaur's horns. Hugga Hugga bellowed in response. Again, Asterux struck. In six strokes of the stone, Asterux had broken the horns on each side. Hugga Hugga leaped back into the hole. Still he was stuck. A guard entered the room and raised his club to strike Asterux. Asterux moved to the side. The club struck Hugga Hugga on the head. The blow was all he needed.

The Minotaur slid bellowing down the chute.

෴

In the yard, under the shadow of the tower, Darrow stared into the black pit below. The stench was strong and Darrow was sure he would faint. As quietly as possible, he lowered a large bucket, attached to a rope. The rope was attached to a crank, which could be turned to lift the bucket back up. Darrow listened carefully. When the bucket struck the surface, he stopped.

Darrow looked down and fell to his knees. Grasping the rope, he swung the bucket gingerly, as close as possible to where he believed the hole might be. Cinders rose in the air from the stable fire, lighting the yard. Now, he could see the hole. He clutched the rope with both hands, keeping enough tension so that neither warrior would fall into the terrible ooze below.

The sky burned brighter still and cinders darted about like lunatic stars. Carefully, ever so carefully, he positioned the bucket and set the rope tight. He peered down into the hole and waited.

Suddenly, a black ball shot out of the wall and into the muck. Timwee missed the bucket but managed to grab its side. Darrow reached for the crank and began to pull. Soon, Timwee was standing on the ground.

"How do you like the smell of freedom?" Darrow asked.

Timwee stuttered, "Just fine to me."

"Where is Hugga Hugga?"

"I don't know. He was right behind me."

Darrow peered into the pit. The sky was bright with embers. One of the embers fell into the pit. Suddenly, flames rose from the liquid below.

It had been several minutes since Timwee had been lifted from the muck. Darrow looked nervously across the yard.

"We should go."

"No, wait. He will find a way."

The rope tightened in his hands. The old Minotaur had caught the bucket. He was heavier than Timwee and almost pulled Darrow into the pit. The bucket fell into the muck. The ripple stirred the flames. Then the bucket itself was on fire. The Minotaur bellowed a low moaning cry.

Together, Darrow and Timwee pulled at the crank. Slowly, too slowly, they lifted the bucket upward. Darrow looked down and there were flames on the rope. Another moan arose from the pit. The stubs of his broken horns burning with flame, Hugga Hugga reached toward the wall of the pit. There was a loud snap and the bucket fell into the depths below. The Minotaur hung by one hand that gripped the wall.

Darrow and the dwarf grabbed both arms and lifted him out, then rolled him across the ground to put out the fire. As the Minotaur grimaced in pain, Darrow led him across the yard. They arrived at the small door that was the gong farmer's exit.

Darrow looked back at the palace. The ground was littered with garments and cups where the goblins had celebrated only hours before. A reflection caught his eye. He ran from the exit and retrieved a small sword.

When he returned, they ran to the opening in the wall where the gong farmer dumps his cargo. Through the opening, across the moat, and the three lone soldiers of Sonnencrest disappeared into the night.

· 20 ·

The Band of First Believers

Darrow looked at the sky, noticing the streaks of orange appearing in the east, then indicated a nearby wood. It wasn't safe for the warriors to be on the road during the day, and they needed to find a place to rest.

Neither Hugga Hugga nor Timwee had walked more than the length of a room in ten long years. But in the previous evening, they had traveled miles from the dungeon, through fields and woodlands, in an attempt to avoid the roads where goblin patrols traveled.

Hugga Hugga wobbled ahead, his legs thin and stiff. His ribs showed through his chest and his back sagged under the weight of his enormous head, now adorned with a crown of stubs and splinters that had once been his horns.

But it was the dwarf, Timwee, who had suffered most. In the night, he had fallen and broken a shoulder. Each step sent a sharp throbbing pain through his chest and down his arm.

The party came to a small brook, and Timwee collapsed in the streambed, frantically scooping water into his mouth with one hand. For a long time, Hugga Hugga just sat on the bank, too tired even to relieve his thirst.

"Wait here," said Darrow. "We need a place to hide."

Darrow followed the brook upstream through the forest. Darrow stepped faster as the brook crossed open fields, but for the most part, the woodlands sheltered it from view of the road. He passed a few farmhouses but dared not approach. There was nowhere the goblins would not search. Anyone caught aiding a prisoner would surely face death.

The sun rose higher and the birds burst into song. Darrow barely noticed. He stepped frantically, scanning the landscape for anywhere to hide.

At the edge of a field, Darrow heard a voice. Fearing goblins, he moved behind a tree. He listened closely and realized that what he was hearing was not the sound of someone speaking but sobbing. He stepped out from behind the tree and could just see a small shed beyond the field.

Darrow approached the shed with slow steps, his eyes darting in every direction. The sobs grew louder. The shed was small, as long as two men lying end to end and half as wide. The door was gone from the hinges, and it had no windows at all.

Darrow eased his head into the doorway. Curled up in the corner was a cave troll. The size of the creature frightened Darrow, who jumped back. But the troll looked up at Darrow, sad-eyed and motionless. Darrow took a slow step inside.

"Who are you?" Darrow asked.

"Naark," the troll answered, his voice thick and gravelly.

"What are you doing here?"

"I have nowhere to go."

"And where did you come from?"

"The dungeon," Naark answered, and continued his pitiful sobbing.

Darrow quickly looked around the shed. It was a shed where a farmer had once stored corn, but it was a long time since it had been used. It was not much of a hiding place, but it would have to do.

"Stop crying," Darrow said gently. "Come with me."

The troll staggered to his feet and followed Darrow downstream. Hugga Hugga and Timwee were asleep. The cave troll let out a cry when he saw the two warriors, but Darrow assured him that they were friends. Naark lifted Timwee to his back and the four warriors headed to the shed.

They spoke no words; within seconds of arriving, they were all asleep, piled up on one another in the tiny confines of their hiding place.

⟡

It was midafternoon when Timwee awoke. He opened his eyes, surprised by his surroundings and the bright light shining through the doorway. As he rose, he grimaced, gripping his shoulder, and remembering the ordeal. He became nervous. The others were sleeping, but he did not care. He shook Darrow. For the first time since leaving the dungeon, Timwee asked questions.

"Who are you? Where are we going? Is the king alive?"

"I am Darrow of Ael. I freed you because I need soldiers to drive the goblins from Sonnencrest. And the king is dead," Darrow answered calmly.

Hugga Hugga opened his eyes and, upon hearing these last words, blinked sadly. Naark snored.

Timwee looked down at his shrunken body and across at Hugga Hugga, who looked no better than he. He looked at Darrow, a boy who walked with a limp but spoke so bravely.

"Who sent you?"

"I came on my own."

Hugga Hugga reached over and touched Timwee's arm, giving him a stern look.

"Have you fought before?"

"Never."

Hugga Hugga and Timwee exchanged nervous glances.

"Where is the army?" Timwee asked.

"The army is us," Darrow replied.

Darrow looked at his bewildered comrades with fierce, determined eyes.

"You need not tell me that the road ahead is hard. I am young. I walk with a limp and there are many who are stronger than I. But no strong warrior has stepped forward to lead our battle. If you want to save our kingdom, you'll have to fight with me."

The warriors just stared.

"Look, I just rescued two of the greatest warriors of Sonnencrest."

Timwee's face took on a more respectful look, but he could think of nothing to say. He wanted to say he was old and weak and could no longer fight. But his pride would not allow it. His head sagged and he looked at the ground.

Hugga Hugga touched Timwee gently and signaled with his hands. Timwee translated.

"What has happened in the last ten years?"

It had not occurred to Darrow that, being locked in the dungeon, they would know nothing of the outside world. So Darrow began by describing how the king and his family had been killed.

Hugga Hugga signaled a question with his hands.

"All of them?" Timwee interpreted.

"All but the littlest princess. She escaped but has not been heard from since."

Hugga Hugga began to weep.

With great passion, Darrow continued to tell, in long detail, how the goblins had killed the innocent, burned the countryside, and impoverished the kingdom.

As Darrow described all that had happened, the two old warriors stirred. Now they were filled with anger. But Darrow was just beginning.

A hundred times, he had considered what he might say to convince others to join his cause. Now, the first three recruits stood before him. His great passion poured forth as he pleaded his cause.

"This tragedy facing our kingdom has little to do with hunger or poverty or cruelty or death. A far greater loss has overtaken our land. Where brave warriors once fought and wise men ruled, tyranny reigns. Our kingdom stands paralyzed by fear and despair.

"The swords of four warriors can do little to the goblins. But our courage can awaken others. Each small victory will draw new volunteers to our cause. Our actions will rekindle powerful hopes. Those hopes can arouse our people and fuel the greater victories to come.

"As we sit here now, there is little that recommends our chances for success. From your years in prison, you are so weak you can hardly walk. I am inexperienced, lame, young. But what we need is not the strength or the experience or the will to fight. That will come later.

"What we need now is the courage to believe. That courage is the beginning. From that beginning we can, I know, inspire a great army more powerful than *three* goblin nations."

Naark just blinked, awakened by all this talk. But Timwee and Hugga Hugga looked at one another, amazed by Darrow's words.

For what must have been three or four minutes, Hugga Hugga made motions with his hands. When he finished, Timwee looked back at the Minotaur and nodded his agreement. Then he turned to Darrow.

"We are weak. We have not fought in ten long years. But we are not defeated. Our hearts remain strong. Win or lose, live or die, we will stand with you in this quest."

"Then join me in a band of first believers—volunteers ready to risk their lives to free Sonnencrest."

Darrow raised his small sword.

Timwee and Hugga Hugga exchanged uncomfortable glances. A strange pause filled the shed. Darrow was confused.

Naark blurted out, "I have no sword."

Darrow realized his was the only weapon. He thought how his large words measured against this tiny force, broken in body and without arms. But he did not waver.

"To launch our band, we must believe."

In a voice so loud and firm that the others feared he might alert goblin patrols, he shouted: "Hold out your swords!"

So Timwee, Hugga Hugga, and Naark, without hesitation, held up imaginary swords and repeated after Darrow:

To this small but mighty band
I pledge my allegiance, my honor, and my life
For a cause more noble and precious
Than the soul of creature or man
To break the chains of fear that enslave our people
To ignite in our countrymen the flames of hope
To inspire the courage of others
To bring a new sunrise of peace, honor, and virtue to our
nation
For these things no price is too large, no sacrifice too great
A band of first believers we shall be
And through our deeds will our people be free.

At the end of the pledge, Hugga Hugga was once again overcome with emotion. Timwee lifted his imaginary sword high into the air and cried, "So it shall be! So it shall be!"

Satisfied, Darrow urged his warriors to rest once more. His first victory had been won.

· 21 ·

Zindown's Mission

In the great room of the palace in Blumenbruch, fifty chairs surrounded a long table. King Malmut refused to sit. Beltar and the great wizard Zindown stood straight and still like statues before him.

"The entire army drunk on rincinnar brew! The prison unguarded! Warriors escaped!"

Beltar glanced at the door. Zindown smiled slyly.

"And have we captured them all? We have not!" The goblin king asked and answered his own question, working himself into a tirade.

Beltar leaned forward and spoke to the king.

"Indeed, it was a cleverly conducted escape, Your Majesty. But only three remain at large."

"It's been a week!" the king shouted, sweat rolling down his forehead.

"Three prisoners can do nothing. One of them is a cave troll."

"But one of them is the Minotaur!"

Zindown's smile grew wider. He leaned forward, his long wrinkled neck lifting his head high above the king.

"Ah, Beltar," he sighed. "I know it must be stressful to have lost so many prisoners on your watch. Perhaps . . ."

"Stay out of this!" snapped Beltar.

"Yes, these soldiers are your concern alone. I have larger issues on my mind. Perhaps we ought to consider who is behind this trouble."

"Yes, yes," the king was practically leaping with each word. "Who?"

"As we know, the prisoners were headed for the forest. I think—"

"I have sent thirty more soldiers to the forest," Beltar interrupted. "It is all the fort will hold."

Zindown turned to Beltar, his eyes narrowing in a look so wicked that even Beltar shivered.

"Oh, Beltar, can you not think beyond the pitiful tools of war? Is the truth not plain? There was no break-in at all.

"No one was injured. Not a sword was lifted against a goblin guard. The warden was found five miles away, delirious, in a cow pasture. I suppose, Beltar, you would call that a military strike?"

Beltar glowered at Zindown but held his tongue.

"Send soldiers if you will, but I sense a more powerful hand at work. The king is right to be concerned. Perhaps, Beltar, you should show more respect for his wisdom."

"These three are nothing!" shouted Beltar.

"Silence!" the king bellowed. Zindown continued.

"Nothing? Perhaps. But these nothings will soon be in the forest beyond the reach of our military might. Perhaps this is no job for a general. Perhaps a visit to Hexenwald is what we need. There we will learn the true nature of the problem we face."

And with those words, Zindown lifted his black robe and swirled it above his head. A puff of smoke exploded into the air. When it drifted away, Zindown was gone.

· 22 ·

Scodo's Mission

Sesha and Scodo sat together inside her wagon. Around them lay scattered a sea of objects in no particular arrangement. Cooking utensils, small sacks, tiny bottles, magic ingredients, large boxes, pots, bedding, and all sorts of things customers in the nearby villages might buy. Scodo himself was wedged between a box of dried spiders and frogs and a bag of griesonaut teeth that poked at his side.

It was Sesha who spoke the first words.

"A young man named Darrow has broken into the Kirstinnex prison. He has freed Hugga Hugga and Timwee. They are coming to the forest. They will need your protection."

"I know those two warriors. I fought with them before the palace fell."

"They are not the warriors you know—not after ten years in Kirstinnex. They can't protect Darrow. You must join them."

"If he freed them from Kirstinnex, he will hardly need my help. He must wield a mighty sword."

"He has never used a sword. He has no experience. Your sword is the one he needs."

"Why is this important?"

"Because he is coming to save Sonnencrest."

Scodo blinked.

"Above all, you must not allow the goblins to kill Darrow. I need you to go to Darrow and join his band today."

"No. I cannot. I will not."

"And why not?"

"What would happen if I joined? Even if this Darrow accepted me, I would only hurt his cause. Who would march with a monster? Who is willing to look at my face day after day? I have lived this before, and I will not do it again."

Sesha frowned.

"Then, if you won't join him, trail him. Follow him. Don't let him out of your sight."

"I don't understand," Scodo responded. "If he cannot fight and he has never used a sword, how can he possibly save the kingdom?"

"There are plenty who can lift a sword. It is not swords that need lifting."

"What are you saying?"

"Words, Scodo. Words are the first weapon. Swords alone are not enough. To defeat the goblins, we must lift hearts and hope and spirit."

"He had better talk fast, Sesha. Against the goblins, neither my sword nor your magic can protect this boy. You know that."

"Scodo, my dear Scodo," Sesha responded. "Perhaps you are right. But trust me. Protect him and you may be surprised."

"I will do my best," Scodo answered. "But only because you asked."

Sesha's face broke into a smile. "Well, my dear Scodo, perhaps this Darrow will have a magic all his own."

· 23 ·

Quinderfill's Cabin

After resting for several days in the shed, the small band of warriors were on the move again. The path through the forest slowed them down, so Darrow led them across open fields, far from the relative shelter of the trees. He led the way alongside Hugga Hugga; behind them, Naark carried Timwee on his back.

Suddenly, the air filled with the sound of hoofbeats. Across the pasture rode two goblins, swiftly bearing down on the four. There was no hiding now. As the goblins closed in, Darrow could see their long curved swords gleaming in the sun. A screeching howl filled the air. Hearing the war cry, Darrow ran for the trees with Hugga Hugga close behind.

Naark looked to Darrow for orders, but Darrow was already on the run. The troll paused, looking left and right, considering his next move. Then he did something that surprised even the goblins. He gently placed Timwee on the ground, and turning to face the riders, he waited.

Looking back, Darrow saw Naark standing still, and wondered if the troll had given up. Perhaps he was sacrificing himself to allow Darrow to run free. But what of Timwee? Heartsick, Darrow counted two brothers as lost.

The first rider was closing fast. He lifted his sword and screeched once more. Darrow stopped, staring as the horses, seemingly in slow motion, closed upon Naark. The rider rose high in his saddle and leaned toward his target. Calmly, Naark drew back his arm.

As the horse arrived, the nine-foot troll launched his fist directly into the horse's muzzle. So staggering was the blow that it almost stopped the animal cold. The horse screamed in pain, and the rider was flung into the air, crashing into the ground thirty feet beyond. He lay very still.

The second rider, seeing the fate of his comrade, tried to rein in his panicked horse, but he lost control and flew out of his saddle, landing at Naark's feet.

Naark could have made short work of the two goblins. Instead, he grabbed them both, one in each hand, and lifted them from the earth. While they shook with fear, the troll carried the two soldiers across the field and into the trees where he tied them together with vines. He returned to the field, lifted Timwee on his back, and followed his comrades into the trees.

ᏨᎢᎢᎢᎯ

A day later, Darrow and his three companions entered Hexenwald Forest. Their destination was a cabin that once belonged to a friend of Asterux's, an old hermit named Quinderfill. Quinderfill spent his life making medicines from a rare mushroom. Once a year, he would travel to the plains to sell his wares to many eager customers. One day, celebrating his good fortune in a tavern, he wandered into the street and lifted his hands as if to address the passersby. But when he opened his mouth, no sound came forth and he fell to the ground, dead.

The old hermit's demise launched a great commotion, as many believed that Quinderfill had amassed a small fortune. Upon his death, brave men and foolish adventurers entered the forest to find Quinderfill's cabin and return with his treasure.

Most became meals for bat spiders and griesonauts. Those who survived returned empty-handed, for the cabin was never found. But Darrow held a map, drawn by Asterux, with elaborate directions. The problem was that Darrow could barely understand a word.

"What is a Mestular tree?" Darrow asked. Hugga Hugga and Timwee had never entered Hexenwald. Darrow did not know. Soon they were lost. Remembering his first trip through the forest, Darrow abandoned the road. Without a path, thorns tore at their legs. Timwee and Hugga Hugga trudged with steps that were painfully slow.

The next day, they reached a brook. Hugga Hugga and Timwee collapsed and, after drinking, lay motionless on the ground. Naark curled up beside a tree. Darrow let them rest, but he knew they could not sleep long. The forest was too dangerous for them to remain exposed.

He tried to rouse Hugga Hugga and Timwee, but they would not move. Timwee's shoulder ached. Hugga Hugga was too tired to move. So Darrow turned to them and spoke: "Tell me about the day the archers fell like rain in the forest."

Timwee and Hugga Hugga looked up, stunned by the question.

"Tell me," Darrow repeated.

"It was . . . awful," Timwee whispered. "They all died."

Hugga Hugga looked away.

"And the ambush outside the forest? And the march to Kirstinnex? How many died?"

Hugga Hugga looked up, his face pained.

"How many?"

"Almost all we knew," Timwee replied, his voice still no more than a whisper.

"And who still lives? Who stands free of the dungeon? We are all that is left of the army of Sonnencrest," Darrow said.

"Every sacrifice. Every death. Every dream is bequeathed to us, to our small and pitiful band.

"I know that your strength is spent—that you can barely lift your broken bodies from the ground. But if we lie here, we will die.

"In our hands, in our hearts, and on our backs rests the one hope of a desperate and long-suffering kingdom. Rise up. Stand. Walk!"

Standing in the shadows, not far from the creek, was Scodo. As Darrow's words rang in his ears, he saw Timwee, Hugga Hugga, and Naark lift themselves from the ground.

"Indeed," thought Scodo, "perhaps there is a magic in this young boy's words."

· 24 ·

Ambush at Frenngravel Creek

*W*hoooowhip! Whoooowhip! Whoooowhip!

The snake owl cried from a nearby tree. And when a dozen species followed, their voices formed a dark overture that spoke of events to come.

Three weeks ago, Darrow and his band had arrived at Quinderfill's cabin. And on this morning, they sat on the dirt floor to consider the enormous challenge ahead.

Three weeks of rest, food, and exercise had made new men of Hugga Hugga and Timwee. Timwee's shoulder had almost healed. Hugga Hugga now walked with firm, steady steps. Naark was as strong as ever and aided the group by taking on all the heavy tasks around the cabin. In the meantime, Darrow had made daily hikes to the edge of the forest to plan their first attack. Now he explained his plan.

"Each day, about an hour before sundown, a goblin wagon enters the forest bringing supplies to the fort. The same driver, the same guard at his side. Both are armed with swords. Sometimes, there is a passenger or two but mostly just the driver and a guard."

Hugga Hugga motioned with his hands and Timwee interpreted.

"What about the patrols? How often do the horsemen or foot soldiers go by?"

"Usually once or twice a day, mostly in the mornings. But these soldiers do not travel with the wagon."

Hugga Hugga and Timwee nodded. Naark still eyed the window, giving the conversation not the slightest thought.

"Is there a hiding place near the road?" Timwee asked.

"Near the bridge that crosses over Frenngravel Creek. We'll have cover about a hundred feet away."

Hugga Hugga spoke frantically with his hands. "Can we block the bridge? Are there logs?"

"Better. There are large stones in the creek."

"So we block the road with stones and charge when the wagon stops," Timwee surmised. "Hugga Hugga will take the driver. I can take the guard. Darrow, you and Naark empty the wagon."

"No," said Darrow firmly. "I will take the driver."

The two old warriors exchanged nervous glances.

"But the driver . . ." Timwee began.

"I have been practicing for two weeks," Darrow interrupted. "A sword is just a piece of metal. I will take the driver."

꘎

The afternoon shadows stretched along the ground. It had rained early in the day and the water in the creek flowed high under the bridge. Darrow looked down the road. They were late. Perhaps the wagon had already passed.

Darrow inspected the road. "No fresh tracks. Let's move!"

Hugga Hugga was the first into the creek, lifting a small boulder and carrying it to the road. The rocks were heavy and only Naark was strong enough to lift a large one from the ground. The others carried smaller rocks and rolled them up the high banks. Darrow looked nervously down the road.

Suddenly, Naark shouted, "The supply wagon!"

The four warriors raced to their hiding place.

From behind the bushes, Darrow looked out at the road. Their stack of stones barely covered one side. So pitiful was the pile that the driver noticed nothing at all. The single guard slept in his seat.

A loud battle cry rang in the air.

Darrow turned to see Naark charging from the woods, far too early, waving a wooden club.

The driver's reflexes were quick. In a split second, he cracked a strong whip over his horses and charged the bridge. When he spotted the stones ahead, he veered hard to avoid them, and came careening back onto the road. Unfortunately, his wheel struck the pile and the left side of the wagon rose in the air, landed on its side, and went skidding across the bridge. The contents spilled out directly into Frenngravel Creek. The panicked horses strained against their harnesses, unable to move the wagon. Seeing the group charge from the woods, the guard bolted for the woods. Hugga Hugga gave chase. Darrow approached the driver, holding the fellowship's only sword. The driver did not run.

The driver was a small man, no taller than Darrow, but with a broad back and strong arms. His face was marked with scars and crevices that spoke of experience in battle. Facing Darrow, he drew his sword and waved it with a confident flourish.

Darrow did not wait; he lunged forward, swinging his weapon in a broad looping stroke that missed its target and sent Darrow stumbling to the ground. He looked up. The goblin stood above him, grinning widely, his sword falling like a hammer toward Darrow's head. Darrow rolled to the side with less than a second to spare.

Springing to his feet, Darrow faced his foe. Both swung their swords, but Darrow's stroke was weaker. Helplessly, he watched his sword fly from his hands.

Again, the driver smiled and reared back to strike the finishing blow. Darrow was backed against the wagon with nowhere to move. Barely a minute into his first battle, he faced death a second time. The goblin turned to bring the sword with full force against his target. Darrow closed his eyes.

But before the weapon could make contact, the goblin's head jolted forward and his body went limp. The sword fell wide of his mark, dropping from the driver's hands.

Darrow looked down. The goblin lay motionless at his feet. His skull was crushed like an eggshell; a rock as large as the goblin's own head lay to the side. Darrow looked up to see Naark, his fist in the air, issuing a cry of triumph. Once again, Naark's powerful right arm had saved the day.

Darrow looked at Timwee, who was standing waist-deep in the middle of the creek, trying to salvage something from the wagonload. He looked up at Darrow.

"One knife. An axe. A short sword."

Hugga Hugga returned from across the field, frantically waving his hands. Far behind him, Darrow saw a party of ten goblins on horseback.

"Run!" he cried as he grabbed the driver's sword and fled. The four of them scrambled through the forest through brush and briars where they knew no horse could follow. After an hour, they stopped to listen. There was no sound of pursuit.

· 25 ·

The Goblins Strike Back

*T*he water gurgled softly in the stream. At either side, the four warriors made not a sound. For four hours, they had moved through the forest, putting distance between themselves and any goblins that might be in pursuit.

Now, night had fallen. Sure that they were safe, they lay exhausted in odd poses across the ground.

The stream was an hour's walk from Quinderfill's cabin, at least in the daytime. In the darkness, their return would be a blind man's journey of groping for landmarks they could not see. Bedding down for the night was out of the question. Nearby lay the wretched bogs from which the griesonauts roamed, and no corner of the forest was safe from bat spiders and their silent strikes.

Darrow looked in the direction of the cabin. Above the stream was a clearing, lit bright by a full moon in a cloudless night. Fortune had smiled on his band. Maybe the journey back would not be so bad.

⌒៣៣⌒

Darrow rose and dusted his pants while his band lay motionless on the ground. A noise broke the silence.

Dogs.

It began with one bark, not far away, but others followed and within seconds the howling, snarling, and yelping of bloodhounds came ringing through the trees.

"Up! Up! The goblins are closing in!" Darrow implored in a voice strong but soft, fearing that shouting might alert the dogs to their position. But sleep masks all danger and Darrow was forced to shake his comrades one by one to get them on their feet. And when they finally stood, the barks and howls ringing in their ears, Darrow pointed to the clearing where a fallen tree offered the only defensible barrier.

Frantically, they charged across the clearing. As they approached the tree, they could hear the dogs, quieter now, sure in their pursuit, running close behind. As they reached the barricade, they turned to greet their foe. A dozen dogs entered the clearing and the sight of the men launched a new eruption of their wretched noise.

"Get ready," Darrow shouted, lifting his sword.

But just as the hounds approached, Naark issued a blood-curdling cry. For a moment, the dogs froze in their tracks. Suddenly, the troll lumbered forward to face the dogs, clutching a log as long as he was tall.

The first wave of hounds leaped upward, biting at Naark. He swung his makeshift club, filling the air with flying, screaming dogs. The others reeled and scattered to a safe distance.

A pair of dogs stepped forward, feigning attack. Naark swung his log. They scurried back. Three more dogs circled to the back, nipping at his heels.

"Get back here," Darrow screamed. But his order was too late. Naark was surrounded.

From behind, a sharp cracking noise filled the air and Darrow turned to see Hugga Hugga pounding his axe against a large tree.

"What are you doing?" he cried, but the Minotaur continued his axe strokes against the tree.

Meanwhile, Naark wheeled and swung at the dogs behind him. At the other side, dogs charged his back. He turned in a circle, shaking his log. As he turned, more dogs attacked. Naark's eyes widened. His hands shook. His swings became bigger, more desperate. Sensing their victory, the beasts grew increasingly bold.

Darrow rose to come to Naark's rescue, but Timwee pulled him back, shaking his head.

As the first few goblins appeared in the clearing, Hugga Hugga scrambled back to the barrier, but for Naark there was no return. He charged forward, dogs now hanging from his sides. He lifted his mighty club and swung with all the great power of his body. A great screech arose as the goblin stepped back. Now Naark's opponents were too many. Dogs and goblins charged at once. Darrow turned from the scene, unable to watch. When he looked again, Naark was dead.

Darrow turned to his side to discover that Hugga Hugga was once again gone. Then he heard the axe strike one more time.

A sharp cracking noise rang through the clearing. A giant pine was falling, right into the mob of goblins and dogs. The goblins scattered, but for some it was too late. When ten thousand pounds of pine tree struck the earth, seven goblins were crushed beneath it.

Now the dogs leaped onto the barrier. Timwee and Hugga slew two of them with sword and axe. Again, the dogs retreated.

Darrow counted. Seven. Eight. Ten. And then two more. There were still twelve goblins that he could see.

Darrow considered his situation. There was no hope of victory. What mattered now was how he would die. And he was determined that, in his final moments, he would take as many goblins as possible with him.

Realizing their victory was certain, the goblins took their time to regroup. An officer signaled with his hands, directing the remaining soldiers to the edge of the fallen tree. Clumsily, they stepped through the branches to form a line.

The officer raised his sword and shouted the order. The twelve goblins bolted forward, swords held high, screeching their battle cry.

Darrow tightened his grip, his body tense, eager for the attack.

At the barrier, Darrow attacked, but a goblin blocked his stroke. Again he swung, but this time he lost his balance and found himself on the ground. He cursed himself with the worst words he knew, lying on his back, unable, even at his death, to damage his foe.

Meanwhile, Hugga Hugga, holding the axe, took a broad swing at the first wave of goblins. Darrow looked up at Timwee dodging weapons from every side.

Fire in his eyes, one goblin lifted his long, curved scimitar high into the air, prepared to claim Darrow as his prize. But just as the goblin sword quivered above him, ready to fall, another sword appeared, slashing across the air and cutting the sword and the hand that gripped it from the goblin's arm. Darrow looked up. What he saw made him shudder. It was a face so hideous that he covered his eyes.

Towering above the goblin line stood a monster with the large shoulders and arms of a man but covered with a hard outer shell. Half man, half scorpion, this creature fought like no creature Darrow had ever imagined. Simultaneously swinging his gigantic sword and his darting tail, the scorpion man cut down three goblins at the edge of the line.

The goblins wanted none of this battle. At the monster's first appearance, one cried out, "Scorpion man!" and the others turned to run. Even the dogs fled. Soon the only sound that remained was the crash of panicked feet against the forest floor.

Timwee cried out, "Scodo!"

Hugga Hugga opened his arms to embrace him, and Timwee leaped forward, offering his hand. But Scodo gave only a nod of recognition and slipped quickly back in to the forest. But just as he left the clearing, he stopped and turned again to face the three surviving warriors.

"Bless you, my friends," Scodo said softly.

Then he was gone.

"Who was that?" Darrow asked, bewildered.

Timwee answered, "The finest warrior Sonnencrest has ever known."

Then the three warriors, heartbroken and weary, buried their friend Naark and hiked back to Quinderfill's cabin.

· 26 ·

The Magic Sword of Darrow

"**H**opeless."

Sesha folded her arms and pressed her lips together, shaking her head at Scodo's bleak assessment.

"He is brave. He speaks with beautiful words. But what does that matter? He'll be dead in a week."

Scodo turned his head, not wanting to see the disappointment in Sesha's face.

"He will get better," Sesha shot back.

"He is small. He can't lift a sword. He walks with a limp."

Sesha winced at each word. Then she asked, "And the others?"

"The cave troll is dead. The remaining two were once great fighters, but they are old."

A long silence filled the wagon.

Sesha lifted her chin, a sparkle in her eye. "Then somehow we must make a fighter of our man Darrow."

"He would need a sword as light as a feather," answered Scodo, almost laughing in despair.

A long silence followed. Then Sesha, eyes twinkling once more, looked up at Scodo. "Scodo, my friend, you are a genius!"

Scodo looked back, confused. Sesha stood up, her smile now a look of determination.

"I must go now. But there is one thing you must do. You must spread the word of Darrow's great victory over the goblins."

"Victory?" Scodo asked.

"Yes, victory. The goblins retreated. Darrow won. Is that not correct?"

Scodo stared back, wordless.

"I can help Darrow fight. That will be my job. But there is something much more important. The people need hope, and they need a hero. This Darrow may not be much, but he is all we have."

"Well, that much is true."

"Scodo, I need you to write down a message about Darrow's victory over the goblins. You must carry this message to every village on the plains. We must spread the word of Darrow's great victory.

"The people must know. They must have something to believe in!"

He looked back at Sesha and sighed. "Okay. I will deliver the messages. I just hope when they learn of their hero that their hero will still be alive."

It had not rained in many days and, as the wagon came to a halt, the air filled with a fine dust that lingered in the air. The old mule, Zauberyungi, coughed and wheezed.

Sesha climbed down and stepped into the road. For a few minutes, she looked down from the mountain to the valley below, remembering the beautiful view she had enjoyed as a child. Then, with slow steps, she walked toward the door. When she reached it, she hesitated again. Mustering her courage, she knocked.

From the other side, the blacksmith and famous pot-maker, Thor, peered through a hole and saw the gypsy girl. She had bought pots from him to sell in the villages. Recognizing her, he opened the door and invited her inside.

"Ah, Sesha, so good to see you today. You must need some new pots. Have they been selling in the villages?" he asked.

"I've sold a few," Sesha replied.

"And how was your journey? May I give you a cup of water or a piece of bread?"

"I have brought *you* some bread." Sesha handed him a small parcel containing a fresh loaf filled with raisins.

"What beautiful bread!" Thor exclaimed, surprised at so fine a gift. "But at least you could enjoy something to quench the thirst."

"A drink of water would be nice."

Thor ladled water into a wooden cup from a bucket next to his table. They both sat down.

"I have a number of small pots," Thor began. "But if you're wanting something bigger . . ."

"Thank you, sir," Sesha replied, "but I have not come for a pot."

Thor looked a bit surprised. "Then how can I help you?"

"I need a sword."

No one had asked Thor for a sword in at least thirty years. He thought of his wife, who died by a weapon shaped by his very own hands.

"I am a pot-maker, young miss," he answered politely. "You must go elsewhere to find a sword."

Sesha sat silent for a time, struggling to find her words. Her silence made Thor uncomfortable.

"And why might you need a sword?" Thor asked, mostly to move the conversation.

"It is not for me. It is for a friend."

"A sword is a sword, young lady. It can bring no good, if you ask my opinion."

"But the sword I need will be too light for any man. Really, it is a toy, hardly a weapon at all. My friend is barely more than a boy. What harm could it do in his hands?"

"There are swordsmiths aplenty throughout the kingdom who will be happy to make you a sword."

"No, it must be done by you. It must be forged in the hottest fire. Here, I brought special materials for the sword." Sesha held out two small sacks of powder.

Thor crossed his arms, his face stern. What did this gypsy girl know about his fire?

"You'd best get going, young lady," he replied, struggling to remain polite. "Please take this business elsewhere."

Sesha's face fell. She reached into her dress and retrieved a sack of coins.

"Please, I can pay you well for this task."

These words insulted Thor.

"No amount of money will make a sword-maker out of me. My work fills the stomachs of children—not the hands of murderers and thieves."

Sesha tried to reply, but the old blacksmith was waving her away.

"Out. Get out."

Sesha retreated from the cabin.

"Out. Out!" Thor was shouting now, pointing toward her wagon.

Still facing Thor, her eyes searching for the slightest softness, she stepped backwards toward the wagon.

Thor stood in his doorway with his arms folded, his expression unchanged.

She reached the driver's seat. She looked back at Thor with pleading eyes. Thor did not move.

She wanted to cry out to him. She wanted to hug his neck and tell him that she was really the princess. She wanted to say that this sword was more important to her and their kingdom than anything else in the world. But she could not betray her secret.

She grasped the reins and looked at the old mule, but her hands would not move. She braced herself, refusing to cry. All the while, Thor stood silently, staring at her.

Then she had an idea. She reached back into her wagon and pulled from the canopy one of the tiny yellow birds. She climbed down. In slow, timid steps, she approached Thor once again, her body shaking with emotion, her hand outstretched, offering him the tiny bird.

Thor knitted his brow, unsure of the meaning of her approach. Sesha moved closer, each step filled with the fear of failing in the great mission that rested upon her shoulders alone. She stood directly before the old blacksmith. She dropped to one knee.

But before she could lift her hands to offer her gift, Moakie appeared, bouncing excitedly around the corner of the cabin, almost knocking Sesha to the ground.

"Moakie, Moakie, Moakie!" Sesha cried, hugging the dragon's neck just as in days past. Moakie's teeth were black and old, but it did not stop her smile. She bounded in circles around Sesha, nuzzling her with her nose. Sesha moved back and forth, stroking the dragon with her hands.

Thor knitted his heavy brow. How did this gypsy girl who sold pots in the villages know Moakie? And when Moakie had calmed down, Sesha dropped to her knee and offered the yellow bird to the old blacksmith.

"I bring you a gift from Princess Babette."

Thor stammered, "How do you know the princess?"

Sesha could not lie to the man who saved her life. So she simply hung her head in silence.

For a moment, Thor considered her words. What if this girl knew Babette? What if Babette needed help?

"It doesn't matter. I will not make this sword." With those words, Thor stepped inside his cabin and shut the door.

⁘

The next morning, Thor rose and drew water from his well. After washing his face, he went to the shed to wake Moakie. Moakie was sound asleep and snoring even louder than usual. Thor leaned over and gave his dragon a gentle shake.

On the floor lay a brush, its bristles worn and stained black.

Moakie snorted and shivered and then lifted her head. When she saw Thor, she broke into a smile and in the soft morning light, her smile sparkled in a way Thor had not seen in ten long years. Every tooth was gleaming white.

Next to Moakie lay two bags of magic powder and instructions for mixing the powder and making the sword.

Thor looked out the window and softly spoke.

"Yes, my princess, you will have your sword."

· 27 ·

The Unlikeliest Hero

In a small clearing, Darrow lifted his hand, shading his eyes against the light. It was morning and the sun had just risen above the trees. Gauging its direction, he placed the sun at his back, and marched to the west, the direction out of the forest and onto the plain.

Nearby was a goblin fort. It was a small structure of logs and a few stone buildings. Normally, it held only twenty or so soldiers. But these soldiers were on high alert. Each and every one patrolled the forest, searching for the thieves who attacked the wagon at Frenngravel Creek.

So Darrow avoided the roads and trudged through the underbrush, setting his direction as best he could.

Two weeks had passed since Naark had fallen. Alone in the forest, three warriors could do little to save a kingdom. He needed volunteers.

His target was the small hamlet of Siegenhoffen, which was near the forest's edge. It was where goat farmers came to trade and buy supplies. Barely fifty people called it home. Most were old. He had chosen the village because it was small and no goblin soldiers were stationed there. After a long discussion with Hugga Hugga and Timwee, Darrow selected it as the place to start.

To convince these men, Darrow would need optimism and belief. But today, as Darrow trudged through the forest, he was almost overcome with gloom.

The vision of Naark falling to the dogs played again and again in Darrow's mind. What was Naark's reward for courage? Only the appearance of the scorpion man had saved Darrow from an equal fate.

The goblin army was at least five thousand strong. They were three. In Siegenhoffen, he would be lucky to find two volunteers. And who might those volunteers be? Who would follow *him*, hardly even a grown man, small, lame, and too weak to lift his own sword?

⌀⫘⊘

A day later, Darrow stepped out of the forest and into the plain. His clothes were torn and ragged. Across his arms and legs were cuts and scratches where the briars had torn at his skin. But these injuries were barely visible beneath the dust and dirt that covered his skin.

In the distance, he could see Siegenhoffen. It was a collection of small huts that seemed to have dropped onto the plain in no pattern or form. Barely rising above the town was the steeple of the church, too big for the village but built when the goats were plentiful and the price was high.

For many months, he had imagined this moment when he would pour forth his vision of a free kingdom. But now, facing this tiny village, he stood doubtful and exhausted.

He thought back to the day that the goblin beat old man Groompus. Some of the anger that began his journey returned and from this anger he found resolve. He lifted his head and walked into the village.

⁂

The afternoon sun beat down on the dusty street. The villagers mostly remained in their houses, small one-room structures with walls of stacked sod and roofs of straw. Many appeared empty. There was the stone church and a couple of wooden buildings. Seeing a man carrying a box, Darrow spoke.

"Good sir, I have traveled far to this village. I would like to speak with your elder."

The man, old but with large arms and strong, thick legs, might have been the elder himself, but he did not answer right away. He took a step back, placed his box on the ground, and eyed Darrow from head to toe.

"And who might you be?" he finally asked.

"I am Darrow of Ael. I have urgent business."

The old man's eyes widened. Nervously, he looked around the street.

"And from where have you traveled?"

"From Hexenwald."

The old man gave a nod and held up his hand as if to say *wait*. He walked briskly down the street, leaning into windows and doors along the way. People entered the street, watching Darrow from afar.

The onlookers gathered and moved closer toward Darrow, taking their measure of this ragged, filthy boy. Darrow wondered if visitors were so rare.

The old man returned, this time not walking but running. Behind him, a gray-haired man, tall and stooped over, struggled to keep pace. The two of them stood before Darrow. The crowd hovered close.

The tall, gray man was the first to speak.

"Who are you and what is your business?"

Darrow looked around and realized that the entire village was standing in the street.

"I am Darrow of Ael." He paused for a moment not sure where to start. Then he said it.

"I have come to enlist the citizens of Siegenhoffen in a great crusade to free Sonnencrest."

A murmur spread through the crowd.

The elder lifted a piece of paper. "Are you the one who attacked the goblins at Frenngravel Creek? Are you the so-called hero who defeated the goblins in the forest?"

Darrow was dumbfounded. The crowd now pressed tight. Every ear awaited his response. For once, words escaped him. All he could summon was a single word.

"Yes."

"Will you please walk to the door of that house and back?"

Puzzled, Darrow did as he was asked, bobbing with his usual gait along the way. The two men whispered to one another, nodding and noting that indeed he walked with a limp.

"Then this is you?" He handed Darrow the paper. His hands shaking, Darrow struggled to read the paper. The crowd pushed at him from all sides. What he read he could barely believe.

Our Battle for Freedom Has Begun

To the Citizens of Sonnencrest: From the tiny
village of Ael, a hero named Darrow has emerged.
Although he is lame and walks with a limp,
he is a mighty warrior who has already defeated
the goblins three times. First, he broke into the
Kirstinnex dungeon to free Sonnencrest's bravest
warriors. Four of them ambushed a goblin supply
wagon and escaped with a supply of weapons.
When the goblins followed them into the Hexenwald
Forest, they defeated an entire army of men
and dogs alike. The battle is known as the Battle
of Naark's Hill, named for the courageous cave
troll who gave his life that day. Now, brave men
from every corner of Sonnencrest are pouring into
the Hexenwald Forest to join Darrow's army and
help bring an end to goblin rule. There is new hope
in our land. Please make copies of this message
and carry them to every neighboring village.

"We received this two days ago," the elder stated. He raised his hands, trying to calm the onlookers. Turning again to Darrow, he said, "Speak to us. Can this really be true?"

Darrow paused, wondering if perhaps he might correct some of the details, but this was no time for small points. He lifted his head and spoke.

"It is true. We have engaged the goblins in a battle to free Sonnencrest. I am here to tell the citizens of Siegenhoffen that we can and will succeed."

There was some applause but mostly murmurs.

"My fellow citizens of Sonnencrest," he began. The crowd fell silent.

"Ten long years of tyranny have left our people broken and in despair. The goblins have robbed our homes, our businesses, and our churches. But they have taken something far more precious still.

"During these years, they have taken from our people the hope that we can change our future. They have stolen the courage we need to stand against the oppressors and drive them from our land.

"Today, in the forest, brave warriors are preparing for battle. In the forest lies a goblin fort housing no more than twenty soldiers. With volunteers, we can take this fort and drive the goblins from the forest.

"With a victory in the forest, we can march onto the plains and assemble a great army. That army will face the goblins in battle and force them from our land.

"I know, as you do, that the goblins are a formidable foe. Their soldiers number two thousand or more. But our greatest enemy is not the goblins at all. Our greatest enemy is the fear and despair that occupies our hearts.

"To lead this quest, I left the village of Ael, far to the west and so tiny that, to us, Siegenhoffen would appear a great city. But from small beginnings, great deeds can grow. Today, in the tiny hamlet of Siegenhoffen, a great journey begins. It is a journey of the heart. It begins with the belief that submission to an evil master is no life at all and that death in the battle for freedom is the highest honor any one of us could possibly obtain.

"And it begins with the belief that we can find our courage, the belief that we can face our foe, and the belief that we can assemble an army and march from the forest to slay our oppressors and restore freedom, honor, and dignity to our kingdom."

As Darrow spoke, the crowd forgot his dirty rags. As they listened to his words, he seemed no longer small but a figure of size and power. Instead of remembering that he was lame, they imagined a great march, the march against the goblin army that this man somehow knew he could defeat. When he was finished, there were few doubters. A great cheer erupted from the crowd.

Only a handful of young men lived in the hamlet of Siegenhoffen, but when Darrow returned to the forest, six of them followed him.

· 28 ·

Volunteers for Sonnencrest

"**S**ix volunteers," thought Darrow. His band had tripled
in size. But when Darrow arrived at Quinderfill's
cabin, he encountered another surprise. While searching for
food in the woods, Timwee had come across four volunteers
who had entered the forest to join Darrow's army. A fifth had
actually wandered to the site of the cabin. One of the men
had traveled from the town of Stiffledorf, nearly three days'
journey away.

"All Sonnencrest hails Darrow," he said solemnly, looking
straight at Darrow.

Darrow looked around. His band was now fourteen strong.

Among the new recruits was a soldier for hire, Kaylin, who
had worked in the armies of three different kings. A tall man
who told many tales and knew many jokes, he delighted the
campfire that evening with stories of hunting for kriezzels,

exotic weasels that could imitate a human voice and confuse
their pursuers in the woods. He was a talented swordsman,
and Darrow assigned him to teach the men the skills of the
blade.

Another of the new recruits was a dwarf named Cedrick,
who had made his living writing songs, at least until goblin rule
began. Under the goblins, singing and dancing hardly befitted
the public mood. So Cedrick took work cleaning chimneys,
which gave him a terrible cough and nearly destroyed his fine
voice. That afternoon, he played his mandolin and sang with
the remnants of his old tenor, much to the delight of the men.
Because Cedrick had traveled the kingdom in the days of old,
performing in villages of every kind, he knew the land and the
people, and Darrow drew on his knowledge.

There was Aisling, a girl of only sixteen who arrived with
a sling and a bag of stones. Her father was an archer who lost
his life when the giant Cyclops rampaged through the Pfimincil Forest. She was an only child, whose mother begged her
to stay at home. But she had had a dream in which her father
told her that she must go to the forest, find Darrow, and fight
for the kingdom.

Then there was Kilgo, a locksmith who traveled from the
city of Kelsner's Plain. Kilgo was an amateur magician who
entertained the fellowship with a grand show.

Timwee had slain two wild boars. And when the meat was
cooked and everyone had eaten all they could, Darrow spoke.

"Gather round, my friends, and welcome to our band. Look
around you. Our army is but a handful of men, most without
experience in battle. But the smaller our band, the larger each
of you stands in achieving the mission before us. You are the

first whisper of a cry we will raise across our kingdom. You are the first flame in a great fire that will drive the goblins from our land.

"Tomorrow more volunteers will arrive. And one day, when we watch the goblins flee before us, all will remember the first warriors gathered here tonight."

That night, with men sprawled around the cabin, Darrow lay inside, considering the events of the day. The admiration of these new recruits had lifted his spirits. But he feared he was unworthy. He had spoken great words and was hailed as the greatest warrior in all Sonnencrest. The revolt he had imagined in his dreams was finally beginning. But what would these people think of him when they saw him perform in battle? Just how many more battles, he wondered, might he survive?

⟋〰〰⟍

When the sun was up, Darrow sent Timwee and Hugga Hugga back to the woods to search for volunteers who might be lost. They returned at noon with another seven men.

After a day of training and drilling, Darrow called his soldiers together. Eagerly, all gathered round the fire. With the weapons they had recovered from the battle at Naark's Hill, Darrow had a good sword for every soldier and he passed a weapon to each.

"Raise your swords," he cried in a voice loud and clear.

Twenty-one swords lifted, each reflecting the flames, sending dancing lights against the walls of the forest.

"Repeat my words: To this small but mighty band."

And twenty-one voices cried out his words.

"I pledge my allegiance, my honor, and my life."

And with each line, their voices roared back, each time louder still.

To this small but mighty band
I pledge my allegiance, my honor, and my life
For a cause more noble and precious
Than the soul of creature or man
To sever the chains of fear that enslave our people
To ignite in my countrymen the flames of hope
To inspire the courage of others
To bring a new sunrise of peace, honor, and virtue to our
  nation
For these things, no price is too large, no sacrifice too great
A fellowship of believers we shall be
And through our deeds will our people be free.

With these last words, the swords did not fall but remained high, quivering at the vast array of stars in this clear summer night. Into this heavy silence, Darrow spoke again.

"Tomorrow evening, my brothers and sisters, we will attack after sunset. We will strike the fort and drive the goblins from this forest."

With those words, all of the pain and suffering of ten years of cruelty, oppression, and crimes, all the broken hearts of all of the families of all of the land of Sonnencrest came together, no longer as heartache and despair, but as a great and powerful yearning for promise and hope.

And this time, the sound surely shook the walls of the goblin fort many miles away.

Sesha waited in her wagon. She had sounded a whistle, a high-pitched whistle that only Scodo could hear. After a time, when Scodo appeared between the trees, running and panting heavily, she clapped her hands and smiled.

"What news do you bring, my mighty Scodo?"

Scodo was silent for a moment, catching his breath.

"The news is all good. Darrow has returned from Siegenhoffen with six volunteers."

"Six! Why there are not six good men in that pitiful little sodpile."

"There are none now. They are at Quinderfill's cabin."

"And who else is there?"

"More and more every day. The messages are working. Men from all over the kingdom are heading for the forest."

Sesha smiled quietly.

"You have done your part well, my friend. Now we will learn what my magic may inspire."

· 29 ·

To the Fort!

Darrow awoke an hour before sunrise. He threw back his bedding and looked around the yard, now cluttered with cloaks and blankets and snoring men. The excitement of the previous day had faded into the reality before him. Today, he would lead his army into battle.

These new recruits knew only his legend. They praised him. They worshiped him. They had left their homes to risk their lives and follow him to war.

But they had never seen Darrow fight.

He wrapped his feet in cloth and reached down for his sword. His hand gripped the handle and the weapon practically lifted itself into the air. Darrow looked down at the weapon. It was not his sword.

The metal of this new weapon glowed bright silver, as though newly forged. The handle fit his hand perfectly. But this new sword was not his. He inspected its markings, but it bore no name. Darrow smiled.

As he gripped this weapon, a warm glow passed through his body. His hand squeezed more tightly and he felt new strength in his shoulders and arms. He thought about the battle to come and no thought of failure entered his mind. He imagined dueling the goblins, his metal clashing against their own.

He raised the sword high above his head. It did not feel like a real weapon—it was too light. Surely, it would shatter on contact. But he liked the way this weapon made him feel.

He walked to the edge of the woods. He swung at a small tree and the sword cut deep into the wood—another stroke and the tree fell. He swung it again and again, each time with more power and confidence.

The first glow of sunrise appeared in the sky. In this better light, he held the sword across the palms of both hands. On the handle, in the metal, was a tiny marking—a figure. A bird. A tiny bird painted yellow. He had seen that bird before but could not remember where. Something told him that this sword with the bird would bring him luck and this he knew to be absolute truth.

Darrow placed the sword in his scabbard and began to walk the camp, brimming with optimism, eager for the day's events. He talked with each of the new arrivals. He asked about their skills, their experience, and from where they had traveled.

He wanted to know how each man had heard of their battles in the forest. They told him that all Sonnencrest was alive with the stories of Darrow's army and his courage in battle. And to each of these reports, Darrow responded with a confident smile.

Not long after waking, Darrow sent Timwee and four others to forage for food. Now they had more than twenty mouths to feed; by midmorning, seven more men had arrived. Two were from Ael, his brother, Mempo, and a friend who had lived in a cabin next to Darrow's.

"Mempo," Darrow shouted, embracing his brother tightly. "How did you know?"

"Your fame has even reached Ael!" Mempo stepped back and looked up and down at his brother. "Everyone is very proud. Even the crippled man, Felbester, tried to join us. Look, here, we have brought gifts."

The friend ran a few feet back to retrieve two large bundles. Nervously, fingers fumbling, he struggled against the knots.

"These bundles are a great load for so long a journey. Surely, you did not carry them by yourselves?" Darrow asked, nodding toward the other man from Ael.

The friend, now standing straight with his head held high, responded, "They were heavy indeed, but we could not disappoint our village."

When the bundles were opened, goods of all sorts spilled out onto the ground. They included bread loaves, some baked with real wheat and blueberries, a delicacy Darrow had never seen in Ael. There were blankets and warm socks, a few shirts made from wool, even a leather belt ornately engraved with the words Darrow of Ael.

In these bundles were valuables beyond any means of the poor and feeble families of Ael. Darrow made a short speech praising his village. And, after a heartfelt thanks, he asked about his father. The men told him that Darrow's dad praised his son's wisdom every single day.

∽∾

Away in the forest, Timwee, Kilgo, and three other volunteers were scouring the forest for wild boar.

"Here's how it works," Timwee explained.

"One of us goes ahead looking for the boar. Step lightly and be as quiet as possible. You will hear them before you see them. They dig for roots and they make loud grunts. The idea is to walk around them and chase them back to the rest of us.

"So, who has the best ears?"

No one answered.

"You," said Timwee, pointing at Kilgo the locksmith. "That way. Step lightly and make no noise. Chase the boar back towards us."

Kilgo glanced ahead nervously, but after some hesitation, he moved cautiously across the underbrush of the forest. He turned back to Timwee.

"How do I chase it back?"

"Make a lot of noise. Call it some names! When we hear you yelling, we will charge and kill the boar."

So off Kilgo went, stepping lightly across the grass, vines, and bushes that filled the forest floor. After each three or four steps, Kilgo would stop and listen.

After about twenty minutes, Kilgo heard a sound. He froze, tuning his ears to the noise. It was not exactly a grunt. More like a slobbering noise. Slowly, carefully, Kilgo stepped ahead.

Now the noise was louder. It was a strange snorting sound. "Could this be the boar?" wondered Kilgo, a city dweller who had barely seen a pig.

Now he circled the sound. The snorting was loud and it was a good thing, Kilgo thought, because there was no way this boar would hear Kilgo above his own noise. Through the brush, he saw the beast for the first time. Its snout was as long as two bread loaves and it walked low to the ground with short legs and webbed feet. There was no curly tail. Instead, its tail was as long as the rest of its body, thick, furry, and tapering to a point at the end.

"These forest pigs are quite different," thought Kilgo. He leaped toward the animal, shouting the most terrible insult he could conceive.

"Out, out, you putrid, dwarf-legged excuse for a pig! The entire swine family retches at your disgusting appearance!"

The animal looked back with an air of disgust, but the sight of this man hurling himself forward, arms and legs flailing and making a terrible racket, told him this was not the place to be. Away it ran.

Its feet were fast and it flowed low like a snake across the forest floor. Kilgo followed, insults and all.

Kilgo saw the bushes move and Timwee's head rise up. A look of terror flashed across this face.

"A griesonaut! Run for your lives!"

Timwee and the three men scampered through the forest. Kilgo, still behind the griesonaut, ran the opposite way. Hoping to keep the creature at a distance, he continued screaming as he ran.

Unfortunately, his cries alerted a goblin patrol. Ten minutes later, they picked up Kilgo and took him to the fort.

Inside Quinderfill's cabin sat a small group of men. On the previous day, Hugga Hugga had visited the goblin fort. Now he reported his plan. As he signed words with his hands, Darrow interpreted to the group.

"We are small in number and the men are untrained. But we have swords for most. There are only twenty goblins at the fort. Here is what we propose.

"We will assemble our men to the west, hidden among the trees. To the other side, we will send Kaylin and Timwee.

"The wall surrounding the fort is made of timbers and these timbers are old. They will burn without trouble. Timwee and Kaylin will set fire to the wall. When I see the smoke, I will put my axe to a great pine that overlooks the east wall. When the tree falls, it will open a hole in the wall and spread the fire. At the moment the timber hits, our soldiers will rush to the opening. Hopefully, in all this confusion, we can force them from the fort. The best soldiers are on the plains and not at the fort."

The door of the cabin burst open. Timwee was breathing heavily. He reported that Kilgo was lost.

"We cannot delay to look for one man," Darrow replied, though it pained him to lose a soldier before the battle had even started. "We will lose many more before this struggle is over."

Timwee nodded as Darrow continued.

"There is one more thing to consider," Darrow added. "If any goblin soldier escapes, word will reach the goblins in three days. They will send an army. We need time to prepare. If no goblin escapes, we might have a week."

"Let's place five men at the gate to block an escape," Tim-wee suggested.

"Five at the gate is five less to attack," Kaylin reminded.

"We can't afford escape. Five at the gate." With those words, Darrow ended the meeting and the men began preparations for the march.

⁓

At the fort, the goblins dragged poor Kilgo inside. Inside his shirt, they found the paper announcing Darrow's great victories in the forest.

One goblin stood on a chair and read the words aloud.

"From the tiny village of Ael, a hero named Darrow has emerged. He is a mighty warrior . . ."

Howls of laughter exploded all around. These goblins had seen Darrow fight. "And has already defeated the goblins three times."

"In his dreams!" shouted one goblin to the laughter and applause of the others. And when the goblins had finished reading the paper, they shoved Kilgo into his cell.

In a fort, deep in the forest, entertainments of any kind are treasured, so the goblins gathered round Kilgo's cell. They mocked him with jokes about Darrow. They asked why the scorpion man did not come to save Kilgo as well. And to great laughter, they asked Kilgo when the day would come that Darrow would actually kill his first goblin.

Meanwhile, Kilgo was in a state of unrest. He had heard there were twenty soldiers at the fort. Instead, there were almost fifty packed tightly inside the walls. He knew Darrow would be attacking soon. Outnumbered and untrained, there was no way they could succeed. Somehow, some way, he must send a signal to delay the attack.

He eyes searched the cell. Its walls were wooden logs and the roof was made of straw. Perhaps that was a way out—through the roof. Still, the goblins crowded at his cell. He pretended to fall asleep. But even a sleeping prisoner proved great fun for the goblins, who shouted taunts and poked him with sticks.

⁓

While Kilgo agonized in jail, Darrow and his men were on the march. Shortly before sundown, they arrived at the fort. Behind trees and bushes, they took their places looking down on the wall.

In the dim light remaining, Darrow could see the entrance to the fort. There were comings and goings at the gate, but Darrow wasn't worried. Night would arrive soon and the fort would grow quiet.

Kaylin and Timwee stepped through the forest to position themselves on the other side of the fort. When the moon rose above the tree line, they would move to the wall and set it aflame.

On the ground, Darrow's men fidgeted and turned with restless movements. Few had held a sword and only a handful had tasted battle. As Darrow waited, he heard a rumble in the sky. He looked upward, noticing the clouds that had gathered. In an instant, rain burst forth, drenching the fort.

Darrow cursed to himself. There would be no fire tonight.

⁓

Inside the jail, Kilgo searched for a strategy to distract his captors. A goblin appeared with brown scales pasted across his face. "See," one cried, "we have a scorpion man of our own! And we have the magic to make one hundred more!"

But Kilgo hardly noticed the laughter that followed. "Magic!" thought Kilgo. His mind went to work. Within seconds, he had a plan.

Slowly and with great drama, Kilgo stood up and turned to face the goblins. His face somber, impervious to their taunts, he gave a great bow. The goblins looked at one another, unsure what to think.

Kilgo held up one open hand so that the goblins could see his empty palm. Then he held up both open hands together. He lifted his right hand into the air a little above his head and paused for effect. Then he reached into his ear and pulled out a small coin. The goblins laughed. Kilgo gave another deep bow.

Kilgo removed his shirt, rolled it into a small ball, and put it in the pocket of his pants. Once again, he held open his hands for all eyes to inspect. Once again, he lifted his hands to the sky. Then he reached into his mouth and pulled from it the sleeve of his shirt, then the body of the shirt and, finally, the other sleeve. This time, the goblins laughed and gave Kilgo even louder applause.

Kilgo bowed again deeply, and when he was again erect, in perfect pantomime, he held up three fingers as if to say three minutes. He took a chair and moved it to the center of the cell. He gave the goblins a knowing smile. In anticipation, they responded with small applause. He threw the sleeve of his shirt over the rafter that crossed the roof of the cell.

Standing on his tiptoes, he tied one sleeve of his shirt to the rafter and the other round his neck. Tugging tightly on the knot, he turned to face the goblins. With his feet, he teasingly wiggled the chair.

The goblins were awed. Was this man truly going to jump from the chair without hanging himself? Kilgo held up two fingers and turned his back. Frantically, his hands out of view, he removed flint, metal, and tinder from his pocket and began firmly striking flint against metal. Sparks flew, but nothing caught. More strikes, more sparks, and finally a spark took and an orange circle appeared in the tinder. Carefully, Kilgo exhaled against the orange. It grew. A flame appeared. He lifted the flame to his shirt and the shirt caught fire. The goblins stepped back in awe. Kilgo ripped the shirt from his neck and hurled it upward against the straw above. Before any goblin understood what was happening, the roof burst into flames.

◠◠◠

The moon was already above the tree line. It was past time to move. But Darrow could not give the order. He wondered if this whole plan was a terrible mistake.

He eyed the dozen or so men looking at him from either side. He signaled Hugga Hugga to take his position by the tree. He lifted himself from the ground and gripped his weapon.

Then he saw it. From within the fort, a billow of smoke arose. The smoke was soon followed by a flame. Through cracks in between the timbers, he saw a flurry of bodies moving in every direction without order at all.

He signaled Hugga Hugga, who buried his axe in a towering tree. The crack of metal against wood sounded again and again. With a pop, a tremble, and a soft whistle, the tree fell through the air toward the fort. When it struck, it crashed through the wall and across the roof of the jail. The flames rose into the tree.

The twenty of Darrow's men gave a mighty cry. At the opening, a few goblins met their advance. But soon another thirty joined their defense.

The goblin swords struck hard and men began to fall. Outnumbered and outskilled, some ran after seeing their brothers fall. And seeing their comrades in flight, others did the same. But just when the battle seemed lost, one volunteer turned back to look.

At the hole in the wall, Darrow stood alone. His bright sword glistened in the flames, flashing here, thrusting there, in a dazzling display of swordsmanship. One after another, the goblins fell. For each one fallen, another stepped to the fore, and the new ones fell as well. Silhouetted in the flames, Darrow appeared a supernatural force, unafraid, untiring, and unstoppable.

Hugga Hugga and Timwee looked up in awe. What had transformed their once-feeble leader? A cry rang out.

"Look to the wall, to the wall. The mighty Darrow is holding fast!"

Heads turned. Feet stilled. "All hail Darrow!" one recruit cried. "To his side," cried another. A surge of emotion swept the men, who grabbed fleeing comrades and rushed back to attack.

Soon, the entire force stood at Darrow's side, fighting with newfound courage and confidence they lacked before. The goblins fell back. Darrow's men poured inside.

The gate burst open and goblins poured out into the forest. No soldiers blocked their path. In the excitement of the battle, these untrained recruits had rushed to the line of battle, leaving the gate unguarded.

Desperately, Darrow gave chase with a small band of soldiers. But the darkness shielded the goblins from sight. They listened for sounds, but the noise of the forest covered the goblins' escape.

Meanwhile, the light from the fire guided volunteers through the forest. When the battle began, Darrow had just twenty men. Seven were lost. But by the end, another forty men and three women had joined his troops. Too excited to sleep, his army celebrated until daybreak. Cedrick, the bard, composed a song to celebrate their great victory.

Deep in the darkest forest,
He found the goblin lair
When smoke commenced the battle
They never had a prayer
His sword was quick and mighty
His bravery tried and true
He helped us find the courage
To see our victory through.

In Hexenwald the forest
The goblins are no more
The great and mighty Darrow
Has shown them all the door!

Again and again, the song rang out through the trees. When the first light of day appeared in the sky, they congratulated themselves once again and began the work of the day. They buried their dead beneath a tower erected with stones from the fort. Then they picked up the wounded and began a tired but triumphant march back to Quinderfill's cabin.

⚬⚬⚬

At the cabin, thirty more had found his band. The new ones were hungry. Many had spent days in the forest, lost and frightened. Not all of their companions had made it to the camp.

Darrow had little to offer, but he ordered his men to give up their remaining pieces of boar. Despite their hardships, these new men were inspired by the news of the victory. And when they met Darrow, they marveled at how this small, youthful figure, walking with a limp, could have driven the mighty goblins from the forest of Hexenwald.

As Darrow was making his rounds, Timwee came with terrible news. Kilgo, the locksmith, had been badly burned when the tree fell upon the jail. The men had constructed a stretcher to carry him back to the cabin. They had wrapped his body and called him a hero. But his injuries were too great. By the time they reached the cabin, Kilgo was dead.

Darrow called together the men and gave a beautiful speech praising the locksmith. He ordered that Kilgo be buried beneath the apple tree behind the cabin. It was a place where Quinderfill surely spent his days enjoying the view of the forest. Three volunteers began digging the hole. An hour later, one of them ran to Darrow, urging him to the gravesite.

Resting five feet deep in the ground was an old chest, barely longer than a loaf of bread but deep and tall. It was made of wood with metal hinges, and the wood was beginning to rot.

Darrow jumped into the hole to inspect the contents. There was no lock. With a knife, he pried open the lid and what he saw made him stand up in wonder.

A great pile of treasure spilled out onto the damp soil. Gold and silver coins, gems, and even a fine silver dagger. Quinderfill's treasure had been found.

Darrow knew right away what this money could mean. He had his men bring the chest into the cabin, and then he called together Hugga Hugga, Timwee, and Mempo. "Our prayers have been answered," Darrow exclaimed, his whole face glowing with the blessing that had fallen into his lap.

"We need swords, but swords cost money. Now we have a fortune. Our men can be armed!"

But Timwee asked the one question that Darrow had yet to consider.

"Where can we buy them? Someone might sell us one or two, perhaps even five swords. But no one has the hundred swords we need. The goblins control every town."

"There must be swords somewhere!" Darrow exclaimed, pounding his fist against the table. "Someone must have swords!"

Mempo suggested that they might travel to Pfisterstellen, the small kingdom that lay on the other side of the forest. But no one knew the way.

"What about the road through the desert?" Timwee asked. But Kaylin explained that the road had been closed since the goblins took Sonnencrest and it was probably not passable.

Hugga Hugga signaled his thoughts. "This treasure has no value for us," he said. "To get our swords, we will have to take them from the enemy on the field of battle."

Darrow was alarmed. "We can't leave the forest without weapons. In three days, the goblin king will know about the fort. An army will be on its way. Against trained soldiers with real weapons and real armor, we will have no chance."

Hugga Hugga once again spoke.

"What chance do we have in the forest? We are out of food. There are no weapons here. Our volunteers are dying. Leaving is our only chance."

All were silent, considering their grim prospects. It was Darrow who finally spoke.

"Hugga Hugga is right," he said, choosing his words slowly. "Time is precious. Tomorrow, we break camp and leave the forest. On the plain, our volunteers can find us. The villages can provide food. Our chance is a small one, but if we don't move fast, there will be no chance at all."

The three others looked at one another, wondering at Darrow's bold decision. A loud cry arose from the camp. Fifty men had just entered the yard. They carried food and wine sent from the villages on the plains. When they heard that the goblin fort had fallen, they cheered and hugged one another, some with tears in their eyes.

Looking away from this scene, Darrow turned to Timwee, Hugga Hugga, and Mempo.

"Believe," he told them. "Nothing is possible unless we believe."

❦

That night, Darrow peppered Timwee and Hugga Hugga with questions about the goblin army. Timwee explained their tactics.

"They are well armored with helmets and breastplates. When they attack, they do so in one line with their shields locked together in a great metal wall."

"How can you break the wall without swords?"

"You can't break the wall even with swords. We must surprise them. Against the formation, no army can succeed."

That night, Darrow considered this advice. How do you surprise an army on an open field? The plains offered no cover at all. How can you break a wall of iron with wooden spears? Darrow had no answers. He tossed and turned, unable to sleep for the longest time.

⌾

When Darrow awoke, the sun was well into the sky. The cabin was empty. The eight or ten men who had slept there had already risen. Panicked, Darrow jumped out of bed and pulled on his shirt. There was so much to do. How could his men have allowed him to sleep so long?

He moved for the door. But before he left the cabin, he stopped and turned back to look at his bedside. The chest? Quinderfill's chest?

It was gone.

He called out to Timwee and Mempo to see if someone had put it away. But neither knew anything of the chest. Frantically, he searched the camp, questioning the men, almost accusingly, but no one admitted any knowledge of where the chest might be. Darrow wondered if thieving men might have entered his camp. Timwee came to calm him.

"The chest is of no use to us. Forget it," he said.

Darrow knew he was right. So he assembled the men and spoke.

"We have won a victory, but larger ones await. There are no more goblins in the forest. We must march to the plains where we can find more warriors. We will arm ourselves in the villages. And when we meet the goblins on the plains, we will avenge all they have done to our kingdom. We will defeat them in battle. We will drive them from our land. And we will bring ten long years of unspeakable tyranny to a just and lasting end."

The soldiers were packed tightly together in the small clearing and Darrow's words made their spirits soars. Twenty of them returned to the fort to search the ashes for swords. The rest began their march from the forest. As their first steps struck the ground, Darrow hoped against hope that somehow his words would ring true.

· 30 ·

Report from the Forest

The soldier stared at his feet, unwilling to look into the eyes of the monarch before him. His clothes were discolored with the mud of the forest and the dust of the road.

"Well?" shouted the king. "Tell me again!"

The soldier cleared his throat but did not lift his head. The great general Beltar and Bekkendoth, the king's advisor, looked on.

"H-h-h-his sword. It was his sword. I never saw such a sword so quick. He was just a little guy, but no one could take him. All fell before his blade."

"You did not fall!" the king cried. "You ran."

"There was no hope," the soldier whispered.

The king turned to Beltar. "One man! Really a boy, not a man!"

"These were not our best soldiers, Your Majesty."

The king barely heard his words.

"Fifty soldiers killed or fleeing like mice before a kitten. My fort in ashes and you tell me I have not a single soldier who can take out a lame boy from some place no one even knows!"

Beltar did not speak.

The king turned to the soldier. "Take him to the dungeon, I say. And drop him in the coward's cell."

Bekkendoth whispered something to the guard as he carried the soldier away.

The king walked to the window. Dark splotches of sweat appeared on his robe. Beltar spoke.

"Your Majesty, Darrow has only thirty men. If they leave the forest, we can crush them in a matter of days."

"And if they don't?"

"They will starve."

"Where is Zindown? Maybe he can fix this problem."

Bekkendoth answered. "He has left Globenwald. I believe he is in the forest now."

The king stood silent, seething. A small puddle of sweat collected at his feet.

"We have already taken action, Your Highness," Beltar continued. "I have sent word by horseback to move five hundred men toward the forest."

"I would recommend more," Bekkendoth suggested. "After all, there are two thousand you can send."

"Two thousand to snuff out thirty peasants? You must be mad." Beltar gave Bekkendoth an angry glare.

"He is a hero now. Others will join him. Why not be safe?"

"He can find a thousand for all I care. How will they fight? With pitchforks and hammers?"

The king looked at Beltar. "Are you leading this army?"

"No, they are already marching toward Hexenwald. I will ride to Blumenbruch tomorrow. He has no army. He is a one-legged rabbit. We will bring him to Blumenbruch alive."

"Alive? What then? What then?" the king sputtered, lifting his arms and splattering the walls with droplets of sweat.

"We will cut off his head. And when we do, Your Majesty, you will be sitting in the very first row."

· 31 ·

Out of the Forest

$\mathcal{T}$he trails of the forest echoed with footsteps. Darrow's army was four hundred strong now, and though hardly any had seen battle, they stepped boldly and without the slightest concern for dangers that lay ahead. In their own minds, they were warriors, lifted far above the common conditions of ordinary life. They were lifted by their belief in a larger cause, men and women who knew without a doubt that they held the great and precious power to transform the future and write history with their very own hands. These were days to which every person aspires but only a few have the privilege to live. These were the days they would treasure until age and death lifted them from the earth.

As the first among them stepped out of the forest and into the sunshine of the plain, he cried out and four hundred more

joined together in the song composed by Cedrick on the trails
of Hexenwald Forest.

All hail the mighty Darrow
All hail his growing fame.
The goblin nation shudders
To hear his mighty name.

Four warriors in the forest
A fellowship began.
They faced a goblin army
And the goblin army ran.

Thirty in the forest
Besieged a fortress strong.
They slew the goblin forces
And righted what was wrong.

All hail the mighty Darrow,
All hail his growing fame.
The goblin nation shudders
To hear his mighty name.

Freedom for our kingdom
Justice for our land
For victory we shall battle
'Til none of us still stand.

For ten long years we've waited
We've suffered hard and long

But tomorrow will be different
When we sing our victory song.

All hail the mighty Darrow,
All hail his growing fame.
The goblin nation shudders
To hear his mighty name.

But while his army forged ahead, drunk with visions of their victory to come, Darrow was a tormented man.

He had his soldiers, four hundred, with more arriving every day. But they were untrained, unruly, and barely armed. Even after ransacking the goblin fort, they held less than a hundred swords and no armor. Their weapons were knives, hammers, pitchforks, axes, wooden clubs, and crooked spears.

Hope. Belief. Optimism. These words had brought him a multitude. But to win his victory, he needed weapons and he needed them fast.

His army surged forward, in high spirits, joined on all sides by new recruits eager to follow his every command. But Darrow's mood was dark. He would soon meet the goblin army—not a paltry force of fifty lesser soldiers assigned to the forest duty that better soldiers refused. Darrow would face an army numbering hundreds at least, maybe a thousand or more. The soldiers? Not an unruly band of raw volunteers but warriors, well trained and battle hardened. Every one would wear armor. In every hand would be a fine sword. And behind their line of hardened shields would stand Beltar, the greatest general of their time.

Outside the forest, there was a great plain with nowhere to hide. Could he tell his men that he had summoned them to disaster? Had his brashness and daring only sentenced his nation to still more decades of tyranny? He had no answers. He had no choices. In a week, maybe days, he would face the goblin line. When he did, he could only hope that courage would be stronger than iron.

· 32 ·

Duel in the Desert

*T*he whip whistled through the air as Sesha shouted, "Faster, Zauberyungi, faster." The mule hardly noticed the whip. It was the urgency in Sesha's voice that pushed him ahead.

The wagon jolted onward in fits and starts. Ahead and behind lay a broken road that crossed a vast, lonely desert. To either side were barren mountains. At odd spots, a scrubby tree broke this landscape of rocks, sand, and starving brown grass.

The road itself was narrow and dotted with craters and fallen rocks. Whole sections had been washed away in some long-ago storm. The road led to Pfisterstellen, a tiny kingdom that bordered Sonnencrest on the eastern side. Fearing the goblins, Pfisterstellen had closed its borders long ago. The road was no longer used.

Across this landscape no houses stood. There were no people or animals. The only sign of life was a small wagon pulled by one mule. The wagon was headed to a small cove on the sea. There, Sesha and Scodo hoped to find Telsinore the pirate, who they hoped would sell them swords.

"How many do you think he will have?" Sesha asked earnestly.

"I don't know," replied Scodo, answering the question for the third time. "A pirate like Telsinore keeps lots of swords. We can only carry two hundred in this wagon."

"Will this treasure be enough?"

"If he does not kill us and steal it, it will."

Sesha and Scodo were silent for a long time. In the wagon lay Quinderfill's treasure. Two hundred swords would not arm Darrow's entire army. But two hundred soldiers with swords might give Darrow a chance. Time was short. They needed to reach the cove and return in three days. It would take a miracle to succeed.

⁘

As Sesha and Scodo drove through the desert, a fine mist surrounded the wagon. It was a strange mist, floating above them, not quite rain but more than a cloud. It extended three or four wagon lengths in all directions. To Scodo, it seemed strange, but Sesha barely noticed at all.

Sesha should have known better. Having studied ten years at Asterux's side, she knew the spells of the great wizards. And this mist was the greatest of all magics, the encirclement.

In the encirclement, the wizard loses all human form and becomes an encircling cloud. The spell has no physical effect, other than the dampness that the victim may feel. But what is taken from those encircled is far more precious than any physical possession. Because the encirclement is a robbery of the mind—a theft of the knowledge, memories, and even secrets its victim cannot recall.

The maker of this spell was Zindown. And so, at that moment, unknown to Sesha or Scodo, their most powerful enemy knew everything.

Even before the encirclement, the evil wizard's spies had told him much. Zindown knew they were carrying Quinderfill's treasure. He knew they were traveling across the desert to meet the evil pirate Telsinore. He knew that they would offer Telsinore the treasure to buy his swords. He knew those swords would be used to arm Darrow's army.

But now he knew even more. Now he knew that Sesha was not Sesha at all, but the escaped Princess Babette. He knew that Babette had learned magic at the side of the great wizard Asterux. And he knew that Babette had used her powers to give Darrow a magic sword.

This knowledge alarmed Zindown.

Darrow was marching from the forest with hundreds of men. At every step, new volunteers were flocking to his cause. In a few days, Darrow might lead a thousand men.

The first wave of the goblin army was marching to meet him. Darrow might have more men, but his men had no weapons. If Sesha and Scodo delivered the swords, Darrow might somehow succeed.

But these were mere possibilities. The job of a wizard is to shape events. And Zindown was determined to write the outcome of this battle with his very own hand.

He had reason to be confident. Against Sesha and Scodo, Zindown had an ally even greater than his magic alone—time.

The goblin army would meet Darrow in three days. Even without obstacles, the task facing Sesha was difficult indeed. And obstacles were exactly what Zindown had in mind.

⁖⁖⁖

Sesha and Scodo leaned into the wagon, pushing it with all their might. A dry streambed, two feet deep, crossed the road. Once, twice, three times they shoved. On the third try, the front of the wagon lifted, Zauberyungi jolted forward, and the wagon fell with a loud plop onto the road.

Sesha and Scodo hardly noticed that the fog was lifting. A slight breeze nudged at the wagon from behind, moving the mist ahead and into the sky. The air ahead began to swirl. Sesha looked up at the whirlwind and wondered if bad weather lay ahead.

She did not wonder long.

In an instant, the breeze reversed itself and menacing clouds collected in the sky. At first, the wind was easy, even soft, but the air slowly gained speed. The breeze became a gale. Sesha grabbed the wheel of the wagon to hold her balance. Scodo's hood blew back and he lifted his arm to block the stinging sand.

Against this wind, Zauberyungi leaned hard, his hooves struggling to grip the road. But the winds reached a mad rage, hurling sand and rocks against the wagon. Sesha's feet lifted from the ground as she gripped the side of the wagon. Frightened, she looked beseechingly at Scodo. Stronger and heavier, Scodo was making small steps forward.

"Zauberyungi! Zauberyungi!" she called out. "You must help him, Scodo!"

Slowly, carefully, the scorpion man moved forward until he had almost reached the old mule. Zauberyungi slipped, falling to his knees in a backwards slide that sent the wagon into reverse.

The jolt broke Sesha's grip, but she managed to grab the back of the wagon. Had her hand missed its target, she surely would have been blown like a fallen leaf across the autumn sky.

Meanwhile, Scodo had edged forward yet another two feet. He turned his body sideways to the wind and planted his tail hard in the soil. With both hands, he pulled his sword from its scabbard and raised his arms high. He tottered and shook, struggling to hold his position. But he regained his balance and with a mighty force, he plunged the sword deep into the ground. Scodo wrapped his large arm around the mule's neck. With one foot steadied against the sword, he lifted Zauberyungi to his feet and held him in place.

Sesha clung desperately, five fingers away from being lost to the sky. Behind the wagon, the wind was at its worst. It blew down both sides and around the back of the wagon, creating an unpredictable swirl that from time to time lifted and shook her body. But amidst the raging storm, Sesha's mind was hard at work.

With a great burst of strength, she pulled her body into the wagon. There, she turned, her face again to the wind, feet pressed hard against the back of the wagon. She lifted two fists into the air, her hands closed tightly, every knuckle white. Her eyes were closed as well, not against the wind or the sand but against everything around her. Her body tight, her mind entranced, she began a low whistle.

The sound had a strange and penetrating melody. It was not quite a tune but a string of notes, barely twenty seconds long.

When these notes reached Scodo's ears, he turned and looked, shocked at the eerie tune that seemed to have entered from a world far beyond.

A small whirlwind appeared, just in front of Zauberyungi. The whirlwind began spinning sand in a circle, and the circle began to grow.

Amazed, Scodo stepped back. Now the whirlwind was larger. It was expanding, exploding in size, by the second. Then he realized what was happening. As the raging winds struck the whirlwind, their power was drawn into its vortex. Its swirl expanded until it became so large and powerful that Scodo feared it would consume him and Zauberyungi and Sesha.

Horrified, Scodo stood tensed, bracing for the worst. But as Sesha's circular storm expanded across the plain, an amazing thing happened. Just like a hurricane, a center of calm opened up inside. The eye of this storm moved back and surrounded the three travelers. Suddenly, there was no wind at all. Outside, in every direction they looked, the new storm blew round and round. But inside, at the center, tranquility reigned. Scodo looked back at Sesha.

"Unhitch Zauberyungi," she cried out, firmly and confidently. Scodo hesitated, but Sesha shouted again and he scrambled to obey.

Just as Zauberyungi was released and moved to the side, the eye of the storm passed by and the wind welled up again, this time from behind. The storm was moving. Now the wind was blowing at their backs. Unprepared for this new surge, Scodo and Zauberyungi were swept into the air. There was no way to stop. As they dropped to the ground, they did their best to recover their feet and run with the storm. The old mule and the scorpion man bounced across the ground and back into the air until, finally, they lay on the ground, the air still and the storm behind them.

Meanwhile, the wagon, freed of Zauberyungi and Scodo, was thrust down the road at a fantastic rate, Sesha gripping the seat as the wagon bounced and rolled far from the road and across the sandy plain. When the wind finally passed and the wagon stopped, Sesha looked back at Scodo and the mule, a good distance behind.

She waved with both arms, trying to get their attention as they looked at one another, dazed by the dramatic events. "Quit your dallying," she teased. "The pirates are waiting!"

∽✲∾

Back on the road, Scodo turned to Sesha with a look of wonderment. "Do you understand what happened?" he asked.

Sesha looked down, not sure what to say.

"You must understand that the wind may not have been a storm," she began, carefully choosing her words. "There are windstorms in the desert but not like that one. I suspect it was the work of a wizard."

"A wizard? How can you know?" Again, with patience and calm, Scodo waited as Sesha considered her words.

"Only a great wizard can move the skies into a raging force. There are only two wizards who could have done this, and one of them is on our side. I believe our journey is being opposed by Zindown."

A chill raced through Scodo's body. Zindown was a legend, both for his evil and his power. He asked the question at the front of his mind.

"But what was that noise? And why did the wind suddenly change?"

Sesha was quiet for a long time, but Scodo waited.

"That was me."

"You?"

"Yes," replied Sesha, reluctant to say more.

"Where did you learn this magic?"

"As you know, I grew up in the forest with Asterux. He is a great wizard, even more powerful than Zindown."

"So you have powers as well."

"Not like a true wizard. I studied only ten years. Zindown may be two hundred years old and his power grows with every year."

Then Sesha told Scodo the story of how she had learned at Asterux's side. She told him about finding forgiveness and the moonflower and how she used the whistle of her little yellow bird to bring the magic alive.

Scodo looked at Sesha, entranced by her story.

"There is magic for both good and evil. Asterux taught me that the evil power is always easier to find and easier to use. Evil requires only temptation and weakness. But to draw on the magic of good requires more, much more.

"There is a great force of good inside every creature. But as we go through life, that power is corrupted and diminished by all we see and experience. When a truly good person of pure heart can tap the power inside, and when that person can grow and nourish the magic over time, he will possess powers far greater than those that arise from evil."

Scodo just shook his head, skeptically. "This is not the world I know. How long did it all take?"

"Seven years."

"Seven years!" Scodo replied, surprised and with new respect. "And after that?"

"After that day, the magic came faster. Each day, Asterux would give me a new task and I would search for a new word, or rather a new whistle, that would summon the magic. I opened bottles, lit fires, and put animals to sleep. Once," she said with a sly smile, "I made Darrow disappear in the forest."

"I bet he loved that!" Scodo laughed.

"Asterux was a wonderful teacher. He is a loving man and his deep goodness is beyond any measure. But after ten years, he sent me on my way."

"Why?" Scodo asked.

"It was time."

Hearing these words, Scodo knew in his wisdom that the answer was not for him to know. He turned back to the problem at hand.

"So you think the wind came from Zindown. Will he be back?"

Sesha looked up into the sky. Her eyes showed strength but also resignation to the trials that lay ahead. "He will be back."

"Do you have the power to fight him again?"

"Zindown is a great wizard. But he may underestimate me. Sometimes small tricks can undo great schemes. We shall know soon enough. He will not give up with one battle."

The wagon continued across the desert, stopping here and there to pass through a gully or dodge a hole in the road. Sesha looked ahead. A great black shadow had fallen on the land ahead. The shadow seemed to move, not forward or backward, but from within, quivering and wriggling.

Zauberyungi snorted loudly, his feet taking on an uneasy gait. Scodo, aware of the strange shadow, looked at Sesha. Sesha said nothing.

Zauberyungi stopped altogether. "On, Zauberyungi," Sesha cried. The old mule began to move again but with uneasy steps, stopping every few seconds before pulling up again.

Sesha cracked the whip above his head. This time, Zauberyungi stopped, stamping the ground. Scodo dismounted to inspect the problem. His eyes searched the mule's body. Then he brushed Zauberyungi's leg and stamped the ground.

"Just a spider," he shouted back.

The wagon moved again, but Zauberyungi stopped once more, stamping one hoof against the road. One hoof joined another and Sesha looked on in horror as Zauberyungi began a strange dance, his four feet beating out a frantic rhythm. Scodo jumped from the wagon and ran to his side.

This time, he brushed his own legs. He jumped back, brushing off his arms.

"Spiders!" he cried. "There are spiders everywhere!"

The wagon stood near the top of a small rise in the plain. From this place, Sesha could see no spiders. But at the top of the rise, the dark shadow appeared again, moving slowly toward them.

Zauberyungi whinnied, bouncing about as if he were standing on a burning stove. Scodo began to flail at the ground with his sword, moving from side to side, circling, shaking his legs one at a time.

A vast ocean of spiders approached. "Curse you, Zindown," Sesha muttered under her breath, and for a moment she thought she heard an evil laugh across the plain.

Turning back, she dove desperately into the wagon, throwing bags and boxes this way and that.

Now Scodo had joined in Zauberyungi's terrible dance, writhing with each painful bite. Worse, the darkest part of the shadow was now only a few feet away, a terrible black mass bubbling like a churning brook.

A sharp pain shot up Sesha's arm and she cried out. She looked down to see a spider, hardly bigger than a mite. But now spiders were in the wagon and more were pouring in. Two more bites shot through her body. She cringed and rolled to her side.

Then she saw it.

Wedged between the canvas and the side of the wagon was a box. On its side were the words DRIED LIZARDS AND FROGS. Frantically, she grabbed the box and ripped it open. With the spiders crawling up her back, she hurled its contents into the air and delivered a soft whistle that rolled across the valley and echoed against the low cliffs at either side.

Nothing happened.

Distraught, Sesha looked at the front of the wagon. Zauberyungi's eyes were ablaze. He let forth a terrible moan. The great shadow lapped at his feet.

Sesha struggled to compose her thoughts. With all of the concentration she could muster, she wiped Zauberyungi and Scodo and spiders from her mind until all that was left were the deepest and purest feelings that dwelt in her soul. She remembered the goodness. She forgave the goblin swordsman who killed her family. She gave her father forgiveness and love. Once again, a low, soft, melodious whistle departed her lips and lingered in the air.

Suddenly, the ground and the wagon exploded with thousands of lizards and frogs. Mouths opened. Tongues flashed. The great feast had begun. In a few moments, they had devoured the spiders surrounding the wagon and surged forward to meet the advancing shadow.

Zauberyungi, his skin cleared of spiders, backed up the wagon a few feet and Scodo retreated to his side.

"Get in the wagon!" Sesha screamed.

When Scodo was at her side, she said quietly, "There are not enough of them."

As Scodo looked about, the battle raged in near silence. But Sesha's words were true, for while her army of lizards and frogs greedily devoured the spiders, the spiders were ten thousand times their number, and they were coming fast. Sesha pulled at the reins and backed up Zauberyungi again.

"Zauberyungi," she called, "run like the wind." She cracked a strong whip in the air over Zauberyungi's head. Sensing no other course of action, the old mule bolted forward and launched the wagon into the dark shadow ahead.

For a few moments, Zauberyungi strained at the load and his start was slow. With speed, the clopping hooves and spinning wheels might escape the spiders' bite. But Zauberyungi's pace was no gallop, just a jittery, jumpy walk. The spiders climbed his legs once again.

Sesha felt the wagon tilt forward slightly and saw that they had reached the top of the rise. Before them lay a long sloping descent. As Zauberyungi tap-danced ahead, gravity took charge. The wagon lurched forward, striking the old mule from behind. Bumped by the wagon, his load relieved, Zauberyungi bolted ahead in a mad dash to stay ahead of the wagon.

By the bottom of the rise, the shadow had passed.

They continued on another mile until they came to a small brook. Scodo unhitched Zauberyungi, who waded in the water while Sesha rubbed a special potion over his wounded legs. There they rested for perhaps an hour. With no time to lose, they forged ahead once more.

Back in the wagon, Scodo comforted Sesha, who was shaken by what had taken place.

"You have dueled with the greatest of wizards and prevailed."

"Zindown is not finished," Sesha responded, her voice breaking, holding back tears.

"Perhaps, but you won this time. Now that you believe you can beat him, you will be even stronger."

"I am not sure I believe that," Sesha answered.

"Then find it inside yourself," Scodo answered. And after a moment's pause, he added, "I believe in you."

At once, Sesha felt stronger.

· 33 ·

The Black Wand

I t is written that victory will come to the strong. Indeed, there are few advantages more formidable than power and might. Where might meets might, the strongest must surely prevail. But strength is only one weapon. Cunning, invention, and surprise are others. And in the face of the unexpected blow, even the mightiest can tumble.

Against the great Zindown, Sesha had twice succeeded. But the wizard was far from finished. In the grim landscape of her journey, a land abandoned by all human form, Sesha faced her greatest test yet.

⌒〰〰〇

As the wagon ambled down the road, Sesha, comforted by Scodo's words, looked ahead with new hope. Perhaps Zindown had abandoned the fight. Perhaps they might yet deliver to

Darrow the swords that he needed. Perhaps victory—an ultimate victory against the goblins—was really possible.

She turned and looked at her friend Scodo. His hood had fallen from his head. His face, covered with a dark shell, looked straight ahead.

"Scodo," she asked, "what if Darrow wins? What if he drives the goblins from the kingdom? What will you do then?"

Scodo looked back at Sesha. The question made him thoughtful. After a long pause, he replied, "I will go back to the forest."

The answer hurt Sesha. She admired Scodo, and the thought of him living out his life alone in the forest made her sad.

"But if Darrow wins," she replied, "you will be a hero. People will celebrate your deeds. You can be accepted for the first time."

Scodo replied, calmly and without the slightest bitterness, "I will never be accepted. The way I look will frighten the bravest men."

"Well, I am not frightened one bit," said Sesha.

"Then perhaps you are the bravest of them all."

They both laughed and continued in silence, but a few minutes later Sesha spoke once more.

"What if magic could change you? What if you could look like any other man? Then what would you do?"

Scodo was silent for a long time.

"I don't believe in magic such as that. But what would I do if I could appear in a way that would allow me to walk into a room and be accepted for who I am?"

"Yes."

"And Darrow won and the goblins were driven from this land?"

"Yes," Sesha answered.

"I would put away my weapons and never fight again."

Sesha was deeply moved but could not find words to respond. For another few minutes, they traveled in silence. Then Scodo turned to Sesha, his eyes filled with the greatest sadness she had ever seen.

"Most of all," he added, "I would try to purge the hatred from my heart."

And with Scodo's words, Sesha wished, more than anything she had ever wished in her life, that Darrow would win and that somehow, some way, she could find the power to heal her friend.

⌇

A sharp clap of thunder echoed across the desert. In the sky, dark clouds gathered together and blocked the sun. Scodo, walking at the side of the wagon, looked up at Sesha. Her hands tightened against the reins and she sat straight in the wagon seat. Warily, her eyes searched the sky. Her search did not last long.

From these clouds, a terrible figure appeared. His body was human in form, but his skin was dark, ashen, and covered with raging flames. Above his flaming countenance rose two black wings that waved slowly in the air.

Scodo reached for a rock and hurled it at the figure. But just as the rock reached its target, the figure disappeared. Suddenly, it reappeared higher in the sky. A thunderous laugh shook the earth.

Scodo grabbed another rock and hurled it straight at his target. But again, as the rock arrived, the figure was gone, reappearing higher still, this time far from the range of even Scodo's mighty arm.

Sesha shot Scodo a scolding glance. "Calm. Stay calm," she said.

High in the sky, red eyes gleaming, yellow teeth reflecting the light of the fire, the monster looked down at Sesha and Scodo.

He lifted a flaming hand that held a black wand. He lifted the wand high above his head and for a moment it did not move. Then, in one swoop, he waved the wand across his chest. In the air appeared six tiny vampire bats, which began to descend toward the wagon.

Again, he swung his wand and six more bats appeared. Again and again and again, he waved the wand until the sky was black with bats and Sesha and Scodo could see the monster no more. Lower and lower, the bats descended, not in a straight line but pendulously, like feathers falling downward through a windless sky.

Scodo looked at Sesha, but she needed no words. Her eyes focused, her lips pursed together in a thin line, her eyes scoured the sky.

"I need to find the monster. I need a clear path!" she shouted, not even looking at Scodo but knowing he awaited her words.

Scodo ran from the wagon, hoping to distract the bats and spread them out. Indeed, some of the bats changed direction, descending now toward Scodo. Still, as Sesha gazed upward, she could not see past the great expanse of fluttering black wings.

Now the bats were upon them. Sesha swatted the air, knocking the first one away. The monster gave a great laugh. He

turned toward Scodo and hurled a lightning bolt that exploded at his feet. A small, gnarled tree trunk burst into flames.

Scodo grasped the flaming tree and lifted it from the sandy soil. He waved its flames at the descending bats and a few retreated. Scodo gripped the roots and began spinning his body faster and faster until, in one great, powerful stroke, he hurled the burning tree across the sky scattering the bats in every direction. For the briefest moment, the sky opened. Sesha looked up and stared at the fiery figure above.

This time, Sesha's face showed no fear, struggle, or pain. Her eyes were bright and focused, undaunted by the terrible demon above. She tightened her fists and pulled them down, elbows bent. On her mouth appeared the faintest beginning of a smile. She began a low whistle, this time vibrating and repetitive.

The sound of Sesha's whistle only amused the monster. And indeed, the creature did not explode, disappear, or fall straight to the earth. No, what happened was at first not noticed by the monster at all. Its great black wings began to diminish in size. At first, these smaller wings carried the monster just as before. But gradually, the wings grew smaller still. And as they did, the monster flapped harder, struggling to remain in the air.

Soon the shrinking wings could no longer hold the monster in the air. The monster fell, slowly at first, but with increasing speed, until it crashed into the ground in an explosion of fire, ash, dust, and sand. The impact was frightful and the bats, one and all, fled for places far, far away.

For what seemed like an eternity, Sesha and Scodo stared at the smoking pile. The smoke disappeared, and from the rubble, Zindown arose. His tall frame seemed to tower above the landscape. His face was twisted in anger, but he was otherwise unscathed. His black robe was shiny and spotless, and his gray hair fell in wavy curls down the back of his robe. The old wizard looked straight at Sesha.

"Asterux had taught you well, Princess. Today, the victory is yours. Savor it if you will. For in the end, fate will never grant your wishes.

"No mule-driven wagon can cross this desert and be back in less than three days. No lame boy, even armed with three thousand swords, can defeat the army of Globenwald.

"And your masquerade, Princess, will continue no more. Because no daughter of Henry X can hide from the goblin king's army."

Then Zindown extended both arms in the direction of the wagon and his body shook. The landscape began to move and Sesha felt the world spin around her with increasing speed. In an instant, there was a flash of light.

Sesha looked down at her body. Her skin was pale. Her toes were long and slender. Her hair was somewhere between red and blonde.

Zindown was gone. All that remained was a cloud of smoke that drifted slowly, slowly across the plain.

· 34 ·

Kelofel

The afternoon sun shone into their faces and a speck on the horizon blurred as if surrounded by fog.

Darrow raised his hand to shield his eyes. The speck should be Kelofel, the first town his army would encounter.

What waited in Kelofel, Darrow could not know. Goblins were stationed there, a handful who kept the peace. These were no match for Darrow's growing band, but perhaps reinforcements had arrived. Perhaps a battle lay ahead.

Closer, Darrow could see a steeple that rose above the town, but no other building stood more than one floor from the ground. A few hundred people called Kelofel home. They were traders and shopkeepers who mostly sold to the nearby farmers and bought their crops in return.

Darrow looked ahead, shielding his eyes against the afternoon sun, searching for signs of trouble. He could make out shapes, wagons and walkers descending on the town. What was the meaning? He could not know.

His followers struck up their song and great voices filled the sky, but Darrow turned and ordered silence. An ambush might await. The company quieted. All eyes watched the village. The only sounds were the footsteps of soldiers, more than five hundred of them, and the rustling of their garments.

Horsemen emerged, a band of five galloping furiously in their direction. Darrow halted his army. Those with swords drew them from their belts. As the riders grew closer, Darrow could make out their shapes. These were not goblins. They were men and they were waving frantically.

Down the long line of marching men and women, the volunteers eyed one another. Then, from the village came a sound.

Church bells.

The first ring was solitary and followed by another, but the rings came faster. These were not rings to mark the time of day or a sad event. These rings were furious and exuberant. The men exchanged curious glances, unsure of the meaning of the sounds.

The horsemen pulled to a stop. A short man of perhaps forty-five years old with a hard face and a short beard dropped from his saddle. The man's eyes searched among the soldiers, looking for a warrior with a polished shield, fine boots, or even clean clothes.

Not finding such a warrior, he looked at the boy before him and said, "I have an important message. Can you take me to Darrow?"

"I am Darrow."

For a moment, the man was surprised to see this small figure dressed in rags. But he dropped to his knee and made a great bow.

"My name is Haidus and I come from Kelofel to welcome the mighty Darrow, who has freed our village from goblin rule."

As they heard these words, the volunteers began whispering to those behind them that the goblins had abandoned Kelofel. Before the news was halfway down the line, a great cheer arose and the soldiers, one and all, knew that Kelofel was theirs.

Haidus offered Darrow his horse. But Darrow refused and asked him to lead his horse and walk with him to the village. The long line began to move again as Darrow peppered Haidus with questions about his enemy and when their army might arrive.

There were only seven goblins in Kelofel. Upon hearing that the fort had fallen, they had fled.

"There are rumors," Haidus added, his face growing dark and worried. "They say a great goblin army is marching across the plain to meet you."

But Darrow paid the rumor no mind. The goblin command in Blumenbruch would only now be learning about the fort. Once they knew, they would send soldiers. He had time. Probably two full days.

Soon they were a short distance from the village. The streets were filled with people and Darrow wondered how a village this small might have so active a market. As they drew closer, children sprinted from the village cheering and jumping up and down like a hundred bouncing balls. They were followed by women and girls and a few men, who carried loaves of bread, pieces of cheese, and even slices of dried meat.

As they came into the village, Haidus again urged Darrow to take his horse and Darrow, having never ridden a horse, declined. But Haidus persisted, explaining that the people must know which of the men was the great Darrow and that, if he alone was on horseback, they would know. So, reluctantly, Darrow climbed into the saddle.

When his horse stepped onto the village street, it was not only the few hundred citizens of Kelofel who had turned out to cheer his army but a thousand or more who had gathered from all parts of the plain. They stood on the rooftops. They sat in the windows. Parents lifted small children to their shoulders to get a glimpse of the leader who sent the goblins running across the plain.

A thunderous cheer erupted through the village. They hailed Darrow's soldiers as great heroes, though barely thirty of them had ever seen battle at all. They reached to touch their garments and hurled flowers in their path.

But most of all, they pressed one another for a chance to touch the great hero or even his borrowed horse. Darrow looked stunned, unbelieving, as if he had entered a strange dream. But it was no dream at all, for with each step, the cheering grew louder still.

When they reached the square before the church, another great cheer sounded from the crowd. There was music with a drum and some instruments with strings, but no one could hear the notes. Darrow's horse was taken to a platform where leading citizens stood. They dressed shabbily, but these were the best that they had. When the crowd had quieted, a woman climbed to the platform and placed a necklace of flowers around Darrow's neck.

Haidus raised his hands to silence the crowd. On behalf of Kelofel, he spoke.

"For more than a decade, the goblins have ruled our village. For ten long years, our people have suffered at their hands. But today the goblins are gone, chased to the west by a great leader and the brave soldiers who have joined his cause. All hail the mighty Darrow! All hail a free Kelofel!"

Another great cheer arose from the crowd. They called for Darrow to speak and their hero did not disappoint.

"I thank you, Haidus, for your kind words, and I thank the people of Kelofel and so many who have traveled so far to greet us and offer encouragement for the battle ahead. Our fight for freedom, however, is only beginning.

"Within days, we will face a large goblin army on the plains. These will be veteran soldiers, experienced, trained, and armed. Our challenge is to meet this army and defeat it. Our challenge is as large as a mountain whose snowcaps surge into the sky. But there are no choices. High as it stands, formidable as it may be, we will find a way to the top.

"We need food. We need shoes. We need bows and arrows. Most of all, we need swords. And today I ask all of you to give us whatever you can to help us in the great cause that we share together.

"Finally, I ask something most important of all. For too many years, throughout our kingdom, our spirits have been crushed by tyrants and our hopes have withered from fear. But today it is time to put those fears aside. Today, it is time to imagine a free Sonnencrest. Today, it is time to find our courage, to believe in our strength, and to forge a new future in our land.

"If you are able, join us. If you have food or weapons, supply us. But whoever you are and whatever you can do, most of all, believe in us. Believe in yourselves. And believe in Sonnencrest and the great nation we can build together."

When Darrow finished, the villagers cheered until their voices were hoarse. That night, every oven baked bread. Every household sharpened knives and made weapons. In the morning, they delivered cakes, daggers, clubs, and ordinary poles they had sharpened themselves.

But in the great stack of goods donated to Darrow, there were only twelve real swords.

· 35 ·

Scodo's Mighty Struggle

Babette, Scodo, and Zauberyungi continued across the plain. For a long time, Scodo walked by the side of the wagon, not looking at the princess at all.

"So you were never Sesha," Scodo murmured, as though he had lost a friend.

"Oh, Scodo, I am the same person, I really am. Asterux made me Sesha to protect me from the goblins. If they had found the princess, I would have been dead."

Scodo eyed Babette nervously. The ugly Sesha had made him less uneasy.

Babette pulled the wagon to a stop and climbed to the ground.

"Don't be afraid, Scodo." But Scodo stepped back.

"How can a beautiful princess be friends with a monster like me?"

Sesha looked at Scodo for a long time. Then she spoke. "Scodo, for your friendship, I would gladly be the ugliest woman on earth. And I would do this because you are the most beautiful man I know."

Then she put her arms around the scorpion man and held him for a long, long time.

∽

For hours, Scodo and Babette rode across the desert in silence. Then Scodo asked, "Will he be back?"

"I doubt it. But who can say? For all I know, he might be a tick on Zauberyungi's behind."

Scodo laughed. "Don't be so sure. I doubt he's so anxious to tangle with you again."

"I don't scare Zindown. My magic could never hurt a wizard like him."

"You certainly hurt his pride."

Babette smiled. "That couldn't be hard."

"I have a question," Scodo continued. "That was Zindown himself in the sky with the wand, right?"

"That's right."

"If he is a wizard, he could disappear and reappear somewhere else. It would seem he could use this power to dodge your spell."

"Not exactly. A wizard does not really disappear. What Zindown did was move faster than you can see."

"I don't understand."

"In that particular magic, there is a system. The wizard lays out a pattern of points. He uses his power to move from one point to the next. It happens so fast that it seems he is disappearing. But really, he is only moving from one point to the next."

"Can you do the same thing?"

"I can't. I can barely get this mule across the desert."

For a while they continued without words. Then Scodo asked, "Can you teach me magic?"

Babette looked up, a little surprised at the request. "It would take too long."

"Can I try something simple?"

Babette paused for a moment, looking down at the reins. "It's not possible to learn magic here in the desert. It requires so much concentration. The wagon is bumping and rattling. Zauberyungi makes noise. There are too many distractions."

"I can try."

"Really, it couldn't work."

"Please."

For a long time, Babette simply stared at the desert ahead, lost in thought. Then she spoke.

"For this to work, you have to block out all your senses: your sight, your hearing, everything. You must retreat completely inside your own mind. That would be really difficult here."

"Let me try."

"Well, let's try just the first step. But just the first step. Here it is. Consider those people who have showed you kindness and love. Just think about them. Feel their kindness. Feel their love. These things give each of us power.

"As you do, go through your entire life. Remember everything. Grasp for every kindness, every good deed, every act of love both large and small. And when you bring these events to life, they will grow a goodness and power you can feel inside. Hold onto that power. Feel it. Grow it."

So Scodo began. With little effort, he blocked out all his senses. Such were his powers of concentration that he was soon separated from all his surroundings. Deep into his memories, he traveled.

His first thoughts were of his parents. He thought of his times as a child alone with his mother and father, in the forest. He remembered carrying stones to build his parents' house. He remembered walking the woods with his father. He remembered the sweet song of his mother lulling him to sleep and the word *vianu*, which meant love and understanding. These thoughts stirred him with warmth and made him feel strong.

He thought of Hugga Hugga, who had accepted him as a soldier and a friend. He thought of the soldiers of Sonnencrest, many of whom had treated him with respect. He clung to these memories and they aroused warm feelings.

His mind returned to his mother. He recalled the moment when he asked her why he was different and if he was indeed as ugly as he seemed. And he remembered that his mother told him that it was she who was a monster and how he was the most beautiful creature of all.

He thought about when Sesha found him in the forest, her friendship, and the kindnesses she had shown him.

He began to weep. Inside, he felt a power stirring in his heart. And that power felt good and right and he knew that that was what he needed to grow.

But as he searched for memories of kind acts, he could go no further. Scodo had known the goodness of others so seldom in his life. So he lifted his head and asked, "Now what?"

"It takes much longer than that, Scodo," Babette snapped.

"My memories of goodness are few. But the ones I hold are strong. Let me try the next step."

Babette did not believe that Scodo could be ready for the next step. After all, this step had taken her years. But she was too tired to argue.

"Think of all those people who have dealt you insults, mocked you, or committed small wrongs. Understand them. Love them. As you do, your power will grow."

Scodo thought of soldiers who had mocked him. He thought of ordinary people who covered their faces before him. He remembered a woman who lifted his cloak to show his tail and called him the devil. These memories were a multitude.

One by one, he looked into the faces of those who had brought him torment and shame. He looked into their eyes and struggled to understand them. What he witnessed made him shudder, for he did not see evil at all. Instead, he saw hurt and injury and pain. He saw disappointments, humiliations, and tragedies that dwelt deep inside his tormenters—each and every one. These experiences made them small and robbed their hearts of kindness, compassion, and love. Almost instantly, Scodo's great mind understood that the wrongs against him were not of his own making. They arose in his tormentors from their own injuries to their own souls.

When Scodo considered these things, he was overcome by a deep sadness that stirred him deep inside. He trembled and he shook. He felt compassion for those he remembered and understood that perhaps their afflictions were even greater than his own. His understanding grew to affection.

His affection grew to love. Warm, positive, wonderful feelings filled him and a mighty spirit arose inside. As it grew, he felt a joy so great and so vibrant that for a moment he was frightened by its force.

These feelings were too new and too strong. But he was nothing if not brave and he clung to this power and would not let it go. Separated from all sensory contact, he lingered in this condition for a long time. Empowered by these feelings, he forgave all of them, that great and enormous multitude that had mocked him and ridiculed him throughout his life. He forgave them all. Every single one.

Scodo looked up again. "I have forgiven them."

Babette could not believe these words, but she knew that they were the right ones. More importantly, she could feel a warmth—a powerful, radiant warmth—flowing outward from Scodo's being. She sensed an enormous power that was almost frightening in its force. And she knew, without a single conscious thought, that she was witness to a miracle so rare and special that centuries might pass before it ever happened again.

Now she understood that inside of Scodo dwelt a powerful force of goodness and magic far more profound than her own. She suspected that Scodo's untapped powers were perhaps as great or greater than those of Asterux himself. This time, without doubts or skepticism, she spoke in a stern, commanding voice.

"Think of those who have done you the most terrible wrongs. Confront them. Understand them. Forgive them. And your power will grow."

Without a moment's hesitation, Scodo's mind descended once more deep into his past. Soon, he faced the terrible mob that had chased him from the goblin village, that had hunted him with torches and dogs. This was the mob that murdered his parents and destroyed the house he had built with his own hands. For many years, he had been unable to face this memory and now he trembled before it.

Suddenly, he became deeply fearful and longed to turn back. But against those fears, his new power gave him strength. For the first time, he looked directly into the faces of the mob and a deeply felt bitterness rose up inside him. Understanding? Compassion? Love? These feelings were far from his reach, but he would not turn back. He peered into their eyes, gleaming with hatred and cruelty of the most vicious kind. He looked into their hearts and wondered what they must contain.

What Scodo saw made him tremble and shake.

Babette looked at her friend and she became alarmed. His hands made fists so tight that Babette feared he might break his own fingers. His body shook so violently that she touched him on the shoulder to offer him calm. But nothing in this world could intrude upon the journey that Scodo had begun.

Hours passed, as the wagon traveled slowly ahead. Babette feared for her friend and decided that somehow she must awaken Scodo from his ordeal. She dreaded that she had unleashed some terrible force so strong that it might destroy him. She feared that he might never awaken. But slowly, his trembling subsided. After a while, his body, remarkably, returned to complete calm.

In her seat next to Scodo, Babette could feel a presence so strong and powerful that it surely stilled trees and calmed creatures miles away. The great power that flowed from Scodo was as real and tangible as the earth beneath them and the raindrops from the sky. She marveled at the strength her friend surely possessed and wondered if he might become the greatest wizard ever known and sow the magic of goodness, justice, and right all across the world.

For a very long time, Scodo remained in his position, his head lowered, his hands holding the seat, with an appearance of total calm. Then, slowly, Scodo lifted his head, opened his eyes, and spoke these remarkable words.

"I have forgiven them."

Babette was awestruck, but she feared the next step. Already, Scodo had done what had taken her years. Could any being endure something beyond what Scodo had experienced that day? But she also knew that the magic was indeed within Scodo's reach. And if Scodo could find the magic, he could not only perform good and wondrous deeds; he might well transform an evil world.

For a few moments, she wavered, unable to decide. Scodo looked at her, not with impatience but with understanding and hope. Without a single word, his expression told her that he placed himself completely in her hands—trusting her, without a single doubt, to do what was right. So Babette turned to Scodo, her decision made. With fire in her eyes and a powerful force flowing through her own body, she shouted words that echoed off the cliffs and ricocheted high into the evening sky.

"Search for the one person who has handed you the greatest evil. Search for the one person who has done you the most grievous wrong. Search for the one to whom you owe the greatest and most terrible revenge. Find him! Understand him! Love him! Forgive him!"

Scodo lowered his head and thought. There were many in his life who had done him wrong. But who was worse than the others? He did not know. Harder and harder he thought, reviewing his life and all of the terrible characters it contained. But there was nothing.

Babette, sensing Scodo's struggle, offered firm instructions: "Don't reach for him. He will come to you. Let him come. Let him come."

Returning to his struggle, Scodo first searched for his power. But this time, his mind was jolted as if by some outside force. In his mind, he was suddenly spinning through space, falling and turning, faster and faster, until without the slightest warning, he was still. And when the falling stopped, his entire span of life raced before him. Hundreds, perhaps thousands, of events flashed by in a few seconds. But he saw each episode with great clarity, in great detail, and with an understanding he had never before known.

When his life had passed, the events began to spin one into another. He saw faces of people and goblins and Minotaurs that did not belong together. They appeared in settings that were entirely wrong. He became deeply confused, and now, instead of goodness and courage, he was overcome by anxiety and fear. For a few short minutes, this great whirlwind of distorted and false memories raged through his mind. Again, he began to shake—this time not with the power of good but with the fear of evil. Inside his mind, the torments of his life grew suddenly large and his heart was racked with terrible pain. All of the awful ghosts of his awful past swirled and raged in a panorama so frightful that he feared he might never depart with his sanity intact.

Then it stopped.

When it stopped, he saw the forest where his parents lived and where his childhood was spent. Standing in the forest, looking directly into his eyes, stood Zindown.

Scodo was perplexed. He had not the slightest understanding of why Zindown might appear. But the second he saw the image, he knew that it was Zindown who had somehow, some way, dealt him his most grievous and terrible wrong. Scodo wondered if perhaps Zindown planned to hurt him in the future, for while Zindown was evil and had opposed him and Babette in the desert, Scodo knew of no other way that Zindown had committed acts against him. But as he considered Zindown, a new feeling arose inside him.

It was the feeling of hate.

Desperately, Scodo fought back with all his new power. He returned to the memories of his parents. He looked into the face of his loving mother, and in her expression he found strength. He thought of Hugga Hugga and Babette and the friendship they had given him and his strength continued to grow. He looked into the souls of those who taunted him and those who were horrified by his very presence and he understood them, loved them, and forgave them once again. And finally, he forgave even the goblin mob and they, too, felt his love. As he retraced each step, slowly, and with all the power inside him, his goodness and his power began to grow. A great, wondrous glow filled his body and surged through his fingertips and toes. With this new power, he felt as if he had soared into the air, breaking even the grip of gravity that binds us to the earth. Now he was stronger and his power raged. He turned toward the image of Zindown again, armed with the most powerful forces the human spirit can create. He considered Zindown for his wrongs and thought of the evil deeds he carried with him every day. He wondered at the terrible burden.

As he searched for compassion, his body trembled mightily with all of the great power he had summoned. But that power was not enough. He could not understand. He could not forgive. He could not love. His spirit staggered backward, reeling in defeat.

But Scodo had stood at the edge. He had reached for the power and it lay only a little beyond his grasp. One person stood between him and the magic. And Scodo would not be denied. Once again, he put Zindown away and went back to his power. He retraced his memories. He nurtured his goodness. Once more, he felt love for his enemies and forgiveness for their actions, this time more deeply and profoundly than before.

When he had brought his power to its greatest level yet, stronger than he could have imagined, he brought this power once again back to Zindown. He faced the image of the wizard anew. And a great struggle raged inside of him.

Babette was once again alarmed. Scodo's body shook so violently that the wagon began to wobble. The wobbling grew and the wagon rocked so hard that Zauberyungi brayed in fear. This time, Scodo did not calm. He shook and trembled as he gripped the wagon with his mighty hands.

Babette feared that she had pushed him too far. On and on, the shaking continued and Babette became afraid that Scodo might never return from the horrific struggle that raged within.

Then, in an instant, he was still. For a long time, he did not move.

Now Babette was hopeful. Perhaps he had conquered his demon. Perhaps this great being that sat beside her would perform wondrous magic that very night. Waiting with eagerness, anticipation, respect, and love, she stared at Scodo.

Scodo lifted his head, and as tears dropped from the motionless eyes on his dark face, he turned to Babette.

"I have failed."

Babette comforted Scodo, who was dazed by all he had been through. She told him he had great power. She told him he would do great deeds that could change the world. She urged him to find patience because he had been blessed with a beautiful gift, greater even than that of Asterux himself. Her words soothed his battered spirit. But for a long time he could not move or speak.

As she whispered encouragements into his ear, she wondered what terrible demon lay inside of him that could resist the awesome power of goodness that Scodo held within.

· 36 ·

Kelsner's Plain

The road was dry and the morning dew had long since burned away. As Darrow looked to the rear, the line of soldiers stretched into the horizon. Their footsteps raised a dust cloud that obscured the end of the line. Darrow no longer greeted each new recruit. They were too many. He wondered how many walked in the line. It must be at least six hundred.

Ahead, Darrow could see a town, bigger than Kelofel, with stone houses, some three stories tall. The town was Pfesthammer and before Darrow had approached the city limits, his soldiers were greeted by well-wishers who lined the road to cheer his success. When he entered the town, the streets were as packed as before. This time, the town had already gathered food and weapons, which they presented with great ceremony in the town square.

When he finished his speech, he inspected the weapons. There were pitchforks, more hammers, and many knives. But when he had sifted through the pile, he turned to Timwee with an expression of despair. No words were needed to convey the terrible news.

In this vast pile of weapons, there were only eighteen swords.

As soon as he was able, Darrow asked to meet with the blacksmiths. "Our hope lies in your hands," he began. "We need swords, as many as you can make and as fast as you can make them."

"But we know nothing of swords," one of the smiths responded.

"It is time you learned," Darrow snapped heatedly. "We are all responsible for allowing the goblins to rule unchecked."

By early afternoon, the men were marching again. Darrow pushed his men hard, desperate to cover ground. They were almost a day's march from Kelsner's Plain, where Darrow expected to spend the night. But the hardships of the march were hardly noticed at all.

The cheers of their countrymen rang in their ears. The hopes of their kingdom soared in their hearts. Alive, eager, and certain of victory, Darrow's ragtag band practically floated across the plain.

⟨∞⟩

The sky was dark as Darrow's company approached Kelsner's Plain, a city that was home to ten thousand people, almost fifty miles from the forest. As they rounded a turn in the road and the city came into view, a man on horseback galloped to meet Darrow. This time, there was no welcome. This man brought a warning.

The goblin army was marching. They would arrive at Kelsner's Plain tomorrow night.

The messenger was unsure of their number. There were reports from many people. Some said a few hundred, others counted as many as a thousand. But whatever their number, they would soon stand before them on the field of battle.

At the edge of the city, Darrow was met by the committee of town leaders.

"You have one day to prepare. Tell us how we can help."

"Bring me every carpenter in the city," Darrow replied. "Tell them to prepare to work tonight and all day tomorrow."

One of the men scurried away to meet Darrow's request.

As they walked the streets, Darrow marveled at the shops. He had never seen a city of any kind. One shop contained bowls and cups and pitchers, all made of glass.

"People drink from these containers?" Darrow asked.

The mayor struggled to suppress a smile.

"They do. In fact, Kelsner's Plain has more glass blowers than even Blumenbruch. These drinking cups are in every house."

They arrived at the mayor's home. A small crowd stood outside and cheered Darrow's approach. But there would be no speeches tonight. For weeks, Darrow had considered this battle. His speeches would slay no goblins.

Inside, city leaders answered Darrow's questions about the whereabouts of the goblins, the size of their force, and the landscape beyond the city. When his questions were answered, he told the leaders what he needed. "We will need volunteers to

work behind our lines." Heads nodded. "We will need con-
tributions from every household in the city." Heads nodded.
Darrow issued his instructions in great detail.

In the next room, Timwee, Hugga Hugga, Kaylin, and
Mempo waited. Darrow entered and gave orders. All soldiers
would assemble west of town at sunrise. They had one day to
prepare and they would need every minute. And when all was
clear, Darrow lifted his sword to repeat the pledge of their
band. Around the table, every sword rose to meet Darrow's.
But before he could speak, a messenger burst into the room.

A wagon had arrived from Kelofel. It contained twenty
swords.

· 37 ·

The Temptation of Evil

Not a single star broke the blackness of the night, only a quarter moon. It hung just above the horizon and its reflection cast a long white line across the water.

Thirty-five hours earlier, Scodo and Babette had begun their journey. Now, long after midnight, they stood at the pirate's cove. To reach Darrow in time, they would have to make the return trip in barely more than a day.

The ground was soft and wet and covered with high grass. They scanned the darkness to locate a ship. They could just make out a dock in the distance. As they approached it, they saw the shape of a ship against the sky.

The deck was littered with snoring, unwashed, unshaven men. Some lay in hammocks. Others sprawled about the deck in all manner of bodily contortions. Scodo looked at Babette. Babette shrugged. What were their choices?

They stepped quietly onto the boat and looked about. Where was Telsinore? Suddenly, a voice boomed in the darkness.

"Who dares trespass on the Trap Door?"

Startled, Babette turned to see the dark shadow of a large man lifting himself from the deck. Knives and clubs hung from his belt. He pulled a sword.

"I've run many a man through for less than this," he said with a hint of pride. "Though you are obviously no man."

The sleeping bodies began to stir.

"We came to see Telsinore," Babette shot back. "We have business to discuss."

"Aye, and what business does a lady have? Perhaps you're an old friend of the Cap'n, come here to reacquaint?"

At the sound of a woman's voice, several men lifted their heads and began to blink.

"Only to do business," Scodo repeated. "We've brought treasure. A lot of it."

At that, the pirate grabbed a rope and sounded a bell. Twelve men stood about the deck, staring at the strange pair.

"You'd best stand back with your hands on your head."

One pirate charged Scodo, but Scodo grabbed him by the shirt and threw him from the boat. The pirates drew their swords. Scodo drew his as well and took a step forward. The pirates stepped back.

Then a voice rang out behind him.

"I wouldn't try that if I were you. Not if you want this pretty lady to keep her head."

Scodo turned. A pirate was holding Babette by the hair with a knife at her throat.

"Put her down," shouted Scodo.

"No, you drop your sword. One wrong move and the missus will be looking for her head."

The pirates snickered meanly. Scodo dropped his sword. In a moment, his hands, arms, legs, and feet were tied with ropes. Then his neck was chained to the mast. Babette was tied, gagged, and carried below.

"Remove his hood," cried the pirate who had been thrown overboard. By now, torches lit the deck. A pirate grabbed the point of Scodo's mask and pulled.

The reflections of the torchlight danced on the dark shell of Scodo's face. His tiny round insect eyes glowed still and red. A gasp spread across the boat.

"We've caught ourselves a monster," said the large pirate, speaking softly and with respect. In the light, Scodo could see this pirate for the first time.

A long scar ran up the side of his neck and behind his ear. He was bald on top and the wide scar made a trail of hairless skin connecting the top of his head with his neck below.

"And it's a monster we'd best dispose of," said another. "He could have evil powers!"

"Well, if he's so evil," replied the scar-faced pirate, "perhaps he should join our band."

A great laugh erupted from the men.

But one pirate spoke out. "I heard of this scorpion man. Be careful of him. He's killed thirty men in a single fight, so they say. These chains mightn't be enough."

The pirates exchanged glances. One or two took a cautious step backward. Meanwhile, Scodo's keen mind was thinking fast.

"Where is Telsinore?" he asked.

"What is it to you, scorpion man?" the pirate shot back.

"Our business cannot wait," Scodo replied. "By morning, the possibility of great treasure will be lost."

"Your business days are finished, scorpion man. You can have your say at sunrise. Be glad of it. They'll be your last words."

But Scodo continued. "Kill me if you will, my friend. But when Telsinore learns of the treasure he has lost, you'll surely be lying at my side at the bottom of this bay."

The pirate eyed Scodo suspiciously. "What are you talking about?" the pirate asked.

"I am talking about wagon after wagon of precious treasures. All of the treasures from a thousand homes and castles across Sonnencrest—the stolen loot of ten years of goblin rule. By the morning, that chance will be gone."

The pirate narrowed his eyes. "I'll not be tricked by nonsense. Still your tongue or I'll pull off your scales with a blacksmith's tongs."

"Threaten me if you will," Scodo replied, "but kill me and my fate will surely be your own."

"You don't scare me, scorpion man," the pirate replied. He sat down on the deck, preparing to sleep. For a moment, he stared out to sea. He turned to look at Scodo, grimacing at the sight. Then he rose to his feet, jumped to the dock, and scampered back toward land.

A few minutes later, he returned with Telsinore.

Telsinore was not a happy man. "Who dares disturb me?" he roared. The other pirate held up a torch. When Telsinore saw Scodo, he stepped back, covering his eyes in disgust. He collected himself, looked upon his captive, and spoke with grim impatience.

"Tell me your business."

"I need swords," replied Scodo calmly. "I have brought a handsome treasure to pay for it."

"If your treasure is in that wagon, it is already ours. Why should I give you swords for something I already own?"

"This is true. You can kill the girl and me and the treasure is yours. But if you do, you will miss a treasure a hundred times its size."

Telsinore raised an eyebrow but leaned closer to hear more.

"There is great rebellion in the land of Sonnencrest, led by a warrior named Darrow. He has driven the goblins from Hexenwald. Every day, a hundred new men arrive to join his army. But to fight the goblins, he needs swords."

At the mention of the goblins, Telsinore spat on the deck. "So this Darrow might kill a few goblins and I wouldn't complain. But suppose you tell me why that means treasure for me?"

"If Darrow wins, the goblins will flee. They will be forced to cross the channel to Globenwald. And when they do, they will carry with them gold and silver stolen over the last ten years.

"Think of it! Soldiers on horseback, their saddlebags stuffed with jewels and gold. The tax collectors and officials will carry boxes of coin. And, in one or two wagons, there will be the greatest treasure of all: chests and chests of treasure, collected in the palace, which belong to King Malmut himself."

"If, if, if!" Telsinore shot back, trying not to appear intrigued. "All of this is based on *if*. Sonnencrest will never defeat the goblins. They are a race of whimpering puppies!"

"Perhaps you are right," Scodo said, "although Darrow has already won great battles. But may I ask a question?"

"Go ahead."

"Are you a gambling man?"

"I am indeed."

"Well, tell me then. What would be your answer if someone offered you a chance at a great treasure? And imagine that this treasure was greater than any you have touched in a lifetime of work."

Telsinore thought, imagining such great treasure. Excitedly, he began pulling his beard.

Scodo continued. "Perhaps your chance was small—maybe only one chance in ten. But what if the price for this chance was small as well? What if, to have a chance at this treasure, all you would have to pay would be two hundred swords? Would you not pay the swords?"

For the first time, a smile crossed Telsinore's face. "I understand your logic, scorpion man. But why should I believe your tale? How do I know this Darrow even exists at all?"

"Perhaps he doesn't," replied Scodo. "But what if the chances are only one in twenty that he exists and can drive the goblins away? If it never happens, what have you lost? Two hundred swords? But what if he does exist? What if the lady and I crossed the desert and boarded your ship for a reason? What if Darrow succeeds? If my words are true, you have the treasures of a whole nation waiting to be robbed."

Scodo could see the glimmer in Telsinore's eye.

"You speak with sly logic, scorpion man."

"I speak with *your* logic, Telsinore."

Telsinore laughed out loud. This monster was amusing.

"Two hundred swords are too many. I will give you one hundred and fifty," the old pirate bellowed with gusto.

"I need two hundred," Scodo shot back.

"Then we keep the girl," Telsinore replied.

"One hundred and fifty and I take the girl."

Telsinore paused for a moment. In his mind, he recalled those dreadful goblins stealing his emeralds on the river. And the very thought made him tremble. He pictured the chaos of fleeing goblins. He imagined wagons loaded with treasure arriving at the channel. Then he pictured his own sword stained with blood and an enormous pile of riches stacked at his side.

These were pleasures too rich to resist.

He looked down at Scodo.

"Scorpion man, you have yourself a deal!"

He turned to the pirate holding the torch. "Untie the prisoners," he ordered.

Scodo and Babette led Telsinore back to the wagon. Telsinore inspected the chest, but his mind was on the channel.

"This Darrow," he asked. "When will he face the goblins?"

"In barely more than a day, we believe," said Scodo.

"You'll never make it," the pirate replied.

"We have to make it," said Babette, still angry and refusing even to look at Telsinore.

Telsinore shrugged and turned to his men. "Get the swords, a hundred fifty of them," he ordered. The men scurried back to the shed next to the dock. Telsinore paused, thinking of the goblins.

"Make it two hundred," he shouted, "and hurry. These people have no time to waste!"

In four short trips, the wagon was full of weapons. While they loaded, Telsinore paced back and forth. When the wagon was ready, Babette gripped Zauberyungi's bridle, prepared to begin the journey back. But Telsinore told her to wait.

He turned to his men.

"Bring the axe."

A minute later, two pirates returned, carrying an enormous battle-axe. The shaft of this axe was as long as the wagon itself. The two-sided blade was as tall as three hands and twice as wide. Across the blade were beautiful engravings of dragons and knights in battle. The metal shaft was decorated with a flowering vine that wrapped round and round from the handle to the blade.

"This should bring you luck and a few more dead goblins," Telsinore beamed. "Go! Go! Darrow is waiting!"

Back in the desert, neither Babette nor Scodo rode the wagon. To lighten the load, they walked, Babette at Zauberyungi's side, rubbing his shoulders and whispering encouraging words. When the road rose, Scodo stood at the back of the wagon, pushing it forward.

Soon after the sun broke over the horizon behind them, Zauberyungi stopped and would walk no more. Babette and Scodo had not slept in more than a day. They lay down to rest.

When they awoke, the sun was high in the sky. By Scodo's reckoning, they had slept almost three hours—two more than they intended. Desperately, they rose and pushed forward again with new urgency.

The return trip moved more quickly. Where water had eroded the road, Scodo now knew how to flatten the sand so the wagon could travel more easily across it. Using their old wheel tracks, the wagon passed more easily through the gullies and back into the road. No wizard threw obstacles before them. By sunset, they had reached the rise in the plain where the spiders had swarmed. Many miles remained, but their progress gave them hope.

ᥴᰘᥲ

Night had fallen, but still Scodo and Babette pushed on.

By Scodo's calculations, the goblins would arrive at Kelsner's Plain in the morning. They were seven or eight hours away. With luck, they would just make it.

From the front of the wagon, Zauberyungi unleashed a long moan and began to stagger. Babette rushed to his side, feeding him grass dusted with strange potions. At first, her magic lifted his spirits, but it gradually lost effect. Hovering at his side, Babette whispered, nudged, stroked, and urged him on. But as they approached a stream, they had to stop once more. Zauberyungi could not take another step.

"Give him an hour," Babette said, and soon all three were again asleep.

When the time had passed, Scodo was awake, shaking Babette and beseeching Zauberyungi to rise again. But Zauberyungi would not budge. Babette knelt at the old mule's side and whispered gently into his ear. But even Babette's sweetest words could not move the mule.

Now, Babette was pleading with Zauberyungi, who looked back with aching eyes. Frantically, Babette pulled grass from the stream's bank, offering it to the mule. Zauberyungi lifted his head to take the grass but fell back once more.

Babette knelt again beside the mule, pleading. Zauberyungi lifted his head, trying to roll to his feet, but his body sagged to the earth.

Scodo and Babette looked at one another, wondering if their journey had come to an end.

"We need your magic!" Scodo cried to Babette. "Find it. Bring Zauberyungi to his feet."

Babette looked back at Scodo without expression. "I have no magic for Zauberyungi," she said.

Scodo was on his feet, stomping angrily in the sand.

"Where is Asterux? If he is such a great wizard, why is he not here to help? The force of evil can visit us three times. But not once does the great and mighty Asterux bother to help! Call him!"

"It is not necessary to call him," Babette replied. "He will know."

"He can't know. If he knew, he would be here!"

"Don't be angry. There are things you don't understand."

"What things?"

"A wizard for the good possesses great powers. It is important never to use those powers as long as any person can find it within himself to succeed. The power of good must always make room for what lies in each of us."

Scodo sat in the sand, his face in his hands, shaking his head in disbelief. They were at the end. Zauberyungi lay motionless on the ground.

For ten, maybe twenty minutes, Scodo and Babette did not speak. Babette looked, unmoving, at the sky. Scodo stared at the ground below.

Scodo rose to his feet. Without hesitation or delay, he walked over to the old mule. For a moment, he looked down at Zauberyungi, wondering if perhaps he was dead. Then he leaned down and placed his arms around Zauberyungi's belly. With all of the might that remained in his body, he lifted. And ever so slowly, the mule was raised from the ground.

Stunned, Zauberyungi tottered for a moment and staggered backward, but he found his footing. Scodo put on his harness. Two deep breaths later, Zauberyungi stepped firmly ahead. The wagon was under way again.

Across the desert, the sun was casting the first shadows of the day. In a few hours, Darrow would face the goblins at Kelsner's Plain. Miraculously, Zauberyungi had pulled all night. Scodo and Babette, almost too exhausted to walk, had helped by pushing the wagon from behind. Now they were two hours away.

Scodo guessed that the goblins arrived last night. They knew that Darrow was marching from the forest and that Kelsner's Plain was the place that the two armies would most likely meet. With luck, their wagon would reach Darrow's army just in time.

Onward, onward, Babette urged the old mule. As they walked, her words to Zauberyungi were constant, gentle, but urgent. Zauberyungi could sense in Babette's voice that their goal was near, the ordeal was ending, and that reaching this end, whatever it might be, was more important to Babette than anything in the world.

"My beautiful Zauberyungi," she whispered. "You are the hero. The hero of us all!" Forward Zauberyungi surged.

The wagon passed out of the long valley and through a canyon that opened into the plains. Kelsner's Plain was barely an hour away.

"Onward, Zauberyungi, onward!" Babette whispered, nuzzling his neck as they walked. "Onward, you beautiful boy."

But just as the wagon entered the great grassy plains of Sonnencrest, the wheel lifted over a rock, crashing into a rut. It twisted to one side and the weight of the swords shifted hard. For a moment, the wheel leaned at a deep angle away from the road. A snapping sound split the air.

A wheel fell from the wagon and struck the rock. The weight of the wagon followed.

Scodo lifted while Babette inspected the damage. The wheel was shattered, utterly beyond repair. Zauberyungi whinnied loudly. Wild-eyed in frustration and disbelief, Scodo lifted a rock and hurled it far into the distance. Babette fell to her knees, muttering words Scodo could not hear.

Then Babette rose. "Unhitch Zauberyungi," she stated quietly. She looked back down the canyon and to the desert from which they had come and spoke not a word for a long time.

Out of his harness, Zauberyungi collapsed on the ground. His chest rose and fell with each breath but otherwise he lay without movement. "I don't know if he will live," said Scodo with deep emotion.

Babette looked at her beloved mule. Angry, she turned back toward the desert, staring into the sky.

"Curse you, Zindown. Curse your evil soul."

As these words passed across the plain, black clouds once again gathered in the sky. Scodo looked at Babette with alarm.

Three bolts of lightning crisscrossed high above and thunder shook the ground. The clouds began to swirl until, off in the distance, a black tornado appeared. Spiraling, towering, high into the sky, the funnel began to move straight at the wagon.

"Run, Babette, run!" Scodo screamed, his legs clawing at the sand as he scrambled desperately to get away. "Run!"

But Babette did not run. Her face was unmoving, her feet planted firmly on the ground. With her hands curled into fists, she braced her body against the wind. From her mouth came her strange whistle. Above the roar of the storm, her whistle sounded clear in Scodo's ears. But the tornado did not stop. Its movements were slow and jagged, but its direction did not waiver. When it arrived at the wagon, Babette refused to move, still whistling, hurling her magic against a power far mightier than her own.

When it struck, it threw Babette into the air. She landed far away, her body crumpled on the ground. The wagon lifted into the air and, with the tornado, disappeared from sight.

☙

As Babette lay unconscious on the sand and grass, a voice called softly.

"Awaken, Babette."

Babette tried to look up, but her head was heavy and her eyes would not focus.

"Awaken, my princess, your work is done."

This time, her eyes opened slightly. The sun glared from above, and at first, she could make out nothing at all. A shape

appeared: a short, round man. She squinted again to focus and lifted her hand to shield her eyes from the sun. Now she could see.

It was Asterux.

The terrible events of the last three days raced through her mind. She was broken in spirit. Her head would barely lift above the ground. Summoning her strength, she spoke.

"Asterux, Asterux, I have failed you, I have failed Darrow. I have failed our kingdom."

"My dear, you have failed no one. You have made me prouder than you will ever know. As I speak, Darrow is fighting the goblins. It is time to return to the forest and wait."

Blinking, confused but too tired to argue or understand, she climbed to her feet. "Where is Scodo?" she asked.

"He has gone to join Darrow in battle. Come. It is time to go."

No other words passed Babette's lips. She rose and began to follow Asterux to the forest. But after a few steps, she stopped and turned to stare at Zauberyungi's lifeless body laying on the plan. She lifted her arms and tightened her hands into fists. A low whistle drifted into the horizon.

When Asterux turned to look, Zauberyungi's body was gone.

· 38 ·

Against the Goblin Wall

By the time the sun peeked above the horizon, not a single soldier was still asleep. Seven hundred and fifty men stood ready on the plain, pacing to and fro, inspecting their weapons, and wondering when their first battle might begin.

They called themselves soldiers, but almost none had looked across at the enemy and summoned the courage to charge headlong into the possibility of death. The cruelty of battle was beyond their imagination. That their weapons were useless they could not know. But from their innocence came power. Blind to the ordeal that lay before them, they were still able to believe.

There were some who held swords, but most held the weapons of the primitive tribes that roamed the plains many centuries ago. Sticks as tall as a man sharpened to a point without metal or even stone tips. Others held clubs carved from the

branches of trees. And many held pitchforks, the weapon most available on the plains, as if the goblins were little more than hay that might be piled in a great stack and set ablaze.

Two days ago, cows grazed on the pasture where they stood. On either side of this pasture, the land rose upward to form hills just tall enough to look down on the pasture but rare in this long, flat landscape. This was the site Darrow had selected. Here, on this ground, the fate of the kingdom would rise or fall.

⁋

The stone was round and flat, barely bigger than a walnut. In the soldier's hand, it journeyed down the edge of a long blade, curved and half the length of a tall man. Again and again, the stone stroked the metal until the morning sun danced at its edge. When the blade could not be made sharper, the soldier rose and dropped the sharpening stone into his pocket. As he did, across the goblin camp, five hundred more did the same.

A scout, at rigid attention, stood before the goblin commander Decidus.

"Twenty minutes from where I stand. More than seven hundred, as best I could count."

The commander nodded. He was no general, but he had been handed the mission to round up Darrow and his thirty men. Now an actual army waited across an open field.

"Seven hundred of nothing," he scoffed. Decidus knew war and he knew what lay ahead. Before the goblin swords, sticks and pitchforks would stand no chance. He smiled and wondered who would carry so many bodies away. There was a second reason for Decidus' smile. This larger force would make him a hero. Fortune had touched his career. His victory would be celebrated throughout the kingdom.

⁂

In the distance, Darrow could see the dark blur that was the goblins' advance. The sun in their faces, shrouded in dust, they glowed like an image from a strange dream. Darrow's men, seeing their enemy for the first time, let out a great cheer.

Darrow scanned the field and inspected his line. His soldiers were adorned in rags. Above their heads, they hoisted their wooden spears. Here and there, a few torches sent fingers of smoke into the air. Behind them stood about a hundred townsfolk, recruited the day before and now guarding an odd assortment of boxes and barrels.

Darrow wondered how many swords they held. Perhaps two hundred? It was no use counting.

"Form the lines," Darrow ordered, and across the field all scrambled into the unruly formation they had practiced again and again the day before.

Soon the goblins halted their march. In their line, there was no disorder. Each soldier stood motionless with a forward gaze, standing erect, expressionless, and proud. Each was armored with breastplate and helmet. All held shields, and in almost every right hand, held in exactly the same position, pointing upward and parallel to the body, stood a gleaming sword, almost thirty inches in length, with a curved blade honed to a razor's edge.

Scattered among the troops were five cave trolls. Towering over the goblins, holding large hammers, the cave trolls grunted and snorted at their foe.

Darrow's men were quieter now. In recent days, they had sung brave songs, but now they looked ahead, awed by the gleaming metal that painted their opponent's line.

What was the power of a wooden club against an armored soldier wielding a fine sword? What damage might a wooden spear inflict against a breastplate of iron? Darrow's weapons were courage, passion, and belief. So as his troops girded for battle, he climbed to the top of a fence post, balanced gingerly on his short leg, and began to speak.

"The power of the sword is great indeed. Men and women will die today on this field. But no cold metal blade will extinguish the fire that burns in our hearts.

"What weapon has more power than the passion of the heart? Our hands today shall write a new history for our kingdom. And through centuries to come, all shall remember this day on Kelsner's Plain when we drove the goblins from the plains of Sonnencrest and marched to our capital to restore freedom to our land."

A great cry arose. Once again, Darrow's words made his men proud and sure. For what they felt in their hearts was suddenly larger than what they saw with their eyes.

Across the field, the goblin formation stood unmoving and ready. Darrow lifted his sword to signal the advance.

His sword high in the air, a scream arose from the far end of the line.

"Tornado!"

Goblins and men alike looked to see a dark funnel weaving its way toward the field. On both sides, the soldiers retreated and shielded their eyes as bits of grass and dirt flew about in the air. Soon, the noise raged like a swarm of a million locusts.

Into the field between the two armies, the dark funnel came. As the soldiers looked upward, it reached so high that the top was beyond their view. For a moment, the funnel seethed in place as if anchored to the land. Then, ever so slowly, it moved to the center of where Darrow's army had once stood. It hovered for what seemed an eternity and then, strangely, its winds began to slow. No longer supported by the wind, a great object dropped and crashed into the earth. The sound of clashing metal rang across the plain.

All that remained was a great cloud of dust. More than a thousand soldiers, human and goblin alike, stood wide-eyed and speechless, not sure by what miracle the storm had disappeared.

A low breeze swept across the field, slowly clearing the dust from the rubble. What Darrow saw, he could not believe: a pile of metal resting on a shattered wooden frame. Two hundred swords, the bounty Babette and Scodo had transported across the desert, lay there for the taking. Standing upright and high over the pile like a flag of victory was the great battle-axe.

Darrow's men scrambled to the pile, picking through the weapons and raising them high in the air. Timwee mounted the pile and pulled at the battle-axe. It was too heavy to lift, so, walking backwards, his back straining against its weight, he dragged it across the ground to where Hugga Hugga stood. Then Hugga Hugga lifted the axe, quickly and easily, as if it were a toy made for a child.

When all had armed themselves, they reformed their lines and stood ready once again. Darrow lifted his own sword and the line began its advance. Shields locked in a ribbon of silver, the goblins awaited.

There was no headlong charge. Across the line, soldiers beat swords against wood in a primitive rhythm that guided their steps. When they had traveled a third of the distance, Darrow ordered a halt.

Decidus, the goblin commander, looked across the field, surprised by the order of their march but puzzled by their decision to stop. Eager to be done with this riff-raff, he spoke.

"If they will not charge our line, we will charge theirs."

So the goblin line began its advance. *Boom, pattattattat. Boom, pattattat.* The goblin drums sounded and feet followed. One step forward, a pause, and another step. With each step, the wall of metal shields moved forward. Darrow's men likewise resumed their advance. Like a pair of centipedes in a sidestepping dance, the two armies edged closer and closer together.

The goblins stopped. Decidus cried out an order and a great volley of arrows rose into the sky. When those arrows landed, soldiers of Sonnencrest fell all across the grass.

Another volley of arrows struck. More soldiers crumpled to the earth. Now the goblins moved forward again with gleaming metal and frightful swords. The two lines were a long stone's throw apart.

At the front of Darrow's line, a voice moaned.

"We are going to die."

To their sides lay fallen comrades begging to be carried away. Ahead stood a wall of shields that neither sword nor wooden spear might break. And when the first voice cried out, others followed, and the men began to run from the field.

Soon, Darrow's entire front line was fleeing the battle. Decidus turned to order pursuit. But from the corner of his eye, he noticed something strange. As Darrow's men departed, they revealed a wall of wooden shields and these shields stood unmoving before them. The shields spanned the length of the line, sheltering another row of soldiers armed mostly with pitchforks and spears.

This wall did not waver. Instead, it stepped forward toward the goblin line.

Decidus looked left and right. The soldiers ran with their weapons, disappearing over the hills on either side. Some goblins gave chase, but most looked back for orders. Perhaps it was a trick. But when Decidus looked ahead, the wooden wall stepped forward once more. For a moment, Decidus was silent. Then he shouted his command.

"Forward." And with these words, the goblin line stepped ahead with new resolve.

Now the sun was far above the plain and its rays reflected against the goblin shields with a blinding light. Behind their wooden barrier, Darrow's men steeled for the assault. The goblins stepped forward and this time Darrow's line stepped back. In the meantime, Darrow counted, "Seven, eight, nine . . ."

A great thud sounded in the air as the wall of steel met its wooden foe. Again, Darrow's line retreated, first one step, then another. Swords flailed at the wood while pitchforks jabbed at the advancing foe. But there was something strange about this wooden barrier, for these were not shields at all but one wooden wall carried by the entire line.

Again, the goblins struck and metal buried itself deep into the wood. Chips flew into the air and pitchforks fell, severed at the handles.

Behind Darrow's line, some soldiers ran. But the wall, hammered together across a grand expanse, did not break. Darrow counted, "Thirty-eight, thirty-nine . . ."

Once again, the wooden wall stepped backwards and, when it did, the pitchforks withdrew. From behind, townspeople rolled barrels to the line and those barrels emptied themselves, painting a great line of cooking oil, lamp oil, and even pig fat across the ground. Again, the goblins surged. But this time, the wall retreated three steps. Torches dropped and a row of fire erupted between the lines. The shield-bearing goblins tried to step back, but pressed by the comrades from behind, they fell into the fire and the air was filled with chilling screams. Shields fell. Soldiers erupted in flames. But others took up the shields. The metal wall reformed and, when the flames had fallen, the goblins stepped forward again.

"Eighty-seven, eight-eight, eighty-nine . . . ," Darrow continued.

Another row of townspeople hurried to the line, carrying boxes filled with bottles, bowls, pitchers, and glassworks of all kinds, collected from a thousand homes throughout Kelsner's Plain. These boxes were emptied behind the wall. Again, Darrow's line stepped back and, as they did, the wall dropped to the ground with a great crashing sound. Shards of shattered glass flew into the air and across the ground. Again, the line stepped back. Again, the wall struck the ground. A sea of broken glass lay across the goblins' path.

Decidus could not see the trap Darrow had laid. He saw only backtracking and he gave the order.

"Advance!"

The goblins pressed forward, pushing the shield-bearers onto the glass-covered ground. A great cry filled the air, shields fell, and Darrow's pitchforks found their mark. This time, fewer goblins stepped forward. The wall was broken.

"One-hundred forty-eight, one-hundred forty-nine . . ." But before Darrow could say the final number, from over the hills came a great charge and three hundred soldiers returned, most armed with swords, to strike the goblins from behind.

At the sight of this charge, Darrow issued his order. The wooden wall fell forward across the glass and Darrow's band poured into the goblin line.

Standing unprotected by shields, the goblins met Darrow's charge with courage and iron. But their breastplates provided no protection from behind. As Darrow's men returned from the hills, even the wooden spears proved a deadly weapon.

Darrow stepped into the fray.

Now it was his sword that reflected the sunlight. Now it was his weapon that spread fear. Dancing through the air, blocking, cutting, stabbing, Darrow's blade put on a wondrous display. Where Darrow stepped, the goblins fell back, shrinking from his terrible skills.

Meanwhile, the cave trolls and their hammers were taking a terrible toll. But standing on a pile of shields, sling in hand, Aisling felled one troll with her stone. A band of dwarfs from Pfesthammer took two more by swarming their feet, stabbing them with daggers until the giants stumbled and fell. The remaining trolls, fearful and confused, simply ran away.

Decidus ordered his soldiers to form a circle, but in the roar of the battle, his words went unheard. Here and there, groups of goblins gathered shields and locked together against the Sonnencrest advance. But from Darrow's line stepped the Minotaur wielding his enormous axe. Rearing back, he unleashed his weapon in a mighty stroke that shattered shields and sent veteran warriors scrambling in retreat.

Decidus ordered his soldiers to retreat to the north where the fewest enemy troops stood. Swords flailing, they broke the Sonnencrest line. But once beyond the battle, these goblins did not turn to fight. They ran from the field. Soon, chaos reigned as each goblin battled not for kingdom or comrades but for his own escape. With victory beyond his grasp, Decidus made a decision of his own.

He ran.

Suddenly, there were no more goblins on the field. Swords were dropped, armor discarded, shields thrown at the advancing foe—all sacrificed to make a desperate dash for life.

The battle was a rout. And for the rest of the day, Darrow's men, crazed and triumphant, chased fleeing goblins across the long stretches of the plain.

· 39 ·

Scodo Arrives

While most of Darrow's band chased goblins, a few hundred remained, celebrating in the pasture.

"To Blumenbruch!" one soldier cried.

"To Blumenbruch!" the others responded.

New men arrived from every direction. Some, disappointed about missing the battle, had joined soldiers pursuing the remnants of the goblin force. News of this victory would travel fast. Within a few days, Darrow would have fifteen hundred, possibly two thousand men. And with the swords taken today, many would be armed.

A wagon arrived from Pfesthammer.

"How many?" Darrow asked.

"Thirty-five swords," said the driver. "But we promise more tomorrow." In Kelsner's Plain, the blacksmiths were hard at work.

Another wagon arrived, this one from Blumenbruch. To avoid the goblins, it had traveled north to the edge of the mountains then down a small road to reach the scene of battle. Darrow could not believe its cargo—two hundred swords. For the first time in his campaign, Darrow had more swords than men.

From Kelsner's Plain, more wagons appeared, and women and girls climbed down, offering breads and sausages for the troops. People on foot poured down the road, laughing, cheering, and joining the celebration. Some brought wine, which the men drank greedily.

Darrow sat on a rock, smiling, taking in the scene. For the first time, almost since the day he had marched from Ael, he felt no urgent business, no pressing concern. Mempo stopped to ask when they would march on Blumenbruch. Darrow just shrugged.

Over the small hill, a band of soldiers appeared, waving helmets and breastplates captured on the field. Others ran forward to hear their report and cheer their exploits. From a corner of the crowd, a fiddle and flute burst forth with lively music, and some of the townspeople began to dance.

A scream brought the music to a halt.

At one edge of the crowd, people staggered backwards. Soldiers reached for their swords. Those not at the edge covered their eyes. Stepping slowly across the ground, barely covered by the tattered rags that were once his cloak, was the scorpion man.

Swords lifted in every direction, but Scodo did not react at all. Slowly, purposefully, he moved forward into the pasture, his hideous face scanning the scene. He seemed to be searching for some specific person.

One soldier stepped into his path, his sword drawn and ready to strike. The scorpion man stopped, eyeing the soldier with complete calm. For an instant, the soldier stepped back, confused. Then the soldier moved toward the monster, his weapon raised high.

Before the sword could strike, a voice broke across the landscape. It was Darrow's voice, and it spoke one clear and determined word.

"Halt!"

The soldier froze, a little relieved but concerned that Scodo might still attack. Scodo froze as well, not sure for whom the order was intended.

All eyes turned to Darrow, who walked purposefully across the field, the crowd parting before him. They looked on in wonderment as Darrow approached the monster, a great smile opening on his face.

When he reached Scodo, Darrow stopped. For a few seconds, he just looked at Scodo, not with fear or horror but with a long and admiring gaze. He stepped forward, opened his arms, and seized the monster in a great embrace. The onlookers gasped.

For long moments, Darrow held Scodo tight. When he finally stepped back, he looked again at the scorpion man with a welcoming smile. It was Scodo who first spoke.

"I have come to join the battle to free Sonnencrest," and he paused uncertainly, his head hanging. "If you will have me."

There was no hesitation in Darrow's reply.

"I have carried your fighting spirit in my heart for many days. It will be our greatest honor to have you march at our side."

Then Darrow turned to speak to a bewildered crowd.

"Today, a great and mighty warrior has appeared among us. He has battled for our cause from the earliest day. Deep in the forest at the top of Naark's Hill, we faced death at the hands of the goblin army. Only the appearance of this great soldier turned the battle. Single-handedly, he rescued not just our tiny band but the fate of our kingdom as well.

"Before the fall of Blumenbruch, he was Sonnencrest's greatest warrior. And today he is our greatest warrior still. In the history of Sonnencrest, the name Scodo shall rank among our greatest heroes. All hail my friend, all hail my brother, all hail Scodo, the greatest fighter among us."

For the briefest moment, the crowd remained silent, but when Hugga Hugga and Timwee took up the cry, the crowd roared forth to hail the mighty Scodo. Soldiers and people drew close, patting Scodo on the back, praising his courage, and offering congratulations all around.

Darrow looked at the brave and mighty Scodo and wondered how Scodo, who had known little but horror, disgust, and repugnance, would feel as he was embraced and celebrated that day by his fellow soldiers there on the field.

· 40 ·

Zindown's Plan

"Tell me, oh great and mighty Beltar, can you tell me . . ."
Beltar, eyes narrowed and lips pressed together,
waited as the king's words poured forth.

"Tell me, how can a great military genius lose in battle to
an eighteen-year-old cripple barely the size of a wolfhound?"

The king stood, hands on hips, eyes burning so bright they
might set Beltar afire.

"I wasn't there," Beltar replied, looking away from the king.

"And why did we send five hundred to face an army almost
twice our size?"

"No one knew he had swords," replied Beltar, ignoring the
king's faulty math.

Dark green splotches rising from his neck, the king turned
to Bekkendoth.

"A pipsqueak, one-legged boy from Wail! And where is this Wail anyway?"

"To the south in the mountains below the Pfimincil Forest," Bekkendoth replied, wondering just why no one remembered that he was the one who said more soldiers were needed. "It's Ael, Your Majesty, not Wail."

The king sank into a chair, his chest heaving. When calm returned and his eyes had faded to gray, Beltar spoke.

"Your Majesty, we are indeed facing a formidable foe. Mistakes have been made. But can we now move forward to crush this revolt and give this peasant just what he deserves?"

The king rose again and walked to the window. His back was wet with sweat. He stood at the window for a long time. Beneath his feet two small puddles formed. When he finally spoke, his words came in a whisper almost too faint to hear.

"Yes, the plan. Tell me the plan."

Beltar unfurled a roll of paper and spread it across the table. His long finger stabbed a place on the map.

"Here is Darrow, still at Kelsner's Plain. His force is growing. He now has at least a thousand and maybe fifteen hundred men. He is a shrewd opponent. That I will admit. Now he has blacksmiths all across the kingdom working overtime to produce swords."

"We arrested three of them yesterday—in Blumenbruch," Bekkendoth added.

The king looked back, wiping his forehead with his sleeve.

"His army is growing, but they have not faced cavalry. They remain without armor. We can move in at night and surround their camp with locked shields. Our archers will wake them with a hail of arrows. When we follow with the cavalry, they will have no chance."

The king looked back at Beltar. "Here is what I want. I want a guarantee. Can you guarantee victory?"

Before Beltar could answer, Zindown interrupted.

"I can give you a guarantee. I guarantee that this plan will fail."

King Malmut's body shook with anger.

"I am sorry to deliver this news, but I have been to the other side."

Beltar rolled his eyes and glared through the window.

"First," Zindown began, "you must know that Princess Babette is alive."

"Alive!" screamed the king. "Then kill her!"

"It is not an easy task. She has magic of her own. But we cannot kill her now. I need her for my plan.

"Second, you must understand we cannot win in open battle. Darrow's army is fifteen hundred strong but growing every day. By the time Beltar attacks, Darrow will have two, maybe three thousand or more.

"But it is not numbers that make them strong. These soldiers know little of battle but are driven with a passion and belief. For this Darrow, this runt as you call him, they will fight like madmen. Beltar can surround them. But they will break his wall on every side."

Beltar looked up, his face whitening in rage. The king surged from his chair.

"Well, listen, my world-famous magician. Will you tell me just one thing? Why is this Darrow boy not dead? Just one little murder, is that too much to ask?"

"Your Majesty, would you have me hurl spells at every criminal? Murder by the hand of the wizard is reserved for only the most personal vengeance. But why concern yourself with who does the deed? Murder is exactly what I have in mind.

"To kill Darrow, to destroy his army and crush this rebellion, there is really only one course of action."

"And what is that?" Beltar shot back.

Zindown smiled, pausing for effect.

"Surrender."

Beltar rose from his chair, glaring at the wizard. The king looked confused.

"Not a real surrender. I mean a trick."

Beltar returned to his seat. Remembering his victory at Tolenbettle, a smile slowly crossed his face.

"If we surrender, we can lure Darrow away from his army and when we do we will slay him with a sword. With Darrow dead, we can attack with our full force—all in a great surprise. Without their great leader, these peasants will flee for their lives, scattering all across the plain. Cut off the head, the beast will die."

The king liked this image but was still puzzled.

"Who could slay him? Who is good enough to defeat Darrow?"

"I think Beltar would do just fine." Zindown gestured Beltar's way. "I think he is brave enough for this task."

Beltar straightened to speak, but the king interrupted.

"This Darrow—his swordsmanship is legendary."

Zindown lifted his chin and touched together the fingers on both hands.

"And a legend is all that it is, Your Highness. Darrow is a pathetic weakling. He is lame and small and can hardly lift an ordinary weapon."

"So how has he slain scores of my finest swordsmen?" Beltar scoffed.

"Because he carries a magical sword." He looked straight into Beltar's eyes. "But when you face him alone, his sword will be gone."

For a long time, the room was silent as the monarch and his general contemplated Zindown's strange plan. Beltar was the first to speak.

"I understand your plan. If their army is rejoicing, we can strike at the most unexpected time. Perhaps Darrow cannot fight without his sword. But how will you lure him from his army? This is the part I don't understand."

Now, Zindown was positively gleeful. He had waited the entire conversation to deliver his line.

"Yes, my good general, that is indeed the critical part. And for this challenge, I plan to employ a tactic that in my lifetime of wizardry I have seldom used."

Beltar and the king leaned forward in their chairs, eager to hear.

"To lure Darrow from his army, I plan to tell him the truth."

And with a great howl of laughter, Zindown exited the room.

· 41 ·

Surrender

At the edge of Kelsner's Plain stood a sentry. In the distance, he could see a small cloud. "Perhaps a horseman," he thought. There were still few horses in camp and this volunteer would be welcome.

As the rider approached, the sentry could see a white flag of sorts waving above the horse. The rider wore garments of black and green. "A messenger from the goblins," he thought and hurried into town to notify Darrow.

In the streets, word traveled fast, and men and women gathered to see what might come.

The white flag high in the air, the rider galloped into the street and brought his horse to a stop. A soldier took the bridle and led him to the house where Darrow slept. Behind him, a crowd gathered to see and hear what he might say.

Darrow emerged from the house, limping as usual. The goblin looked down at this small figure and grimaced, unwilling to believe his kingdom had been humbled by so meager a foe. When he had dismounted, he stood before Darrow, not looking in his face.

"I travel under a flag of truce. I carry a message from His Royal Highness King Malmut of Globenwald."

Necks stretched and heads bobbed, straining to get a view and hear each word. Darrow signaled silence. He accepted the scroll, broke its wax seal, and read the contents aloud.

> *To Darrow of Ael, Great General of the Army of Sonnencrest:*
> *On behalf of the great nation of Globenwald, I extend to you our surrender.*

At these words, a great murmur moved through the crowd and a few soldiers launched a cheer. But Darrow raised his hand for silence. When the crowd quieted, he continued.

> *You have handed our nation a terrible defeat. Too many sons of both Globenwald and Sonnencrest have lost their lives. Your army grows with each passing day.*
> *So, in exchange for safe passage from your kingdom, we agree to remove all troops from Sonnencrest and will begin our departure today.*
>
> *King Malmut II*

When Darrow spoke the king's name, there was not a whisper in the air, as if more words must surely follow, telling them that this strange news could not really be true. But a few voices began to cheer and those cheers became a thunderous roar. Some ran from the scene to spread the news. Others hugged one another and tears flowed down many cheeks. Hands reached toward Darrow, for no words could be heard and touch was the only way to convey, not just congratulations, but their deep and lasting gratitude for the mighty deed he had achieved.

When he could again be heard, the messenger pulled out a sword and handed it to Darrow.

"This is the sword of Beltar," he said. "The victory is yours."

Darrow himself stood silent, his expression dazed, struggling to make sense of this message. Hands reached beneath his legs and suddenly he was lifted in the air and onto the shoulders of his men. Now people poured into the streets. Carried above the crowd, Darrow was surrounded by a cauldron of joy, teeming with bodies bouncing with energy beyond their ability to contain. Through the streets he flowed, his presence drawing the crowd to its hero like a whirlpool flowing through a choppy sea.

When they reached the town hall, he gave a beautiful speech thanking the families of Kelsner's Plain who donated cooking oil and glassworks and even manned the battlefield. He spoke of the kingdom to come and how freedom would reign and that the tables of Sonnencrest would once again be filled with milk, wheat bread, and grapes from their fields.

"All hail, King Darrow!" a voice shouted. A thousand voices joined this chant.

But Darrow's mind was elsewhere. When he had finished, he turned to Mempo, his expression grave, and snapped, "Get me back to the house."

⚬⚬⚬

At the house, Darrow called for his circle, but only Scodo, Timwee, and Mempo could be found.

"Brother, why so gloomy?" Mempo asked. "A happier day is hard to imagine."

"Sit. I want to talk."

The four sat facing one another.

Scodo spoke first.

"It is a trick. I cannot prove it, but I believe it beyond any truth I know. Why would they leave Sonnencrest after one small battle? Are they cowards? Do they care for our well-being? Give me one single reason why they would do such a thing."

"They are afraid of you," Mempo responded, his back straight and his head held high.

"Perhaps it is a ploy," offered Timwee, "but what are we to do? Messengers are running to every corner of the kingdom. Do we tell our soldiers that our victory is not real? Do you tell this mob that war continues? They promised to leave. Let's see if they do. In the meantime, we remain on alert."

Darrow looked at each of the men, weighing their advice. "It is a trick. This is what I believe and we should tell the people the truth."

"We don't know the truth," Mempo shot back.

"They are setting a trap," Darrow snapped. "When we march to Blumenbruch, drunk with our victory, their entire army will be waiting."

Timwee repeated his advice. "Maybe we don't march to the capital. Maybe we wait here, on alert, to see if they really leave. In three days, we will have a thousand more."

Darrow nodded. "Three days. That is what we will give them. If they remain in Sonnencrest, we will march to Blumenbruch and give them a farewell they won't forget."

～⚬

The afternoon sun was falling in the sky and shadows of the crowd fell through the curtains and into the room. At the door stood a sentry. Inside, Darrow, Timwee, Hugga Hugga, and Scodo stood hunched over a map.

There was a knock on the door.

Darrow turned, his face strained and unhappy, but he remembered the sentry.

"Who is it?"

The door opened. A face appeared in the crack.

"A messenger. I asked him who it was from, but he won't say."

"Send him away," said Darrow, but Scodo went to the door. The messenger stood tall, almost the height of the door, and he was dressed in fine clothes. He did not speak.

"Who sends a message to Darrow?"

"I cannot say," replied the messenger, still at attention. "But he knows the sender well."

As Scodo turned to go back inside, he glanced at the envelope. On it was a small picture of a yellow bird.

"Let this man inside."

Darrow looked up from the map, emitting a long sigh.

"You may want to read this one," said Scodo.

Darrow turned and snatched the envelope from the messenger. As he read, his mouth opened and his jaw slowly dropped.

My dear nephew,

You have made me the proudest uncle in all Sonnencrest. From your walk through the forest when the skriabeasts brought you to my home to your wonderful impersonation of a gong farmer at the Kirstinnex prison, I saw qualities of courage and wisdom that I knew would make you succeed.

But now, as you stand at the edge of our kingdom's greatest victory, there is something you should know. Princess Babette is alive and is ready to take the crown. Before proceeding to Blumenbruch, it is important that you meet with her to discuss the kingdom, its future, and the establishment of government when the goblins are gone.

This messenger will take you to a secret place barely a day's walk from Kelsner's Plain. No one must accompany you on your journey for there is a great ransom on the head of the princess— so great that even one of our own might strike her dead. Please trust me in this matter. As always, I am forever at your service.

Asterux

All waited for the message, disappointed that Darrow had not read it aloud. When he was finished, he looked up and spoke.

"Princess Babette is alive."

"Who is Princess Babette?" Mempo asked.

"Some say she escaped from the palace the night Sonnen-crest fell. She is the one survivor of the royal family."

Timwee objected. "These are legends. Any imposter could make this claim. She was only eight years old."

"It is true. I know her."

All eyes turned to Scodo.

"How could you keep this secret from us?" Mempo shouted.

Darrow lifted his hand. "Do not doubt this message. It is from my uncle. It says things that only my uncle would know. I will leave to meet the princess tomorrow morning."

"I will join you," offered Scodo. "We will bring our twenty best men for protection."

"I must do this alone."

"Don't even think about that," said Timwee. "What if this is just another trick? If they kill you, then where would we be?"

"Without you, Brother, we will all be dead," Mempo concluded.

Darrow looked back at his friends, angry that they would doubt his judgment. Almost shouting, he said, "This message is no trick."

Scodo and Timwee exchanged looks of alarm. But there was no chance to speak. Darrow spoke so firmly, no voice would rise in response.

"Tomorrow I leave alone."

⟨⟩

A low wind rose across the plain and stalks of high grass bowed their heads and shivered before its presence. Darrow leaned forward in his saddle. He was not used to a horse and the long ride made his body ache. All day, the messenger had spoken hardly a word.

They reached the house and dismounted, tying their horses to a carriage. It was a fine carriage, fit for a princess, thought Darrow, but he noticed an emblem on the door—a bat spider painted in shining green.

The messenger spoke.

"You are about to meet a princess. You cannot do so dressed as you are."

Darrow protested that he had no other clothes. But the messenger reached into the carriage and withdrew a fine robe.

Darrow knew nothing of royalty or its customs. So, not wishing to offend, he accepted the offer. The robe was too long for Darrow. Its hem dragged the ground and it had no place for a sword. So the messenger also pulled out a fine belt with engraved leather and metal trim.

"Here, you can use this to hold your sword."

Darrow took the belt. It was heavy, very heavy, in his hands.

The messenger explained that the craftsmen had buried a metal inside the leather so that it would not be possible to cut the sword from his side. While he buckled the new belt, he handed the messenger his sword to hold.

The messenger marveled at Darrow's blade.

"This is as fine a sword as I have seen. Do you mind if I examine it?"

"Not at all."

The messenger turned his back and faced the carriage. He lifted the sword lying across his palms.

"It is so light. It must be terribly fast."

"Indeed."

The messenger opened a compartment on the wagon. There were several swords inside. He lifted one, placing Darrow's sword inside.

Holding his own sword in both hands, he said, "Even my lightest sword is no match for your blade." Then he reached in the compartment and placed Darrow's sword in the scabbard on his new belt.

"Wait here," he said. "I will inform the princess that you are ready."

Darrow paced nervously in the yard. His new belt felt heavy. From the house came not the slightest sound.

The door opened.

What Darrow saw made him gasp.

Standing before him was no messenger and certainly no princess. Before him stood a goblin, tall and broad-shouldered. His hand gripped a weapon, the blade almost as tall as Darrow himself, curved upward and no thicker than a moonflower vine.

"So you are the boy wonder, Darrow."

Darrow stepped back and grasped his sword. In his hand, the weapon felt cold. No warmth stirred his body.

He pulled the weapon from the scabbard. The point fell downward, almost too heavy to hold with one hand. But it was not the sword that most occupied Darrow's mind.

"Who are you?" he demanded.

"I am Beltar and I am here for a special purpose."

"Do I have to guess?"

Beltar laughed.

"My dear Darrow, I am here first and foremost to offer congratulations. Your swordsmanship is wondrous. Your speeches have brought a downtrodden kingdom to its feet. And your battlefield strategy stands with the best of our time."

"You flatter, my good general, as well as you fight."

Now, Darrow's moment was at hand. The great goblin general stood before him. Without Beltar, the goblins would be a weaker foe. In the next minutes, two swords could write the history of his kingdom.

From the moment, Darrow found new strength. In his shoulders and arms, a new power surged. With both hands, he lifted his sword slowly. It was no longer as heavy as before.

As the two opponents faced one another, Darrow looked deep into Beltar's eyes. For a moment, he thought he saw doubt. And that doubt made his power grow.

The two warriors, swords lifted high, stepped sideways in a circle like two roosters in a ring. Darrow attacked first, swinging his sword hard across the sky. Beltar stepped back, easily avoiding Darrow's stroke. The goblin countered with a sideways and downward stroke that barely missed Darrow's head and nipped his shoulder. Blood trickled from the wound.

Again, they circled. Again, Darrow was first to attack. Spinning his body in a full circle, he brought his blade sweeping across Beltar's side. Beltar stepped back, avoiding the blow.

Beltar's strategy was simple. Under the weight of his heavy sword, Darrow was sure to tire. The longer the fight lasted, the better were the goblin's chances. Carefully he stepped, inviting Darrow's attack, dodging his thrusts, and measuring his opponent's strength.

Darrow stood before him, his sword upright before his face, his hands and arms extended forward. Again, Darrow charged. Again, Beltar dodged. And after many more thrusts,

Darrow lifted his sword once more. Beltar saw a quiver in his blade.

Darrow charged again, his feet slower, almost clumsy. Beltar stepped easily to the side. Now, Beltar stepped closer, offering just enough target to invite another thrust. Each time, Darrow responded.

Beneath the weight of his sword, Darrow's feet were heavy and lumbering. Beltar saw his chance.

Towering over Darrow, almost twice his size, Beltar unleashed a mighty swing that sent Darrow staggering back toward the house. Again, Beltar charged with a bold thrust, and Darrow stumbled to the side, barely dodging the blow. Beltar attacked with a wide stroke aimed to crash across Darrow's shoulder. Metal met metal in a thunderous clash. Both swordsmen staggered back.

When the two warriors looked up, only Beltar held his sword. Mouth open, hands empty, Darrow circled toward his weapon, which lay twenty feet away. His hand trembled, his face was white.

Beltar stepped into his path. Standing between Darrow and his blade, he stroked at his target in short, controlled swings. Defenseless, Darrow dodged.

A great smile spread across Beltar's face. This boy, this fraction of a man, with one good leg and words so bold, had handed his armies humiliation and defeat. The sight of him, helpless and scared, was far too joyful to end.

Patiently, sure of victory, Beltar paced slowly around his prey. Here and there, he offered a thrust, not to fell his opponent but simply to watch him scamper away. His eyes twinkled. A low laugh rose from his chest.

Suddenly, Darrow lunged at Beltar's feet. Smiling, Beltar stepped to the side. He could have slain him right there, but why? Untouched by Beltar's sword, Darrow rolled behind Beltar, diving for his blade. Desperately, he grabbed it with both hands, his left hand gripping the blade. Suddenly, he was on his feet, but blood from his hand poured to the ground.

Darrow circled, back in the fight, fire in his eyes, his steps marked with a trail of blood. Beltar feigned attack. Darrow jumped to one side. Beltar jabbed in the air. Darrow ducked. With slow and steady steps, Beltar moved directly toward his foe.

Darrow did not retreat. As Beltar's sword came crashing down, Darrow's rose to meet it and spun in a circle, swinging his own sword in reply. Beltar stepped to one side, barely missing Darrow's stroke. Pressing forward, Darrow feinted, lunged, stroked, and swung with new mastery that forced Beltar to retreat.

Darrow's sword was quick and his feet were light. Suddenly, he was a dancer, bobbing up and down with wondrous movements across the ground. But as he lifted his weapon to strike again, his shorter leg caught the hem of his robe. He spun to break his fall. When Darrow found himself on the ground, his sword lay inches from his wounded hand.

He looked up. Beltar towered above him, smiling once more. For the briefest moment, Beltar stared into the face of his victim, savoring that timeless moment between life and death. Gripping tightly with both hands, he brought down his weapon, like a hammer, toward his foe.

But Beltar's moment was Darrow's chance. His left hand, caked with blood and mud, found his sword. He swung it

across his body and there it met Beltar's stroke. His parry was weak and it ricocheted off Beltar's blade. But its force was enough not to block but to change its course, sending Beltar's weapon deep into the ground.

Beltar tugged to pull his weapon free. Darrow was once more on his feet. Gripping his weapon with both hands, blood streaming down his arm, he launched a powerful swing. When the stroke was finished, the sword was streaked red.

Beltar lay dead on the ground.

⚬⚬⚬

The dark water rose and rolled against the ship, sending a great shower across the deck. At the wheel stood a thin man with a small pointed beard, stripes of pasty white skin showing through.

At his side was a sailor with a scarred face. He stared into the wind, looked back at the captain, and asked, "Why Sonnencrest? The goblins stole everything."

"Ah, we shall see, mate," replied Telsinore. "With a little luck, this trip will be one to remember. Ten years of evil deeds have built a mountain of treasure. The riches of an entire kingdom, puny though it is."

"That sounds awfully sweet."

"True enough, true enough. Riches are sweet indeed. But a treasure rising high in the sky cannot settle every account. This crime has a victim I have owed for some time. The gold in my chests will be a fine reward. But settling my debt will be the sweetest joy of all."

· 42 ·

The Flight of the King

"Where are the messengers? I'll have their heads if they don't arrive soon!"

In the palace where King Henry once ruled, the goblin king paced nervously across the room. Other than the shouts of the king, the palace was strangely quiet. Goblin soldiers stood twenty miles from Blumenbruch, waiting to ambush Darrow's victory march. Dignitaries had made the journey to watch the battle unfold.

But the king knew more. Beltar had fought Darrow two days before, and the outcome, which he did not know, would shape the battle to come.

The king stormed onto the balcony. He leaned on the railing, rising on his tiptoes to see. There, he could view most of the city. More important, he could see the road to the east that would bring a rider with the message he waited to hear. His eyes scanned the far distance. The road was empty.

"Bekkendoth!" he cried.

"I want a horse sent to meet the messenger on the road and return with the news!"

"With all due respect, Your Majesty, the two riders will only meet and return together. You won't learn the news a minute sooner."

Again, the king looked hard into the distance. He detected something, a small speck. It was a dust cloud. Soon, he could detect a slow rhythm as the cloud advanced. Within the hour, his messenger would arrive.

Beltar would win. He was certain. But what if he didn't? The king's face began to twitch. Why was Beltar so special anyway? Every general could be replaced.

The rider drew closer. He was now entering the city. "Open the gates," the king ordered, even though the rider was still fifteen minutes away. A servant scrambled down the stairs. A small crowd of soldiers and palace staff gathered, curious about the king's order.

Malmut looked again. Three specks appeared on the road. All of them seemed to be moving at a rapid pace. The king wiped his brow. He cursed Zindown. Darrow had better be dead; if not, the wizard would pay for his harebrained scheme.

On the avenue leading to the palace, the rider appeared: a goblin soldier in full uniform, his horse galloping at break-neck speed. "This is a great messenger," thought the king, admiring the horseman's speed.

Closer and closer, the rider approached the gate. The small crowd had grown. All eyes fixed on the soldier and his mount. But as the rider reached the gate, he veered to his left, passed the gate, and disappeared down the road leading away from Blumenbruch and toward the border.

Nervously, the king looked again at the faraway road. A whole host of dust clouds, not moving in any orderly way, approached the city.

He marched inside and screamed at the servants. "Who chose this messenger? I want to address this person now."

No one offered an answer. Out toward the gate he stormed, the crowd parting at his approach. A horseman entered and pulled to an abrupt stop, gripping the mane to stay in the saddle. The animal was soaked with sweat. Foam glistened at the edges of its mouth. The rider warily eyed the crowd. When he saw the king, he became afraid.

"What is the news?" demanded the king. "Tell me, tell me!"

The rider looked down, unable to answer.

"Are you mute?" cried Malmut.

The rider did not lift his head and spoke his words in a quiet voice.

"Beltar is dead."

A murmur swept the crowd. Through the crowd, eyes searched for horses and wagons that might bring escape.

"Surely there is a battle raging," the king sputtered.

"Battle?" The rider was confused. "Your Majesty, I thought we surrendered. A copy of your letter of surrender was sent to our commander by Darrow himself. Now, the army is fleeing. Surely, Sonnencrest will want revenge."

The king cursed Zindown's foolish ploy. It had backfired. All was lost.

Goblins began tiptoeing from the crowd.

Indeed, as the king looked through the gate, he saw horses pass, one here and another there, and then in groups without formation or order, a chaos of frightened riders sure to be followed by wagons and goblins on foot.

Silently, the king shivered with rage. Large wet stains appeared on his clothes.

The king charged into the palace, almost colliding with Bekkendoth.

"Where is Zindown? That mole-brained circus magician will pay for this blunder!"

Outside, the yard was almost empty.

"We have no time for Zindown, Your Highness," Bekkendoth replied. "We must leave right away."

But the king walked to the balcony and shouted, "Bring me Zindown."

A grim expression filled Bekkendoth's face. Darrow's army would soon be upon them. He looked out the gates. The road, once filled with riders, was now packed with wagons and carriages and even a few soldiers running on foot. In the distance, he saw plumes of smoke.

An attendant burst through the door.

"Zindown's carriage has arrived."

The king scrambled down the empty stairs. In the yard, only Bekkendoth and three soldiers remained. There stood the carriage, black with the green bat spider painted on the door. The driver was a statue, hunched over staring at his feet.

"Where is Zindown?" the king demanded.

The driver lifted his head.

"Zindown is gone."

But before the king could consider what it might mean, Bekkendoth was at his side, his hand on the king's shoulder, whispering, "We must leave. We are no longer safe."

"Bring the royal carriage," shouted the king.

"The royal carriage will make you a target. We must use another."

"My soldiers will protect me," the king insisted.

"Your Majesty, the soldiers are gone."

The king made no reply.

"Put him in Zindown's carriage," ordered Bekkendoth.

Two soldiers, holding the king's arms, guided him to the carriage door. The king shook as he walked. Then he turned back.

"A king rides in a royal carriage!" cried the king, his voice trembling. The servants looked back at Bekkendoth. Bekkendoth nodded and the servants shoved the king inside.

Now the king leaned through the window. "My crown! My jewels!"

"Your Highness, all the riches of the world will be no good if we do not escape."

But the king would not yield. So for twenty minutes, they waited while servants rushed inside to retrieve the crown and three large chests of treasure, all looted from the homes of Sonnencrest.

When the wagon was loaded, it pulled up to the gate and stopped. Bekkendoth looked out. A soldier ran by, his shirt stuffed with candlesticks. A goblin carrying a box of coins was stabbed in the back by another, who took the box as his own. The acrid smell of burning houses entered the carriage and the king launched into an uncontrollable cough.

Seeing the road ahead blocked with wagons and fleeing goblins, Bekkendoth wondered if escape was possible.

After a long time, the carriage jolted forward. In fits and starts, traffic began to move. When the first hour passed, they were almost a mile from the palace.

A sharp noise sounded from the side of the carriage. The king looked up, startled. Outside, three goblin soldiers waved swords.

"Out, you mud lizards. This carriage is ours."

"Go away," said Bekkendoth, peering from the window.

"Get out," one soldier replied, "or you will be dragging on a rope from behind."

Bekkendoth looked coolly back at the attackers. "The great wizard Zindown is inside," he replied. "Would you like me to convey your message?"

The soldiers scurried away.

A rider passed, screaming that Darrow's cavalry was coming up the road. Horsemen and foot soldiers scrambled from the road and into the woods. Others simply ran faster through the brush at the side.

Bekkendoth looked back. As far as the eye could see, wagons and goblins filled the road. How could Darrow advance? But the rumor cleared traffic. Now the carriage moved at a steady pace.

Another hour passed. The horses, which had pulled all day, no longer responded to the whip.

"Stop there at that farmhouse," Bekkendoth ordered.

While the driver threatened the farmer with his whip, Bekkendoth harnessed two fresh horses. They charged back into the road.

These new horses were good ones. Pastures and trees, now graying in the fading light, moved past the window at a rapid pace. Soon, there were no wagons at all, only riders who led the retreat. Bekkendoth took a slow, deep breath. Perhaps they would make it after all.

At twilight, the great pines appeared, separated by scrubby grass that lined the road on either side. The carriage lifted sand from the ground and Bekkendoth could taste salt in the air.

He looked across the carriage at the outline of the king. Loud snores echoed in the cabin. The carriage rocked with a slow, reassuring rhythm. Bekkendoth's eyelids were heavy. His head nodded. Soon, he was unconscious in his seat.

How long he slept, he couldn't tell. He was awakened by a loud banging on the side of the door. He lifted his head, eyes blinking against the light. For a moment, he struggled to remember where he was.

"Out of the wagon, you slimy louts!" cried a large, muscular man with a scar that ran from his neck to the top of his bald head. There was a ring in his nose.

"Out, I told you! Unless you wish to be carved alive by my own little dagger, the Red Princess."

"The princess!" cried the king, suddenly awake and confused.

"Shuddup in there, I tell you or I'll fill your wagon with blood!"

Bekkendoth pulled at the arm of the king and led him out the door. The glare of torches surrounded the carriage. To his left, he saw the moon reflected in a vast expanse of water. Then he cringed.

Across the road lay a pile of wreckage. There were saddles, weapons, and wagons, overturned and broken, their contents emptied on the ground. Amidst the rubble were bodies, dead goblins, scores of them, cut and disfigured in gruesome ways.

The king's own driver lay on the ground, a boot pressing the center of his chest. His eyes were shut tightly and he shivered.

From the torchlight, a man stepped forward. He was tall and thin with a scraggly, crooked beard. The light behind him made his face a dark shadow, but Bekkendoth could see a great gold chain on his neck that supported the largest emerald he had ever seen.

"Who are you, and why have you stopped my carriage?" stammered the king.

Bekkendoth shot the king a stern look. But the man just laughed, lifting his saber in the air.

"Ah, but the question you pose is backwards. Who are *you*, and what are *you* carrying in this carriage?"

Bekkendoth hung his head and answered in a low voice.

"I am a simple wheelmaker fleeing Sonnencrest. This man with me is the brother of a man who sells wagons to the king. He is wealthy. You can have his treasure. But be gentle; the man is disturbed." Bekkendoth paused. "He thinks he is the king."

The king began to protest, but Bekkendoth slapped him across the face. Stunned, the king quietly babbled to himself.

"Get on with it. Run them through!" shouted a voice behind a torch. But the pirate's sword was in no hurry.

"First, let's see how fine a storyteller this gentleman might be. Search the carriage."

Three men scrambled forward and began opening the doors and compartments inside.

"Three chests, big heavy ones!"

The trunks were removed and the men pried at them with their swords. A grand display of riches spilled out onto the ground. For a moment, the pirates could only stand and stare.

From the carriage door, another man appeared. In his hand, he held the crown of the king. Smiling broadly, he placed the crown atop his filthy, lice-ridden head.

"Well, well, well," said the pirate, eyes sparkling. "Perhaps he is king after all."

"I suppose that it is time for introductions, though our acquaintance may be brief. I am Telsinore, captain of the world-renowned Tarantula pirates."

Telsinore made a deep bow. As he lifted his body once again, he swept his sword backhanded across Bekkendoth, whose severed head dropped to the ground.

"The fate of the liar is cruel indeed."

Amidst a chorus of laughter, the king's eyes grew wide.

"And the driver?" said Telsinore calmly. The sword point thrust into his neck.

Telsinore looked at the king. He lifted his sword high. The king crouched, his arms covering his head. Just as Telsinore's sword quivered above the king, the old pirate lowered it unexpectedly to his side. The pirate laughed out loud.

"You know, I have fought many a duel but never with a king. It would be terrible to murder a great monarch without giving him a fair opportunity to fight. Don't you agree, boys?"

From beneath the torches erupted cheers, catcalls, and applause.

"Grab a sword and I will give you a sporting chance."

But the king stumbled backward against the carriage, desperately shaking his head.

"Grab a sword, I say."

The king shivered wordlessly before him.

"There, hanging from the side of the wagon, is a sword. Take it or I will saw off your toes."

The men laughed uproariously at this threat and this time the king looked up at Telsinore, still unable to speak. He turned to the wagon. Squinting so tightly he could barely see, he laid his trembling hand on the weapon that hung from its side.

As he touched the weapon, a strange calm entered his mind. His hand closed on the handle. Still shaking, but less than before, he lifted it from the wagon. As he did, the trembling stopped completely.

He looked at this strange weapon. It was light, so light it almost floated in the air. On its handle was a tiny yellow bird. Warily, he turned to face Telsinore.

The sight of the king holding a sword set the pirates laughing again.

"Careful, Telsinore, a mighty swordsman awaits," shouted one and the laughter that followed sent two rolling on the ground.

"So, you are going to make a fight of this?" Telsinore bellowed in a mocking voice. "I bet you trained under the finest swordsmen in all of Globenwald." More laughs.

"Have you nothing to say? A last request perhaps?"

The king stood silent and still.

"Well, we might as well begin, if you afford me no fun." And with those words, Telsinore swung his sword lightly in front of the king.

The king lifted his blade and brought Telsinore's weapon to a halt.

"A skillful defense, if I have ever seen one!" shouted Telsinore. Again, the pirate swung his sword, playfully, almost in jest. Again, the king parried the blow.

Telsinore swung once more, this time a little harder. The king responded, stilling his blow.

Now Malmut's eyes focused. His expression hardened. The shaking was gone. His knees bent and his body crouched; he waited for the next stroke.

But the next strike was hard and true as Telsinore brought his sword downward in a mighty stroke at the king's side. The king moved to his right and blocked.

Telsinore looked down at the king. The king looked back. And for the first time, the king smiled.

Telsinore moved boldly against the king. One after another, his strokes were hard and true. Each time, the king's sword was quicker in response.

A bright red color filled the pirate's face. He gripped his sword with both hands and swung diagonally, across the king's shoulder, with all his might. And when his blade struck the sword of the king, it shattered, scattering fragments through the air.

The king faced Telsinore, his smiled broadening. For the first time, he moved forward and attacked. Telsinore dodged and one of the pirates threw him a new blade.

Now Telsinore defended. As the astonished pirates looked on, the king, his sword flashing left and right, up and down, backed Telsinore around in a circle and drew blood from his left arm.

As the king advanced, Telsinore hastened his retreat, circling the edges of the torchlit ground. Moving like a man possessed, the king pressed Telsinore, hastening his retreat. From the debris of a wagon, Telsinore kicked a board directly into the king's path. When the monarch stumbled on the board, a pirate shoved him from behind.

Now Telsinore leered over the king. He thought for a moment of the war he had launched ten years ago. Telsinore smiled. This monarch had delivered him more riches than he had ever dreamed of. He admired the king's fight. So he spoke.

"My dear King Malmut, you have fought bravely and well. And mercy pays few rewards for a bandit of the sea. But there is something you must know.

"I killed Rildon. It was my trick that launched this war. Now, you have lost Sonnencrest and perhaps your kingdom as well.

"You stole my emeralds. Now I have done you much worse. So I will spare your life. Drop your sword and run. No one will follow."

The king's face reddened and he rose slowly from the ground. He hurled a fist full of sand directly into Telsinore's eyes. A split second later, the Sword of Darrow had brought Telsinore to the ground.

The king reeled to face the pirates. Stunned and disbelieving, they stood motionless, absorbing the sudden turn of events. Into the darkness, the king disappeared.

⌒⟋⟋⟍⟍℃

Malmut raced madly into the blackness of the night. On the uneven ground, he tripped and fell but each time scrambled desperately to his feet. He was surrounded by trees that blocked the moonlight and his head struck a branch. He fell backwards against a rock. When he rose, a sharp pain shot up to his shoulder and a terrible aching seized his wrist.

He saw the moon and he followed it to the water's edge. Not stopping to consider strategy or direction, he turned and ran down to the shore. He thought he saw the outline of a small boat. When he reached it, it was tied to a tree and barely large enough to hold two men.

His wrist ached terribly, but he lifted the sword and cut the rope. Into the boat he dove. Seeing the sword on the ground, he leaned over the bow to retrieve it. He cried out as he slipped, his broken wrist striking against the rail. Angrily, he hurled the sword into the grass.

His right hand could not grip the oar. So he nestled the oar in his elbow and began to pull. His strokes were feeble. At first, the boat merely rocked in place. But desperation made him stronger. The boat began to move. Across the channel lay Globenwald, an unseeable blackness two miles away.

The boat entered the channel. The tide was moving out to sea, tugging at the boat. He pulled harder against the oars. Faster, the boat moved. He heaved great breaths and his wheezing sounded across the silent sea. His arm ached. Sweat poured down his back and into the boat.

But in this ordeal, the king was lifted. For the first time ever, his fate would be decided by the strength of his own will.

Forward the boat surged. In the distance, he could make out the far shore. His boat moved midway through the channel, still nudged by the tide but pulled far more strongly by the king. He looked again and he knew. Globenwald was in reach.

The king marveled at the man he had become. Those who doubted him would see. He had slain the feared Telsinore. He had braved the sea. Everyone would know of his heroic deeds.

But as he reveled in these thoughts, the sky crackled above him. Lightning flashed across the heavens.

The king looked upward, fearing a storm. He pulled on his oars with new purpose, all but forgetting his pain. Again, the sky thundered, and this time the lightning struck the water and the sea exploded in a flash of silver. Wide-eyed, the king's strokes took on a frantic pace.

Measuring the coming storm, the king again looked into the heavens. A deep shudder rolled through his fame.

There, amidst the clouds, he saw the outlines of a face. It was a face he knew. The wizard Zindown stared down from above.

A new bolt of lightning flashed, followed by a brief explosion of fire. The king and his boat were gone. All that remained was a puff of smoke that floated slowly into the horizon.

⁊⁊⁊

Back on the highway, Telsinore lay bleeding and bandaged in a makeshift bed. The sword had taken its toll, but this pirate had more lives than a family of cats. Even magic could not do the deed.

A young pirate held a drinking cup to his lips. The old captain gulped his water greedily as the younger looked on.

After a long pause, the young pirate spoke.

"That king, he could have walked away. Why would he risk his life and refuse your offer?"

For a long time Telsinore looked into the sky and fingered his crooked beard. Then he spoke.

"Ah, there are passions that cause men to act in foolish ways. And indeed the king's vengeance has struck me a blow. But such men, blind to their own interests, are easy prey to the coldhearted scoundrel. So be glad of it, my friend," said Telsinore wistfully. "For nothing rewards the evildoer more than the hand of revenge."

· 43 ·

Scodo's Magic

Deep in the forests of Globenwald, not far from the palace of the king, stood a small castle. It was hidden amidst the trees, far from the road, with only a small path leading the way to its door. No moat guarded this castle. Instead, a necklace of thorns, black and the height of small trees, circled its walls.

Its entrance, a door bearing the image of a bat spider, stood high behind twenty stone steps. On the bottom step sat a figure, no more than a shadow on this starless night.

With the morning, a figure came striding up the path. He was tall with a flowing black robe and a long black walking stick, beautifully carved. He walked proudly, his steps large and forceful. When he arrived, he looked down at the visitor seated before him.

"Why, Scodo, what a surprise!"

"You must be used to them by now."

The scorpion man rose to his feet and stood directly before the wizard. Zindown laughed out loud.

"Ah, Scodo, I suppose you did not read the surrender. All goblins receive safe passage home."

"I read it," Scodo shot back. "There is not a word about wizards."

Zindown spun into the air, howling in laughter.

"But a wizard needs no protection, even from the wrath of the great scorpion man!"

With those words, Zindown hurled a great ball of fire at Scodo's feet and the ground burst into flames. But Scodo, shoeless, his skin exposed, walked directly into the fire and emerged from the other side, glaring up at Zindown, his body smoking, his scales blackened, his expression unchanged.

Zindown laughed again. He vanished from the sky and appeared on the ground. He reached down and picked up a rock. As he hurled the rock at Scodo with all his terrible might, the rock became ten rocks. Scodo lifted his sword to protect himself but the rocks struck on his face and body with loud thuds.

Still, Scodo stood unmoving, scales broken and hanging loosely from his frame. Blood trickled down his legs. He looked back at Zindown and spoke, "Really, Zindown, is that the best you can do?"

Zindown knew Scodo possessed no magic, for in the desert he had visited Scodo's mind. He knew he could slay Scodo at that very moment. But first, he wanted to take some measure of the pleasure Darrow's victory had taken away. In a flash, he appeared in front of Scodo.

"There, there, Scodo. Why don't you just put an end to me right now?"

Scodo thrust his sword forward, but his motion had barely begun when Zindown was gone. He reappeared ten feet away, a little to the left. Suddenly, Scodo's body was engulfed in flames. Scodo cringed with pain but spoke not a word.

"Quicker, Scodo." He howled with laughter. "You must be quicker."

Scodo picked up a rock at his feet and hurled it at Zindown.

With the rock in midair, Zindown disappeared. In what seemed the same instant, he reappeared, this time further to Scodo's left, almost within reach of his sword. But when Scodo jabbed, Zindown was not there but in a new place far to the right. Laughing, he vanished again, reappearing, not quite in front of Scodo but about eight feet back and still a little to his right. He reached down and flung a handful of sand with the force of a tornado.

Scodo trembled. The sand delivered a terrible sting and blood poured from his wounds. But he still didn't speak, because all this time Scodo's mind was at work.

He remembered the long ride across the desert and how Babette had talked of wizards and the tricks they performed. He remembered Babette saying that wizards do not disappear at all but move from place to place with blinding speed. Scodo realized that he could never strike the wizard where he stood because the wizard was too fast. But if he could aim his throw to where the wizard would appear next, then perhaps his sword might reach its mark.

Scodo took two steps forward and spoke, looking deep into Zindown's eyes.

"Oh mighty Zindown, I am only a creature and not even a man. But my hands are quick. Surely, you will give me yet another chance to strike you dead."

Zindown laughed so loudly that the trees shook and the door of the castle rattled against the stone. Suddenly he stood before Scodo—directly in front, within reach of his sword. Again, Scodo lunged with his weapon, and in a flash Zindown appeared back and a little to his left, exactly as before. A large rock struck Scodo in the face, almost knocking him to the ground.

Scodo staggered in place, afraid he might fall. He lifted his head, looked at Zindown, and recalled Babette's explanation of how wizards disappear by moving rapidly in a pattern from place to place. He concentrated, determined to work out the pattern so that he could catch Zindown unawares.

He hurled another rock, eager to see where Zindown might appear. His memory told him that Zindown would next appear a little more to the left, a few feet further back. That was exactly where Zindown appeared, howling in laughter, mocking his pathetic foe.

Trembling, Scodo struggled to collect his strength. Now, he knew the pattern. Now he knew where Zindown would next appear.

"Please, oh mighty Zindown, please give me one more chance." Zindown laughed yet again.

As he did, Scodo lifted his sword as if to stab at Zindown's image but instead he pivoted and threw his sword with such wondrous force that the leaves on the trees rustled in awe.

The sword arrived just as Zindown appeared. It struck him straight in the heart. The wizard crumpled dead on the ground.

Scodo stood and stared at his vanquished foe.

Scodo had never understood the deep hatred he felt for the old wizard. He never learned that it was Zindown's spell that made him a monster at birth. But he did know, better than Babette or Darrow or any other, that the kingdom of Sonnencrest would never be safe as long as Zindown was alive.

Dark clouds formed in the sky. Lightning rattled across the horizon. With Zindown's death, his spells were broken. All at once, a thousand acts of terrible magic were undone.

As Scodo stood motionless beneath the trees, the scales fell from his skin. His tail snapped from his body and dropped to the ground, withering away until it disappeared into dust. The claws dropped from his toes and his feet took on a new shape. His head, that terrible insect head, dropped its shell and reshaped itself with new features, all covered with smooth skin and dark black hair. When the changes were finished, he bore not the slightest resemblance to the monster who had stood in his place only moments before.

But Scodo did not cry out in joy. His mind was in a place far away. Quietly, he looked at Zindown's corpse and he began to think. He thought of his parents and his friend Hugga Hugga and, of course, of Babette, who cared for him so much. And he felt the power of goodness grow inside of him.

He thought of the tormentors, the mockers, the taunters, and all who turned from him in horror. He found understanding for their actions and he gave them forgiveness and love. Once again, deep inside, his power grew.

He thought of the mob that hunted him in the forest and killed his parents. He felt compassion for their fears and love for their souls. And now a raging, burning, exhilarating power filled his body and flowed almost violently out of his fingers and his toes.

Now, he looked down at his greatest enemy and most evil foe. He gazed upon Zindown with sad eyes. He wondered of how it must have felt to carry the heavy burden of so many evil deeds. He ached with pity for the old wizard. He hoped in the afterlife or in some life to come that Zindown might rescue his soul and perform good and wonderful deeds. Looking down at the corpse, he did the one thing he was never before able to do. He gave the wizard his compassion, his forgiveness, and his love.

Now his body trembled with awesome power and that power demanded its release.

He recalled Babette's instructions and knew he needed words to express the magic that burned within. He searched for the most beautiful memories of life and his mind went straight to his mother who, throughout his whole childhood, never once looked at him with anything but adoring eyes. And he remembered the day he asked her if he was indeed a monster.

"No, my love, you are the most beautiful child of all. It is we your parents who have been cursed because we do not look like you. You carry the beauty of the *vianu* in your soul." That word, *vianu*, meant peace. It meant beauty. It meant love.

When Scodo heard this word leaving his mother's lips, he knew he had the only language he would ever need.

For a short moment, he looked back at his life—at the fighting, at the killing—and he felt the burden of his deeds lift from his soul. He took his sword in his still-powerful hands and walked to the steps of Zindown's castle where he placed it on the stone.

With all his concentration, he lifted the power from his body, and he felt great elation, as if his very spirit had rocketed far into the heavens above. For a few minutes, he reveled in these feelings and marveled at these forces that raged so beautifully inside him. Then he turned to face the sword.

He tightened his fists and extended them in front of his body. He was exploding inside. The force was so great that he feared it might tear him apart. He pulled his fists tighter, and with all of the enormous concentration of his mind, he stared directly at the sword.

"Vianu."

A great flash of light exploded over the rock. The sword, a large, heavy weapon as tall as a small man, broke into thousands of tiny pieces, which rained down on the castle and its grounds. When the light was gone, all that remained on the rock was a small smattering of metallic dust. Across the ground, the remnants of his weapon sparkled like diamonds in the sun.

Scodo's life was freed of weapons, but that was only the beginning. Released from the hatred he had carried through his life, he smiled, a great and gentle smile that covered his new face. It was a handsome face, as handsome as the face of any man in all of Sonnencrest.

· 44 ·

A Free Sonnencrest

The late summer sun baked the road, the grass was brown, and a haze of dust hovered above the road. But the heat could not quell what filled the hearts of the citizens of Sonnencrest. Along the road to Blumenbruch, they gathered and waited for the moment when Darrow and his army would pass.

When the army arrived, they lifted homemade banners, blue and yellow, sewn in the late evening hours and hung from sticks and poles. With one hand, mothers handed bread to the men. With the other, they held back children who tugged with all their might, hoping to break free and march behind.

And indeed, men and women alike joined in the march and soon it was less an army and more a procession of joyous folk, young and old, men and women, heading to Blumenbruch to celebrate the great victory.

In the city itself, every house stood empty as the people gathered in the streets to greet the arrival of the great man. As the first soldiers arrived at the edge of town, the crowd pushed close and Darrow, finding no path through the crowd, mounted a horse, and led his procession in single file, weaving back and forth like a bright, tiny thread in a great tapestry.

When they finally arrived at the gates of the palace, the mayor stood waiting. He bowed deeply before Darrow and with great ceremony he opened the way, allowing Darrow to enter the palace grounds. As Darrow stepped inside, there were no leaves or rubbish on the ground and the dirt was marked with the tracks of a hundred brooms. The walls of the palace had been scrubbed clean, flowerpots stood in the windows, and everywhere banners of blue and gold were proudly displayed. Those who waited inside looked intently at Darrow, hoping that he would approve.

But Darrow hardly noticed. As he looked up at the great castle with its tall stone towers, he blinked. His eyes had never seen a building so grand. For a moment, he stopped, taking in the beautiful stonework and he wondered if the winter wind seeped through the stones like it did in Ael.

But there was no time for wonderment. The mayor grasped him by the arm and pulled him ahead, into the palace, up the stairs, and out onto the balcony where Henry X and his family were last seen. From the gates, the people poured in, and soon a great crowd waited beneath him. They stood on barrels, sat in wagons, and jostled for position across the great walls. Not an inch of ground stood vacant.

While he waited, Darrow thought back to where his journey had begun. He recalled his first steps from Ael, limping his way to faraway places he could hardly imagine. He remembered when the sword fell from his hands at Frenngravel Creek and he saw Naark's body lying on the ground. Who was he, he wondered, to deserve this adulation? But at that moment, in an almost dreamlike state, he saw his mother. She looked at him without speaking, but seeing her face told him all was well.

The crowd roared for their hero. And when Darrow spoke, his words were so inspiring and beautiful that throughout the kingdom of Sonnencrest they would be quoted for centuries to come.

◎〰◎

One week after Darrow's triumphant march into Blumenbruch, the people filled the streets once more. The long-lost princess, the only surviving heir to the throne of Henry X, had returned. A week later, she was crowned queen.

Her coronation began with a great parade. Her long curly hair, somewhere between yellow and red, bounced as she waved through the window of her carriage. The carriage moved slowly, but after a block or two, Babette opened the door and stepped out to greet the startled crowd. She walked slowly among them touching, embracing, and offering gentle words. The once-eccentric little girl now moved with grace and poise. From her manner, the people of Sonnencrest sensed right away that she was an unusual leader of deep goodness, who would protect the peace and bring prosperity to their land.

Within a month of her coronation, Queen Babette did something that shocked her kingdom. Against the warnings of every royal advisor, she journeyed to Globenwald. Among the goblins, her visit was greatly feared. Surely, she came to threaten conquest and demand reparations. But when she met the new goblin king, she instead offered him a gift.

She brought artisans and stone carvers, who built a monument to honor the goblins who had died in her land. When the monument was unveiled, the goblins were deeply moved and there was much weeping and rejoicing. Queen Babette's visit forged a great friendship with the new goblin king and began a long era of peace.

⟨⟩

One year after Darrow entered Blumenbruch, a third celebration gripped the kingdom. In the great cathedral of the capital city, Queen Babette was to be wed.

Waiting for the queen, dressed in a great white robe, was Asterux, whose responsibility it was to give her away. And upon seeing Babette, so beautiful in her wedding dress, Asterux, who had never married and had no children of his own, knew at once all of the deep emotions of a father on his daughter's wedding day.

Babette gave Asterux a great hug. He offered his arm and waited for the music to begin. But at that moment, the queen gave a low whistle. Yellow birds, Annisan Serenaders all, burst into the church and offered a song so beautiful that the orchestra dared not interrupt. When their song died and the music began, Babette and Asterux walked slowly down the aisle to meet the groom.

Asterux gave Babette's hand to the groom, and the couple knelt before the priest.

"Do you, Babette, take this man to be your lawfully wedded husband, to love and to cherish, in sickness and in health, until death do you part?"

Babette said, "I do."

The priest turned to the groom and began, "And do you, Scodo, take this woman . . . ?" When the question was complete, Scodo turned and replied, "I do."

Babette and Scodo lived long and happy lives and had many children. Babette ruled Sonnencrest with great wisdom. But Scodo, disdaining the palace life, learned the skills of a carpenter and spent his days in the kingdom building houses for the poor.

Sometimes, at birthday parties, Queen Babette would delight their children with a marvelous magic show. She would whistle mysterious sounds and wondrous events would unfold. The children would squeal with excitement and it was all great fun. But Scodo, standing nervously to the side, would loudly remind the children that "the hand is quicker than the eye."

Under Queen Babette's rule, Hugga Hugga and Timwee held positions in the army, and their deeds were celebrated each year on a special holiday honoring their service. Over the years, Hugga Hugga gave rides and played with the children of Babette and Scodo. For a while, Thor and Moakie moved to the palace, and Thor became the royal blacksmith. But palace life was not for him and he and Moakie soon returned to the mountains.

∽∭∾

But what of Darrow?

Before the palace stand two great statues. One is the likeness of Sir Fenn, whose goodness founded the nation. The other is of Darrow, whose courage to believe restored its freedom. Darrow was chosen as the Grand General of the Sonnencrest army. But after his great early adventures, he grew bored with running an army in so peaceful a land. One day, he retired from the army and wrote a book.

His book is the story of a girl, tall and strong, who wielded a great sword. She sought to free her land from invaders. But while the girl possessed vision and cunning, she was shy and spoke poorly before crowds. In the forest lived a young prince, a magician, who helped her find the words, inspire her countrymen, and bring freedom to the land.

The book closes with these words:

There are no true heroes. They are ordinary persons, perhaps possessed of some skill or another, lifted by people who need to believe that somewhere, someone possesses a magic that can rewrite the future and leave them in a better place. These heroes have no magic of their own. But the belief in the hero, true or not, allows each of us to become larger than we are. For it unlocks the true and powerful magic that lies in our very own hearts.

Acknowledgements

The authors would like to thank the following friends who read early drafts of the book and whose comments both improved the story and encouraged us to pursue publication: Eduado Cavalcanti, Ryan Coughlin, Matthew Dooman, Sam Dooman, Skyler Leonard, Liam Barclay, Lukas Eigler-Harding, Elizabeth Rosenbaum, Elizabeth Pankova, and Noah Tunador.

Reviewers

ALABAMA
Abbey Johns
Abigail Ketchem
Aisley Chapman
Alexander Roman
Austin Richerson
Brayden Moore
Camryn Banks
Chloe Adkins
Clayton McCown
Connor Ferguson
Corey Mitchell
Daniel Bracker
Dawson Savage
Dee Taylor
Devin Burke
Emma Kate Gramling
Erin K. Ellis
Gianna McDowell
Heleena Stamaris
Jacob L. West
James Jeffers
James Marsh
Jennifer Pate
Kelby Wilson
Kessler Tharp
Kyle Sloane
Landon Craig
Landry Tharp
Leighton Riley
Lillie Harris
Mackenzie Holtcamp
Madison Cotton
Max Kearley
Megan Saalwaechter
Michael Belcher
Nevaeh Tigue
Peityn Dishaw

TJ Lander
Trey Hamilton
Youri Ferraro
Zachary Montgomery

ALASKA
Ethan Armendariz
Jonathan McBroom
Joshua Andrews
Katherine Fox

ARIZONA
Andrew Chambless
Abigail Whitlock
Alex Cox
Alex Ivey
Alexander N Burstrem
Alexis Lanni
Alexis N. Say
Andrew Bell
Anelise Cunning
Angelia Rose Bautista
Ashlin Bradford
Baxter Bruce
Brian Lynch
Catriana Murty
Chloe Cobb
Chloe Twombly
Christopher Todd Jr.
Colin Morris
Cortlyn A. Elton
Devon Black
Dylan Clark
Dylan Sikes
Eli Kitch
Elizabeth
 Vicoryosmanson
Ella Gerardo

Ellie Robbins
Emily Hilton
Emma Kennedy
Emma Lowe
Erin Benites
Ethan Anderson
Fletch Fangman
James L. Cosby III
Jaycie Anderson
Jessica Stringer
Jon Witthoft
Joseph Gonzalez
Joseph Poznecki
Joshua Hilton
Julian Carter Carvalho
Kaitlin Slusher
Katelyn Robert
Kendra Mongeon
Kymberleigh Shepherd
Lauren Clark
Levi Barker
Lily Sandoval
Logan McCallum
Madison Kurko
Madison Uber
Max Walker
Mystery Finley
Nathan Catanach
Neil R. Banerjee
Nicholas Dodt
Nicolas Hort
Owen Buck
Peyton Humbert
Robert Whitlock
Ryan Corrigan
Sage Cutler
Sami Lin Ortiz
Sarah Gee

REVIEWERS

Scarlett Nelson Melle
Starr Secor
Sydney Cash
Tatiana Corbitt
Tatiana Corbitt
Taylor Doran
Travis Davenport
Trevor Buck
Walker Kitch
Zachary Gurrola
Zane Walker
Nicole Potter

ARKANSAS
Alyssa Morgan
Amber Marler
A'Meisia Hampton
Andrea Wright
Bobby Joe Phillips IV
Cameron Flanery
Cameron Walderns
Cheyenne Keck
Cory Parsons
Dylan Hicks
Ethan Amos
Heath Moore
Ian Corder
James Engle
Jodie Seaborn
Justin T. Webb
Katie Vonderheide
Lily Williams
Lindsey Keck
Madison Prescott
Makayla Parsons
Mayme Mosteller
Melissa Besaw
Nathan Spears
Ruby Trinidad
Simon Tursky
Tally W. Richmond
Taylor Clayton

Tyler Manning
Zach Tarver

CALIFORNIA
Abigail Ibarrola
Adam Davis McMorris
Adeline Ennis
AJ Juarez
Akhia Triplett
Alex Paloma
Alexander Kessler
Alexandra Singer
Alexandria Gille
Alora Duran
Amanda Badger
Amanda Lund
Amber Holloway
America Arellano
Andrea Ramirez
Andy Suh
Angelina Aldama
Angelina Oseguera
Anna Horrocks
Antonio Ibarrola
Asher Jamil
Ashley Palacios
Ashlyn Healey
Ashton Potts
Athena Lily Stanfield
  Caile
Austin Salyers
Azar Richards
Bella Deguilio
Blake Sorensen
Braden M. Wu
Bradley Otherson
Brayden Dawson
Bree Myers
Brendan Su
Brett Damkroger
Bryan Juarez
Bryan Ontiveros

C.M. Juarez
Cailyn Araiza
Cameron Britt
Cameron Rishel
Cameron Rix
Camron Herrera
Ceira Sponenburg
Cenjay Davis
Chad Thomas
Chaim Weinberg
Charles Robertson
Chazz Dial
Christian Palmquist
Christine Davis
Cody Olivo
Cole Duman
Colton Nelson
Connor Winter
Cozette Ming
Cristian Camargo
Cristian Castro
Damian Montreuil
Darren Lee
David A. Silver Jr.
David Eaton
David M. Gogue
Derek Byrd
Destiny Galloway
Devin Hogate
Devon Warrington
Dominic Bailer
Dominick Korenthal
Efren Meraz
Elias Ellery Ortiz
Elijah Call
Emelie Moya
Emerson Lee
Emily E. Stone
Emily Volpone
Erika Wilson
Erin B. Wu
Esly Preciado

REVIEWERS

Frederick Cuneo
Gabe St. John
Gabe Elton
Genesis Taylor
Brennan Gillon
Gino Barba
Hannah Owens
Hannah Schoenrock
Harmony Turner
Ian Kelsey
Victor-Antonio
  Robertson
Isabella Marquez
Isaiah Call
Isaiah Webb
Izabella Villalvazo
Jacob Gibson
Jacob Heaton
Jacob Richards
Jacob Robertson
Jaden Renner
Jake Paulson
James Reinaga
James Yang Jr.
Jared Lee
Jason Yeh
Jayden Brown
Jayson Hall
Jenna Corryn Lawton
Jeremy Walters
Jimmy Call
John Austin
John Villalvazo
Jordyn Fahey
Joseph Bartoni
Joshua Amador
Joshua Kortje
Julia Teymouri
Julian Costilla
Julianna Travierso
Kailee Smith
Kaitlyn Bean

Kaitlyn Christine Scadina
  Mansfield
Kaitlyn Todd
Kallysta Tyler
Katie Davis
Kayla Cunningham
Kayleigh Pollard
Keith Garver
Kelly Otherson
Kendal England
Kenneth Rangel
Kerragan Guilliatt
Kevan Baird
Kevin Humphrey
Kylie Stockard
Leah Van Well
Leon Tanguay
Levi Murtaugh
Lexi Huddleston
Liam Fallon
Liberty Landrus
Lindsey Thomas
Logan Tree
Lola Kanester
Luis Marrufo
Luke Ernst
Lusas Engwall
Maddie Reese
Madison Boling
Madison Hirst
Maile Di Paolo
Majdi Rayyan
Makoi Netane
Malaika N. Buhlmann
Marcus Gaona
Maria Mirza
Marlie De Troya
Mason Hirst
Matias Moreno
Matthew Dugan
Max Myers
Megan McDaniel

Miae Cho
Mialy Rasetarinera
Michael Chu
Michael Ito
Michael Ringgold
Mikey Call
Mitchell Holloway
M.L. Streutker
Natalie Wang
Nathaly Munoz
Nathanael Chow
Navya Mishra
Neo Amadeus Price
Nic Church
Nicholas Middelberg
Nicholas Truong
Nicholas Wells
Nicky Caldwell
Nina McAdoo
Nolan Belanger
Paola Arellano
Payton Huhtala
Peter Beardsley
Peter Chau
Phyllis Battaglia
Piper Hatton
Rachael Rickling
Rachel Warner
Renee Lemont
Ria Kelsey
Robert Evans
Roman Casillas
Ryan Buchanan
Ryan Doerr
Sam Bernstein
Sam Duman
Samantha Justinich
Samantha Lewis
Samantha Travierso
Samuel Turner-Stakes
Sasha Cooper
Serenity Wood

REVIEWERS

Seth Murray
Shawn Bradbury
Siena Pamplona Villegas
Signa Mascot
Simon Haswell
Skye St. John
Spencer Stone
Starr St. John
Stephen Calhoun
Stephen Jan
Steven Christopher
  Otherson
Sydney Garcia
Talon Mahosky
Tanner Kearl
Tatianna Calhoun
Taylor Hospodarec
Terri Goad
Timothy Youngman
Tre Presidente
Trent Coppa
Trevor Alexander Smith
Tucker Dunbar
Tyler Benedict
Tyler Koenigsberg
Tyler Sanders
Vanessa Vega
Willow Mina
Zachary Casillas
Zachary Fletcher
Zachary Winter
Zoe Toves
Zoecyn Priwer

COLORADO

Abigail Maria Andrade
Alexa Rath
Alexander Caswell
Alyssa Roberts
Amelia Stevens
Angel Y. Rodriguez
Ashley Faith Larson

Benjamin Suparat
Braeden Shively
Brayden Maroney
Brennan Watts
Brock Herring
Caleb Cline
Camlin Ames
Chloe Meyer
Chloe Williams
Devin Alton
Duncan Brasa
Emma Claire Zeiler
Hunter Brown
Jack Sheeder
Jacob Burge
Jacqueline Herring
Jaden Quillen
Jamie Forde
Jaret Roberts
Joey Huston
Joseph Prindle
Julia Archuleta
Kacy Addison Moen
Kaius Fox Damata
Kalob Lincoln McConnell
Kelsey-Jo Thibodeau
Kyra Correa
Luke Dickinson
Madelyn Crowley
Madison Bradshaw
Marcus Tyler Catlett
McKenna Schafer
Megan Engel
Michael Uchida
Mikaela Matzen
Miles Louison
Natalie Rose Thompson
  Ivaniszek
Nathan Meyer Jr.
Neiomi Rodriguez
Noah Crowley
Reagan Webster

Riley Vallot
Ryan Huston
Sonja Singelstad
Taryn McGraw
Taylan Shively
Trevor Butcher
Trevor Smith
Tyler R. Lindblad
Wesley Herring
Zachary Bolyard

CONNECTICUT

Alex Dallen
Alexa Stinson
Alexander Kent Seese
Alexander Preble
Alysha DeGennaro
Amelia Henriques
Amy Garceau
Anthony Martino
Caleb Leventhal
Caleb Rollins
Chris Centurelli
Claudia Victorino
Elisabeth Brockman
Eric Ciskowski
Erik Rosati
Gerald Camp
Hailey Anne Strom
Jeffrey Bowman
John Kronenberg III
Joseph Santese
Kaya Pascucci
Lanie Barnett
Lindsay Salvati
Maddie Mason
Mathew Pierce
Megan Ory
Michael Melillo
Mr. Kahn Carter
Nasarel George
Nicolas Brockman

REVIEWERS

Nicole Cislo
Noah Stone Pereira
Nyshant George
Samantha Barter
Samuel Posner
Simon Neal
Timmy Engstrom
Timmy Longueira
Tony Longueira
Trevor MacGinitie
Whitney Grace
  Hathaway
Xavier Joseph Rivas

DELAWARE
Cassidy Cornish
Elisabeth King
Jessica Price
McKenna Seitelman
Nicholas James Istenes
Noah Wydeven
Tasneem Bootwala
Zane Rego

DISTRICT OF
  COLUMBIA
Graham Roberts
River Jordan Yearwood

FLORIDA
Alec Gobel
Alex Brown
Alexa Laxton
Alexei Mattson
Alissa Darling
Allison Davies
Allison Davies
Alyssa 'Ally' Scott
Alyssa Main
Alyx Nicole Harrison
Amanda Stevens
Aminata Thiam

Anaiah Lugo
Andrew Rosebrock
Andrew Urso
Andy Pradilla
Angelina Nguyen
Anna Dickinson
Anthony Venezia
Ashley Smith
Aspen Reyes
Audrey Shuler
Autumn Ragan
Bailey Woolverton
Barbara Kate Schmitz
Benjamin Dobbins
Bianca Dvorsky
Blake Brennan
Bradley Batdorf
Breanne Hopkins
Brianna Manfredi
Brooklyn Armstrong
Bryce Herrera
Byron W.R. Lorton
Cameron Kocan
Carmine Guerra
Carson Gould
Chloe Gabrielle Oakes
Chloe Oliver
Christian Foshie
Christian Maldonado
Christian V Torres
Christian Walsted
Ciara Rubie
Claire Garill
Clara Schwall
Clayton Annis
Collin Clay
Collin Johnson
Connor Smith
Courtney Kreisler
Courtney Urban
Cristian Jumelles
Dallan Cox

Damian and Dayton
Damian Mark
Danielle Snyder
Danny A. Rogers
Daphne Eguidin
Dayton Southall
Dru Thompson
Dylan Galin
Dylan Worley
Elexious Childs
Elliana Gamb
Emily Bohannon
Emily Del Negro
Emily Hitaffer
Emily Payne
Emily Thompson
Emiy Mills
Emma Oberle
Eric Moser
Ethan Anthony Mapes
Evan Wilk
Gabriella Fawell
Gabriella Marcisak
Garret Johnson
Garrett Wynn
Gatlin Tomanek
Grace Barcza
Grace Messemer
Gregory Smalley
Hailey Alysa Dean
Haley Keane
Hannah McLaren
Hector Sanchez
Henry Tibble
Hunter Ryan
Jaclyn Briskin
Jacob Bishop
Jacob Elder
Jacob Fantauzzi
Jacob Foster
Jacob Rodriguez
Jacobe Bell-Miller

REVIEWERS

Jake Becker
Jake Schmitz
JaQuesta Adams
Jared Suarez
Jessica Graham
Jevin Johnson
Joanna Duhigg
Joey Sendra
John Beiser
Jonah Robert Fink
Jonah Smith
Jordan Tucker
Kaitlyn Thompson
Kaleah Shaarda
Kaleb Mapes
Kambree Dalton
Katelyn Rogers
Katelynn Hatfield
Katie Beason
Kelsey Winiarski
Kireina Kates
Kole Badeaux
Krystal Stewart
Krystal Torres
Kurt Nochowicz
Kyle Woolley
Lane Wilber
Lauren Spradlin
Liliana Pita
Lillian Childs
Lindsey Dale
Liv Thompson
Logan Armstrong
Logan Gagne
Lucas Compton
Madeleine Chitty
Madison Mills
Madison Percey
Malachi Potts
Matt Scarborough
Matthew Hart
Max Olander

Megan Meerleveld
Mia Evans
Michael Nieves
Michaela Shimer
Mikey Bychek
Mischa Groner
Mr. Charles Hoe
Nalanie Gayle
Nathan Hyde
Nicholas Maycumber
Nicolas Suarez
Noah Carrier
Nolan Drake
Olivia Cicco
Olivia Long
Orion Tighe
Rachel Elizabeth Muller
Rachel Ramos
Raul Ros
Raymond Martinez
Rayven Caitlin Toonk
Rebecca Zeno
Regan Chamberlain
Remy Searfoss
Rheana Martinez
Riley Graham
Ryan Concannon
Samantha J. Siwiec
Sammy Bookhardt
Samuel McAnally
Sara Hostelley
Savannah Kiwacz
Sean Cutter Dimotta
Sebastian Stevenson
Serenity Ahr
Shane Cote
Shannon Hill
Shelby Suarez
Skylar Oney
Skylar T. Jay
Spencer Newcombe
Stephanie Bell

Steven Stewart
Sydney Hostelley
Sydney Smallwood
Tayden Serr
Taylor Cote
Taylor Liverman
Thomas Tomanek
Tiffany Dobbins
Timothy Rocha
Timothy Russell
Tricia Means
Tristan Thacker
Tristian E. Rivera
  Marquez
Tyler Pastor
Victoria Blount
Victoria Ritt
Wade Twyford
Wynter Ragan
Yan Michael Epps
Yesenia Ivelese
Zachariah Kopstad

GEORGIA

Aaron Rieck
Abbigail Hayes
Aiden Bailey
Alamanda Mooney
Alexis Crawford
Alma Cuellar
Amaya A. McFadden
Amina Glass
Annalisa Sookar
Anniston Hall
Arabella Barnes
Ari Miller
Ariel Johnson
Asia Curtis
Audrey Jenkins
Brandon Connor Bass
Brandon Pocchio
Brendan Sigmund

Bria Butler
Brittany Mooney
Caitlyn Blanchard
Caitlyn Rogers
Caitlyn Wigington
Cameron Balli
Carlie Hendrix
Cathleen Hill
Charlie Faramarzi
Chloe Hendrix
Christian Jesse Robinson
Christina Skipper
Christina Wetherbee
Connor Bell
Connor Dyer
D'Asia Funches
Dalton Skipper
Damien Andrews
Danielle Alderman
Dawson Corey Mills
Destiny Harrington-
  Young
Drew Walker
Elizabeth Hamrick
Ellisa Dove
Emily Mospan
Emma And Mary
  Axelson
Emma Wilson
Ethan Faulkner
Evan Shadoff
Gabriel J. Mendez
Gabriel Mavromatidis
Garrett Stigall
Graham Hammontree
Hannah Cline
Hannah Neissel
Hannah Simmons
Holly Ahlquist
Ian Phillip Stuckey
Isabel Herrick
Izzy Brown

Jack Freund
Jack Travis
Jacob Boronczyk
Jacob Elswick
Jake Zemansky
Jala Smith
James Hood
James 'Jimmy' Sokol
Jenna Hauser
Jeremy Burton
Jeremy Mavromatidis
Jocelyn Thomas
Jordan Moore
Jordyn Nahass
Josephine Hightower
Justin Boutwell
Kaylin King
Kelsey Whitehead
Kenna Weber
Kevin Carver
Koi Peters
Kristofer Carpenter
Kylie Geller
Lauren Patterson
Lexie Hargrave
Liam Christian
Liam Gargano
Madison Freund
Madison Mermelstein
Makenzie Boremi
Mary Butker
Michael Bodin
Mikah Harper
Miss Ty Price
Mitchell Palmer
Morgan Alexander
Naia Vincent
Nathan Zappulla
Nieko Ward
Noah Adams
Noah Glenn Grillo
Noah Harris

Raj Patel
Raven Hepler
Rebecca Elswick
Rebecca Faulkner
Riley Caldwell
Riley Swab
Ryan Trull
Sam Cross
Sam Mckinney
Samuel Mendez
Sarah Clark-Henderson
Shayla Fullwood
Spencer Sigmund
Steven Thompson Jr.
Sumer Crapps
Taelah Oliver
Tanner Hillman
Taylor Mckinney
Tracey Williams
Victoria Yanez
William & Matthew
  Blanchard
Zane Roberson
Zyan Allen

HAWAII
Ariana Fletter
Austin Rogers
Austin Sprague
Caleb Cameron
Jonah Dilliner
Kawika Akutagawa
Olivia Kedrowski

IOWA
Abigail Hammer
Aidan Feldman
Alex Cline
Alexis Moellers
Alexis Strait
Alexxis Foreman
Alyssa Fowler

REVIEWERS

Alyssa Oberfoell
Amelia Balk
Andrew Casady
Andrew Hill
Andrew Oleson
Austin Witten
Ava Grace Osterhaus
Bailey Massa
Bayleigh Hughson
Blake Richards
Brianna Carlson
Caitlin M. Kline
Camden Paul Boyde
Cassie N Kline
Cassie N. Kline
Connie Eddy
David Warrington
Destiny Schwartz
Drew Snyder
Emily Follmuth
Emily J. Hammer
Erik Ramker
Evan Balk
Gage Zabel
Haily Collins
Hunter Xavier Kennedy
Jackson Shoars
Jade Peterson
Jeremy Smith
Jesse Vandeusen
Jordan Combes
Katie Hirv
Kaylee Eick
Kennedy Bombei
Kyla Wilson
Lexie O'Brien
Logan Combes
Madesyn Michelle
  Flenker
Makaela Richards
Mercedes 'Sadie' Mathes
Micaela Ariel Dennis

Palmer Robbins
Quentin Seger
Rebecca Sparandeo
Rhianna Maakestad
Ryan Byrd
Seamus Raney
Seth Hanson
Spencer Rose-Tolstedt
Wyatt Wolford
Wynter Knowler
Zach Kreider

IDAHO

Abbey Teeter
Abbigail Horne
Aiden Rojas
Amanda Benningfield
Andrew Radford
Brandon Woltkamp
Brianna Fernandez
Caly Thurston
Channa Beaton
Chuck Tatman
Daniel Hastie
Daniel Philippi
Emily Long
Jade Ingram
Jaren Palmer
Jay Alex McArthur
Jenna Bodily
Joshua Ursenbach
Katrina Clark
Keegan Ashley
Kristopher Heimgartner
Logan Daniels
Madison Olds
Madison Richmond
  Walker
Malachi Witherwax
McKell Hendricks
Nathan Jackson
Trent Daniels

ILLINOIS

Aaron David Cohen
Aaron Tandy
Abigail Akers
Abigail Gray
Adam Bougher
Aidan Fitzpatrick
Aidan Meier
Aidan Petroshus
Allie Sofolo
Amber Dellacqua
Amber Moore
Anand Shah
Anas Ouri
Angela Isom
Angela Langys
Angelica Leal
Angelina Ivy
Angelina Pancottine
Anna Wagner
Ashari Means
Ashley Shelton
Austin Alexander
  Mendez
Austin Wood
Benjamin Levin
Brandon Turner
Brendan Lucas
Bryan Ohrt
Bryce and Celestine
  Wenzel
Caitlin Ruehle
Carson Rupp
Carson Vath
Catherine Tandy
Collin Christensen
Connor Lasalle
Courtney Arp
Cristina Teruel
Danae Jaggard
Danielle Jayne
Danny Holley

REVIEWERS

Deepshika Kovvali
Devun Schneider
Devyn Whalen Male
Elijah Page
Elise Parkman
Elizabeth Barnes
Elizabeth Kalafut
Elizabeth Schaller,
Ella Pierce
Emily Andrews
Emma Rose Robison
Ethan Buck
Ethan Saunders
Evan P. Miller
Evan Race
Evelynn Hankosky
Gabriela Leal
Gabriella Meade
Gage Lowe
Gianluca Caruso
Gina Wingfield
Gregory Smith
Gunner Silliman
Halleigh Pritchard
Hamza Khan
Hannah Dietz
Hannah Koehlert
Hannah Thurman
Helena Hansen
Hunter Cogswell
Hunter Melton
Ian Elliott
Isaac Thor Wilson
Jack Janik
Jack Otto
Jacob Lafferty
Jacob Ohl
Jarrett Hartwell
Jarrod Khoo
Jasmin Zangara
Javier Lara
Jeremy Litberg

Jessica Freres
John Sheridan III
Jonah Koehlert
Jonathan Love
Jordan Cruz
Josephine Johnson
Joshua Swanson
Josie May-Fenton
Justin Weisner
Kaila Brugger
Kaleigh Nimrick
Kathryn Stacy
Katie King
Keith Skilling
Kel Winchell
Kellan Smith
Kevin Froelich
Kye Brooks
Kyle Johnson
Kyle Nimrick
Kyle Perkins
Kyonte Johnson
Kyree Standifer
Lainie Levin
Landen Bryant
Lauren Blodgett
Lauren Wietermann
Liberty Koester
Lily Ohl
Logan Sheridan
Lukas Klipp
Lydia Ludington
Mac Lang
Madison Lewandowski
Madison O'Neill
Manuel Tena
Mary Kloser
Matthew Wheeler
Max Kopinsky
Maxx Froelich
Mckennen Tobin
Melissa Richmond

Michael Jaggard
Michael Kloser
Michael Wostmann
Nate Rackow
Nathan Koehlert
Nicholas Bennett
Nicholas Veith
Nickolas Slobodian
Nicole Gottlieb
Nicole Kleronomos
Paul Burkhalter
Paul Van Gemmeren
Payton Thomas
Phoebe Ori
Rachel Ohl
Raya Coleman
Robbie Stacy
Rosemaria Devenuto
Sanjana Sivakumar
Sarah Calvert
Sarah Larsen
Scarlett Karen Lucas
Seth Crispens
Shauna Burkhalter
Steven Trinco
Tara Parkman
Tavis T. Johnson
Taylor Moll
TL Kapinos
Tori Bechtel
Treyton Edwards
Trinity Filut
Tristan-Arman Taccad
Vince Obrill
Violet Ohl

INDIANA
Adam Copp
Adam Corbett
Alexander Foust
Allie Wayne
Allyson Goble

REVIEWERS

Alyssa Swangin
Anna Motteler
Anthony Spoor
Antonia Dusevic
Ashley Cencebaugh
Austin Moles
Baylee Green
Ben Littlejohn
Blake R. Jones
Breanna Woodard
Brianne Gilbert
Caitlin Cox
Cameron Rasmus
Carly Flint
Chase Turner
Christopher Kusnierek, Jr.
Chyna Ferguson
Collin Zonker
Connor Brinkley
Cynthia Earls
David Emmert
David Littlejohn
Dustin Moles
Elizabeth Eubanks
Emily Swangin
Grace Lantzy
Griffin Collins
Gus Kellerman
Gwenivere Seegers
Hanna Afarin
Hannah Perry
Holden Rahn
Hunter Culver
Isabel Braun
Izak Lewandowski
Jackie Peil
Jacob Farmer
Jacob Jimenez
James Hebert
James Sopiarz
Jerimiah Craig
Joseph Culbreath

Joseph M. Landon
Joshua Burton
Joshua Solis
Julie Settecase
Kaaleigh A. Krieger
Kaitlyn Brueggert
Katie Settecase
Keenan Myers
Kelsey Cencebaugh
Kendall Abernathy
Kirsten Stenger
Liam French
Lucas A. Ramsey
Lucy Gotwals
Mackensie Ray Chilton
Madison Dahltorp
Makayla Leach
Mary Kate Shultz
Mason Acton
Micah Arnold
Miles Marshall
Noah Evanoff
Noah Hodous
Owen Dossett
Patrick Daugherty
Pierce McCammon
Rachel Steele
Rebecca Rodman
Rebekah Cencebaugh
Robyn MacKenzie
Ross Beatty
Savanna Rutter
Skyla Smith
Sophie Arnold
Sophie C. Braun
Sydney Jean Robinson
Sydney Moore
Tabitha Fay Chambers
Tanaja Ferguson
TJ Valiant
Tyler Taylor
Tyshawn Grauvogl

Victoria Lewandowski
William A Ramsey, Jr
Xondrais Glenn

KANSAS
Abby Schiller
Alexander McVey
Allison Kruse
Alyssa M. Patterson
Avery Stuever
Brook Bradford
C. J. Malsbury
Caitlyn Claussen
Casandra Johnson
Charlie Martin
Christian Lang
Claire Patterson
Dakota Milner
Elaine Sisco
Elizabeth Remington
Evan Ordiway
Grace Schuster
Grace Shelinbarger
Harrison Lowe
Jacob Rubesch
Jake Callier
Jakob Ferreira
Jakob Richardson
Jasmin Bryant
Jasmine Seiberling
Jayden Cook
Jaydn Richardson
Jennifer Lynn Jones
Jonathan Forbes
Joshua Ferreira
Juliana Martin
Kameron Zimmerly
Katie Stanger
Keaton Donaghue
Kristin Anguiano
Kylan Scheele
Lauren Kruse

Logan McKenzie
Maggie Felch
Mckenna Ferreira
Mercedes Berumen
Ryan Bradford
Sarah Cross Wagner
Tatum Gegner
Todd Marvel
Tristan Hogan
Wesley M. Rogers
Weston Johnson

KENTUCKY
Alessandra McLoughlin
Alex Carpenter
Allie Roberts
Alyssa Jamison
Andrew Batten
Athena Rahorst
Avery Hacker
Benjamin Adams
Benjamin McPherson
Blake Stringer
Brianna Wallace
Brittany G. Ashley
Brooklyn Lawson
Bryce Figley
Caleb Scott
Cameron Brown
Cassidy Weickert
Christina Bowman
Christopher Brown
Corbin Allender
Corey Martin
Cory Adams
Daniel Batten
Dylan Cook
Gabrielle Hadley
Grace Baker
Grace Yates
Hannah Gates
Hannah Honaker

Jacob Church
Jamie Freize
Johnny Fields Jr
Kaelyn Short
Karleigh Branscome
Karli Jo Messer
Kasey Eastridge
Kaylen Green
Keith Travis
Lane Hartman
Lauryn Butler
Layla Phillips
Levi Jakob Cadle
Lucas Adams
Luke Wedding
Nicholas Corneilson
Parker Faulconer
Patrick Lepore
Patrick Valsted
Preston Williams
Rebecca Mahlum
Richard Hay
Shayla Duerson
Tristan Littleton

LOUISIANA
Aaron Ray
Ashley Sidaway
Bailey Wilson
Beau Matheny
Caroline Kirk
Chloe Bishop
Gabrielle Honeysucker
Hayley Owens
Jon Boyett
Justin Lewis
Kiley Hebert
Liam McCloy
London Harp
Lucas Gilmer
Peyton Breanna St.
  Romain

Sarah Bailey
Sarah Sinclair
Tahj Foster
Tristen Ray

MAINE
Alexa Mitchell
Amber Lindberg
Annaset Jackson
Anthony Evans
Brody Pond
Caitlin Hodgkins
Cara Nierle
Chenoa Jackson
Colby Berren
Edward Mitchell
Elizabeth Trefts
Eric Cowan
Eve Corbett
Hunter Bertone
Hunter Lindsey
Jacob McCluskey
Jacob Stevens
Jorden Fowler
Joseph Moore
Joshua Thibeault
Luis A. Roldan
Madison Rose Bragdon
Mariah Moore
Miles Michaud
Myka Adams
Natasha Pond
Taitem Lindsey
Trevayne Jackson

MARYLAND
Alex Strong
Alisha Desai
Amber Kennedy
Anisa Howell-Bey
Anthony Fares
Ashli Taylor

REVIEWERS

Benjamin Jablon
Benjamin Williams
Braden Huntoon
Cheyenne Watts
Chloe Houck
Crystal Cleven
Dallas Curry
Daniel Kim
Ethan Dempsie
Evan Powers
Grace Dimock
Kaden Harvey
Kaden Nelson
Kaley Broome
Kaylee Grimes
Kylie Enten
Lauryn Jackson
Leah Crisco
Lynn Coles
Madison Leichtman
Mara Taylor
McKenna Dean
Miles A. Centeno
Nathan Lapka
Nicholas Feehley
Nick Blitz
Nidhi Naik
Rafael Curry
Sarah Taylor
Sianna A. Westley
Stanley A. Hollowak
Tori Grimes
Troy Eismann
Tyler Melvin
Victoria Tsygan
William Cogle
Yisroel Simon
Zachary Houck

MASSACHUSETTS
Abigail Mohr
Aidan McCarthy

Aidan McInerney
Aidan Reinhold
Alanna Burke
Alex Kennedy
Alexander O'Roak
Alyssa Fayerman
Andrea Donnelly
Andrea Leigh
Andrew MacMaster
Annie Stein
Asha Seemungal
Austin Windell Hardy
Autumn Garlick
Becca Hilson
Billy Bracken
Britney Canary
Caitlin McCarthy
Caleb O'Connor
CJ Ryan
Conner Barrett
Danielle Pellegrino
Davis Britland
Dayna Britland
DeAundre Wiggins
Dennis Haughton
Elizabeth Emerson
Elizabeth Lavoie
Emma Tilley
Ethan Chan
Ethan DeForge
Fionn O'Connor
Grace Audette
Hadley Wilson
Haley Couch
Isabella Costantino-
    Carrigan
Ivie Parsons
Jack Holcomb
Jade R. LaBrecque
Jakob Shearer
Jason Fratalia
Joel Vered

Joelle Robinson
Jonathan Eberhardt
Jonathan Tolub
Joshua DeLuca
Juliette Belliveau
Katie Gullicksen
Keith Perry
Kellen Nye
Kyle Mcnamara
Liam DeCastro
Lily Elkind
Lily Goodspeed
Macy Lipkin
Maddie Delande
Marissa Burke
Matthew Clark
Matthew Peljovich
Max Bernstein
Megan Kenney
Michael MacDougall
Mitchell Turner
Molly Doherty
Mya LaBrecque
Myles St. Jean
Nathaniel Devereaux
Nicholas Sparks
Osmanee Offre
Owen Nipoti
Rachel Belliveau
Rebecca Malcolm
Rebecca Marie Gullotto
Richard Mundel
Rohan Patel
Rory Dubin
Rowan Sloan
Ryan Brown
Ryan Gambell
Samantha Pellegrino
Sarah Gotbetter
Scott Robison
Sydney Hall
Taylor Desormeaux

REVIEWERS

Tim Geary
Timothy Camelio
Tommy Weld
Tori Wyeth
Victoria Tucker
Walker Dalpe
Zack R. McCain, IV

MICHIGAN

Aaron Browning
Adam Belanger
Aiden Jerome
AJ Absolon
Alan Bickel
Alec Avery
Alex Bach
Alex Lewis
Alex Smith
Alexander Borowski
Alexis Wagner
Allen Brownlee
Allison Newsted
Alysha Spencer
Amy Shelley
Andrew Eppler
Anthony Bielas
Anthony Branson
Ariana Foster
Ashleigh Weiszbrod
Ashley Haralson
Ashley Yagley
Austin Jorrey
Austin Watson
Avery B. Miller
Ayla Kimrey
Bailey Robert Stark
Bailey Smith
Benjamin Laubach
Bishop Taverner
Brandan Puckett
Bret Thomas
Brett Kenter

Brian Knudsen
Camden Ferguson
Cameron Bigelow
Cameron Lowe
Camren Decaire
Carson Russell
Carson Smith
Charles Setter
Chloe Bos
Christian Zeitvogel
Christopher Shields
Claire MacKenzie
   Hendon
Colin Wright
Connor Millina
Cooper Smith
Corena Kalinin
Cruz Schroeder
Dakota Shay
Dallas Coleman
Damien Davis
Daniel Rosales
Desiree Dianne Kandler
Domonique Hooker
Drew Lewis
Emma Paletta
Eric Murray
Ethan Bastian
Ethan Russell
Gabby Cook
Geneva Hall
Grace Charnesky
Grace Woodward
Grant Lightfoot
Hailee Alexis Mellon
Hannah Borton
Hannah Travelbee
Harmon Nieuwstadt
Hunter Bradley
Hunter Michowski
Ian Erickson
Ian Garlick

Ivan Schury
Jace Nohel
Jacob Hecksel
Jacob Kruisenga
Jadyn M. Blackburn
Jailen Gills
Jake Fox
Jamie Blackwell
Jared Beil
Jeffery Nohel
Jenna Gayle
Jeremy Roediger
Jonathan Carlson
Jordan Golds
Jordan Paletta
Jordan R Stairs
Joseph Catton
Joseph Timothy Hunter
Justin Gayle
Justin M. Marentette
Kaitlyn Bradley
Kamren Martin
Kara Porter
Kathie Atkinson
Kathryn Graham
Kaytlyn Mittag
   Woodrum
Kimberly Reece
Kyle Short
Landon Taverner
Lauryn Carlisi
Leslie Adams
Lexie Staal
Lia Goodell
Lilly Holda
Lily Florian
Lily Simpson
Lindsey Allison Mullen
Lisa Purdy
Lydia Vanderstelt
Madalyn Norris
Maddie Zyski

REVIEWERS

Madison Avery
Madison Dunn
Madison Thompson
Mak Romak
Makayla Gendrolis
Marissa Buitendyk
Marley Pina
Martin Taverner
Matthew Newton
May Amelia Shapton
Michael Bartz
Michael Riffe
Montana Care
Nataleigh Gell
Nathan Thomson
Nicholas Painter
Nikolas Hurd
Noah Belanger
Noah Burton
Noah Dye
Noah Tackett
Nolan Swantick
Philip Baudoux
Rachelle Ignace
Raeanna Ratliff
Raeanne James
Riya Shah
RJ Bredikis
Robert Walker
Sam Wilber
Samantha England
Samuel M. Fisher
Sara M. Blanton
Savanna Lee Duncan
Sebastian Burman
Sebastian Metzger
Seth Ostrander
Sierra Maury
Sofia Seewald
Sterling Weeks
Summer Schultz
Taylor Dunn

Taylor Hines
Tiffany Reece
Tony Gazzarato
Tyler Dallas
Tyler Davis
Tyler Hallenbeck
Tyler J. Barnes
Tyler Wright
Waverlee Baron-Galbavi
Wieland Norris
Zhanin Ruseva

MINNESOTA
Abigayle Waters
Aidan Dalzell
Aiden O'Neil
Alex Gill
Alex Theis
Alexa Krumm
Alexia Engels
Allyce Fries
Alyssa Hollen
Angela McDonnell
Ben Harrington
Ben Weiner
Bently Casey
Brandon Hunter
Brayden Weinzierl
Breelyn Carlson
Brianna Payne
Bryce Birkholz
Casey Shawstad
Charles Matteson
Christopher Garlitz
Cody Snyder
Cole Brandner
Cole Johnson
Cole Linson
Cora Clark
Dalton Hegemann
David Chromy
Dillon Vogt

Elise Edwards
Emily Dodge
Emily Halverson
Emma Markquart
Fiona Simning
Gage McCarty
Gracie Shawstad
Grant Laski
Gunner Shawstad
Hunter Gill
Ian Templin
Jace Moeckly
Jack Lewandowski
Jackson Cross
Jade Ochu
Jared Port
Jeffrey Goodwin, III
Jeremy Lashinski
Jonah Amundsen
Joshua Gabrick
Kalib Koons
Lee Fischer
Liam Wolfe
Lucas Shawstad
Luke Shogren
Mackenzie Jacobson
Madalyn Luebke
Madison Walters
Madisyn Vanasse
Mahalee Partner
Makayla Sever
Makenna Hammer
Mariah Smith
Max Jergerian
Michael Heiling
Michael Templin
Moira Weiland
Morgan Frederick
Natalie Haspert
Nick Hoover
Nick Petersen
Noah Sy

REVIEWERS

Noah Thompson
Rachel Drenckhahn
Rachel Schmidt
Raissa Bronstein
Ryan Behnke-Nead
Sam Taylor
Solveig Rodlund
Sophia Zimmerman
Sydney Nelson
Tannor Alexander
  Emison
Taylor Brandt
Trenton Antinozzi
Tyler Monville
Wesley Ford
Whitney Weichelt
Wyatt Kormick
Zachary Betzler
Zyteijah Clayborne

MISSISSIPPI
Alyssa Catherine Smith
Anjolique Kennard
Ashleigh Williamson
Bonnie Rae Dorman
Brandon Ballard
Emma Siler
Grayson Hewes
Haley Marino
Hannah Belle Lillo
Hollis Hewes
Hudson Poole
James Patrick Jubera
Kai Christie
Kelsey Mayhan
Kevin Meadows
Marissa Wilt
Nason Parkman
Nicholas Callahan
Nicholas Winstead
Nick Counts
Nicole Ewing

Owen Rice
Rob Beuker
Ryan Breaux
Victoria Bryant

MISSOURI
Alex Evets
Alexandra Smith
Alexis Ann Yeager
Alicia Sutton
Alyssa Adair
Andrew Bolstad
Andrew Wyatt
Anna Hirst
Anna Rose Sorsby
Austin Cochran
Autumn Hanning
Benjamin Valencic
Brad Jewell
Brent Hibbits
Brianna Jacobs
Bryan McNeely
Cael Spohn
Christopher Mallett
Corbin Beyer
Dakota Shultz
Danielle Smith
Darby Waligorski
Deacon Gierer
Declan Jones
Devin Kraisan
Emily DeClue
Emily G. Horn
Frankie Robinson
Guillaume Williams
Hannah Hartman
Haven Bennett
Heaven Fullington
Hunter Bennett
Hunter Studer
Ivan Dyreng
Jacob Bradley

Jacob Schott
Jade Davidson
Jeremiah Sweeney
Jordan Lynn Nokes
Joseph Blanks
Josh Bast
Josh Camp
Joshua McAtee
Julie Lafata
Justin Lee Stewart
Kaitlynn Webb
Kalliesta Heafner
Katie Kraus
Katie Loida
Kelsey Keling
Kerstin Adelt
Kyle Daly
Lauren Jewell
Levi Carl
Liam Ruff
Logan Hann
Logan Hunt
Mackenzie Henson
Maddison Webb
Marie Williams
Matthew Craig
Michael Cox
Natalie Temple
Nathan Lalli
Noah Collins
Olivia Dougherty
Renee Wild
Sierra Rowlan
Taylor Byers
Taylor Pipenhagen
Trace Beeman
Trever Thomas
Trevor Graf
Will Graham
William Meyers
Xander Edwards
Zachary Litton

REVIEWERS

Zachary Roberts
Zane Klausing
Zoe Belknap

MONTANA
Jennie Rimmel
Sam Moll

NEBRASKA
Aiden Martinez
Alan Houk
Alison Dassner
Anthony Matney
David Boyle
Elijah Bates
Faith Simcox
Grace Mittermeier
Graciela "Grace" Grote
Grant Dassner
Izaiah Baker
Jack Neussendorfer
Jade Barnes
Jay Schubert
John Feeney
Joshua Brott
Kaitlyn Houk
Keegan Olson
Kristi Keller
Lucas Watson
Melissa Hodde
Nicholas Christensen
Noah Fowler
Paige Stroh
Sean Snyder
Solace R. Johnson
Sophia Harder

NEVADA
Abby Buchanan
Alekken Lamont
Ananya Dewan
Austin Michael Driscoll

Cameron St. Hilaire
Contessa Ulibarri
Eban Cormier
Eden Hall
Evans Gunyah
Hayley Werme
Jaimee Chancy
Jared Buchanan
Jarrod Perez
Jeb Buchanan
Jordan Chandler
Jozsef Abarr
Kaleb Crawford
Kyla King
Lucy Burnham
Madison Nevarez
Matthew David Prince
Matthew Thompson
Nikolaos Collins
Noah Shamy
Richard Campbell
Ryan Eberle
Staci Thompson
Stephanie Janes
Susan Russell
Symantha 'Samye' Lloyd
Taylor Martini
Thomas Campbell

NEW HAMPSHIRE
Alex Poirier
Anastacia Marks
Andrew Winn
Ashley Marks
Benjamin Henson
Bradley Connor Barbarisi
Clayton Thomas
Duncan Scott
Dylan Callahan
Emily Shanteler
Hailey Haskins
Hillary McDonald

Jared Kierstead
Kierra Dean
Lisa Webb
Madeleine M. Tucker
Nicholas Turgeon
Ryker Joshua Lagrenade
Tyler Gardner

NEW JERSEY
Abigail Heinz
Alana Gerdes
Alexa Yong Yow
Alexander M. Cutillo
Andrew Keklak
Arin Weinstein
Arushee Sinha
Ashley Vitiello
Ava Rivera
Brendan Mcnally
Cameron Dowling
Cameron Hills
Caroline O'Sullivan
Catie Waguespack
Celeste Roman
Christine Mayo
Christopher Vega
Clayton Jenson
Daniel Rios
Danielle Steff
Devon Osgood
Elena St. Amour
Emani Blocker
Erin Ryan Meyer
Francis Chiocca
Gabriel Chaves
Gianna Arias
Grace Twaddell
Haley Calderaro
Hannah Joyce
Jack Besnoy
Jack Radley
Jamiya Walker

Jayden Walker
Joseph Raffaele
Julia Fiskin
Jury Russo
Kayla Judge
Leonard Simon Jr.
Marc Berran
Mark Tuccillo, Jr.
Meredith MacLean
Natosha Miller
Nicholas Cali
Nina Casselberry
Rachel Losito
Rachel Rumsby
Rebecca Waguespack
Richard Kreidel
Selena Mendez
Tosh Barker
Willem Price
William Bailie
William Fama
William Rosseter
Zachary Price

NEW MEXICO
Caleb Ostler
Chloe Sandlin
Jesus Cardoner-Meijer
Kailey Wilson
Kaitlyn Hope Maley
Kirsten Lee Jones
Kyle Gabaldon
Kylie Anne Jones
Samuel Harris
Timothy Russell Garcia
Danielle Walker

NEW YORK
Aalia Syed
Abbigale Fetterly
Akiva Sturm
Alexander Riley

Alexandra Harper
Ali Damm
Alista Daneault
Allison Yee
Allyson Dennis
Alyssa Befumo
Anastasia LaPeruta
Andrea Julia Nyiri
Andrew Deocampo
Andrew Woska
Andy Katz
Annmarie Rigoroso
Anthony Cruz
(Anthony Scandura
Ashleigh Rahuba
Austin Cirrincione
Ayanna jenkins Yates
Azrael Korb
Bailey Pierce
Bee Curran
Benjamin Austin
Benjamin Graham
Benji Mayer
Bethany Sionkiewicz
Branden Mosquea
Brandon O'Connor
Brooke Remsen
Caitlyn Kerst
Callalilly "Lilly" Macina
Camie Ainsworth
Campbell Chaplin
Camryn Traeg
Casandra Gilbes
Cecelia Martin
Christian Richter
Christian Strohman
Ciara Hubler
Cody Swanson
Colby Giles-Monnell
Colin Reynolds
Dakota Anderson
Dakota Godek

Dalaney Stahrr
Damion Mitchell
Daria Algier
David Slover
Dayten O'Donnell
Devin Silverstein
Dimitri Smith
Dominic Eannacony
Donovan Eannacony
Dylan Vanhouten
Edwin Brian Lindhe Jr.
Emily Burkhard
Emily Kimoto
Emily Murray
Eric Surprenant
Faith Evans
Freida Lorber
Gabriella Shank
Garrett Hedden
Heather Hinson
Hunter Hinson
Ian Allen
Isabella Renzi
Jabari Duncan
Jack Stanton
Jacob Wilson
Jacqueline Oh
Jamie Del Rosario
Jennifer Sharyl Sescil
Jess Kwong
Joey Beard
John Hagan
John Hodges
John Pareis
John Romero
Jonathan Torres
Joseph Dozier, Jr.
Justin Hatch
Kaileigh Wielgos
Katy Geiger
Kaylee O'Donnell
Kimberly Attanasio

REVIEWERS

Kwesi Etienne
Kyle Mercier
Laura Doak
Laura Rigoroso
Laurin Silverstein
Leigh Murphy Mulverhill
Lesley-Ann Lawrence
Lily Ernst
Madison Ceccarelli
Madison Lavocat
Madison Martin
Maggie Fetterly
Marcia LeTourneau
Marissa Finn
Mary Durocher
Mathieu Boucher
  Strohman
Matthew Ruotolo
Matthew Scipioni
Matthew Welsh
Melina Algier
Michael Himes
Miranda Kelly
Natalie Cartagena
Natalie Sheehan
Natania Pribis
Nathan Lustik
Nathan Sorbello
Nathaniel Calo
Nicholas Pape
Nicole Hayden
Nicole Schofield
Nika Gurwitz
Nina Tedeschi
Noah Wood
Olivia Blarr
Patrick Gore
Peter King
Philip Kwong
Robert Tringone
Sabrina Mittelstadt
Samantha Rose Bystrak

Samantha Rose Bystrak
Samantha Stephan
Sarah Austin
Sean Donnelly
Sebastian Jesmore
Sebastian Jesmore
Shaina Harkins
Shane Davis
Skylar Louch
Sophia Marie Selvaggio
Sophie Gurwitz
Talia Morchower
Tara Sudol
Thomas Shields
Trey Cornish
Victoria Cobb
William Burks
Zachary Darrow
Zoe Foery

NORTH CAROLINA
Abigail Roark
Adam Allard
Alana Weston
Alexis Browning
Allyson Leigh Cowen
Alyssa Gardner
Amanda Fredo
Amanda Tillman
Andrew Dragen
Annemarie Marshall
Ashley Davis
Ashley Hiser
Austin Wilkes
Bailey Ervin
Bailey Poole
Bobby Fields
Brandon Bates
Brandon Fann
Brandon Gibbs
Brianna Holland
Brianna Rhodes

Brycen Columbus
Caleb Mccraw
Caleb Medlin
Carter Norfleet
Chance Evan Collison
Chandler Bosket
Christopher Kennedy
Corrine Collison
Daniela Nickerson
Darian Green
DeeAnne Sander
Dylan Ortloff
Emily Benoit
Ethan Walters
Felicia Sander
Gavin Martinez
George Mason Ellis
Holiday Harvey
Jacklynn McFadden
Jared Gibble
Jaritt Cook
Jarod Dinh
Jessica Reynolds
Joel Freeman
Joey Pennington
Jonah Wilkes
Jordan Loftis
Justize Hunter
Kailey Alyssa Ratcliff
Katie Hicks
Katie Hill
Kayla Webb
Kayla Williams
Kaylei Portscheller
Kelsey Lane
Landen Pepi
Lauryn A. Hill
Leah Carroll
Logan R. Connolly
Maddie Beck
Maddison Wright
Madison Mcmasters

REVIEWERS

Madison Skye Maynard
Matthew Garman
Melanie MacDonald
Melissa Soots
Michael Scamardo
Montana Moss
Name-Sonia Rao
Natalie Bowers
Nicole Long
Noah Foster
Nora Nichols
Patrick T. Kelly II
Peter Aagaard
Reese Stoffo
Rioghan O'Toole
Romeo Martinez
Saajan Shah
Saorla O'Toole
Sasha Griffin
Savanna Wright
Savannah Poole
Scarlett Wright
Sean Condie
Sheldon Campbell
Stacie Williams
Timothy Hedrick
Trevor Allison
Trinity De Risio
Trinity Martin
Tyler Stills
Tyra Jade Cunningham
Xiao Lin
Zoe Gonzalez

NORTH DAKOTA

Brandon Prestriedge
Clayton Nelson
Devin Jacob Askim
Gabriel Skrydlak
Hannah Kinneberg
Hope Geiger
Jonathon Wilson

Liam Dorsch
Seth Owens
Turner Nelson

OHIO

A. Broom
Abby Humphreys
Abby Rosen
Adam Ley
Adam Nance
Ahnna Wickstrom
Alex Coldiron
Alexander Boozer
Alexander Hauser
Alexis Campbell
Alexis Cornell
Alexis Dendy
Andrew Sizer
Annaleise N. Champion
Austin Haynes
Austin White
Bella Bodenstein
Ben Cimino
Braiden Cooper
Brandon Hall II
Brett Dobransky
Brianna Prether
Brooklyn Lint
Caleb Dyer
Cara Singleton
Carlie Haynes
Cassie Dailey
Chance Smith
Chandler McCroskey
Cheosung O'Brien
Chloe Sickman
Cheyenne Kunder
CJ Ketron
Cory Bodkin
Danielle Russell
Darrell Brown
Destiny Wilson

Eli Holbert
Elijah Wood
Ellie Coldiron
Emily Heiberger
Emily Scheckelhoff
Emma Grace Widmer
Ethan Archer
Ethan Whitt
Evan Auburn
Evan Snyder
Garrett Bastian
Hailey Kuhbander
Haley Marie Schlomer
Hannah Bailey
Hannah Shane
Hannah Westfall
Hayden Twining
Hunter Vaught
Ian Smith
Isaac Stephani
Jacob Gill
James Elliott
James Jackson
James Lantier
Jason Keller
Jaykob Cave-Stevens
Jeffrey J.D. Spitaleri III
Jeremy Wenzel
Jesse Brown
Jessica Orozco
Jessica Payne
Jocelyn Pinegar
Joey Duncan
Joey Neibert
Joseph Mccoy
Josh Culbertson
Joshua Custer
Joshua Jones
Justin Lindstrom
Justin Rak
Justin Schumacher
Kaitlyn Dawn Smith

REVIEWERS

Kaitlyn Means
Kaleb McConnell
Kaylan Spaulding
Kerry Steele
Korban Berezne
Kyle Cox
Lauren Goodman
Leah Bailey
Liam Roche
Lilly MacDonald
Logan Brittain
Logan Dotson
Logan Keller
Logan Rock
Logan Vitovich
Luke Stephen
Maddison White
Mateo Randall Wantland
Matthew Berning
Max Coulter
Mckenzie Mcknight
Meg Samuel
Megan Knox
Megan Tomlinson
Michael Fackler
Michael Grau
Michaela Rush
Nathan L. Raber
Nathan Lazich
Nia Harris
Nicholas Steinhoff
Nolan Anthony Cramer
Olivia Banzhaf
Paige Murphy
Patrick Jennings
Paul Lantz Jr
Rad Murray
Reece DeAnna
Remy Moss
Rhea Dawson
Rithvik Potluri
Ryan Dugger

Samantha Godfrey
Samantha Widmer
Samuel Steinhoff
Sarah Kerekgyarto
Sarah Perkins
Savanna Davis
Savannah Brown-Barkey
Shayla Harbottle
Shea Barton
Shirley Hummer
Sierra Harrison
Skylah Hullum
Symon Gallivan
Tabitha Sexton
Taggart D. Spurlock
Tara Prabhu
Tiffanni Bailey
Tre Westfall
Trent Fairburn
Tyler Carpenter
Tyler Guess
Tyler Hunt
Wesley Nixon
William Chan
Zaccaheus Hunter
Zachary Cino
Zachary Mollohan
Zachary Timmons
Zachary Wilson

OKLAHOMA

Aaron Scott Kohout
Abby Detar
Alex Drummond
Alexia "Lexi" Holderbee
Alison McKee
Allison Kimbrell
Baylee Crego
Bethany Calhoun
Blake Martin
Braeden Pruett
Brandon Gravitt

Caitlin Suarez
Chloe Becker
Christan Matthews
Christian Jadwisiak
Christian Morales
Collin Veit
Corbin Walker
Declan Jay Gilbreth
Genesis Jolly
Giovanni Penna
Hunter Hatley
Jacob Gentry
Jaelyn Pickering
Jaicie Clayton
James Tapp
John "J.T" Thurman Jr
Julia Pickering
Juston Clark
Kaden Bradshaw
Kate Park
Kelsey Beesley
Kody Rhodes
Kyle Watson-Trahan
Kylie Mayfield
Lilly Lewis
Logan Longacre
Luz Mercedes Castillo-
    Trevino
Mikey Butenhof
Natalie Williams
Naveen Thavathiru
Quinten Roller
Rachel Strassberger
Sean Maycumber
Sheridon Duerson
Spencer Pearce
Tehmina Cheema
Tiki Turner
Trey Ortega
Tyler Miller
William Kimbrell
Zachary Miller

REVIEWERS

REVIEWERS

Jessica Fellion
Joey Goist
Jordan Sherry
Katelyn Temple
Kevin DePietro Jr.
Kevin Roberts
Kimia Javaherneshan
Klaryssa Kolbeck
Krista McNeil
Kyle Kirby
Lane Henry
Lexie Vath
Lindsey Sabo
Loribeth A. Thomas
Lucas Huynh
Lucian Francis
Luke Adelman
Madison Hough-
  Korowicki
Madison Meiser
Magie Maye Ridilla
Mandi Bouton
Maria Diaz
Marisa Joy Matlin
Max Dlhopolsky
Megan Beam
Megan Clancy
Mikki Gifford
Myranda Mamat
Nadia Martin
Natalie Kay Nixon
Nathan Baublitz
Nathaniel Gunderman
Nia Lewis
Nicholas C. Brown
Nicolina Cuzzola
Owen Youse
Paige Umbel
Paige Vizzini
Preston Kiester
Rachel Thornton
Rebecca Gibson

Rhiannon Harbold
Robert Driscoll
Robin Reynolds
Ryan Ellis
Sean Cramer
Sean Darroch
Sean Waltman
Shailyn Moore
Sharon Allgood
Simon Stockdale
Sophie Goldberg
Stephanie Gamverona
Taylor Kelsey
Thomas Chung
Tim Mattaboni
Trent Smith
Tyler Scott
Victoria Warkentin
Zachary Chast
Zachary Kolumban
Zachary Sikov

RHODE ISLAND
Abby Stark
Andrew Bernier
Audriauna Greeno
Connor Holmes
D'andre LaMay
Emily Lotter
Fiona Mitchell
Frederic Butler
Jaidyn Martinez
Julia Martinez
Julian Jensen
Miguel Figueroa
Olivia McMahon
Scott Chase Jr.
Sebastian J. Shoup

SOUTH CAROLINA
Alex Bower
Alyssa Goodall

Alyssabeth Bolm
Andrew Gamble
Anthony Garcia
Ashley Hooker
Ava McDonald
Becca-Ann Hoff
Benjamin Kennedy
Bentley Kemble
Brady Wakefield
Brandon Grubbs
Caeli Preston
Carter L. Floyd
Coen Najmola
Colton Finley
Daiquan Staggers
Debra Miller
Derek Dolbee
Devyn Freeman-Crump
Elizabeth Albright
Elizabeth Hendrix
Elizabeth McWhorter
Gabriel McWethy
Garrett Scott
Gavin Cook
Haley Grubbs
Hannah Grace Hyler
Izaiah Kahl
Jack Malone-Grippe
Jenna Chapman
Jeremiah Coleman
Josephine Danby
JT Rowlands
Kaitlin M Milam
Kimberly Glover
Liam Noonan
Mackenzie Truitt
Madison Avalon Claudy
Michael D. Mongillo
Mitchell Januchowski
Nathan Hyler
Nicholas King
Sadyne Marks

Shaany Nola Delport
Shayla Lear
Shianne Abdoo-Shaurette
Stefany Hooper
Taylor McWhorter
Tegan Tumbleston
Terry Milam
Thaddeus Davis
Tyler Lane
Tyler Tice
Zackary Hooper

SOUTH DAKOTA
Amber Litke
Blaine Wittrock
Conner Knepp
Daamen Kalwat
Dylan Arneson
Ian Helgeson
Natalie Douvier-
  Jankowski
Rebecca Lynn Neumann
Trinity Jankowski

TENNESSEE
Alex Jensen
Aline Dungey
Allie Young
Alyssa Smith
Amanda Seaton
Andrew Turk
Bailey Georgia Kittle
Benjamin Selby
Brandon Smith
Caitlyn Hargett
Chance Williams
Chris D'Ambro
Dalton Allmon
Deonte Eason
Destin Creech
Devonn Moore
Donovan Eason

Eli Ward
Elizabeth D'Ambro
Elizabeth Vimuktanon
Emily Green
Gavin Francis
George Rummel
Hailey Gremillion
Hayden Gann
Jacob Gremillion
Jacob Meadows
James Bigler
Jerry "Trey" Hooper
John Hutchinson
Jon Wade
Joshua Sheaf
Justin Gilliam
Kameron Thomas
Layla Usmonova
Maddox Thigpen
Maggie Moore
Makayla Lerner
Matthew D. Foutch
McKaela Garrett
Melissa Boyd
Morgan Nolan
Nathan Moore
Nicholas Holland
Nikolas Kip Hunt
Patrick Charlton
Perry Lane
Peter De Wolfe
Sam Lyons
Sam Sweeney
Sarah Hutchinson
Sarah Ward
Scott Donahue
Taylor Buena
Teagan Murphy
Tennessa Parsley
Trey Oliver
Trinity Amabile
Tristan Neilson

Zachary Kilpatrick

TEXAS
Aaron Aguirre
Abbigail Celeste Duran
Absalom Delaine Jr.
Aine Mellor
Alex Gonzales
Alex Rembisz
Alex Villar
Alexandra C. Chavez
Alexys "Lexy" McDowell
Ali Imran
Alissa Piefer
Allison Bennett
Alyssa Lucas
Amanda Lawson
Anna Hafemeister
Aradia Merritt
Arianna Acuna
Ashley Flournoy
Ashley Sanchez
Ashton Major
Asli Gulen
Audra E. Hicks
Austin Demore
Austin Primeaux·
Austin Riis-Due
Avery Kubecka
Ayesha Khan
Ben Young
Benjamin Jacob Cagle
Blakely Annarino
Brendan Roth
Briana Peeler
Brianna Noelle Curl
Brianna Robinson
Brittany Martin
Bryanna Briley
Bryce Speciale
Camdyn Jackson
Cameron Kennedy

REVIEWERS

Cameron Larsen
Cara Martin
Carey Gomez
Catalina Bouchard
Chandler Dillon
Chase Stuhldreher
Cheyenne Rohmann
Chris Goff
Chrissa Hibbitts
Christian Kelly
Christopher Eddy
Christopher Fitt
Christopher Shaddox
Clark Michael Givens
Cobi Jones
Coby Paul Roberts Jr
Colin Andrews
Colton Tyran
Colton Wade
Courtney Stuhldreher
Craig Vincent
Daley Williams
Dalton Dooley
Darin Lerma
David Knowles
David Soto
David Williams
Davin Abraham
Davis O'Brien
Dennis Eardley
Derek Price
Destiny Murphy
Dillyn King
Duce Harris
Dylan Chandlee
Dylan Dolenski
Dylan Marchette
Edward M. Alvarez
Elisabeth Mooney
Eliseo J. Quiñones
Elizabeth Craig
Emily Vetvick

Emily Welch
Eric Demore
Eric Donavan Payton Jr
Erin Oplinger
Ethan Carberry
Evan Palmer
Gabriel Ramirez
Gabriella Maldonado
Gavin Eyerly
Gene Taylor McAda
George Tighe
Gilbert Herrera
Griffin Harman
Gwendolyn Clary
Hanna Dinkel
Hareni Ravikumar
Hayley Cannon
Irene Rivera
Ivy Mangrum
Jacey Shawver
Jack Boller
Jackie Brumfield
Jacob Barth
Jade Chandler
Jade S. Newton
Jake Alner
Jake Herod
Jakob Beheler
Jason Turner
Joey Langton
John Burkett
Jonathan Cunningham
Jordan Mckibbin
Jory Robinson
Joseph Hamm
Joshua C. Hutchins
Julia Chavez
Kaden Drake
Kasey Knowlton
Katie Hradek
Kayl Powers
Kaylee Rigg

Keaton Espich
Keegan Brumfield
Kelli Lynn Champlin
Kendall Wann
Kennedy Shallenburger
Kenny Rodenberg
Kerstin Andrews
Kevin Holan
Kim Justice
Kimberly Carmona
Kinsler Haden
Kip Olson
Kolby Sumlin
Kristen Valentine
Kyla Dermody
La Tifiana Roberson
Larissa Looney
Lauren Ahern
Laynee Abbott
Leonard Kovacs
Logan Gregory
London Terry
Luke Epley
Maddie Alva
Madeleine McGowan
Madison Navarro
Madison Wissing
Maire Mellor
Makenna Marshall
Mark Kittelson
Mason Adams
Mason Houston
Mason Roth
Matthew Blanton
Matthew J. Washington
Matthew Leek
Matthew Woodring
Maxwell Roman
McKenzie Ochoa
McKinlee Reynolds
Mike Harris
Mikey Staffieri

REVIEWERS

Morgan Espich
Natasha Moore
Nate Whitworth
Nathan Tate
Nathan Wells
Nicholas Barth
Nicholas Kircus
Nicky Truong
Nolan Anderer
Olivia Johnson
Paige Schweighardt
Parker Doyle
Patrick Kelly
Patrick Mellor
Paul Bennett
Philip Becker
Phillip Brackins
Quinn Keith
Raymond Smith
Reagan Haydon
Rebecca Hinojosa
Reese Alexander
Reiley Hansen
Rhys Soto
Ricky Lopez
Rose Boller
Rowan Ostrowicki
Ryan Hubbard
Sara Elizabeth Saldana
Sara Verstuyft
Sean Hinckley
Sean Holler
Seth Epley
Shane Cunningham
Shaunn Greenlee
Shelby Schmidt
Skylar Meadows
Spencer Tabor
Sydney Bertrand
Sydney Espich
Sydney Morgan
Tabatha Hughes

Tai Chandler
Tatiana Patton
Taylor Larsen
Theodore Knight
Trinity Harris
Tristin Massey
Tryston Obevoen
Ty Gressett
Yesenia Delgado
Zachary Carlson
Zachary McFadden
Zion Ash

UTAH
Abigail Hill
Ady Jakins
Alex Holling
Allison Russell
Austin Van Dyke
Bailey Stevens
Baleigh Ames
Ben Silvia
Ben Tuinei
Ben Wenzel
Benjamin Belnap
Brad Talbot
Braden Roberts
Breck Pratt
Briana Bartholomew
Britney Shunn
Brooke Elizabeth De
  Palma
Brycen Mackay
Caitlin White
Cameron Buss
Carli Hogan
Chaz Greenfield
Christina Dario
Christopher Fish
Christopher Nielsen
Daniel Lee
EJ Reives

Elijah Belnap
Elijah Gehring
Elijah Reives
Eric Anderson
Ethan Neas
Evan White
Hazel Faccenetti
Hunter Douglass
Jacob Maag
Jacob Ward
Jakob Kempema
Jared Harwood
Jared Johnson
Jennifer Erickson
Jessica Felter
Joseph Hall
Kailee Tea
Kaitlin Bowman
Kaitlynn Wicker
Kaleb Myers
Kaylee Belnap
Khristapher Memmott
Kylie Saxton
Lance E. Shunn, II
Matthew Maag
Megan Headrick
Nicholas Kirby
Noah Jones
Paige Tanner
Rachel Wilcox
Sam Kottler
Sariah Schriever
Satchel Sproul
Shale Goodrich
Statton Davis
Summer Van Moorlehem
Sydney Korzep
Sydney Mayhew
Talia Kottler
Tyler Newman
Tyler Tea
Victoria Stephens

REVIEWERS

Weston Schirado
Wriley Renouard
Zack Elzey
Zoe J. Pankratz

VERMONT
Eva Rocheleau
Nathan Fraser
Simon Bohan

VIRGINIA
Abigail Harvey
Alexander "Xander" Will
Alexander Kauffman
Alexandra 'Ally'
  Thompson
Alexandra Paxton
Alyssa Hodum
Andrew Basden
Ashton Leigh Will
Austin Quick
Bethany Duffer
Brandi Pleasant
Brandi Shaffer
Briana Forest-Russell
Caitlyn Marie Knutson
Caitlyn McDaniel
Catherine H. Tadlock
Chantal Miles
Chase Robert Ables
Cherokee Rice
Christian James Mulcahy
Connor Johnson
Daniel Laux
Derek King
Devon Wyatt
Emily Helfrich
Eric Filer
Eric Cheatham
Erik Covington
Evan Boger
Gabriel Meadows

Gabriella Rocha-
  Fernandez
Gabrielle Alger
Gregory Harvey
Gretchen Baldwin
Hunter Smith
Jack Olsson
Jacob Garner
Jacob Willis
James Boe
Jeremy Christian
Jonathan Cauthen
Joram Stanley
Joshua And Cameron
  Darnell
Joshua Cauthen
Kennedy Broy
Kiana Perrigan
Kieryn Burton
Kyle Forren
Kymberlyn Mitchell
Kyra Brindle
Mackenzie Cecil
Madison A Stockman
Marcus Dean
Michelangelo Mansfield
Nathan Faust
Nick Papakostas
Phyllis Davis
Riley Russell
Robby Mau
Ronald Collins
Roshan George
Samia Mansfield
Samuel Huber
Sarah Crites
Sequoia Tiemeyer
Shea Courtwright
Taya Gray
Taylor Erin Evitts
Taylor Maroney
Tim Layton

Tyler Smith
Veronica Holmes
Zachary Rodrigues
Zack Sandklev
Zoe Tilman

WASHINGTON
Aaron Jackson
Abby McGowan
Abby McGregor
Alainnah Knight
Alex Sugi
Alexandra Chance
Alisha M Hayward
Amaya Udager
Anthony Fontes
Arereona Murray
Aria Freiwaldt
Aric Pasquier
Bradford 'BJ' Weber
Branden Spurlock
Brianna Houtman
Brittani Ann Vombaur
Cade Paullin
Caitlin Bertelsen
Caitlyn Crocker
Cary Bonnett
Christianna Valnes
Clarice Bean
Cody Redinger
Cooper Graves
Devon Baldwin
Devon Piovesan
Easton Mathews
Eitan Younker
Emma Johnson
Ethan Bertch
Ethan Edwards
Ethan Redinger
Ethan Rego
Evan Werner
Everett Lund

REVIEWERS

Felicity Buss
Gabriel Hammond
Gaeble King
Ilan Coberly
Jacob Crowder-Funk
Jake Gray
Janessa Heimbuch
Jarod Miner
Jeffrey Niquette
Jeremy Snyder
Jerry Balch
Jon Mitchell
Joseph Fontes
Joshua Dougall
Joshua Gelderman
Josie Richey
Kaia Kihn
Kaitlyn Marie Orosco
Kaleo Redman
Katie Shabatina
Keely Franchini
Kelten Rimmasch
Kierna Sprague
Laura Nutter
Lily Price
Lindsey Pasquier
Lucia Mathews
Madelyn Johnson
Maren Ferris
Masada "Sadie" Younker
Matthew Houston
Michael Jarvi
Morgan Pasquier
Naoki Masuda
Nataly Green
Nathan Waggoner
Olivia Pineda
Owen Hughes
Paul Bruemmer
Riley Banta
Robert Payton
Sarah Standley

Savion Collins
Scott Nutter
Sean Bonnett
Sean Melton
Tabatha Hale
TaMara Smith
Taylor Christopherson
Taylor Wight
Tea Serack
Townsend Judd
Tyler Oliver

WEST VIRGINIA
Aidan Zampino
Aiden Jones
Alexander Anderson
Alia King
Andrew Jones
Bailey Dubinsky
Bethany Grace Null
Bradley Anderson
Caleb Lamb
Cheyanne Bonds
Dennis Aliff
Derek L. Ballengee
Emily Amos
Izabella King
Kaitlin Morrison
Kayley Mason
Matthew Robert
  Heavener
Mitchell Lee Shepard
Rose Weikle
Sarah Fresquez
Serena Zampino
Sydney Wiley
Trevor D. Jones
Trevor Matheny
Zachary Shepard

WISCONSIN
Abigail Gehring

Anna Holley
Anthony Piotrowski
Anya Grace
Austin Ramiah Casey
Ben Mighall
Bryce Nelsen
Bryn Disch
Caleb Willy Richter
Cameron Pauli
Carter Dieckhoff
Cedric Blackmore
Chanel Juedes
Christian Dirks
Cody Blauwkamp
Cody Nitardy
Corbin Desjardins
Cory McCabe
Dallas Palosaari
Damon Braatz
Deacon Leer
Devon Gaber
Dustin Palosaari
Dylan L. Hoard
Emily Blomquist
Emily Gehring
Emily Winkler
Emily Wolfe
Emma Laskowski
Emma Theisen
Ethan Burns
Ethan Townsend
Gracie Holley
Jack Lila
Jacob Kostelecky
Jared Wondra
Jarod Quigley
Jonah Luksich
Joshua Moczynski
Juell Jahnke
Kaden Cabe
Kaitlin Bonesho
Katya Mikhailenko

REVIEWERS

Kayleigh Bonlander
Kiara Hardy-Wright
Kylie Schedler
Lauren Coffield
Lily Belle Lowndes
Madeline Gehring
Madeline Mews
Max Parmaker
Maximillian Niebler
Maxximus Thorson
Maya Cubias
Megan Baumgartner
Megan Rinehart
Micah Rivers
Milo Brunette
Morgan Marie Peters
Nate Breitzmann
Nathan Bigna
Nicholas Hapka

Nicole Witbrod
Nikole Blomquist
Noah Treptow
Olivia Zietlow
Paul Couillard
Reid Kuenzi
Robert Murray
Ryan Dicke
Ryan Palosaari
Samantha Ploeger
Samantha Poborsky
Samantha Schiereck
Seth Stariha
Shauna Opseth
Shaynea Haakenson
  Johnson
Sophia Caitlyn
  Donnermeyer
Steven Noffke

Tara Holte
Tristan Moctezuma
Warren Misek
Zachary Clark
Zackary Smerchek
Zaynab Hassan

WYOMING
Allison Hirdning
Kassidy Morales
Logan Brown
Michaella Christensen
Noah Achenbach
Ruben O. Colon
Sebastion C. Leeper
Tanner Jones
Ty Ramirez